UNQUIET SPIRITS

Clare Bainbridge

Pear Tree Press

Book 2 in the Roma Capta Series

peartreepressdevon@gmail.com

and http://clarebainbridge.com

Discover more novels by Clare Bainbridge:

Saturn's Gold

Dramatis Personae

The Great Ones: Three Men Controlling the State:
Marcus Antonius: a distant threat, ruling the Eastern Empire
Octavian: desperately struggling to rule Italy
Lepidus: In Italy too, but trusted by no-one.

Their Generals and Supporters:
Lucius Antonius: Marcus' younger brother, consul
Fulvia: Marcus Antonius' wife, a very forceful lady
Ventidius and Pollio: Antonius' generals in Gaul, unsure of themselves
Agrippa, Salvidienus Rufus, Maecenas: generals for Octavian.
Aulus Manlius Torquatus: friend of Octavian, reluctant finder of dead bodies

Everybody's Enemy:
Sextus Pompeius: son of Pompey the Great, in Sicily.
Lucius Domitius Ahenobarbus: has a navy, but whose side is he on?

The Torquatus Household:
Cornelia Balbi: Torquatus' wife, not a dog-lover
Manlia: his sister, Ahenobarbus' wife, in an awkward position
Lucius Cornelius Balbus: Cornelia's father, wealthy friend of Octavian
Vibia: Torquatus' mother, who finds him unsatisfactory and says so
Felix: a slave, and also Torquatus' half-brother
Trofimus: a steward, imperturbable, in charge of everything
Fortunatus: a very expensive cook
Victor: a slave who knows his master's togas inside out
Rachel: Cornelia's maid
Catus: a groom who likes dogs
Becco and Pulex: Torquatus' bodyguards.

From Mevania:
Quintus Fiscilius: an impatient young man, grieving for his sister
Fiscilia: a dead sister with a surprising story
Canidia: their aunt, very sweet but a lawyer's nightmare
Calliste: Fiscilia's slave
Tiro and Nestor: Fiscilius' slaves
Titus Fulvus: a potential bridegroom.

From Formiae:
Marcus Ampudius: grieving for his brother and crossed in love.

Also featuring:
Nereis: a wealthy freedwoman with a past
Epictetus: a freedman who knows more than he's telling
Nar: a dog, untroubled by his fleas but always hungry.
Lollia: a lady with a flat to let
Ancilla: a caretaker
Quintus Acutius: friend of the Fiscilii
Claudius Erotes: a local magistrate
Spurius Malens: a bad man
Margarita: a midwife.

And some undertakers, soldiers, musicians, ostlers, secretaries, dock workers, doctors, managers and tenants.

MAP OF ITALY

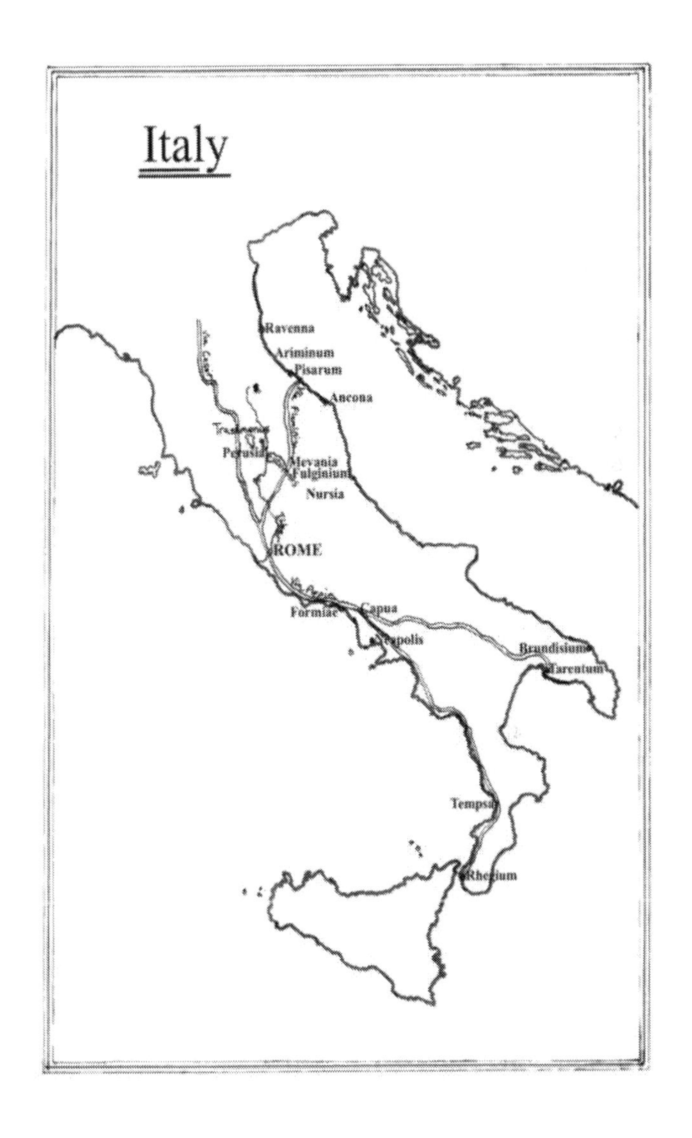
Italy
Ravenna
Ariminum
Pisarum
Ancona
Mevania
Nursia
ROME
Formiae
Capua
Brundisium
Tempsa

Chapter 1

It was going to be another blindingly hot day. Annoyingly, the shrines of the Argei that were nearest to the priest's own house on the Quirinal had been on yesterday's route. Either of those would have been an easy walk for the priest's tired feet this morning. One of the tiny, ancient places was actually in the courtyard of the temple of Quirinus. The temple itself had been burned down in one of Rome's spasms of civil war two years ago and never rebuilt, so that the shrine sat among tall weeds; another was placed in a dusty little garden behind the statue of the ancient deity known as Semo Sancus.

In the middle of March he had walked this same route, as twenty seven man-shaped figures made of reeds had been placed in the little shrines. What the function of these figures was no-one could now say with certainty, but whatever it was they had now fulfilled it.

Yesterday sacrifices had been made and prayers said at twenty one of the shrines, leaving a little group dotted around the Caelian hill and the centre of the city for this morning. Behind the priest, a long tail of local worthies straggled, chatting quietly, or breaking off from time to time to encourage the strong young men whose task was to carry the lumpy reed figures in procession around Rome, and finally to throw them into the river.

Dawn had broken some time before, and the last few streaks of pink in the sky were fading away. There was still a slight freshness in the air, but that wouldn't last. Although it was only May it felt more like August, the heat fraying tempers and creating a feeling of exhaustion which hung like a fog over the stinking city. The priest straightened his back and put out of his mind the hot slipperiness of his feet in their patrician boots. The procession was slowing as it began the ascent of the Caelian: only three more shrines to visit, three more repetitions of the incomprehensible ancient prayers, three more sacrifices to make. What would it be this time, he wondered? A piglet, a lamb? In poor districts it was sometimes only a chicken.

The shrine was visible now in the growing light. But there was something wrong, he could see. Instead of the quiet, respectful gathering he'd been expecting, figures were hurrying here and there as if they hadn't noticed his arrival. And for a moment his nostrils caught for a moment a scent that always had the power to frighten.

Smoke. The fire must be out, however. Nothing but the occasional lazy wisp of white showed where it had been.

As the priest noticed this someone up ahead caught sight of his party and came running down the hill, shouting. His face red and sweating in the warming air, his clean toga streaked with soot, he stood for a moment gasping for breath. It was clear that he was the man in charge. The priest waited patiently for him to speak.

'I am the magistrate here,' the man gasped out at last. 'What ought we to do, lord? This is such terrible bad luck.' He looked as if he were on the point of tears.

'Why? What's happened?'

'The shrine, lord. Someone's set it on fire. They've burned the reed man. What shall we do?'

The priest shivered. Nothing could be more inauspicious. The men behind him exclaimed in dismay.

'This happened when?' he demanded.

'In the night, lord. I checked that everything was in order yesterday evening. This morning, when I arrived just after dawn, I could see smoke coming out of the doorway.' As he spoke the two men walked up the last few yards to the little building. It was one of the most ancient he'd seen, the priest thought: not much more than a stone hut built against the back of the great temple of Minerva Capta.

'Doesn't seem to have harmed the building,' the priest pointed out.

'No, lord. That's because - you'll see,' and he snapped his fingers at a slave for a small clay lamp, its tiny flame invisible in the sunlight. 'Shall I lead the way, lord?'

The priest nodded and the magistrate hurried inside. The priest, much taller, ducked his head under the crooked old stone of the lintel and followed him. There was barely room for two inside the little hut, and the magistrate politely pressed himself back against the door-wall to make space for the visitor. In here the air was even hotter and heavy with the acrid smell of burning. The walls were black and running with water. Along the bottom of the wall opposite the door a heavy shadow lay: the reed man. Almost overwhelmed by the heat and smell, the priest nodded, said curtly, 'Get someone to bring that out,' and ducked back out of the doorway again.

The reed man, when exposed to the light of day, was a sorry-looking object. One side of it had been partially burned away, and what was left around the burnt edges was loose and blackened. Flakes of sooty material blew off it and tumbled about the street in the warm breeze.

'I'd have thought it would have burned like a torch, but it's gone out,' the priest observed. 'I suppose when it fell over it went out, and after that it just smouldered. You were lucky you came along, though. It would have broken out again eventually.'

The magistrate nodded. 'I think it helped that it was made by a different man this year,' the magistrate explained. 'This one's bound very tight, which would slow the fire too.'

The priest nodded. The figures were all roughly the same size and made in the same way: a bundle of reeds as tall as a man was made to look human by being tied around the waist with a cord. Some localities took a lot of trouble with their man, shaping a neck and a neat waist. Some hardly bothered with the details. All, however, tied their bundle just above the bottom, so that reed men appeared to have their feet tied at the ankles. This figure had been carefully made, the waist drawn in hard with tough cord and the neck and ankles formed the same way. It was unpleasantly realistic. The magistrate suggested, from the position of the burnt section, that a flame must have been held to the bundle quite close to the waist.

'You're right, I think. There wasn't enough air for the thing to catch light properly. You're lucky.'

'But what should we do, lord? We can't offer this man, can we?'

'No. I'm sure you can't.' The priest glanced over to where a group of his own slaves stood. 'Felix! Run down to the Forum, will you, to the Regia. Tell the chief priest I need advice, urgently.'

The boy nodded, and was about to run off when his master called him back, because two more slaves from his own household were hurrying up the hill towards them. The first man reached them, beginning speaking even before he'd come to a stop. 'The shrine on the Palatine, lord: it's been burned down.' He turned to the second man. 'Davus had only just left, lord, when more news came in: the shrine on the Velia has been burned too.'

The priest turned to the murmuring crowd. Raising his voice so everyone could hear, he said: 'Someone has attacked our city and its gods. I will go the Velia and will take advice from the chief priest there. Your magistrate can come with me. In the meantime I suggest that you clean the shrine and have it ready to fulfil the ritual.' He turned away. 'Felix,' he said in a softer voice, 'ask the chief priest to come to the Velia, will you? It'll be a lot easier for him.' The boy nodded and shot away.

The men in the procession crowded around him asking what should be done next.

'Take your reed men back to your own shrines, and tomorrow bring them here again. Whatever is decided we can do nothing more until a new reed man has been made to replace each of the burned ones. We will then be able to complete the ritual and so placate the gods.'

He hoped that was true. Rounding up his men with his eyes, the priest turned away and headed back down into Rome. He beckoned the slaves who had brought the news, and as they walked together he asked for more details.

'We heard about the shrine on the Palatine first,' the slave told him. 'They said it was gutted, the whole building gone. No-one had seen anything. The building wasn't guarded, and it wasn't until well after dawn that anyone went there, I gather.'

'The shrine there is just a thatched hut, like Romulus' hut,' the priest said. 'In a little grove of trees. It would be easy to attack, and would burn well. But they can't have started the fire by burning the reed man, because we took it away yesterday.' The priest frowned. 'So I wonder' -

Another man was hurrying up. 'Not more arson?' the priest asked.

'No, lord. I'm from the shrine on the Velia. I've been sent to say that we've found a body.'

'A body?'

'Yes, lord. Inside the shrine. Must have been the arsonist.'

'I suppose so. He went in there, set the reed man on fire, got trapped and died himself.'

'Yes, lord.'

The Velia was almost in the heart of the city, but although the street was crowded, everyone was keeping well clear of the ruined shrine. It was a sorry sight, its door opening onto nothing. It sat in the middle of a puddle of water tainted with soot, now rapidly drying in the hot air, in which pieces of tile and blackened timbers were scattered here and there. A few lazy twirls of smoke still rose through what had been the roof, but some building workers had already begun to pull some of the collapsed roof-beams through the doorway. To one side, a well-dressed crowd, balked of its chance to celebrate, was enjoying the catastrophe. The Velia was a wealthy area, and its households must have raised a good sum of money even in these hard times, because the chosen sacrifice was a large lamb, washed quite clean. It was bounding about among a group of laughing children, who were trying to stop it eating the garland of flowers round its neck.

The local magistrate came over with a self-important frown and introduced himself as Marcus Claudius Erotes. He was a prosperous-looking man with a belly suggesting that whoever went hungry in hungry Rome, he did not. He wore the cap of a freed slave, and a green tunic with a woven border, stretched rather too tightly across his belly. At the moment his expression was one of extreme distress. The toga he would have worn for the ceremony had been thrown over a small statue, extinguishing it.

'I see you managed to put the fire out anyway,' the priest observed.

'Yes, lord. I was just about to come down to make the final arrangements for the day when a message came that the shrine was on fire.'

They walked across to the remains of the shrine together. A large man was inside, his feet protected by heavy boots, tugging the free end of one of the fallen beams, while another man tossed over the walls the tiles that had cascaded down when the roof fell in.

'Who discovered the fire?'

'Well, that's the strangest thing of all. My assistants were actually there in the street when the fire started. They saw a girl go in, but no-one else. The arsonist must have been inside already, I suppose. They were busy talking to the butcher, because he had the lamb that was to be sacrificed in the back of his shop. Then smoke began pouring from the doorway, and while they were still trying to work out what to do the roof went up. The reed man must have been dry and warm, I suppose, and went up as soon as the flame touched it. The roof had fallen right in by the time I arrived. The only thing I could do was to make sure it didn't set the Porticus ablaze. I got a bucket chain organised from the nearest fountain.' The priest could see how easily the Porticus Margaritaria, where vendors of every kind of luxury goods had their shops, could have gone up: the shrine was almost under its overhanging eaves. Perhaps the Palatine fire had been set first: it had burned out, after all. Then the man must have run up to the shrine on the Caelian and set that alight before coming down here.

It must have taken some time.

As he turned to Erotes to tell him so, the man who'd been working inside turned and scrambled out over the jumble of beams.

'There's only one body in there,' he told them.

'Where can the girl have gone?' Erotes asked.

'No. It's the girl that's in there.'

The priest stared at him. A girl! Whatever he'd imagined, he certainly wouldn't have supposed a woman would have done this. Drunken young men, perhaps, for a prank, or someone with a grudge against Rome. There was no shortage of them.

'A woman did this?' The incredulity in his voice prompted a sympathetic nod from the magistrate.

'I know, lord. It's not what you'd expect.' He turned to the sweating workman. 'Get her out as soon as you can.'

'We will, but we've got to move some stuff off her first.'

'So she was still inside when the roof fell in,' the priest said. 'I wonder why? The reed man was at the back of the shrine?' The magistrate nodded and the priest walked over to look in through the doorway. He went carefully into the shrine, and stepped over a fallen timber onto a clear patch of the neatly paved floor, feeling the heat of it strike up through the soles of his boots. The little building was nothing but a stone box. On one wall a blackened inscription laid down the boundaries of the district responsible for the upkeep of the shrine. Facing it another listed the local freedmen who had served as its priests. He noted the plain paving of the floor, and then stood very still, staring down. There was nothing intrinsically shocking, of course, in the sight of a woman's foot in a well-made sandal. But here, protruding from under a pile of timbers, streaked with blood and sooty water, it brought him up short. He climbed a little further, and stopped again, so suddenly he almost fell over. The men had cleared some rubbish away from around the woman's head. Golden hair: rich golden hair such as he had seen on his own pillow this morning. Corn-coloured hair like this was rare in Rome. It was streaked with dirt and water and lay over the face. He bent over, gently putting the veil of hair aside. No, of course this was not Cornelia: how could it be? He straightened up and stood still, waiting for the pounding in his heart to slow, conscious of the sounds of Rome going about its business. He noted the girl's dress, of which a shoulder was visible: torn and dirty it might be but it was of the finest cloth. This was no vagrant or prostitute, as he had assumed. He turned to go, and stumbled over a stone or something: looking down he saw it was a small clay lamp, the kind in use in all Roman houses. It had a single spout, no handle and the dished top had been filled with a charming little scene: a lively goat stretching up to steal grapes from a vine. No doubt this was what had lit the fire. He scrambled back out, the lamp still in his hand.

'She's just a girl,' he said to the magistrate, puzzled.

'Well, no-one cares what she was,' the magistrate told him. 'They want her out.'

The priest looked around and saw a group of men waiting with hooks like the ones used in the amphitheatre for dragging dead gladiators from the arena. He shuddered. 'No,' he said. 'No.'

The magistrate stared at him. 'What do you mean? We've got to get rid of her.'

The priest hardly knew why he felt so offended. 'Of course. But we shouldn't assume this girl lit the fire she died in. She must have a decent burial unless we can prove she was guilty.'

The crowd muttered. 'We saw her go in! And then the place went up. What more proof do you want?' one man shouted and another called out, 'What about us? What luck will we have, after this?'

The priest straightened himself, conscious of his soiled and dusty toga, his sweating face. He became aware of the lamp in his hand, and passed it quickly to one of his slaves. 'The rituals will be concluded properly, I assure you. The gods will be pacified. And I will look into this myself.'

The crowd did not challenge him. They did not see an overheated, soot-stained, exasperated young man wondering if he was about to be lynched. They saw a tall patrician, Aulus Manlius Torquatus, wearing a senator's toga and carrying the staff of a priest. They knew him to be powerful, a trusted friend of Octavian, one of the Three Men ruling Rome. Young as he was, he was not to be touched.

For a moment you could feel the silence, disturbed only by a loose shutter somewhere high above, tapping against a wall in the hot breeze. Then the crowd found its voice again. The questions surged towards him in a great wave.

'Who is she? What's happened? Why did she do it? Why? Why?' And, the thought that had also occurred to Torquatus: 'Will the whole ceremony have to be done again?' Silence fell at this. All the money collected for the purchase of a fine lamb, the effort put into cleaning and preparing shrine and feast, was all this to be wasted? Whenever a ritual has been polluted, it must be repeated in full, with a more generous sacrifice: that has been the rule since time immemorial. Otherwise the gods might be offended and Rome would not - could not - prosper.

The crowd's interest swung away to the shrine again as one of the building workers came out through the doorway with the body of the dead woman in his arms, the head dangling loose, the body barely covered by the remains of the expensive dress. On one side it was badly burned, shrivelled and blackened: on the other, the side which had been against the ground, it was almost untouched. Torquatus winced as the man threw the girl roughly to the ground, and the men with hooks, waiting in the background, pushed their way to the front. Then, before they could speak, Felix was back, a tall, handsome man behind him: the chief priest and Octavian's colleague, Lepidus. The usual entourage of slaves, freedmen and clients trailed after him and the crowd shuffled out of his way with a kind of sullen respect. Torquatus stepped forward.

'Thank you for attending so promptly, and for coming yourself,' he said, projecting his voice without effort for the crowd to hear. 'As you can see, this shrine has been burned. This and the one on the Palatine are ruined, and the reed men here and in the shrine on the Caelian have been violated.'

Lepidus nodded irritably. 'So I've been told. The sacrifice is profaned,' he declared. 'It must be done again from the beginning.'

'All of it? All over Rome?' Torquatus watched the man's fine lips tighten as he realised the implications of the question.

'No. The sacrifices at the other holy places have been accepted. In those cases, then, there has been no pollution. On the Palatine, too, the gods have shown no displeasure at the sacrifice?' There was a slight question in Lepidus' voice, and he shot an enquiring glance at Torquatus, who shook his head. The sacrifice yesterday had indeed been perfectly normal. 'In these two cases, however -' Lepidus paused, thinking. 'A new reed man must be made for each place, and the shrines must be thoroughly cleaned. The rituals can be completed tomorrow. What was the sacrifice here? A piglet, I suppose? Oh, a lamb? Then a sheep will be appropriate, to appease the anger of the gods. The same will be needed on the Caelian. Clear the shrines today, clean them thoroughly. Put the new reed men in their places tonight, under guard. Tomorrow you will do what you would have done today, and the ceremony can be concluded at the bridge as usual. The remains of the half-burned reed man must be taken to the charnel-grounds on the Esquiline and burned: it is impure. Let the procession disperse for today, and conclude its business in the morning.'

Lepidus shot Torquatus a keen look as if to check that he'd understood, then turned without recognising the presence of the magistrate or the people, and began to walk off, his entourage falling in behind him. But before he'd taken a couple of paces, the crowd broke out angrily.

'We'll throw her in the Tiber!' a man called out, and there were shouts and catcalls of approval.

Torquatus said clearly, 'No. I will not allow that.'

Lepidus turned back, looking surprised, and the crowd, seeing this, redoubled its demands to be given the body. Torquatus, not sure himself why he felt so strongly about what happened to a criminal's body, wondered whether Lepidus would overrule him, but after a moment it seemed that priestly solidarity was more powerful than Lepidus' own instinctive feelings. He moved back towards the younger man with a look of enquiry.

'I think there are aspects of this affair that need to be investigated,' Torquatus told him softly. 'I want to examine the body.'

'You think there's some doubt about her guilt?'

'I don't see how there can be. But the sequence of events is hard to understand. I could see that her neck was broken, for instance. How did that happen?'

Lepidus shrugged. 'As you wish,' he said, in a tone of voice that clearly expressed his refusal to get involved. He turned and left.

Torquatus sent two of his slaves to borrow something to carry the body on, noticing that the magistrate from the Caelian had already hurried away, and turned his attention back to the sandal-maker, who was looking appalled.

'You heard what the Chief Priest ordered. The shrine must be cleared and cleaned and a new reed man must be made and placed in it before dark. You are to guard the shrine with lights and prayers throughout the night. And send to the market for the best sheep you can find, to appease the anger of the gods.'

The man looked as if he might burst into tears. Torquatus

turned away to his own slaves, sending some to the bridge to tell the Vestal Virgins and the priestess of Jupiter that the ceremony could not be concluded, and one to the house of the senior aedile, responsible for order in the city, who needed to know of this unexplained death.

Then he turned to what was left of the crowd, and his own procession. 'Tomorrow at the first hour after dawn we shall offer sacrifice on the Caelian hill, then at this shrine, before the procession continues to the Sublician bridge as usual. There the reed men will be offered to Father Tiber, and the rites will be concluded. Rome will be made whole once again.'

Where in Jupiter's name was he going to send the girl's body, though? Only one possibility presented itself. Torquatus stepped forward, holding up his hand.

Not a moment too soon. The mood in the crowd had turned ugly again. Most had gone home, leaving behind only the small group that were determined to have their way with the girl's body.

'She doesn't deserve a funeral,' the man who had brought her out insisted.

'She should be treated like the traitor she was,' an old woman agreed, clutching her cloak round her. 'Drag her through the streets, I say!'

'Yes, and then to the Tiber!' another added. There was a chorus of agreement throughout the crowd. Torquatus knew they were right, and yet it seemed unbearable to allow this broken and bruised body to be treated like rubbish, kicked and spat on in the street. Was it because of the girl's golden hair? He didn't know.

'You may not assume the woman's guilt,' he said, his dark face stern. 'That's not the Roman way.' Not that Romans always followed their own rules, he knew.

The crowd fell back, muttering. But what was he to do with this body lying at his feet? The moment he turned his back they would be on her with their hooks again. Where could he send her?

There was only one possible answer. He would have to take her to his own house. It would have to be purified after the funeral, but he could see no alternative, and there might be some advantages to having the body under his own roof, if he was to find out what had happened. He discovered that he did indeed want to investigate the mystery. Already questions were rising in his mind.

Erotes was still wittering at Torquatus' elbow. He turned to the man impatiently. 'I advise you to send for your fresh sacrifice and your reeds as soon as possible. You will need to be ready before nightfall.' Torquatus snapped his fingers at his bodyguard Pulex, who was about to lift the body onto a shutter borrowed from one of the shops, demanding his purse. He emptied it into the magistrate's hands, and a stream of coins came tumbling out. A man in his position ought to be generous, of course, but this was perhaps excessive. No matter: Torquatus could easily afford it, and he could hear a little ripple of appreciation run back through the crowd. Reminding them to reassemble at dawn, he fell in behind the makeshift bier and began the long walk back to the Quirinal.

Chapter 2

The boy Felix had run on ahead to alert the household, and Torquatus, as he walked through the searing heat with proper senatorial dignity, wondered gloomily what in Hades had come over him. He just hoped his mother wouldn't get to hear that he had given house-room to the body of a girl who had set fire to the sacred places of Rome. But he couldn't help wanting to know how a rich girl could have become involved in sacrilege, and against the Argei, of all things. The cult was one for the poor citizens and freedmen: the only men of Torquatus' own rank who troubled themselves about such things were a few eccentric gentlemen who, seeking safety from political turmoil on their country estates, filled the gap in their lives with speculations on the history of the Latin language and culture. Such speculations tended not to lead to arson. He hoped that her family would not be too ashamed to come forward. If they did they would be able to provide some at least of the answers he needed.

As he relaxed Torquatus allowed himself to recognise feelings he hadn't known he possessed. Because the real shock he'd had that morning had been his own response to the gleam of golden hair. His heart had contracted painfully: he had imagined for an agonised moment that it was Cornelia lying tumbled on the ground, and the sudden surge of emotion had thrown him off balance. Love and marriage had nothing to do with each other, of course, and he had never claimed to love his wife. He had married her for the usual reasons. Her father, Balbus, was rich and powerful. He had been Julius Caesar's trusted colleague, and was now just as close to Caesar's heir, Octavian. It had been at Octavian's behest that Torquatus had asked for Cornelia. Torquatus had never regretted his marriage, Cornelia proving to be the sort of wife any man would want: sensible, competent and good-humoured. She was also, he had come to think, beautiful.

Not that he'd seen very much of her in the year and a half since their wedding. He'd been away from Rome, leading troops under Octavian's most senior commander Salvidienus Rufus. They had fought a frustrating and ultimately unsuccessful sea campaign against Pompey the Great's son Sextus, currently based in Sicily, from which he was able to block Rome's grain supply. Afterwards he had sailed across to Macedonia with Marcus Antonius and Octavian himself, to fight the ultimate battle of Rome's civil wars against Caesar's murderers at Philippi. And now at last those civil wars seemed to be over, and in February he had come home to help Octavian with the task of settling time-expired soldiers from his and Antonius' campaigns on farms in Italy, while Antonius restored order in the eastern provinces.

Torquatus had come home to a house at peace: it struck him now how remarkable that was. Rome's senatorial families had been devastated by decades of civil war, in which father had fought against son, brother had killed brother, and whole families had been eliminated by warlords desperate for money. But in his house two women lived together without rancour. On her marriage Cornelia had come to share a home not only with him but with his sister too, a sister he adored, and whose life seemed wrecked by the civil wars still tearing Rome apart. Both capable, decisive women, he could see that they could easily have fallen out. They hadn't done so.

But respect was one thing, love quite another. He thought back to his wedding day. True, there'd been a delight in it. When the veil was lifted off Cornelia's face, and he saw her for the first time, hadn't he imagined for an instant he saw a goddess? Then he'd seen she was better than that, a warm, vital, happy woman. Perhaps, even if you hadn't intended it, you might find you loved the woman you lived with, not just with affection but with passion too? Sharing a bed with Cornelia had brought him great pleasure, but passion had never been something he'd associated with marriage. And no wonder, when he thought of his own parents.

The Manlius Torquatus family had once been among Rome's leaders but its best days had seemed to be behind it. Every noble Roman's ambition was to become consul, and Aulus' father had managed this, but only after he and his son by his first marriage had succeeded in getting the election winners disqualified for bribery. It was not quite the ringing acclamation Lucius Torquatus had dreamt of. Lucius had married again during his year as consul: his political success had cost him more than he could afford. Less than half his age, his young wife Vibia had found herself at once at the top of Rome's social tree. The ladies of Rome had never forgiven this rich, plain girl from Ancona for snatching such an eligible man from under their noses. But the pair had had nothing in common. Vibia couldn't understand why her elderly husband was so fussily protective of his dignity, while Lucius distrusted her choice of friends and tendency to gossip. Once the dowry was handed over and Vibia had done her duty by presenting Lucius with a daughter and a second son, Aulus, they had lived largely separate lives.

With a sense of relief Torquatus let his parents slip back into the past and turned in to the cool reception hall of his house, where water gleamed in the pool and the mosaic floor echoed underfoot. Across the wide space of the hall he saw that a side-room had been made ready for the young girl's body, with a bed-couch covered in white cloth to make a bier. Slaves were lighting the lamps at each corner, the flames almost invisible in the afternoon light pouring in slantwise through the high, barred window, while at a side table his steward Trofimus carefully measured out incense into silver pots. Decorous and simple, it was just right. To have placed the girl in the reception hall would have felt wrong. She was not one of his family, and she was a criminal. Anyway, she wouldn't be there long. Whatever she'd done, he supposed someone would come to claim her.

Torquatus had never been so alive to Cornelia's presence by his side as he was when they stood looking down at the girl in the golden afternoon light. How could he have thought she was like Cornelia? His wife was sturdily built, with a rich, warm complexion and brilliant, expressive blue eyes. This child's hair was a lighter gold, and in every way she was smaller, thinner, paler, as far as he could judge from what was left of her. For now that the body was laid out on the white cloth the full extent of the damage was exposed. It was a hideous sight. All the left side of the body, from the hips upwards, was a mass of charred flesh, red and blistered in places, black as charcoal in others, with fragments of cloth stuck to it in places. The left arm was almost unrecognisable except by the blackened bones visible where flesh was burned right away. The left side of her face, too, had been almost melted in the fire, leaving the teeth visible and the eye-socket a mass of burned tissue. There was no hair left on that side of her head, and the skin had become a glassy red. On the other side, however, the beams and tiles that had fallen on the girl had saved her from the flames, so that the beautiful face Torquatus had glimpsed under the dust and soot of the shrine could clearly be seen. Torquatus picked up the girl's right hand, noting the neatly trimmed nails and soft skin. After a moment's revulsion at the thought, he gently slid his hands under her head and lifted it. It flopped loosely, as he had noticed earlier, and his fingers noted the softness of her skull just above the nape of her neck. He laid her head down again and straightened it so that her one blue eye gazed up into the roof, as if the answer to some important question might be found there. Cornelia at once moved forward, drawing the eyelid gently down.

The slaves were muttering to each other as they began once again to pull the body this way and that, to dress it in the long white tunic in which the girl would go to her funeral. Torquatus picked up the ruined dress they'd thrown over a stool. He thought, with a shiver of horror, that he'd seen his sister or maybe his wife in dresses like this one, made of very soft fabric in a lighter shade, sea-green in this case, over a darker, heavier under-dress. Even though what was left of it was torn, filthy, and bloodstained, he could see that it must have been very expensive. A bit Greek-looking; he supposed it must be the fashion. It would drape beautifully when she stood, but she wouldn't be doing that, ever again. Torquatus dropped it back onto the stool and wiped his hands.

You could see, from the half of her face that wasn't ruined, that the child must have been beautiful, with delicate, classical features that even the heavy bruising she'd suffered couldn't mar. A sprinkling of freckles over her nose gave her a childish charm, and her hair, tumbled now, had been arranged in the decorous way girls wear it, parted in the centre, the golden wings softly framing her cheeks, the back hair drawn into a knot behind her head; but her mouth was the mouth of a woman, delicately shaped, soft-lipped, kissable.

'I wondered if you might have recognised her,' Torquatus suggested. 'Whether you might have seen her at some friend's house?'

'No. I know what you mean, though: she looks like the sort of girl I might know. Poor child.' Her eyes sparkled with tears, and he put his arm around her.

'What madness could have made her do such a dreadful thing?'

'What indeed. That's the question, isn't it?'

Cornelia twisted in his arm to look up at him. 'You're worried about something, Aulus?'

'Well, I wouldn't say worried. But I don't quite understand what's happened here.'

'Isn't it quite straightforward? Apart from her motive? She went round the three shrines in the dark, setting fire to them. Then, at the one on the Velia, she found herself trapped in the shrine. Maybe the reed man there burned more fiercely than the others, or maybe it didn't, it just made a lot of smoke, and she collapsed because she couldn't breathe.'

Torquatus looked down at her. 'Her neck's broken. I can't quite work out how that could have happened.'

'Perhaps one of those roof-beams fell on her?' Cornelia suggested.

He shook his head regretfully. 'If she had collapsed from smoke inhalation, and was lying on the floor when the roof fell in, a blow on the back of her head like that would have smashed her face against the paving. You can see that hasn't happened.'

'Could she have fallen and broken her skull against the wall or something else?'

'There's nothing in those shrines, Cornelia. If she'd fallen and hit her head on the wall her skull would have been smashed much higher up. And I don't see how she could have been trapped: the reed man was propped against the back wall of the shrine. She'd have had nothing to do but turn and run, if the fire had flared up suddenly. Or if she'd gone in and found the reed man burning.'

Cornelia stared at him. 'Are you suggesting you think she was murdered?'

'I don't see how she could have been. There wasn't anyone else there. That's one thing we do know: she was seen going in there. And why should anyone murder her? She's just a girl.'

'It's hard to imagine what kind of a threat she could pose,' Cornelia agreed. 'Unless she disturbed them?'

'She might, of course. Though that just leaves us with two people playing silly buggers in shrines at dawn, instead of one. And no-one came out of the shrine after the fire was started. No, she must have done it.'

They had moved out of the side-room as they talked, and now settled themselves on the marble bench at the head of the pool in the reception hall. The drowsy heat of the afternoon seemed increased by a slight hot breeze from the great doors that stood open as always. Pigeons fussed about on the edge of the roof where a hard blue sky promised more searing weather to come. In the distance, the voices of slaves could be heard as they cooked or cleaned or whatever slaves did at this time of day.

Cornelia took his hand quietly. 'I think you said that in two shrines she'd set fire to the reed man, but in the other one the man had already been collected?'

Torquatus sighed. 'Yes, that's another thing I noticed straight away. Doesn't make sense, does it? Burning a shrine after the sacrifice has been made and the offering accepted is just stupid. Besides, if you want to attack the gods of Rome why not burn down one of the big temples so everyone would notice? I mean, the Argei!'

Cornelia considered this. 'Well, the big temples are always busy, and surely they are guarded? It wouldn't be so easy to harm them. But tell me about the Argei: I'm just a foreigner, you know, and I don't really get what it's about.'

She was smiling up at him. It was true that she had been brought up in Spain by her grandparents until she was fifteen, but she seemed to him as Roman as his sister. He suddenly wondered if she had found it as hard as his mother had to find her place in Rome. He put the thought away to be considered later.

'I think it's a sort of afterthought to the Lemuria' he told her. 'The spirits of the dead, the lemures, are attracted to light and life and always want to come back to join us if they can. That's what my father told me, anyway, and it certainly feels pretty uncanny; the spirits are there all right, bound up in those reed-men.' He shivered slightly. 'The ritual must be very old; the prayers are in ancient Latin. Let's hope the gods still understand it, even if I don't. Then there aren't any real rules about what should be offered, which is hardly surprising since it isn't clear which god we're offering to. Mostly people offer white beasts, but in one or two of the shrines they've given black ones, suitable for the gods of the underworld. I've no idea who's right. And maybe it's not about the lemures at all. Perhaps it's a way of asking the gods to protect the crops, or keep floods away. It could even be some kind of remnant of old human sacrifice from the old days: some people say Argei comes from the word for Argives, and that originally it was Greeks who were sacrificed. All I know is that we always do it, and I'll be glad when it's safely over. Speaking as a priest, the idea of an attack on those reed men makes my skin crawl. I wouldn't have been surprised if Lepidus had said we had to offer again at every shrine. She must have had some overmastering motive.'

'Or perhaps she was doing it to please someone else?' Cornelia suggested.

'Somebody got at her? Perhaps. But it doesn't make any difference. You don't play tricks like that on the gods.'

'And we mustn't forget,' Cornelia insisted, 'that she may not be guilty. She may just have disturbed the arsonist.'

'Who was seen by no-one. And what would a well-brought-up girl have been doing hanging around a shrine at dawn?'

'She might have gone to meet someone,' Cornelia suggested, and Torquatus' heart sank.

'A man, I suppose' he said. 'A man who's not going to come forward. But who would have made an assignation in such a place, and on the very day of the festival, too? Still, let's say it happened: first the arsonist slips in unseen before dawn. Then the girl goes in too, just as the preparations are about to begin. If the arsonist's the man she's come to meet and he's already lit the reed man how come she doesn't just turn and run? If he hasn't, do they have a chat before he hits her on the head? It would only be a short chat, from what the people there say. How does he get out without anyone seeing him? Or maybe the man she's come to meet isn't the arsonist. So then we have three of them dodging about. Maybe this other man, the one she's come to meet, does hear a sound and bunks off. Meanwhile no-one saw him doing so, nor anyone go into the shrine except the girl.'

He let out an exasperated sigh.

Cornelia gave his hand a reassuring squeeze. 'I think we need to wait until her body is claimed. There's no point in trying to understand it all until then.'

Torquatus grunted. 'This isn't going to be straightforward, I can feel it in my bones.' He got up and they wandered back into the side-room, glancing down at the beautiful, damaged face. He spoke the thought that had been in his mind for some time. 'I'll tell you what, Cornelia. I'd bet you any money no-one comes to collect her. I wish I hadn't had her brought here. She's ill-omened, and will bring the house bad luck. But what else could I have done?'

Cornelia smiled. 'Well, if they don't, we'll arrange her funeral for her. You'll feel better when you've had a bath. And, look, here's Trofimus with a jug of wine.'

Not just 'wine', Torquatus realized, but an excellent Caecuban, laid down by his father. One of his steward's best qualities was his ability to judge his master's mood, to know when ordinary wine would do, and when something special was needed. A couple of cups of the Caecuban and a leisurely bath - not too long in the hot room, in this weather, and a cold plunge to finish with - left him feeling relaxed and refreshed, though no nearer to finding answers to the many questions surrounding this strange and sudden death. He just hoped his instinct was wrong, and that the girl's parents would turn up with an explanation which would make sense of the whole stupid situation.

When he wandered back out into the gardens again, cool and sweet-smelling, Cornelia reminded her husband that Manlia was paying a duty visit to her mother, and that they had no dinner guests tonight, for which she seemed to be thankful, but which made Torquatus anxious. Since his return to Rome he had done a fair amount of entertaining: Octavian needed to remind everyone he was in power, and those around him needed to show they were his friends. But the city they'd returned to was angry, nervous and hungry. Sextus Pompeius' ships were already doing their damnedest to stop the corn supply from getting through. Supplies were perilously low, and there had been sickness too in the unexpected heat of the spring. After an initial flurry of dinner-giving, things had gone very quiet: it seemed inflammatory to lay on feasts when the people were hungry, and a good few of the senators had been so seriously unsettled by the situation that they'd hurriedly decided that life on the Bay of Neapolis would suit them just now, and had disappeared with their households, letting it be known that they feared an outbreak of plague.

Now the senators were returning, though nervously, like chickens who've just seen one of their number caught by a fox: fortunately for Octavian they were too divided among themselves to offer any real opposition. Their lives had been turned upside down. Some, who had been vocal in support of Caesar's murderers, were keeping quiet and hoping to pass unnoticed; others were waiting for the day when Antonius returned to eliminate Octavian, a wretched little provincial in their view, who traded on his name as Julius Caesar's great-nephew and adopted son, and whose precocious success they viewed with hostility and astonishment. Others again seemed to believe that if they sat back and did nothing, Antonius and Octavian would slaughter each other, after which normal life - including regular consulships for themselves - would be resumed. Still others hoped that Sextus Pompeius might come to their aid, or that Octavian might be killed by the angry men whose land had been seized and given to the soldiers. It was not a time for convivial dinner-parties. But at the same time every senator needed to have his reception hall filled every morning, his dinner couches filled every evening. These were the markers of his political and social eminence, and without them he was nothing.

Since they were not entertaining Torquatus and Cornelia dined outside. In Torquatus' Roman home there were no banqueting couches built into the garden, such things being more suited to the leisurely life of the seaside villa, but Trofimus had made the slaves carry out a couple of reading-couches and a table, and it was pleasant to eat in the warm shade, listening as the birds began to roost in the trees around them. Water bubbled from the open mouth of the bronze dolphin which reared out of the pool. The sweet heavy scent of roses filled the air, sharpened with rosemary. Torquatus lay on his back for a moment, his wine-cup on his chest, noting that the blossom had faded long since from the apple and pear trees and sleepily surveying the little round fruit-shapes standing out among the pointed leaves.

'We shall have a good crop of apples,' he said with a yawn.

'Lovely,' Cornelia agreed, though rather absent-mindedly. He threw her a questioning glance, and she sat up decisively. 'I think I might come down to the bridge and watch the ceremony tomorrow.'

'Really? It'll be very crowded, and hot again, from the looks of it.' And indeed the sky was fading into soft pink and gold bands, promising another scorching day. 'And the whole thing's pretty incomprehensible, you know. I can't see why you'd want to.'

'It's something I've never seen, that's all. Girls don't go to that sort of thing, because of all the rough men in the crowd.'

'Whereas married ladies love rough men, is that it?'

Cornelia snorted. 'I just think it would be interesting. I can take a slave to guard me if you like,' she offered.

'You certainly will. Not just one, either,' Torquatus said and just at that moment Trofimus padded out of the shadowed colonnade with a bowl of fruit in his hands, followed by a younger slave carrying a chair. 'The lady Manlia, lord,' he announced, with a paternal smile, and Torquatus looked up as his sister came briskly towards them. 'Manlia!' He held up a hand to her and she bent down and kissed his cheek. He breathed in the scent of the rosemary wash she used on her hair, something he never did without searing memories of the terrible time, two years ago, when he had seemed doomed to ruin and death, and only Manlia had helped him. 'I wasn't expecting you back so soon. Nothing wrong, I hope?'

Cornelia and Manlia kissed, and Manlia sank gracefully into the chair Trofimus had placed for her. Torquatus was a big man where Manlia was small and slender, but in many ways she was very like her brother. Her curly hair was piled into a great dark mass on her head, though tendrils of it were escaping now, as always. Torquatus found the only way to manage his own curls was to keep them cropped aggressively short, which had the added advantage of gaining him approval among old-fashioned types who thought that aggressively short was the only appropriate hairstyle for a Roman man. Her dark eyes, longer and more almond-shaped than her brother's, were set under the same arching brows; though hers were plucked so that they did not meet over her aquiline nose, as her brother's did. Those eyes were glancing sideways at Torquatus, full of laughter.

'Oh no, there's nothing wrong at all, except the usual. Mother's fine.' She made a face, which Torquatus understood. Their mother was not a congenial woman, and she had never forgiven Torquatus for supporting Caesar in the civil wars, when his father had been a staunch republican. He himself visited Vibia very seldom, meanly leaving to Manlia the task of keeping the family together.

'No, thank you Trofimus, I have eaten,' she was saying, smiling up at the steward. 'I'll just have some of that fruit, and some water. Really cold water: I'm dreadfully thirsty.'

Trofimus bowed and walked away.

'And Iunia?' Torquatus asked without enthusiasm. His sister-in-law was not improved by sharing a house with his mother, he felt. Cooped up together in a small but elegant house on the Caelian Hill, the pair of them seemed to do little but feed each other's resentments.

'I feel for her,' Manlia said, with a reluctant smile. She tucked an errant strand of hair behind her ear. 'She's had a horrid life. Widowed while she was still young, with no children, her chance of a second marriage lost when her lover was forced into exile. I do try and be patient with them both, but oh, it is hard. Especially when Mother's always criticising you.'

'Tell me something I didn't know,' Torquatus replied with a shrug. 'What have I done now?'

'Got mixed up with a dead girl. A criminal dead girl.'

'Gods! Did they know about that already?'

Manlia paused, her hand hovering over the fruit bowl, then

looked up suddenly with a snort of laughter. 'The slaves had heard about it. Don't they always? And of course when I heard what you'd done I had to hurry home and see if I could help you in any way.' She caught her brother's eye and laughed again. 'Oh, very well, then, I was just inquisitive. And I felt I didn't really need an excuse to come home early.' This was said with a challenging look and a slight lift of her eyebrows which made Cornelia laugh too.

'You certainly don't', Cornelia told her. 'Did you have a chance - being inquisitive, you know - to take a look at our dead visitor as you came in? Do you know who she is?'

'I did. And no, I'm sorry, I don't recognise her. She's a horrible sight, but I think I'd know if I'd seen her before. But really, Aulus! Bringing her here is so unlucky for the house. What made you think of such a thing?'

'I know it is.' His dark face was sombre. 'But if you'd seen that baying mob, hanging about there with their hooks to drag her round the streets, just waiting for me to leave, you'd have done the same.'

'But if she's guilty of sacrilege - ?'

'I know. But even if she was I can't help thinking that someone put her up to it.'

Manlia saw the political dimensions of the situation, as Torquatus had known she would. 'An attack on Rome's gods is an attack on the state, of course. The state, in Italy at least, meaning Octavian. I see why you need to get to the bottom of this. He'd expect it.'

Torquatus had already uncovered a conspiracy against Octavian, almost two years ago.

He said thoughtfully, 'If this is a plot, it seems at first sight a pretty incompetent one.'

There was a silence as all three reflected on this.

'I can't understand it.' Torquatus poured himself some more wine, then waved the jug at the two women who shook their heads. 'Someone must know who she is. She's been away from her home for a day at least: the fire was discovered in the early hours. Why hasn't her family been running round Rome, kicking up a huge fuss over their missing treasure?'

'Perhaps they don't want to admit their daughter's a criminal?' Manlia suggested.

'I suppose that's it.'

'Perhaps she doesn't live in Rome?' Manlia suggested. 'Or

maybe she does - did - live in Rome and went out on the pretext of going to visit a friend, or something. Her family wouldn't know anything had gone wrong. Even when they realised she was missing they wouldn't identify their daughter with a mad arsonist.'

'I suppose not,' Torquatus agreed.

'But as time goes by they might put two and two together. If Mother's slaves knew all about it, her parents will find out where she is easily enough, once they do.' She turned her head to smile at Trofimus, who was just placing a misted jug of water and a cup on the table in front of her.

'I had to bring her here,' Torquatus said, frowning, 'There wasn't anywhere else. But I wish I hadn't. I have enough problems, without a murder to solve.'

Manlia's eyes met Cornelia's. 'You will, though, won't you?' Cornelia asked. 'You've already pointed out problems in the official narrative. You know you won't be happy till you've sorted it out.'

He sighed. 'It's quite interesting,' he agreed. 'The question of how exactly she died; the choice of that shrine, on that day. But I really don't have much time.'

Cornelia patted his hand, saying comfortably, 'I'm sure you'll find out who did it,' before turning to her sister-in-law. 'Do you fancy going to see the ceremony at the bridge tomorrow?'

'Oh, it's been put off, of course. I must say, I've never been. What exactly do you have to do tomorrow, Aulus.'

Torquatus was yawning in the warm evening air. 'I have to go back to the Velia, and make sacrifice again. You should have seen the magistrate's face when Lepidus said he'd have to offer a sheep this time.'

'Poor souls,' said Manlia. 'That would cost them.'

'Yes, well, I gave them a handsome donation towards it, so they needn't complain. Thank all the gods there are that Lepidus didn't decide the whole bloody thing had gone wrong. Just imagine if all over Rome we'd had to set up new reed men, make more sacrifices, repeat everything. Luckily he didn't, so tomorrow I skip down to the Velia - sorry, I mean I progress in a dignified and orderly way - and then the whole procession moves off to the Sublician Bridge, where, I very much hope, the Vestal Virgins, a praetor, various other priests from my own college and the Priestess of Jupiter will all have gathered, and we can chuck those effigies into the Tiber and good luck to them.'

'Odd that it should have been that particular shrine,' Cornelia observed. 'There was some fuss about it recently, wasn't there? I seem to remember hearing something. I can't think what, though - oh, I know! I was asked for a donation towards rebuilding it. Or maybe refurbishing it? Something like that. It wasn't much.'

'You have property down there?' Torquatus wasn't surprised. Cornelia was a very rich woman, with property all over Italy, and with accountants and stewards of her own to manage it. Nor was she the kind of woman to leave it all to them: she would know if she had been required to contribute to the rebuilding of a shrine.

'All I know is that my agent told me the tenants in my block down there were upset, because some of them were asked for a contribution too. And now, no doubt, even more money will be required.' Cornelia shrugged, and tipped water into her cup, before turning to Manlia. 'I was just telling Aulus I intended to go and watch the ceremony when you arrived, and he was being very prissy about it.'

'Never mind,' Manlia assured her brother kindly. 'I won't let Cornelia come to harm.'

Torquatus was frowning. 'It's pretty rough. Although the praetor and the priest and the Vestals perform the rituals, it's mainly run by the slaves and freed slaves in each part of the city: people like us don't have much to do with it, unless, like lucky me, they happen to be the priest appointed. It's a rite that has to be performed, but I don't think you'd be amused. Next you'll be saying you want to go drinking and fooling about at Anna Perenna's festival.'

'Making bowers of branches with our boyfriends,' Manlia declared, and Cornelia laughed and shot a mischievous look at her husband.

'We'll take care, and we won't drink too much or get into trouble, I promise.'

'You won't, because I shall send Becco and Pulex to guard you both.'

'Won't you need them yourself?'

'No, I shouldn't think so, and I'd really rather they were with you.'

Manlia gave him a sceptical look but Cornelia laid a hand on her husband's arm. 'I'm very glad Aulus cares for our safety. Rome isn't such a peaceful place these days, after all, is it?'

Chapter 3

No-one knocked on the door during the night. Next morning promised to be hotter than ever, and for a few moments after the great house-doors were thrown open at dawn Torquatus enjoyed the coolness of the air: all too soon the sun would be burning in a cloudless sky. He wasn't sitting in his ivory chair waiting for his morning visitors today. They'd been told to stay away yesterday, and no doubt they'd all heard by now how the ceremony was interrupted. Instead he was standing surrounded by the group of slaves, clients and freedmen who would accompany him down to the Velia once again, where they would be able to complete yesterday's interrupted ritual. He spread the word among his followers that the girl now lying in the side-room was not to be presumed guilty of the dreadful crime. He asked them all to tell everyone they knew that he wanted to speak, in confidence, to the young woman's family and friends. They were to emphasise that he had not declared the girl guilty. Maybe that would bring someone forward to tell him what they knew.

Cornelia was talking quietly to Trofimus and the doorman, and he saw with dismay that she was dressed for going out, with a light veil thrown over her hair to protect it from the dust. He turned his energies, as his armed bodyguards came clattering into the reception hall, to persuading her that she really didn't need to see this ceremony, and that in any case he could take her another year when he wouldn't - may the gods grant it - be officiating.

'Chucking the old men off the bridge, it's been going on for ever,' he pointed out. But as the words left his mouth Manlia walked in from the back of the house dressed in a cool and floating gown of a soft pale pink. She was clearly ready and eager to go. Torquatus gave up. He hid a smile at the sight of Manlia's burly slave, waiting patiently behind his mistress with a pink parasol held carefully in one enormous paw, then summoned the bodyguards Becco and Pulex to go along with the ladies once they were ready to start, and not to let them out of their sight. An angry, hungry Rome is never a safe place, and the more muscle his womenfolk had around them the happier he'd be. He'd bought the two ex-gladiators a few years ago, and had never regretted it. Becco was a man whose kindly nature was hidden in a body so large and shambling as to deter any potential attackers. Pulex was smaller, but built of solid muscle, an unsociable man with mean cold eyes, who spent every minute of his spare time exercising his already formidable physique.

With a brief distracted kiss for Cornelia, Torquatus gathered his own group of slaves and set off, wrinkling his nose at the smell in the airless street. The Quirinal is highly respectable, the streets wide and the air clean, but even here the odd passer-by will nip into a side street to relieve himself. And that's in the daytime. After dark, of course, any front door, however imposing, might be a target for the passing reveller. The city needed a good thunderstorm to clear the air.

On the Caelian he found the shrine purified and clean, the sacrifice ready. The ritual was completed without mishap: it seemed that the gods were happy enough.

Torquatus felt his stomach tighten with anxiety as he approached the Velia. What if something else had gone wrong? As if in a dream, he arrived at the little temple, which looked very different today. The smoke-blackened walls had been thoroughly washed, the litter of burned reeds, tiles and charred wood swept away. Apart from the absence of a roof, the little building looked quite normal. The magistrate, apparently also in the dream, came forward once again, bowing and rubbing his hands. Torquatus shook himself out of his stupid mood, and prepared to do his duty.

'You've worked hard,' he said, looking round. If it wasn't for the shrine having no roof, no-one would guess what had happened yesterday. The crowd was larger than yesterday's: obviously he wasn't the only one expecting that there might be more to see than an archaic rite. 'And your sacrifice is all ready?'

The magistrate preened himself a little. 'Everyone's been working really hard, lord. And thanks to your generous donation we were able to buy a very fine sheep. I always say, you can't beat the community spirit you get in this city.'

Torquatus nodded. The sheep, a large one, looked depressed, as if, unlike yesterday's jolly lamb, it foresaw its fate. Better get on, then, and dispatch it to the gods. Twitching the fold of his toga over his head he raised his voice so all could hear the incomprehensible prayer.

Nothing went wrong. The slaughter man knew his work; the sheep died without protest; the entrails were perfectly healthy; the new reed man was brought out from the sacred place, with nothing but a certain freshness and sweetness to distinguish him from the ones leaning at various drunken angles against house fronts and pillars as the procession waited to restart. No messengers had rushed up to tell him of further arson attacks, which seemed to make it more likely that the arsonist was, however improbable it seemed, the girl now lying dead in his house. Torquatus nodded them on, and a buzz of talk and even a few cheers broke out as the new reed man was lifted up by the two chosen bearers, who yesterday had gone instead to fetch a litter for a young woman's body: not that they seemed to remember that today, as they joked and laughed with bystanders. It was all going just as it should, and what was it he'd feared, after all? More arson attacks? Even if the girl hadn't burned the shrines, no criminal would commit more outrages at a moment when they would be guarded. He glanced around as the procession moved off, scanning the crowd jostling good-naturedly behind him, looking for something unusual: a sinister stranger lurking in a portico, perhaps, or a hooded man with a dagger half-hidden under his cloak? He knew this was absurd; then, passing the butcher's shop, the flash of a cleaver caught his eye and his breath caught for a moment. The man was only working on the sheep, jointing it for cooking so the neighbourhood could enjoy its feast. He quickened his pace a little - butchers' shops, like fishmongers' stalls, were best avoided in hot weather.

They lurched their way across the Forum before heading off down the Vicus Tuscus, the procession growing by the moment, scooping up those people who hang around the Forum most days hoping for a trial, a speech, a meeting, a fight: anything that might get them a free cup of wine at their local bar, and who were quite content to walk to the Sublician Bridge behind a priest and some bundles of reeds. There was some singing and a bit of shouting at first, but that died away to an uncertain silence as they approached the bridge. If they'd been doing this yesterday the procession would have had to negotiate its way through the chaos of the market, but this wasn't a market day and the big space was empty except for dollops of ox-dung and drifts of straw and yellowing cabbage-leaves. The procession came at last to the river-bank, lined with warehouses: grain stores, the double-locked depots of spice-merchants, a sawmill where sweating slaves were cutting up great baulks of timber unloaded from a ship lying close by, a yard full of amphorae, its gate guarded by a heavy-set man and a dog whose hackles rose as they approached. It scrambled to its feet and showed its formidable teeth, but the unsmiling guard pulled off his cap and nodded to Torquatus as he passed.

And on the bridge a slightly bored-looking group awaited him: the urban praetor and several other priests from Torquatus' own college in one group, the Vestal Virgins, their white veils contrasting with the dark heads of the men, in another. And, standing a little to one side, the priestess of Jupiter. Torquatus couldn't help a superstitious shiver at the sight: her grey hair was hanging loose, her eyes cast down, her clothes plain, poor and dark. A patrician woman - a priestess - in mourning. But for what? There was something in this rite, some connection with the dead, which made him anxious.

Torquatus stepped forward, waited for the buzz of talk to die away. 'The Old Men are here,' he announced, and heard the words bounce back off the surrounding buildings. The river's stink was choking in the heat, and he could feel the sweat running down under his tunic. The Chief Vestal stepped forward and bowed her head. 'And to their deaths the Argei must go.' She made an odd gesture with her hands, then stood back to let the bearers of the reed-men approach the parapet. The crowd pressed closer: this was what they had come to see. One by one, the little groups of men brought up their reed-men in the same order as they had been collected. The first group took a run up onto the bridge, their man held as if lying on his back. When they got to the middle they stopped and lifted him up, showing him off to ragged cheers. The men turned and jogged back into the crowd. Then they ran to the parapet again, and again made as if to throw the reed man over. On the third rush, they lifted their man higher, held him aloft a moment, and threw him over amid a storm of cheers and clapping. There was a moment's silence, a splash, and a final burst of cheering.

With twenty-seven reed-men to be dispatched, the whole business took some time. The Vestals began to look hot and bothered, and even the Chief Vestal was red-faced and sweating. Only the priestess of Jupiter still stood aside, silent, unmoving, her unbound grey hair almost concealing her face. The crowds began to melt away, drawn no doubt by the neighbourhood feasts awaiting them. Only three more reed-men to go; and then there was the new-looking one from the Velia; and it was over. The Chief Vestal hurried through a final prayer, nodded to Torquatus, and led her young colleagues away. The priestess of Jupiter was smiling and saying something to the slave who was tidying her hair which made the girl laugh.

'Cup of wine at the Regia,' said the priest standing next to Torquatus. 'We always do it.'

Torquatus nodded, but his eyes were scanning the rapidly thinning crowd, looking for his wife and sister. They would have stood out in that crowd of workmen: they must have found the whole thing unbearably hot and dull and gone home. He turned with relief to his neighbour, Publius Aurelius Cotta. 'You had this privilege last year, didn't you?'

Cotta grinned. 'I did. It wasn't as hot, but even so - I'm very glad there was someone even newer than me to get it this time. Especially since you had these problems. Tell me about that - it's hard to believe anyone would do such a dangerous and stupid thing, isn't it? Apart from anything else, if she'd been caught red-handed she'd have been lynched, wouldn't she? You need to have a pretty strong reason for that sort of thing. A protest against the regime, perhaps?' They headed off the bridge, a straggling group of senatorial types. A cup of wine would go down a treat.

No-one called to claim the dead girl that day, not even to say under cover of anonymity that they had known her, that they would never have believed she could do such a wicked thing. No-one came the next day, or the one after. On the fifth day after her death, Torquatus ordered the amount of incense burnt to be doubled, and flowers to be placed around the body. Roses, lilies, anything with a good scent: in the hot thundery air of that unseasonable heatwave the smell of putrefaction was becoming nauseating. He should have had her put in the reception hall after all: at least the air there was constantly refreshed from the open doors and the open roof. He cheered himself up by thinking that she must be buried on the seventh day, and that since no relatives had come forward he would go ahead and make the arrangements himself. He had seldom longed for anything as he longed to get this unlucky body out from under his roof. A pyre up on the heights of the Esquiline, he told Trofimus: pay for a decent site, away from the common pits. It wasn't likely there'd be many mourners, if any. And buy in a good-quality marble urn, a plain one, for the ashes and fragments of bone. There didn't seem to be anything else to do. There ought to be a banquet on the night of the funeral, but who could he invite?

On the evening of the sixth day after the girl had died,

Torquatus, Manlia and Cornelia dined out in the garden again. None of them had needed to say that the smell in the house made the thought of eating there made their stomachs turn. The evening air had been made cooler and more refreshing by the gardeners, who had watered the flowers just before dinner to bring out their scents: honeysuckle and rose the sweetest, but behind them the sharp scents of the geranium, rosemary, sage, rue and hyssop grown for use in the kitchen. They were just checking over the arrangements for the funeral, not wanting to omit anything needful, when Trofimus appeared from the shadows of the colonnade, moving rather quickly for him. He stepped aside to reveal the man who'd followed him in.

'Quintus Fiscilius,' he announced with a flourish, as if Quintus Fiscilius were a surprise after-dinner entertainment.

The young man who stepped out of the shadows turned out to be a scruffy-looking person, with a mop of dusty curls and an untended beard. His tunic looked as if he hadn't changed it for some time, his hands were grimy and there was a little smear of dried blood on his right forearm. Seeing how travel-stained and weary he looked, Cornelia said quietly, 'Bring some wine, Trofimus.'

The visitor licked dry lips. 'My sister?' There was a look of horror in his eyes.

'You are looking for the girl who - who was found in the shrine of the Argei on the Velia a few days ago?'

'Was that where she was? They told me - I must see - .' He stopped, gulping.

Torquatus got up slowly, but Manlia said, 'Are you sure? Perhaps you should sit, have a cup of wine, rest for a moment. Because you must understand that she was found in the remains of a burned-out shrine. She isn't a pleasant sight. No? Come, then.'

They processed in a rather awkward silence through the darkening colonnade back into the house, the gentle splashing of the dolphin fountain dying into murmurs behind them, their feet too loud on the mosaic floor. Even out here the smell came at them in waves. The lamps at the corners of the bier guttered and flared as they walked into the room, the little flames trembling in the heavy, poisonous air. Torquatus hadn't been in there since the previous day, and he noticed that the girl's skin had become white and waxy-looking, with an unpleasant shine on it like sweat. Cornelia had overseen her laying out, getting the slaves to put pads of cloth under the body once they'd washed it down, to catch the fluids that would leach out of it. Every day since the slaves had wiped the body down regularly with vinegar. Torquatus was thankful for her care: this unfortunate young man was going to see a bad enough sight as it was. The girl's dreadfully damaged face had become bloated and puffy after a day or two. The bloating had now gone but she no longer looked as if she might be simply sleeping.

Suddenly Torquatus realised that the last body to lie here in his house awaiting its last rites must have been his father's. A familiar feeling of guilt swept over him. He hadn't been there. He had fallen out with his family, and his father had thrown him out. They had never spoken again and a couple of months later old Lucius Torquatus was dead. Putting the thought aside, he moved to allow Fiscilius to come up to the bier.

'How well you have cared for her,' Fiscilius whispered, as if he might wake the girl from her eternal sleep. 'If she'd been laid out at home we couldn't have -,' He broke off, suddenly still; then cried out, a high thin wail which made the others freeze. He half-turned away from the bier; for a moment Torquatus saw his face chalk-white behind the messy beard, before he crumpled and fell to the floor with a crash, bringing down one of the lamp-stands with him. Torquatus knelt quickly at his side, feeling for his pulse. Behind him he heard Trofimus quietly telling a slave who had cried out in shock to pick up the lampstand and mop up the spilt oil. Cornelia was directing another to fetch water. In a moment or two, Fiscilius began to come round.

Cornelia turned to the steward again. 'Trofimus, our guest here has been travelling. He will need food and wine, and a bed. Are the baths still hot enough for him to use if he wishes it?'

Fiscilius groaned, and her attention returned to him as he sat up.

'I'm sorry,' Torquatus said. 'The shock of seeing your sister's body so badly burned - .' He broke off, staring, as Fiscilius' hysterical laughter echoed round the empty hall.

The young man stopped with a visible effort, gulping to control his sobs, scrubbing at his face with a dusty sleeve. He took a deep breath. 'I'm sorry. As you say, it's the shock. My poor sister -'

Manlia took Fiscilius' hands in hers and held them firmly, and Torquatus could hear his breath slowing, becoming steady.

Trofimus came forward with a cup of water, and Fiscilius took it in a shaking hand, and drank a little.

'What was your sister doing in the shrine of the Argei? Apart from committing arson?' Torquatus asked.

Fiscilius sighed. 'Did she?' he asked in a flat voice. 'I didn't know. I didn't even know she was here till a couple of days ago.' He sighed again and passed a shaking hand over that dusty hair.

'No. Don't say any more just now,' Torquatus told him. 'My wife's right. You need to bathe and eat and drink before you explain. Which would you like first, a bath or some food?'

The young man's colour was gradually returning, and he gave them a hesitant smile. 'A bath and a shave would be wonderful. And then I suppose I ought to eat. Thank you. But before that - may I look again? It's just that I can't quite believe it.'

He rose to his feet as he spoke and Torquatus moved aside. Almost reluctantly Fiscilius inched closer to the bier. 'Yes, that's Fiscilia. That's not her dress, is it?'

'No. That's a tunic of mine,' Cornelia told him. 'Her own was a double-layered dress of light over dark green, and it was too badly burned to cover her decently. You can see it if you want.'

Fiscilius sighed. 'I know the dress you mean: it was a new one, and more grown-up than my aunt generally allowed.' He swallowed hard. 'She was so proud of it. The last time I saw her - at home in Mevania - she insisted on putting it on and coming to show me, twirling round and laughing -'

Manlia held up her hand. 'No more now till you've bathed and eaten, or we'll have you out cold on the floor again.'

Thick hot darkness had fallen over the garden before the little party came outside again. The torchlight rendered Fiscilius' face into a skull, Torquatus thought, till Trofimus brought more lamps and the skull turned back into a young man's face. He was a handsome man, his light brown hair now neatly clipped over a broad forehead, his rather pointed chin smooth. Only his hazel eyes seemed strained, as if they still held the horror they'd seen. One of Torquatus' tunics hung a little loosely on him. Trofimus proposed bringing out another couch, but Cornelia said she would share her husband's, and now lay in front of Torquatus as if they were dining, though rather closer as the couch was designed for reading, not eating. Fiscilius toyed with the simple meal Trofimus had rustled up: bread, a sharp fresh cheese, a dish of olives and another of artichokes in oil, and bowls of dried figs and nuts.

When he'd done they passed the wine-jug around and waited for Fiscilius to tell his story.

'Perhaps you'd better start with who you are.'

Fiscilius smiled back at Torquatus, a tight, nervous smile. 'My name you know.'

Torquatus smiled. 'Yes. And your family? You live in Mevania, you said? How old are you? And how old was Fiscilia?'

'What a lot of questions. My family home is just outside Mevania, but we have a house in the town as well, of course. We have been the leading men in Mevania since time out of mind. I'm twenty-one, and I've been the head of my family since my father died last year. My sister is - was - eighteen.'

As he spoke, a cold finger touched Torquatus' neck. He knew something of Mevania, a one-horse town on the western branch of the via Flaminia, about twenty miles from Perusia. He'd been discussing it with Octavian only the other day. If Mevania was involved this case was about to become a great deal more complicated. He took a mouthful of wine to steady himself, and signed to Fiscilius to go on.

'My father had a number of business interests, of course, brick-making and potteries, weaving and dyeing, that sort of thing. But most of our wealth and position comes from our land.'

Torquatus lay very still, waiting for what must come next, grateful for the solid warmth of Cornelia's body against his. The young man swilled the wine around in his cup, then drank it down in a gulp. 'I don't know if you know Octavian?'

'Caesar,' Torquatus corrected him gently, his eyes as dark as peat-pools. 'Yes. I've known him since we were not much more than boys.'

Fiscilius gripped his lips tightly together for a moment. Then he laughed, though there wasn't much amusement in it. 'Then you'll know how he's taking away the lands of our city. Including mine.'

This was indeed exactly what Torquatus had been discussing with Octavian. The city of Mevania, like seventeen other Italian cities, was being stripped of all the land around it, to fulfil the promise Antonius and Octavian had made to their soldiers. Many of the men had fought for Julius Caesar, going for years from one campaign to the next. Many of the men had long ago lost touch with their families: some no longer even had families to go home to. Julius' promise to them was that when the fighting was over each of the men would be set up for the rest of his life with a farm large enough to support him and his family. And now those promises had to be made good. So while Antonius settled disputes among the client-kings of the eastern provinces, and tried to repair the ravages of years of violent exploitation they'd suffered at the hands of both sides in Rome's apparently endless civil wars, Octavian had come back to Italy to find the land the soldiers were expecting, but without the money to pay for it.

'I'm sorry. It's a hideous situation, and not one of Octavian's making.'

'Well, he's the one who's set up this commission to strip the cities of land: it's his commissioner whose signature is on every fucking document the soldiers show to my tenants and clients. He's the one making families homeless and leaving men like me powerless, if not ruined.' Fiscilius' voice had sharpened and he had raised himself on one elbow.

'It was Julius Caesar who promised these men their land,' Torquatus said calmly. 'Oh, and before him Pompeius did so, and let's not forget Marius and Sulla, if you want to go that far back. In any case, I don't see what this has to do with your sister.'

Fiscilius sighed and lay back on his elbow. 'You're right, of course. I don't know for certain that there is any connection between my family's ruin and my sister's death.'

'But you think there might be?' Torquatus asked.

'Well, perhaps. I'm not sure.'

'You'd better start at the beginning,' Manlia suggested with a smile.

'I was away when she left,' he explained. 'There wasn't anything unusual, that I'm aware of. I left Fiscilia at home with my aunt. Just as usual.' He shook his head, as if baffled.

'She had an aunt who cared for her?' Manlia asked.

Fiscilius nodded, sighed, and seemed to relax a little. He flopped back onto the couch. 'My mother's sister. She came to live with us .'

'Your mother's dead too?'

'Oh, yes. She died when I was thirteen. Canidia moved in a couple of years later, I suppose. Yes, that's right, it was when Fiscilia was twelve. She's been with us ever since.' He stopped, staring into space while he turned the cup round and round in his hand, then seemed to return to himself with a start. He reached for the wine jug as if to cover his awkwardness, and refilled his cup, then, blushing a little at his own lack of manners, he pushed the jug towards Torquatus. 'When I got back, my aunt told me that Fiscilia had gone off that very day to visit a friend at Spoletium. She'd assured Aunt Canidia that I'd agreed to the trip. Fiscilia is - she was - pretty good at getting her own way, but all the same! I don't know how I kept my hands off Aunt Canidia.' He put down his cup so hard it rang on the table and there was a flash of ruby red as the wine slopped over.

'You didn't like her going off like that?' Cornelia asked curiously.

'Of course not. I'd have gone with her in the proper way, if she'd waited till I came home. This is no time for women to be going about the country on their own. I didn't know what in Hades she was playing at.'

'So you went to Spoletium, I suppose?'

'I certainly did. Only to discover that our friends there hadn't seen her and weren't expecting to. I spent the night with them and the next morning came a letter, which Fiscilia had been kind enough to leave and which Aunt had only discovered after I'd left. In it she said she was going to Rome. So then I came on to Rome, with no idea where to look, to discover that people were talking of a girl, a young girl, who'd burned down three shrines and had been found dead in the last one she'd torched, the shrine of the Argei in the Velia. When I couldn't trace my sister I asked at the aediles' office, and was directed to you.'

'Why did you assume the dead girl must be your sister?' Cornelia asked.

'I didn't, of course, not at first. How could I believe Fiscilia was a criminal, an arsonist, a blasphemer, a traitor who had tried to damage Rome? But when I couldn't find any trace of her -.' Fiscilius broke off, licking his lips. 'Tell me, did she die in the fire she'd lit? Or what? Why that shrine, when she'd - apparently - successfully burned two others?'

Torquatus' face was grim. 'Maybe she was hit by a falling beam. Or she was trapped by the heat and smoke. She would have died quickly, I think we can be sure of that. The fire was intense.'

Cornelia looked up at her husband, wondering why he said nothing about his own observations of the girl's injuries.

Fiscilius had nodded and now went on. 'I've been here for a couple of days now, looking everywhere I could think of, getting nowhere. And at last I realised I would have to come to you and see for myself. Whatever she'd done she was my sister and I was afraid the body would be burned and I never would know for sure if it really was Fiscilia.' Fiscilius licked his dry lips again, before seeming to become aware of the cup in his hand. He drank deeply.

Cornelia nodded sympathetically. Torquatus gave him an abstracted glance, then said: 'You haven't explained why she came to Rome.'

'No,' Fiscilius agreed. 'I don't think I really know myself. But she must have come to burn the shrines.'

'There's no doubt she did burn them. She was seen going into the last one, just before it went up.'

'I see. In her letter she was ranting a bit. Saying that the gods would punish Rome for its behaviour. It was a pretty furious letter. She was going to try and get the soldiers settled somewhere else.'

'Jupiter!' Torquatus exclaimed. 'How in Hades did she think she could manage that?' Manlia and Cornelia had cried out too.

'That's what she said she was going to do.'

'You're really telling us that your sister came here to try and persuade Octavian not to settle troops at Mevania?' Manlia asked. 'That's just ridiculous.'

'Really? Well, it's true. I've got her letter. You can see it if you want.' Fiscilius sat up and clapped his hands. His slave, when summoned, unearthed the letter from his master's bag. It was short and to the point. It was also quite unambiguous. Fiscilia had decided that the only way to get the settlement on their land rescinded was through direct appeal to Octavian, and this was what she proposed to do. She hoped she would be able to make him see that stripping Italian cities of their land was a deeply irreligious act, and one that would do the city no good in the long run, since the gods would punish Rome severely for this wicked deed. How they would do this was not for her to say, but their revenge would be swift and sure. Aunt was not to worry about her as she would not be alone, and in the meantime she was Aunt's loving niece Fiscilia.

Torquatus lay back on his couch, apparently speechless.

Cornelia sat up, very brisk. 'Very well, then: we know why she came. She'll have had slaves with her, of course? Her maid Calliste, and two men. Good. Now, how did they travel and when did they arrive? Do you know where they might have stayed?'

Fiscilius looked rather taken aback at this sudden volley of questions. He shook his head as if to clear it, and ran his hand over his hair again. 'She took my light mule carriage.'

'Driving herself?'

He nodded. 'I suppose so - she usually did. The men were on horseback. Calliste would have been in the carriage with her. I think they must have arrived the day before the Ides.'

'And the slaves?'

Fiscilius shrugged. 'Vanished.'

'Really? That doesn't look good, does it?' Cornelia said.

'They wouldn't risk coming back even if they were innocent, would they?' Torquatus put in, listening in some amusement. 'I mean, I don't see how they could have stopped her running round Rome burning down shrines. But they can't have counted on Fiscilius seeing that.' Cornelia glanced back at him and shook her head.

'As to where they all stayed, I've no idea,' Fiscilius went on.

'You don't have property in Rome?' Torquatus asked.

'My father used to keep a flat here - well, we owned the block, actually, but we kept one flat back for ourselves. It was useful for elections.'

As the leading men in Mevania they would probably have been citizens well before the other men in their city were enfranchised; going off to vote in Roman elections would have been a visible sign of the family's importance.

'Where was the flat? You don't still have it?' Cornelia seemed to have recovered from her dismay at the slaves' flight. She was sitting up straight and had swung her feet back down to the floor, very much in control of the situation. Torquatus lay back and let her get on with it.

'No. I sold the whole block a year ago, when the times were so bad, to a couple. She was called Lollia. I don't remember his name: she seemed to be the one in charge, anyway. It was right by the Sanqualis gate.'

A short walk from his own house, Torquatus knew, but in another universe socially. The Sanqualis gate opened onto the crowded and noisy Subura.

'You haven't asked around that area? Well, I think we should. Someone might have seen her. She said she wouldn't be alone. Maybe she's got friends you weren't aware of, among your old neighbours, perhaps?' Fiscilius shook his head, and shrugged. 'What does it matter anyway, where she stayed?'

'It probably doesn't,' Torquatus agreed. 'But at the moment we just have the two statements in Fiscilia's letter explaining what she was doing in Rome: she'd come to get the settlement at Mevania moved and if she couldn't the gods of Rome would carry out some sort of revenge. Presumably the burning of the shrines was that revenge. Incredible. But if we can find someone, anyone, who saw her or maybe let her stay with them, we might begin to understand what was in her mind. And it would be even better if we could find those slaves of hers.'

'Of course I've checked with the few people we knew in Rome. They haven't seen her,' Fiscilius told him impatiently. 'And she'd only just arrived, she didn't have time to meet anyone new. But I don't understand about this arson - if that really was her. There wasn't even a reed man in one of the shrines. So what would be the point of burning that one down?'

Torquatus yawned. 'Yes, that's an added complication.'

'And yet she must have been intending an act of sacrilege? A deliberate attempt to pollute the ritual.'

'Let's leave it for tonight,' Torquatus said. 'Tomorrow we mourn your sister, and you need sleep before you can go through that.'

'You're right, of course. Fiscilia's dead. And she was my sister, whatever she did.'

'I'm only sorry that your aunt won't be here. I'll write to her tomorrow: she might able to help us make sense of your sister's death.'

Fiscilius' face looked taut and grey, the skull Torquatus had imagined earlier. He said seriously: 'I'm grateful to you, Torquatus. I can't say what it means to me that you've done everything that I as her brother should have done.' He broke off for a moment before passing a shaking hand over his face. 'Whatever she'd done. I'll try and sleep, as you suggest.'

The ever-watchful Trofimus stepped forward to lead the visitor to his room and Torquatus watched them thoughtfully as they walked away.

Chapter 4

Victor, the slave in charge of his master's wardrobe, had dug out a spare mourning toga from somewhere, so Fiscilius was able to appear as his sister's chief mourner correctly dressed. The young man looked, unsurprisingly, as if he had not slept well.

Torquatus himself was relieved to be getting the unlucky girl out of the house: the stench was unbearable. It was hotter than ever, though an ominous line of black clouds lay along the horizon. The funeral procession didn't need to go through the Forum to get to the Esquiline, where the burning grounds surround the temple of Venus Libitina, goddess of death; from Torquatus' house it would have been just as quick to walk up the Alta Semita a little way, take the street called Ad Malum Punicum, and make their way across the Viminal. Torquatus was tempted to direct the procession that way, for fear of unseemly disturbances once people discovered whose body was passing by. But he reflected that possibly the sight would stir someone's memory, and he chose the Forum route. They made their way slowly through the crowds. People stood well back to avoid the smell; then they heard the body was that of a young girl, and made soft sympathetic sounds; finally they realised that this was the arsonist who had tried to harm Rome, and they either fell silent or catcalled and whistled their disapproval. Torquatus and Fiscilius walked together through this uneasy crowd, preceded by the thin tweetling of flutes.

They left the city through the Querquetulan Gate and swung left. As they climbed up to the burning-grounds Torquatus noted that the line of clouds had rolled closer, and hoped the coming storm would hold off until after the burning. It's a horrible thing, and inauspicious too, when rain puts out the fire before the body is consumed. If Fiscilius wasn't too long-winded, they might just avoid a soaking.

He needn't have worried. There generally wasn't that much you could say about an unmarried girl, but Fiscilius used all the conventional tropes. His sister had never had the chance to become a woman and fulfil her destiny, she'd been a rosebud nipped by frost untimely, and she had loved her home and worked wool. Nothing, Torquatus thought, amused, to give his hearers any idea of what his sister had actually been like, no hint of the young woman who had pinched her brother's fast mule carriage and driven off to Rome alone. Let alone of the girl who had run about

Rome in the dark, risking her life to threaten Rome's gods. And anyway, he remembered sadly, Fiscilius' speech was addressed to no-one who had known her.

Then a torch was thrust into the pyre, gusts of hot wind fanned the blaze, the flames roared, fuelled by a generous allowance of incense, and great gusts of smoke roiled up into the overcast sky carrying that smell of roasting flesh, resinous wood and frankincense which the wind so often blows down into the city. Once they'd processed solemnly round the pyre in a silence only broken by the lamentation of the paid mourners, everyone stood as far off as they decently could, sweating in the tremendous heat, watching respectfully through the wavering air.

The fire burned furiously at first, then settled into a steady blaze. Torquatus wished that Fiscilius had arrived sooner. If they'd had time for the news of Fiscilia's identity to become known, some friends or neighbours of hers might have come to the funeral. Her aunt could have come down from Mevania. As it was there were only his own slaves and freedmen, and a gathering of strangers who'd followed the funeral procession up from the Forum out of curiosity. A few brief questions convinced him that none of them knew anything. The strangers gradually drifted away.

The mound of wood was beginning to collapse in on itself, exposing its white heart. There had been nothing to see of Fiscilia's body for a while. The undertaker, a young man who looked as though he were constantly having to suppress a naturally cheerful demeanour, now came across to Fiscilius. 'The pyre's dying down now, lord. You will soon be able to take the piece of bone you need.' The undertaker's slaves were raking out some of the ashes at the edge, to cool them. The undertaker pointed to a flat piece of bone, part of a shoulder-blade perhaps, and the sweating slaves threw water over it so that it sizzled and steamed. That little piece of bone would be buried: the rest of the ashes would be collected once the pyre was cool and placed in the Fiscilius family tomb.

It was at this auspicious moment that the storm-clouds which had been gathering overhead burst. There was a flash which for an instant turned everyone into ghosts and paled the fire. At almost the same moment thunder shook the ground, and the rain came down in sheets. What was left of the pyre dissolved into stinking smoke. Fiscilius scooped up the piece of bone the undertaker had pointed out. It wasn't quite cool and he passed it from hand to hand, watching as the others ran for cover.

'Come,' Torquatus said. 'They can gather the rest of the ashes later.'

Almost everyone else had vanished by now, either into the temple, or simply towards their homes. Even the undertaker had scuttled away somewhere. Fiscilius and Torquatus looked at each other, their togas heavy with water, their faces streaming, their feet squelching in their boots. It hardly seemed worth taking shelter, so they gathered up their slaves and began the long walk home.

Manlia had not attended the funeral. Her position in Rome was an extremely sensitive one, since her husband, Ahenobarbus, was one of Octavian's most effective opponents, a naval commander suspected of working hand in glove with Sextus Pompey. Ahenobarbus had become the head of his house after his father had died fighting against Julius Caesar at Pharsalus, the great battle which had seen the end of Pompey the Great. Caesar, having forgiven old Ahenobarbus once, would not overlook his continued enmity, and that ancient and noble family had been despoiled of everything. Octavian had honoured Torquatus' decision to shield his sister from the ruin that had engulfed her husband, and always treated her courteously. For her part Manlia returned the compliment: she took no part in public activities, lived very quietly, and kept Ahenobarbus' son Lucius out of Rome. His maternal grandmother was one of the formidable Cato women, and he lived with her in Lucania. Lucius might have been only fifteen, but Manlia knew that if he came to Rome he would say something inflammatory during a drunken party or drag his stepmother into the political arena she so carefully avoided, or just behave boorishly and embarrass her. Even a funeral, she felt, was best avoided if there was no pressing family reason for her to go.

Cornelia, too, had decided to stay at home and make sure everything was ready for the funeral dinner-party the next day. This banquet ought to have been held at Fiscilia's home and on the same day as the funeral. But Fiscilius' only long-standing acquaintance in Rome was away. He was due to come home tomorrow, and his steward expressed confidence that his master would be happy to attend the dinner, if it could be postponed for one day. Torquatus was happy to oblige. He hoped that Quintus Acutius would have things to tell him about the Fiscilii. The main banquet, the one that would mark the end of the mourning period in nine days' time, would take place in Mevania and would be Fiscilius' responsibility. Torquatus very much hoped that by that time he would have found out why Fiscilia had taken such a reckless course.

If Torquatus wondered vaguely why Cornelia felt she needed to oversee the preparations, given that they had a houseful of well-trained slaves, and the incomparable Trofimus in charge of them, he didn't have to wonder for long. A considerable bustle greeted their arrival: slaves ran about with towels and dry clothes and hot wine, and soon they were sitting comfortably in one of the rooms looking out over the garden, while thunder continued to crash overhead and the water poured off the roof of the colonnade in narrow spouts. Manlia had come in just before the storm burst, and she and Cornelia wanted to know everything that had happened at the funeral. Torquatus told them, finishing up with: 'We need to talk to that woman who bought your flat, Fiscilius. She seems to be the only clue we have so far.'

'Well, you won't.' Cornelia sat back, looking rather smug. 'She lives in Campania, according to the caretaker.'

'You've been there?' Torquatus stared, incredulous. 'How did you know where it was?'

'Fiscilius said it was just beside the Sanqualis Gate, so it wasn't hard to find. I've just got back. Oh, don't worry. I was most discreet. And I took the litter, and my maid, and a couple of the men, so I was quite safe, if that was what you were worried about.' Her voice was sedate but her eyes were full of laughter. Torquatus was speechless.

'You might have got wet,' he protested, sounding feeble even to himself.

'I have to admit, though, that I couldn't get in,' she added regretfully.

'You astonish me. You didn't manage to search the whole building? And find out what Fiscilia was playing at while you were at it?'

'I didn't, I'm afraid. And the caretaker would only tell me what I've just told you. She wouldn't even confirm that the flat was empty. I've got Lollia's address, though.'

'Empty!' Torquatus and Fiscilius stared at each other. 'Tell us exactly what happened.'

'I went in, with my slave. The woman was sitting at a little counter, the way they do. I asked her if I might see the lady Lollia.

She told me that Lollia doesn't live there any more, but she still owns the place. Then I said that if Lollia's flat was empty I'd like to see it, as I was looking for somewhere for my husband's brother, who was coming to Rome for a few months. She asked if I wanted to make an arrangement to view the flat so it must be empty. I didn't make any arrangement. I thought I might be treading on your toes if I did that. I said I'd tell my husband it might be available.' Cornelia cast down her eyes and gave a very passable impression of a wife whose only wish was to please her lord.

Torquatus tried to repress a smile. 'We need to talk to Lollia.'

Fiscilius was scowling. 'So what if the flat was empty? Fiscilia couldn't have been staying there. How would she have got in?'

'Lollia can tell us that,' Torquatus said. 'Let's send a message down to her.

Next morning, Torquatus was coming to the end of his morning visitors when a couple of unexpected guests appeared before him. Among the toga-clad, business-like clients and petitioners they stood out: he tanned and fit-looking, his toga slung on rather casually as if it wasn't something he wore often, she plump and smiling in her modest brown gown and stola. They were looking round them rather anxiously. Fiscilius, standing next to him, started forward. 'Lollia! How are you? This is extraordinary. Surely you haven't come in answer to our letter? No, of course you couldn't have done. But how - ?'

Lollia looked confused. 'Letter? No, I've had nothing like that. But I'm afraid I've got bad news.' Torquatus listened more carefully.

'We just came up for a few days, to see my new little niece and do a bit of shopping. We're staying with my sister because the flat's unfurnished at the moment. Obviously I sent a message to Ancilla, the caretaker at the flats, as soon as I arrived, thinking I probably should go over there to check that everything's in good order, and to my surprise she came over to see me. You'll never guess what she told me?'

'Something about my sister Fiscilia, I suspect,' Fiscilius suggested.

'That's right, though how did you know? Ancilla told me that Fiscilia had been staying in my flat, and using what she said was my key. It certainly wasn't. And she said Fiscilia's dead. I can't believe what she told me: that Fiscilia burned down some shrines, and died doing it. I was so shaken I had to sit down. It can't be true?'

'That Fiscilia is dead, yes. Her body was found in one of the burned-out shrines. As to the flat we suspected that she might have gone there,' Fiscilius told her. 'Simply because she didn't know many people in Rome.'

'Whatever was she doing? I've never heard of such a thing.' Lollia was so distressed that she picked up the end of her stola unconsciously and began to fan her face with it.

'That's what Aulus Manlius Torquatus and I are trying to find out.' The woman dropped her stola and bobbed awkwardly when she was introduced, and her husband eyed Torquatus nervously.

'We are trying to find out if Fiscilia met someone here in Rome,' Torquatus told them. 'Someone who perhaps led her on. But she did leave a letter, a very angry letter, threatening revenge against Rome for the settlements.'

Lollia shook her head. 'Well, I wouldn't have believed it. I mean, I didn't know her myself, but for a girl to have dared to come to Rome all by herself! Whatever did she think she could do? And the danger: even though those dreadful proscriptions seem to be over now, there's still so much violence. It's hard to feel safe with soldiers everywhere, especially when they've been drinking.'

'Which is pretty much always,' her husband put in gloomily.

'Was that what led you to sell up so soon? I hope you didn't find the investment a disappointing one?' Fiscilius asked.

'No, not at all,' said Lollia's husband. 'And we haven't sold up, just decided to let the flat. Living in Rome's expensive, and we've lost business. Hasn't everyone? When Lollia's father died a few months back and left us the family farm, we decided we'd find a tenant for the flat and go and live in the country.'

'Very traditional,' Torquatus agreed.

'I feel a lot more comfortable now,' Lollia said. 'My husband says I'm a silly woman, worrying about nothing, but I'm glad to have left Rome. '

Fiscilius smiled. 'You're not silly at all. There'd be plenty of people alive today if they'd left Rome while they still could. But I don't quite understand how Fiscilia could have been using your flat?' He left a slight question in the air, and Lollia rushed into speech again.

'Well, so many people have died, or left Rome, that it's not so easy to find good tenants now. So when Fiscilia wrote to me, asking if she could use it - ,'

'She wrote to you?' Fiscilius exclaimed. 'I'd no idea. When was this?'

Lollia and her husband stared at each other, dismayed. 'You didn't know? That's just what I was afraid of!' Lollia exclaimed. 'I feel so guilty, but how could I know what she planned? About a month ago, it must have been: something about coming to Rome for a few days, and asking if the flat was let or not. She offered me money. I wrote back and said she was welcome; I told her it was empty, and promised I'd let her know when it was let. I assumed she wanted it for both of you, and anyway, I never heard from her again.' Her eyes filled with tears.

'Would you let us borrow the key, Lollia?' Torquatus asked. 'I think we need to go and look at it.'

'Of course. I thought you might want to do that, so I brought it with me. I never lent it to her, though,' she added anxiously. She fumbled under her stola, coming out with a large and handsome key. 'I don't know what there is to see. All the furniture's gone, of course, and surely they'll - I mean her slaves, I suppose - will have taken Fiscilia's things away?'

'Who knows?' Torquatus said, looking round with satisfaction at the empty hall. 'We'll go straight away.'

They called up Becco and Pulex, as well as the litter, and the bearers padded off through streets that smelled fresh after yesterday's rain. Fat clouds still sailed across the sky, and whenever they crossed the sun the inside of the litter filled with shadows. Fiscilius was on edge, shuffling about in his seat.

'I don't see how Fiscilia could have got into the flat. We handed over the keys when it was sold, obviously. She couldn't have had one. Someone else must have been involved.'

'The caretaker would know Fiscilia, I suppose?'

'Yes. If it's the same woman, of course.' He sighed and shifted again. 'How long will it take us to get there?'

It didn't take long at all: it wasn't far to the Sanqualis Gate. When they arrived at the little block of flats, the caretaker wasn't in her booth at the entrance. For a moment they looked around at the clean but featureless entrance-hall. Then Torquatus got out the key they'd been given and headed off up the stairs. The key was a new one of a sophisticated design, beautifully cast in bronze with a star-shaped group of stubby spikes at its end, designed to fit into a matching set of holes at the end of the door-bolt. Torquatus wasn't surprised when it slotted smoothly into place and the bolt slid back at the first turn. He pushed the door open very gently, as if someone might be waiting inside with a weapon.

There wasn't anyone, of course.

The door opened into a little antechamber, through which the living space was visible. They could see quite easily because one of the window-shutters in the living-room hadn't been fastened properly and had swung open, letting in a beam of watery sunshine. The place was exactly like hundreds of others in Rome, and everywhere Romans live: the living space fronting onto the street, with two tall shuttered windows, each with a narrow balcony. Behind it, accessible through archways which would normally, he presumed, be curtained off, were a couple of small rooms, lighted only from the main room. The building had been crammed into a space between the arch of the Sanqualis gate and a larger, older building, so there wasn't much light. There must be a staggering amount of noise on a normal day: what it would be like at night when wheeled vehicles were allowed into the city, Torquatus shuddered to think. But it felt solidly built, and it offered a reasonable amount of space, for Rome. In normal times such a place would be easy to let. These were not normal times.

They walked into the living room, their boots like thunder on the floor. There was, as Lollia had said, no furniture, though marks on the walls showed where chests and beds might have been. But the room was not empty. Two large boxes lay empty on the floor, their lids flung open. Women's clothes were scattered all around: a fine tunic in soft, cream-coloured wool; another in dove-grey; a scarf with little spangles embroidered on it which flashed in the light. Torquatus walked across to the window which was still dark and threw open the shutters, glanced at the empty balconies, and continued round the walls to the back rooms. He kicked aside a heavy shoe, half-hidden under a cloak.

'This wasn't Fiscilia's, surely?' he asked, picking it up. It was the clumsy kind that fastens with a thong passed through holes all round the top, making a kind of leather bag.

'Calliste's, I suppose,' Fiscilius said, without really looking. 'It looks as though she left in a hurry,' he added. 'But why didn't she take any of Fiscilia's things?'

Torquatus thought it looked more as if the room had been ransacked. He threw the shoe back down, then with an exclamation picked up something lying nearby. 'I've seen one of these before,' he said. 'In that burned-out shrine on the Velia.'

It was a small oil lamp with a relief of a goat picking grapes on its top.

Fiscilius brushed away tears. 'Well, that seems to confirm it. We've got several like this at home. It really was Fiscilia who burned down the shrines.' He turned away and made a show of folding up a tunic and laying it in the box.

'I suppose it does,' Torquatus said slowly. 'But we still need to speak to the woman downstairs,' said Torquatus. 'Did she see Fiscilia go? Did she have Calliste with her? That's what we need to know. And there's a huge question here that we haven't even asked yet. Where are the other slaves? Did they all stay here? Surely there can't have been room?' He shrugged. 'Too much speculating. I want some facts. I'm going to see if I can find any of the other tenants. Why don't you go and look for that damned caretaker?'

The curtained-off recess downstairs was still empty when Fiscilius went downstairs. He glanced into her little room. A small and rather battered table, with a chipped Arretine-ware plate on it holding what must be the caretaker's set of keys, a heavy stool and a shelf holding a plate and a cup made up the room's furnishings. On the plate was a key just like the one they'd borrowed from Lollia.

Meanwhile Torquatus had walked up a narrower and darker set of stairs to a corridor with two doors facing each other in the middle of it. Two poky little flats, no doubt, each providing a small living room with a single window at the front and a single dark room behind. Could anyone find a space like that adequate? For a moment he was appreciative of the airy spaces of his own house. He knocked on the door on his left, an authoritative, imposing knock. No-one came, but almost at once the other door opened behind him. He spun round. A young man had stuck his head out of the door without fully opening it, his dark curls tousled and his eyes heavy with sleep. The word boy would be more appropriate, he thought: the creature smelled stale with wine and cheap perfume and sex, his eyes underlined with smudges of eye-black, his lips still faintly tinted carmine. His tunic was of silk, but soiled and crumpled, and far too short for decency. He looked as surprised to see Torquatus as Torquatus was to see him, and shot him a quick up-and-down look that took in the stranger's expensive toga. He giggled, one fine, long-fingered hand over his mouth. 'And what can I do for you, lord?' His voice was very soft, with an insinuating tone that made Torquatus' skin crawl.

'I'm looking for a woman,' he said curtly.

'Oh, what a shame.' The creature pouted and fluttered darkened eyelashes.

'A young woman, or two young women, who stayed here, briefly, last week. Did you see them?'

'No, dear, I didn't. I'm not terribly interested in women. Anyway, I'm out at night, mostly, and in the day I'm sleeping it off.'

'Since they were in the flat below you, perhaps you might have heard something,' Torquatus insisted.

'Might have, but didn't. I hear the bloody carts going through the street all night long. Who doesn't? And someone's been leaving a door or something to bang in the wind, the last few days. Otherwise, nothing. Who's asking anyway, if it's not a rude question?'

'I am Aulus Manlius Torquatus, priest and friend of Octavian Caesar.'

The boy's eyes widened. 'This place is a bit low for you, then, I'd have thought. Anyway, if I'd heard anything, which I didn't, I probably wouldn't have paid any attention. That's one of the good things about this room. My clients can sometimes be' - he smirked - 'a little bit noisy. The landlord doesn't bother us if the rent gets paid, and that woman downstairs couldn't care less if someone was murdered as long as it doesn't leave a mess.'

'Someone has died, and I need to find out why.'

The boy's eyes widened. 'I'm guessing one of the ladies you mentioned?'

Torquatus nodded. 'The lady Fiscilia, from Mevania. And if your memory should improve you can come to my house on the Quirinal and tell me about it. I can reward you if you do.'

An avid, hungry look suddenly swept across the young man's face, ageing it, and taking away all its superficial prettiness He laid an urgent hand on Torquatus' sleeve. 'If you're a friend of Octavian Caesar's, I bet you know Maecenas too, don't you?'

'Of course. What's Maecenas to you?'

'I've heard he gives wonderful parties. I'm a musician,' the boy said. 'Really good. I only do this -' and he gestured to the room behind him - 'for some extra cash. If I could just get to play for him -,'

'I can't promise anything, but we'll see.' Torquatus pulled his sleeve free. 'I'd like to have a look in your flat, please, just in case you're concealing any dead bodies, you know. And I'd like to know who lives in the other flat.'

He thought for a moment that the boy wasn't going to let him in; then he shrugged and stepped aside with an ironical bow. 'The old man over there's a teacher. Out all morning drilling kiddies in the Basilica Aemilia, then in the afternoons he goes to rich people's houses, I think, pushing culture into their sprogs, lucky him.'

They went into the small living-room, choked with surprisingly rich furniture: two tripod tables with finely carved lion feet, one holding a jug of wine and two chased silver cups, a lounging-chair with fine bronze scrolls in the armrests, covered in a crimson silk cloth with gold tassels and fringes, a silver mirror, a bird in a cage singing on the balcony among some pots of geraniums, a reading-couch with a bag of book-scrolls on the floor beside it, and on it a splendid cithara, its sound-box inlaid with flowers of moony, gleaming shell. The whole place reeked of incense, cassia, lilies. He stuck his head in at the bedroom door, the boy fidgeting anxiously behind him, and to his surprise saw a man asleep in the bed. A man he recognised, too; a distinguished elder senator, and one rather given to speechifying on the subject of our frugal and virtuous ancestors. Well, well.

Torquatus stepped out into the living area again, and went in silence to the door. The boy wouldn't have allowed him in, he knew, had his lover been awake.

'Thank you for your help. And I mean what I said: if you can help me find out anything about those two unfortunate women I'll help you.'

As he was about to step out into the corridor he turned and added quietly, 'I'm just interested in investigating a crime, by the way. Nothing else. I've never been a great admirer of old Cato.'

The boy looked puzzled, then his face cleared and he smiled.

This was a very small block, by Roman standards, and he was on the top floor. Torquatus went downstairs to Lollia's flat in a thoughtful mood, to find Fiscilius standing by the window looking down into the street. Torquatus wandered across to join him.

'Did you find the woman?' Torquatus asked.

'No.'

Fiscilius went over to the small rooms at the back. 'I don't think there's anything here,' he said, peering in. 'Do you?'

Torquatus was just about to go and look when he stopped, his eyes on the loose shutter. 'No wonder the shutter was hanging open: the bolt's broken.'

It was a standard fastening: an iron bar on the shutter swivelled to drop into a socket on the frame. It had been forced so hard that the socket had been torn from the frame, taking a splintered piece of wood with it, while the bar had been bent so that it no longer turned. Torquatus, looking closely, noted a small brownish discoloration on the splintered edge. 'You'd hear that, wouldn't you?'

At this moment a shrill voice sounded from the doorway. 'And who gave you leave to come in here?' the caretaker demanded, bustling in. She was a big woman, her grey hair in what might best be described as a military bun. Torquatus' two huge slaves, left outside on guard, trailed along behind her looking sheepish. Then the woman took in the mourning togas, and went very quiet. Fiscilius moved out of the shadow of the back room, smiling. 'You know me, Ancilla, don't you?'

She gasped. 'Fiscilius! I suppose I should have expected to see you, lord. There's something wrong, isn't there? I don't know why Fiscilia was here, or where she's gone, but -,' She stopped, looking from one of them to the other.

'We need your help, Ancilla,' Fiscilius said, and she nodded, rubbing her hands together nervously.

'When did Fiscilia arrive?' Torquatus asked.

'Oh, I feared it would all end in trouble! It must have been the day before the Ides, or maybe the one before that, lord.' She paused, her lips working silently. 'The day before the Ides, that's right.'

'You recognised her?'

'Yes, lord, of course I did. But why are you asking? Has something happened to Fiscilia? Oh, gods! It wasn't Fiscilia who did that dreadful thing?'

Torquatus stepped forward. 'Who burned three of the Argei shrines? I'm afraid it was. And we're trying to find out how and why. What slaves did she have with her? Did they come here too?'

'They did, of course. There was Calliste, her own maid, and two men, I believe, but I never saw the men. Fiscilia said she'd sent them off to the stables with the carriage, and they must have stayed there, I suppose.' There were plenty of stables around the gates of Rome, of course. Torquatus hoped they weren't going to have to search too many of them.

'They can't have brought the carriage through Rome during the day?'

'No, lord. Lady Fiscilia arrived after dark, quite late in the evening. She said they'd had to wait a while before the gates were opened: quite cross about it, she was. Anyway, she said Lollia had given her permission to use the flat, held up the key to show me and went straight off upstairs. I went after her with Calliste and helped carry up her mistress's bags.'

'She had Lollia's key?'

'That's right.'

'How many copies are there of that key?'

'Just hers and mine, as far as I know.'

'I see.' He looked at her thoughtfully for a moment and her eyes fell.

'And you haven't been upstairs since they left, to check the rooms?' Torquatus went on.

'No, lord. I didn't know they weren't coming back.'

'Very well. Then tell me what happened on the day Fiscilia came. Had you been in your room downstairs before they arrived?'

'Oh yes, lord. I was there all the time.'

'All the time? You're sure?' Torquatus asked.

'Yes, I think so - although, no, I went out for a few minutes. A man came in, a slave, said he needed to find good stabling for his master's horses, and could I point out the direction of the best place. I just stepped out for a minute to show him the way.'

'You went out of sight of the building?'

'Well, I suppose so, but only just. I walked through the gate with him, and pointed the way. Then I came back and soon after that the lady Fiscilia came in. She seemed quite as usual, though, as I said, a little put out by the delay. She and her slave went up to the flat, and I didn't see her any more that day. Calliste went out to buy some food from the bar up the road. I lent her some plates, since there wasn't anything upstairs.'

'You didn't think it odd that a young lady like Fiscilia should stay in a flat where there was no furniture?' Torquatus put in.

'Of course I did,' she replied tartly. 'The whole business was weird. But if the lady Lollia and her husband had their reasons for letting Fiscilia stay there, what business was it of mine?'

Torquatus looked at her thoughtfully for a moment. 'So when did you discover that your own key to the flat had gone missing?'

Fiscilius stared at him, but if Torquatus had hoped to throw Ancilla off balance, he was disappointed.

'It isn't, lord, as far as I know.'

'I saw it in the plate downstairs,' Fiscilius put in.

'I've never lost a key yet,' Ancilla said. 'We don't have a big problem with security round here, although it does seem that strangers can come wandering in. I should be more careful in future, I suppose.' She sniffed, and shot Torquatus a hostile glance.

He met her eyes impassively. 'Surely there's supposed to be someone in your room at all times?'

Her eyes fell. 'Macro - that's my slave - he usually covers for me. But he's sick today, and I thought the place wouldn't come to any harm for a little while.'

'And in the meantime anyone can walk in. No wonder Lollia had a better key made.'

She looked as if she might reply, but then seemed to think better of it and turned to Fiscilius. 'I'm very sorry for your loss, lord. I wish the lady Fiscilia had told me if she'd been in any trouble. But I still can't understand what would make her do what she did.' She shook her head.

Fiscilius' eyes filled with tears, but he asked quite steadily, 'Did you see Calliste leave?'

'Yes, I did. I was downstairs, and I looked up just as she walked out.'

'She didn't speak to you?'

'No. Actually I was just tidying up, and - and looking for something I thought I'd dropped on the floor. She came downstairs and hurried past my booth to the door. I thought it was Fiscilia at first, then realised it was Calliste.'

'I see. What day was this?'

'The Ides. A little before noon, I suppose.'

'And then,' Torquatus persisted, 'no doubt you got up from the floor to find that the key to Lollia's flat wasn't lost after all, but was back in the dish where it ought to be?'

Ancilla blushed but met his eye. 'I never lost the key, lord.'

Fiscilius had been paying no attention to this. 'Fiscilia must have gone out very early,' he said. He turned to Ancilla. 'You didn't see her? She must have left well before dawn.'

'Oh, no, but then I probably wouldn't. Macro guards the place at night.'

'He does, does he?' Torquatus said. 'Then we'd like to speak to him. I think that's all we need for now. We'll send someone to collect Fiscilia's things. I suppose no-one came to see Fiscilia that night?'

Ancilla shook her head.

They all moved downstairs, Torquatus locking the door behind them. In the entrance, the woman leaned in to her booth for the dish of keys. There were two very simple ones, no more than a metal hook to lift a latch, no doubt belonging to the two top flats, and one or two heavy iron things that looked like store-room keys, and one that stood out: bronze, well-made, just like the one Torquatus had in his hand. Ancilla held it out, and he nodded. She didn't meet his eyes.

'Thank you. Keep it carefully, please.'

'I always do,' she said with a toss of her head. 'I don't know why there's all this fuss: the flat was empty, there was nothing there to steal, even if someone had taken the key.'

'There were two young women in there,' Fiscilius burst in.

'Well no-one took it, as I say. Who would? I haven't seen any strangers at all, not until you came in yourselves.'

'Really? Are you sure?' Torquatus' voice was sharp.

'Quite sure.'

Macro, when Ancilla dug him out from a sour-smelling bed under the stairs, proved to be a short man, almost as wide as he was high. His eyes were bleary, his skin blotched and his mouth pursed like a baby's, and he didn't seem happy to be questioned. 'I don't know what happened days and days ago,' he whined. 'As far as I can remember, nothing did. No, the door isn't locked at night, why should it be?'

'There was a young lady staying upstairs: she went out sometime before dawn, we think. Surely you would have noticed such a thing?'

'I would. If it happened. So as I didn't notice it, it can't have happened, can it?' Pleased with his own wit, Macro gave an unlovely smile which displayed a few brown teeth and a lot of gaps.

'If you were awake,' Torquatus suggested. Macro pursed up his little pink mouth but said nothing.

Torquatus turned suddenly on Ancilla. 'Have you ever had trouble with him falling asleep when he was on duty?'

She blushed painfully. 'Well, I - I mean, not often.'

He gave her a cold look. 'And you haven't heard anything? Anything like a break-in? Anything that might have caused this, for instance?' He held up the broken window-bolt. She took it, turning it over in rough, reddened hands.

'This came from the shutter up there?' He nodded. 'It wasn't like that before.'

'When did you last check?'

'When the lady Lollia left. That would be before Saturnalia. It was all clean and tidy, so I shut the place up again once I'd seen over it, and I've never been back again. Why should I?'

'So this could have happened any time after Saturnalia?'

'I suppose so. Although I'd have thought I'd have noticed from the street if one of the shutters was open.'

'And are you really telling me you've never been up to look into the flat in all the seven days since Fiscilia and Calliste - left?'

Her face was closed and cold. 'That's what I'm telling you, yes.'

Chapter 5

'What in Hades do we want with the stables? 'Wherever they are now, those slaves aren't going to be hanging around waiting for us.'

The two men were standing in the entrance to the flats, wondering which way to go next. Torquatus nodded. They certainly wouldn't. A slave really couldn't win. It was his duty to do without question whatever his owner commanded; if that owner commanded him to do something illegal he would almost certainly be tortured, because a slave's testimony was worth nothing in the courts unless it had been tortured out of him; if he ran away that was even worse. Nothing could excuse flight, and if the slave was caught he'd be put to death. Or, if he was lucky, given back to the master he'd fled from, to be punished as the master saw fit. So would Fiscilius' slaves turn up again in Mevania, abject and appalled, and desperate to explain how their mistress had gone mad? Or would they make a break for freedom? Looking at Fiscilius' scowling face, Torquatus knew which he'd do.

'We still need to check when they left,' he said. 'And - if we can - where they were going. Your sister was a clever girl, wasn't she?'

'Clever?' Fiscilius was staring at him.

'Don't you see? Lollia said there were only two keys: hers and Ancilla's, and Ancilla agreed about that. Fiscilia certainly didn't have Lollia's key, so she must have had Ancilla's. So how did she get it? The man who came in to ask about stables must have been one of your slaves. That got Ancilla out of the way. Then Fiscilia popped in and took the key as soon as the woman's back was turned: she'd know where the keys were kept, after all.'

'But how could Fiscilia know it would work?'

'She couldn't, of course. But it would be worth a try, wouldn't it? And if Ancilla came back too soon, she'd pretend she'd just arrived and find some reason for why she needed to borrow Ancilla's key.'

Fiscilius looked stunned. 'I thought I knew Fiscilia. But I'd never have dreamed she'd behave like this: leaving home with just a couple of slaves, stealing keys, camping in empty flats.' He shook his head. 'Let alone turning criminal.'

'Your sister was a forceful character, wasn't she? She'd have got on like a house on fire with Cornelia and Manlia. I can believe

- just about - that a girl like that might decide to try and intervene to get the settlement at Mevania moved. I struggle with the idea that she would turn arsonist. And yet she did.'

The two men passed under the darkness of the gate and turned left. There's a road around Rome that runs just under the walls, of course, but it's never been a prestige project for some patrician family, so it's a lot more like the twisted, narrow streets inside the walls than the arrow-straight, splendidly-surfaced roads that bind our city to her empire. You'll find tanneries and dye-works there, smelters and brickworks, and people making glue from fish waste and bones: anything that stinks and will upset the neighbours. There are piles of muck taken straight from Rome's latrines: dealers sell it on to farmers for their fields. And there are stables and dealers in horses, mules and carriages. There are even a few little farms, with a dejected urban scrubbiness about them. Torquatus noted one with a sign falling off it, declaring that it represented a fine business opportunity, a development presumably impossible in the economic climate of the last couple of years. Coups, extra-judicial killings, civil disorder and continuing food shortages hardly provided the environment for speculative building. Not to mention the glut of looted property which had depressed the market since the proscriptions began.

Ancilla's directions were good. A large, well-built block of stables came into view, its business announced by the row of carriages which stood gaily in front of it. There were a couple of tiny, flimsy cisia, painted yellow with the wheels picked out in red. This was the kind of vehicle Fiscilia had so daringly driven, bouncing along behind a couple of mules. The biggest carriage was a heavy ox-drawn carpentum big enough for a family and its luggage, freshly painted in scarlet and vivid green, its top and sides closed in with leather curtains, at present tied back. Behind them, stable-doors lined three sides of a courtyard, their upper halves standing open. From some of these, horses looked out, apparently enjoying the late afternoon sun. A wiry little man who had been rubbing down a riding-horse put down his wisp of straw.

'Good afternoon, gentlemen. What can I do for you? Horses for you all, perhaps?' His eyes passed speculatively over the group: one very superior senatorial type, cavalry experience no doubt, another similar, but not so grand - and Becco and Pulex. The sweeping gaze stopped suddenly as if he was wondering where he could find horses large enough to carry such huge men, and the two slaves looked as doubtfully back. Torquatus had never got those two to feel comfortable on horseback.

'Good afternoon. No, we shan't be needing horses. Or a carriage,' he added quickly. 'What we do need is information.'

The man gave Torquatus the honest look of a man who is not unfamiliar with the authorities and their questions. He called a lad to come over and finish his job - 'And make sure Acer has water, too, will you?' - before turning and leading them to the last of the building's bays: not a stable but a tack-room, with saddles on brackets almost to the top of the wall, each with a bridle hanging from a hook beside it. A short wooden ladder gave access to the highest of these. Against one wall a set of wooden shelves held a collection of odds and ends: one or two lengths of leather strap, a battered measuring jug and a couple of cheap pottery cups with chipped rims. A stool provided somewhere to sit.

'Now then, lords, I'm Conan, and I run this establishment. Who are you and what was it you wanted to know?'

'Aulus Manlius Torquatus and Quintus Fiscilius, looking into the death of a young lady.' Victor raised his eyebrows at this, but said nothing. 'I believe that two men came to you the day before the Ides, in the evening: slaves of a lady from Mevania. They will have had a light carriage, a couple of mules and also two riding-horses. Do you remember them?'

His eyes were bright and sharp but the man asked no questions. 'I don't. Evening, you say: any idea when?'

'It would have been just after dark.'

Conan smiled. 'That's our busiest time, when everything on wheels comes into the city. I can't say I remember them.'

'This is important,' Torquatus told him. 'There's been an attack on the shrines of the Argei.'

'Ah!' Conan obviously knew what he meant. 'So it's that young woman you're asking about. I didn't know she'd come from outside the city. I still don't remember those men, but now I come to think of it, my boy Achilles was on with me that night. Maybe he can help.'

Conan went out, limping slightly. The room was quiet, slowly filling with soft afternoon shadows. The smell of the place - horses, hay, leather - sent Torquatus' mind drifting away to military camps he'd known, in Italian Gaul and Spain and Macedonia, and he was invaded by a sudden foolish longing for the order and clarity of military life, where death was at least explicable.

They waited a while in the quiet, saying nothing; then Conan came back, a large young man in tow. 'This is Achilles, one of our grooms. He was on duty with me, the night before the Ides. You remember them, Achilles, two guys from Mevania?'

'No. Sorry.' The boy gave them a dim stare.

'They will have had a cisium, painted blue and red, pulled by a couple of good mules. Also two Spanish horses, one darker than the other,' Fiscilius explained.

'I think I'd have remembered the mules,' Achilles nodded. 'And the horses. But I don't think they came here.'

There were several other establishments around the gate: Torquatus and Fiscilius tried them all, and received the same answer. No-one had noticed the slaves, the carriage or the animals.

'It's odd,' Torquatus said, as they walked away from the third one. 'They must have put up somewhere round here, if they came in on the Flaminia. The stables cluster round the gates, and Ancilla had directed them to the biggest stables. Why would they go anywhere else?'

Fiscilius was about to answer when Torquatus felt his sleeve tugged and turned to find a rather heated-looking Felix, holding out a pair of wax tablets. He snapped them open and read, his brows drawing together over his nose.

'I'm to go the Palatine: Octavian needs me. You'll have to carry on by yourself, Fiscilius.'

Torquatus half-expected Fiscilius to object, but he seemed happy enough. 'I forget,' he said with a smile, 'that you're really too important to be doing this kind of thing.' He waved an arm at the stables they'd just left. 'Leave it to me. I'll go right round the city, and I'll find out where those men went if it kills me.'

When her husband and his guest had set off on their errand, Cornelia decided to go out on her own account, telling Manlia she wouldn't be long. It was a little while since she'd visited those flats of hers on the Velia, and she was a careful landlord. She owned a great deal of property she'd never visited, in Italy and Spain, but that part of her portfolio that was in the city itself she kept under regular review. A note was dispatched to her manager, a freedman of her father's, and when the man arrived they set off at once, Cornelia and her maid Rachel in her litter and the manager and several slaves walking alongside. As they travelled down into the Forum the manager told her that all the rents were up to date, although one of the tenants, a young widow - or so she claimed - with a child, had had several male visitors. She might turn out to be unsuitable; if she was working as a prostitute and the other tenants objected, he would evict her.

'Well, don't let's jump to conclusions,' Cornelia told him. 'Even if her morals aren't perfect, as long as she's quiet about it, I don't think we should throw her out.'

The manager accepted her verdict, though with a little reluctance. 'That's a very good property, lady, in an exclusive part of town. You don't want it turning into a brothel.'

'No. But one woman going about her business isn't a brothel, is it? Remind me who the other tenants are.'

'Yes, lady.' The agent ran his eyes down his list. 'On the first floor old Articuleius Paetus, he's lived there for ever.'

Cornelia nodded. Articuleius was a crusty old eques: if anyone complained about the young widow and her visitors it would surely be he. 'Do we still have that family - ex-slaves, from Mauretania, I think?'

'Yes, lady. They've turned out to be good tenants, hard-working and quiet. In the other flat on that floor there's a man called Titus Fulvus. Not there very often, I believe, but he pays his rent on the nail and causes no trouble. And on the top floor there are two more families, and a couple of young men. They can be a bit noisy: living on their own for the first time. I've had to speak to them once or twice.'

The inspection produced the usual complaints from the tenants about noisy neighbours, exotic food-smells, and inadequate cleaning of the entrance and stairs. There had also been a young man visiting the one of the upstairs flats and making an unacceptable amount of noise.

'This is a good area,' the grumpy Articuleius told Cornelia. 'Or it was. Now it seems we have to put up with that slut upstairs and young men who haven't the slightest consideration for their elders. How one is supposed to get any sleep I don't know.' He grudgingly agreed that since no-one knew who the noisy visitor had been and since he'd left the next day, there was very little Cornelia could do about it.

Leaving the building, Cornelia told her manager to wait for a few moments. Taking Rachel with her, she walked across to the little shrine where Fiscilia's body had been found. She was expecting to see a burnt-out shell, but the building had already been repaired. The tiles of the new roof glowed red, and the white walls hurt her eyes with their brilliance. It was charming, a miniature Greek temple, correct in every detail, and spotlessly clean. The tiny precinct around it was swept and tidy, and the doors stood open. Cornelia stepped inside, Rachel behind her. Once her eyes had grown accustomed to the dim light, Cornelia could see that there really was nothing here to give any kind of clue to Fiscilia's murder. It was even smaller than she'd imagined. The floor was bare, a neat pavement of stone. The walls were lime washed, and empty but for the two inscription panels Torquatus had noticed. There wasn't a bench or a shelf or a mark anywhere. Nor was there any way in or out except through the doorway where they were standing. Nothing. The sounds of the street were slightly muffled in here: somewhere in the background was a very faint regular sound of water, from the neighbourhood fountain, no doubt. Disappointed, she turned away.

As the party descended into the Forum, they were forced to slow down by a larger than usual crowd. These were not, Cornelia could see as she scanned their faces from her litter, the usual shoppers, gossips and idlers who collected there in the mornings. They looked angry and purposeful. Some of them seemed to have sticks or clubs in their hands. One of Cornelia's burly slaves moved in front of the litter-men to clear a way for them, but with limited success. They moved slowly down into the Forum, the litter swaying a little as the flood of men pushed past.

'Better close the curtains, lady,' the manager suggested, but Cornelia was reluctant. Being shut inside the hot, dim litter, unable to see out, seemed worse than watching the angry crowd milling round her. For a few moments more the situation stayed the same: some blockage ahead made it impossible to move forward. The surging groups of men seemed to get angrier as they were forced to a standstill. Then a great shout went up ahead, and the men on either side of the litter began to move, pushing and swearing and finally breaking into a run. One or two of them took the time to curse her for getting in their way, to push the litter or thump on its roof, and she shrank back into her seat, oppressed by the sweaty, furious crush. Her slaves were powerless to intervene, but when the flow of men died down for a moment they moved the litter so that one side of it was against a house wall, and then got into a line in front of it, so that now Cornelia could only see the backs of her own slaves. She could hear them discussing in an anxious undervoice which way would be best to carry their mistress home.

It was clear from the noises ahead of them that a disturbance of some sort was under way in the Forum. Crashes and shouts suggested that some of the shops were being attacked, and Cornelia could hear screams and cries: clearly those cudgels and sticks were being used. Impatiently, she prodded the slave in front of her in the back, and when the man moved aside she climbed out, shaking out her skirts. Rachel followed her cautiously.

'What is all this about? Can you hear what they're doing?' Cornelia asked her manager.

'Bread riot, I'm afraid.' The man spoke as if this was nothing unusual.

'This isn't the first, is it?'

'No. And until they manage to stop Sextus Pompeius from taking the grain ships, it won't be the last.'

'I see.' Cornelia looked about anxiously. The group of men who'd rushed past them had gone into the Forum, and there seemed no present danger. 'What good do they think rioting will do?'

The manager smiled. 'No doubt they think that someone somewhere has got warehouses full of corn which they won't sell till the price is even higher. Octavian could find out who that is: I wouldn't like to be in their shoes if he did. But maybe they think it's Octavian has the grain?'

Cornelia shivered, hot as it was. The noises were louder than ever: one or two people were now running back up towards the Velia, with bruised and bloodied faces. Cornelia's manager had been talking quietly with the litter-bearers, and now turned back to her. 'We don't normally go into the Subura, but we reckon they're all down there,' and he jerked his head towards the Forum. 'So we'll go up the Argiletum and then cut through to the Quirinal. With a bit of luck we'll avoid the crowds, and keep you safe.' He was sweating, and Cornelia knew it wasn't from the heat. She was a huge responsibility for these men. Her face sober, she nodded and climbed back into the litter. Rachel followed her with relief, and closed the curtains behind them.

Manlia, too, had been out, and came in just as Cornelia's litter was being carried away. They hadn't moved beyond the reception hall when Torquatus joined them.

'Oh, Aulus, you're in armour,' Cornelia exclaimed. 'What's happened?'

Torquatus looked grim. 'Octavian wanted me because he knew there were riots brewing again, and he needed to be sure they didn't get out of hand. I borrowed this kit from his guards. Jupiter! This breastplate's a bit on the small side. I can't breathe.' He winced as Victor the toga-slave fumbled with the unfamiliar buckles, then stretched as the breastplate came away. 'That's better. Just get it sent back to Octavian's, would you? And the helmet and sword.'

'And where is your toga, lord?' Victor demanded.

Torquatus shrugged. 'At Octavian's, I suppose.'

'So you had to take soldiers down into the Forum?' Manlia asked.

'Yes. It's not what Octavian likes. Doesn't look good. But anything's better than having the city burn.'

'Did you have to fight?' Cornelia had her hand on his arm, her face full of concern.

'Not really. There was a good old scrap going on when we got there. The usual stuff, fists and cudgels. When the guys saw our swords they backed off. What Octavian wanted to know was whether there seemed to be anyone organising it.'

'And was there?'

'Yes, I think so. The soldiers went after a couple of men, and they've taken them in for questioning.'

Cornelia shivered.

'Come and sit in the garden, if you're cold,' Torquatus suggested, and they moved off to where Trofimus had already placed a small table with jugs of wine and water and a bowl of dried fruit.

Torquatus drank and put the cup down, refreshed. 'That's better. I wonder where Fiscilius is now. I left him going round all the stables to try and find out what happened to those slaves of Fiscilia's.'

'All of them? But there must be hundreds.' Cornelia pushed the jug towards him again.

'Perhaps not quite that.' Torquatus frowned. 'But I have to say I think most likely the people at the stable Ancilla directed them to simply didn't notice them. Why should they have gone anywhere else? I bet you anything you like Fiscilius comes back empty-handed.'

He was wrong. A little later Fiscilius came in, hot and sweaty-looking, but by no means empty-handed, for in his arms was a small, dusty dog.

Torquatus and Cornelia stared at him.

'I've found them,' he said triumphantly, apparently not noticing their stares and putting the little dog on the ground where it sat, whining softly, at his feet.

'You've got them? The slaves?'

'Oh, no. I haven't actually got them. But I do know where they've gone.'

'Right,' Torquatus said firmly. 'Sit down, have a cup of wine, and tell us exactly what's happened.'

'And where that came from,' Cornelia added, pointing at the dog.

Fiscilius, it seemed, had got half-way round Rome before he'd picked up any trace of the slaves. By that time he'd been on the point of packing up and going home. But at the Capena Gate he'd gone to the largest of the stables. 'And I just knew I'd find nothing there,' he told them. 'It's a huge place, and busy all the time as you can imagine, with all the traffic from the Appian Way passing through it. But luckily one of the stable-boys there was pretty smart. He hadn't seen the slaves arrive, but he'd seen them go. Noticed it because it was an odd time for anyone to start a journey: the men had arrived at dusk on the Ides, and he remembered them because instead of going into the city as he'd expected they'd headed out onto the Appian.'

'The Appian? That's interesting,' Torquatus agreed. 'They'd have no reason to go south.'

'No legitimate reason, no. Anyway, the stable-boy also told me he'd seen the men stop, just outside the stables, right by the gate, to pick up another slave, a woman.'

'So that's where Calliste went,' Cornelia said quietly.

'It seems so. But that's not all. One of the men was driving the carriage, and the other was riding one horse and leading the other. There'd been a bit of an argument when the woman got in, and they didn't set off straight away. Then they dashed off, in a great hurry.'

'Gods! So they really were running away. I wonder how much they know about what Fiscilia was up to.' Torquatus sat back, smiling. 'Well done, Fiscilius.'

'I'll have to catch them. Calliste will know about it all right.

They were as thick as thieves.'

'You haven't told us about the dog,' Cornelia pointed out, looking rather disapprovingly at the creature nestling at Fiscilius' feet.

'He's Fiscilia's dog, Nar.' The young man bent and patted him. 'He was just wandering about, lost. When he heard my voice he must have recognised it, because he came over to me at once. I couldn't believe my eyes. You can't imagine what it means to me to have him back.'

'Fiscilia came to Rome to attempt to appeal to Octavian and she brought her dog?' Torquatus exclaimed.

Fiscilius flashed him a smile. 'Oh, she would, of course. He went everywhere with her. And the slaves would never have dared to harm him or lose him when she was alive. No, they must have fled when they heard what she'd done, and left him behind. And here he is.' He picked up the dog as he spoke, burying his face in the little creature's dusty fur.

Chapter 6

To say that Cornelia didn't take to Nar would be an understatement. Her expression would have made an alp in December look temperate. At the same time both her training and her temperament made it impossible to refuse any kindness to a guest. Her husband watched with some amusement as hostess and dog-hater battled it out. What made the situation all the more piquant was Fiscilius' obvious lack of awareness of her feelings. That his dog might not be warmly welcomed into any house had clearly never crossed his mind. A countryman, he lived among dogs: hunting dogs, guard-dogs, herding dogs. Torquatus was glad that he felt comfortable enough to treat the house as his home, but he could also see it from Cornelia's point of view. Senatorial houses in Rome often had guard dogs: chained up out of doors, kept rather hungry, they certainly weren't pets. Ladies sometimes favoured a little dog which they washed and groomed like a baby; nasty yappy things, in his view. Torquatus himself, like many senators, had a place in the mountains where he went to hunt. The dogs there lived in kennels, but it was true that after a hard day, coming home tired but triumphant with his kill slung on a pole, a favoured hound or two sometimes followed the master back into the house and flopped down at his feet for the evening. They didn't, however, chew up their owners' patrician boots, climb on top of a newly laundered and neatly folded toga to sleep, or leave half-eaten bones lying about the reception rooms. Nar did all of these within an hour of coming into the house. He also had fleas: lots of fleas, picked up no doubt during his days of roaming. Fiscilius' solution to this was to take the dog into the bath suite with him, to give the little animal a good wash and comb. Cornelia said rather faintly that fortunately she had already had her bath, so she need not - in her words - be in his way.

This evening was much cooler: even had there been no funeral banquet, they would probably not have eaten out of doors. The slaves had been working hard: dining couches were set up and elegant tasselled covers laid over them; garlands of flowers were being kept in the coolest of the storerooms, where they were regularly sprinkled with water; and delicious smells were wafting from the kitchen quarters. All was not well, however. As Torquatus, Manlia and Cornelia sat quietly by the reception hall pool waiting for Fiscilius to appear after his bath, they heard a roaring sound, and it was coming closer. Turning their heads in alarm, they saw a terrifying but not unprecedented sight: Fortunatus, their cook, in a dreadful temper. He rarely left his kitchen, apparently feeling that a mere senator (or senator's wife) could come to him if they had anything to say, but now he stormed in, knife in hand, complaining first that Nar, not content with the meal of scraps Fiscilius had ordered for him, had found his way back to the kitchens to ask for more, tripping up a slave carrying a dish of cooked quails intended as part of the feast and eating two of them, and secondly that the hot weather had made the fish go off. It would therefore serve everyone right, he said, vaguely but ominously, if the dinner he was to put before his master's guests was an inferior one, damaging to his reputation. It wasn't quite clear to Torquatus whether it was his own reputation at risk or Fortunatus', but this was clearly not the moment to ask.

'A beautiful turbot, lord,' moaned the cook, 'and absolutely stinking. Those quails, too - gone, just when we needed them more than ever.' He seemed to cheer up as he added: 'Made the dog fucking sick though. He threw them up in the kitchen doorway.'

'Come now, Fortunatus,' Cornelia said calmly. 'You're always at your best in emergencies. We can rely on you to come up with something wonderful, just as you always do. I've no doubt you've found a solution already.'

Fortunatus replied, rather more quietly and with his knife-hand now down by his side, that he had in fact negotiated with their neighbour Atticus' cook for a bucket of fine mussels. But - flaring up again - if he had to have that dog in his kitchen he wouldn't be answerable for it. Slaves, he added ominously, were grateful to be given meat of any description. Torquatus left it to Cornelia to soothe the irritated artist, and noted with amusement that it didn't take her long. Moments later she was able to lead Fortunatus back to his own kingdom, sharing his views on the undesirability of animals in kitchens with such obvious sincerity that the sting of his rage was drawn.

'I don't know why I put up with that fellow,' Torquatus told Manlia.

'You'll remember when you eat your dinner,' she said, smiling. 'Besides, he's been here for ever. You could never get rid of him.'

'Don't bet on it. Much more of that sort of impudence and I might do just that. I'd get a splendid price for him: my friends are always trying to buy him from me.'

There were no further intrusions from the kitchens, and the party that reclined together shortly afterwards ate mussels with garlic and parsley, tender slices of veal, a pair of roast ducks, some little balls of cheese rolled in nuts and fried, scallops, sea-urchins, lettuce, warm fresh rolls sprinkled with poppy-seed, tender young asparagus set in a quivering egg custard, sweet cheese-cakes, plums preserved in honey-syrup; but no quails, and no turbot. As for Nar, Torquatus put his foot down, in the interests of his own comfort and his wife's sanity. He instructed Felix that the dog was not to interrupt the meal, and the boy went off with the clean though quite unchastened creature, coming back a while later to tell his master that Nar had taken a great fancy to Torquatus' own groom, Catus, who had offered to make a bed for him in the stables. His worst enemy could not have accused Nar of being unfriendly: his only redeeming quality, in Torquatus' view. Felix told Torquatus in an undertone, as he helped to serve the first course, that the dog was now sleeping soundly on a piece of sacking in the stables, which seemed unsurprising after a day that had included being reunited with his long-lost family, a ride in a litter, a vigorous bath, and various daring escapades in the kitchen. Catus had promised to keep Nar outside at all times except when his company was especially requested indoors. Torquatus gave an edited account of all this to Fiscilius, reclining in the place of honour, whose eyes filled with tears.

'I can't express my gratitude to you both for all you've done. And now you are caring even for Fiscilia's dog. And yet, I can still hardly believe - and I must catch those slaves if I can. They know what was going on, that's for sure.'

'Well, they may have done,' Torquatus agreed cautiously.

'What chance of finding them, though? They've had days to get themselves to a port and buy a passage to Sicily.'

'I suppose that's what they must have done.' Torquatus shifted uneasily on his couch.

'What else? They were heading south, towards Sicily. They would know as well as anyone else that Sextus Pompeius is taking in all the refugees, slaves included.'

'It might take them a while to get a boat,' Torquatus pointed out. 'Assisting slaves to escape can get you into trouble. Serious trouble. People won't be falling over themselves to help.'

'That depends entirely on how much money they have,'

Fiscilius said cynically. 'I didn't think to look before I left Mevania, but I assume Fiscilia will have taken quite a bit.'

This was a funeral banquet, and a particularly sad one at that, and the general mood was subdued. All the men wore dark mourning togas, with garlands of roses on their heads, most suitable to mark an untimely death. There were three male guests, the only men Fiscilius knew in Rome. The older two were equites, one, Quintus Acutius, a gruff old man, a friend of Fiscilius' father, the other rather younger, a brisk-looking man called Cornutius, whose connections with the Fiscilius family were purely business ones. Both men were accompanied by their wives, and Acutius had also been asked to bring his son, a taciturn individual Fiscilius scarcely seemed to know, which with Torquatus' family made the number up to the nine required for a formal dinner. Along with their freedmen sitting wherever they could on the ends of the couches, and the slaves lining the walls the dining room was comfortably filled. Torquatus' one regret was the absence of Aunt Canidia. She might have had far more to say than any of these polite, rather laconic gentlemen: she was the one who'd brought Fiscilia up, after all. Fiscilius, too. He eyed Fiscilius thoughtfully over the rim of his cup, reflecting on how little they really knew about him.

Over the first course the talk was a little stilted, with awkward silences. It was like travelling down a shallow, sluggish river in a boat which was constantly catching on mudbanks or clumps of weed, Torquatus thought: he, Manlia and Cornelia seemed to be constantly pushing off, setting it moving again. He was relieved when, with the introduction of the second course, the discussion moved on to the politics and interests of the noble families of Mevania. In this Fiscilius took the lead. The settlement of soldiers on their tenants' land was an issue for all of them, and as soon as Fiscilius brought it up every man's attention turned to him.

'Hispellum! A whole new town!' He spat the words out and threw himself back on his couch. 'Imagine it: a gaggle of incompetent soldiers on that land. What a waste.'

'Of course it is,' Acutius agreed. 'Luckily I don't have much land at Mevania any more, but I'm sorry for you and the others who do.'

'Why is Hispellum a waste, more than any other settlement?' Torquatus asked.

'Oh, I'm not just saying that because Octavian wants to put bloody Hispellum on our estates. I'm saying it because it's an unsuitable place.'

Torquatus looked a question.

'They're building the place on a spur of the mountain.'

Torquatus nodded. 'Mount Subasium.'

'That's it. It's harsh land: they might grow olives there, I suppose, but not much else. So to keep the soldiers happy they're being given a big chunk of the plain below as well. And that's incomparable land, lush meadows, perfect for growing cattle.'

'Couldn't the settlers grow cattle too?'

Acutius gave a dry little laugh. 'Not a farmer, are you, Torquatus? For cattle you need plenty of space; so three or four of the leading families have large herds there, in fields on both banks of the river, and very profitable it is. The white cattle of the Clitumnus valley are famous: if you need a large white ox for a sacrifice, chances are it will have come from one of those herds. But when the soldiers are settled, the land's cut up into little parcels. It's an archaic way of farming, inefficient, unprofitable; it only works when the plots have a bit of variety, and even then the farmer needs to be clever and lucky to make a living out of it. No, if the meadows are carved up, those men will find their plots are too wet and heavy to grow the grain they need. So they'll give up: and if Fiscilius here and his neighbours aren't absolutely ruined they'll have to buy the land back from them and turn it back to grazing. Years of lost production, and not good for the soldiers either.'

Cornutius nodded. 'They need to put those men somewhere else. But where?'

Fiscilius shrugged. He said no more, but Torquatus feared they had the estates of men like him in mind.

'The men have been promised land,' he pointed out. 'The days are gone when men signed up for a campaign and then went home to the family farm. We have soldiers who've served in Gaul, Greece, Egypt, often for years on end. Perhaps they shouldn't have been promised land, although it's hard to know what else they could have been offered. I mean, would the Senate have voted to give them sufficient pensions to retire on at the end of their service? I don't think so.'

'That's all very well,' Fiscilius cut in. 'But when you want land, you buy it, don't you? You don't just help yourself.'

There was an embarrassed silence. Torquatus could sense that all the other men agreed, though they were too polite to say so.

'There's no money,' he pointed out. 'Antonius is in the East trying to get the finances of the cities there straight after years of depredation. Octavian's task was to settle the veterans here, and that's what he's doing. And Roman armies are full of men from all over Italy, so of course other Italian cities have to help.'

'Yes!' Torquatus noted Fiscilius' shaking hands. 'It's always the same - we fight for Rome, win an empire for Rome, but it's Italy that suffers! As if our family hadn't lost enough already - if our land goes too -,' He caught Acutius' eye, and subsided. There was a moment's agonised silence. Then Manlia turned calmly to Sempronia, Acutius' wife, just as Cornelia asked Acutius a question about his business in Neapolis. Torquatus heard him say something about grain prices, to which Fiscilius replied at length. He turned his attention to Manlia, who was asking about Fiscilia. The talk began to flow again and Torquatus relaxed.

'Poor child.' Sempronia wiped her eyes. 'Who could have imagined that a young girl would have run off from home, all alone, to do such a dreadful thing.'

'I wish I'd met her,' Manlia said. 'She sounds as if she was a very lively, strong-willed person. Did you know her well?'

'All her life,' Sempronia agreed, smiling. 'We were great friends of her father. And she wasn't frightened of anything. It terrified me sometimes, though I couldn't help loving her for it. It's a pity Canidia isn't here: you'd like her, I think. If it hadn't been for her Fiscilia would never have grown into the warm, affectionate young woman she was. Well, that's what I thought, that she'd have made a wonderful wife - for the right man. Now I don't feel I knew her at all.'

'She was old enough to be married, of course?' Manlia made it a question.

Sempronia laughed. 'Oh, yes. I don't know if there was a husband in the offing. But if so I imagine Marcus Ampudius is the man: an eques, like her father, and a most admirable young man. He lives at Formiae. My husband can tell you all about him.'

'Formiae? That's a long way from Mevania, isn't it? Right down beyond Neapolis. Do the Fiscilii have interests there?' Manlia asked, and was surprised to see Sempronia blushing and biting her lip.

'Ask my husband about it: he can tell you more than I can.'

Not wanting to embarrass their guest, Manlia only nodded. 'I'll do that. He's someone my brother needs to speak to. And of course we want to meet Canidia: she would have been with us tonight if only there'd been time to get her here. She brought Fiscilia up, didn't she? She must have been very close to her?'

'Oh, very. You could say she really saved her. Those children ran wild after their mother's death. That was eight years ago now. No-one but slaves to look after them, and they soon learned to ignore them. Old Fiscilius told me that he'd come in one day to find the pair of them, dirty and tousled, wrestling on the floor, and had suddenly realised that what we'd all been telling him was true. He really did need help with the children. He sent for Canidia.'

'How did she tackle Fiscilia?' Manlia asked.

'Well, one thing she did was to buy her that little slave, Calliste.'

'What difference would that make?' Manlia's surprise was evident.

'You don't see how that could change the child? Well, it made her think about someone else for once. Canidia took her to the slave market, and asked her to choose a maid for herself. I remember her telling me how pleased she was that Fiscilia, instead of choosing the prettiest or smartest-looking slave, picked this little girl who was hanging back. Calliste was a year or two younger than Fiscilia, and not very prepossessing, with lank fair hair and a miserable little face. When Canidia asked Fiscilia why she wanted that girl she said she thought it would be nice to make her happy. She did, too. She took responsibility for the first time in her life, and she and Calliste became more like sisters than mistress and slave. Once Calliste had filled out a bit they even looked quite alike: two pretty blonde girls. Perhaps that was another reason why Fiscilia chose her.'

'If Calliste was so close to Fiscilia, why do you think she ran off with the other slaves?'

Sempronia threw up her hands. 'Ah, now you're asking something I can't understand at all.' She took a sip of wine before turning back to Manlia. 'You've written to Canidia, I suppose?'

Manlia nodded.

'She won't be safe where she is. The estate, the house, everything will be given up to the soldiers. I'm very worried about her, alone there with only her slaves to protect her.'

She turned on her couch. 'Fiscilius, you ought to go and look after your aunt, now the funeral's over. She'd be most welcome to come to us, tell her.'

Fiscilius nodded, though Torquatus didn't think he looked pleased.

As they were drinking their wine at the end of the meal, a messenger appeared, a slave of Octavian's, asking for Torquatus to visit him next day. When the man had gone, another awkward silence fell. Torquatus thought the visitors had been made aware of their host's connections, and were reviewing what they'd said: a thought he didn't care for. He called for the wine to go round again.

The guests didn't stay late. After they left, the others, agreeing that they were tired but not sleepy, retired to one of the rooms off the garden with a jug of wine, leaving the slaves to clear the dining room.

Fiscilius paced about the room. 'Thanks to all the gods that's over.'

Torquatus was settling himself on a couch. 'Oh, thank you, Felix. Yes, just leave the wine and some nuts and raisins. We shan't need anything else.' He turned back to Fiscilius. 'Yes. Not the easiest of social situations.' He filled his cup.

'Well, I'll be off tomorrow, and with luck I'll get those slaves before they escape.'

Torquatus nodded. 'If that's what you want. But I'd like to ask you a few questions first.'

Fiscilius stared at him. 'Questions?'

'Don't look so alarmed. Just what you did after you arrived in Rome, for instance.'

'Right. Well, I told you how I'd travelled to Rome. But when I arrived I couldn't get any information. I asked at the city gates: it's not often you see a young woman driving a cisium, is it? But no-one seemed to have seen her. Then I asked the few people I know here - the ones you saw tonight. I kept hearing of this young girl who'd died. I didn't associate her with Fiscilia at first, but at last I thought I'd better check. And so I was directed here.'

'And where did you stay, while you were searching?' Cornelia asked.

'Oh, I borrowed a friend's flat.' He jumped up and walked restlessly about the room. 'But what does all that matter, when the only people who can explain what Fiscilia was doing are getting away?'

Cornelia said, 'It does matter. I understand why you want to go, but there's so much that doesn't make sense. Can we just go through what we do know? We know Fiscilia came to Rome, leaving a letter for her aunt in which she made threats against Rome. She'd earlier checked that the flat in Rome was still unlet. She had with her Calliste and two male slaves, and arrived on the day before the Ides, with you, Fiscilius, fairly close behind. We know she and Calliste went to stay in Lollia's flat, using the caretaker's key. We know that the men took the horses and carriage to stables on the south side of Rome, though not whether that was Fiscilia's doing. Is that all right so far?'

The others nodded, and Fiscilius shrugged, scowling. He came back to his couch and flopped down, filling his cup again.

'We don't know when Fiscilia left the flat, but it must have been well before dawn on the morning of the Ides. We have to assume she then went to the shrines on the Palatine and Caelian and set them on fire.'

'How did she know about them?' Torquatus wondered. 'It's not one of the festivals tourists come to see, she wasn't a Roman, and the shrines are quite hidden away.'

'True,' Cornelia agreed with a nod. 'Maybe the slaves - when we find them - can help with that. Fiscilia was seen going into the shrine on the Velia just before it was set on fire, where her body was discovered. Nobody else was seen either going in or coming out. We know Calliste left the flat later in the morning. We know that the two male slaves collected the horses and carriage on the evening of the Ides. Calliste joined them. The dog got left behind. They were heading south. That's it, isn't it? Unless I've missed something?' She was looking enquiringly at Torquatus, who shook his head, frowning.

'I don't think you have.'

'Something's troubling you?'

'Lots of things. For instance, I saw something in that flat which wasn't quite right - I can't quite put my finger on it. Oh well, I don't suppose it matters,' Torquatus said. 'But there are some things I'd like to know. For example, we've concentrated on the attacks on the shrines, but we also know from Fiscilia's letter that she was intending to intercede with Octavian on behalf of the family. How was she going to do that?'

'She didn't give any details,' Fiscilius reminded him. 'I

suppose she might have intended to hand him a letter: she'll have seen people doing that often enough, when we've been in Rome.'

Cornelia looked sceptical.

Fiscilius frowned at her. 'You don't believe she did that?'

'No. Fiscilia may have been young but she doesn't sound as if she was a fool. We've all seen people handing in those petitions and letters; yes, and then what? The great man smiles, all benevolence, glances over the letter, and passes it to some slave secretary, to be dealt with later, if at all. If I was really determined to get something done, I wouldn't trust to a letter.'

'I agree,' Torquatus nodded. 'She might have been intending to appeal to Octavian personally, when he appeared in public. The only problem is - ,'

'But surely - ,' Cornelia broke in at the same moment.

'He's too well-guarded,' Fiscilius nodded. 'Perhaps she was planning to meet someone who could help her to a private meeting with Octavian, though I simply can't imagine who that could have been. We hardly know anyone in Rome now. Those men who were here tonight are our contacts here. I shouldn't think they've ever met Octavian.'

'That wasn't what I was going to say, though,' Torquatus said. 'The drawback I was going to point out - Cornelia too, I think - was that Octavian wasn't even in Rome.'

'What?' Fiscilius, who had been wandering around the room, spun round.

Torquatus raised his eyebrows. 'He wasn't here. He often isn't: is that so surprising? He's been recruiting in Campania, and then the Teanans kicked up a fuss about the settlements there, the local commissioners weren't able to come to an agreement, and one of them was killed. Octavian went to Teanum himself to bang heads together.'

There was a heavy silence. Fiscilius subsided onto his couch again. Torquatus gave him a sympathetic glance and filled both their cups again, before going on. 'Let's pretend that Fiscilia didn't burn the shrines, and imagine that she was just going to meet someone in the shrine.'

Fiscilius sighed. 'Oh, very well. But it seems pretty pointless, since we know she did.'

'I suppose so.' Torquatus gave him a thoughtful look. 'Though the wounds on her head weren't easy to explain. And I can't help asking myself why she didn't run out of the shrine once it was burning. There was nothing to stop her.'

Fiscilius stared at him. 'What do you mean? Surely there's no question that she died in the fire?'

Torquatus explained that Fiscilia's skull had been smashed at a low point, which the falling beams could hardly account for. 'If it wasn't for all the evidence of her guilt - and I admit it's overwhelming - I'd have said she'd been hit from behind, and was perhaps dead already when she fell to the ground.'

'But since we do know that no-one else was in the shrine, there's no doubt, is there?' Fiscilius' face was white, his wine-cup disregarded in his hand.

'I suppose not.'

Manlia was brisk. 'Let's leave the sacrilege on one side for the moment. Let's assume that there was someone else at the shrine, and that he managed to get out without anyone noticing. She might have been meeting someone who would help her get her message to Octavian. No, all right, Fiscilius: I know you didn't know anyone like that. But suppose she thought she did? Perhaps she was being cheated. After all, anyone who knew Octavian well enough to have introduced her would have known he wasn't here. But she wouldn't.'

'We don't know whether Fiscilia may have been suspicious,' Cornelia said thoughtfully. 'She didn't take Calliste; I wonder why not. And there's a bigger problem, isn't there? She'd only just arrived in Rome, and had no contacts in Octavian's circle, so how could she have found time to get to know this supposedly influential person? I mean, people who are close to Octavian - you, for instance, Aulus - presumably get requests all the time? Can you get this to Caesar for me? Can you suggest this to Caesar? Could you see if Caesar would agree to that? A stranger couldn't just bounce in and get you to intervene?'

'No, certainly not. Even friends are hard to help, especially just now. This resettlement of the soldiers is a nightmare: no-one, absolutely no-one is going to offer to help an insignificant provincial girl. Sorry, Fiscilius, but this is the truth. The best any of us can do is to help a close friend or an important client, because whenever we ask Octavian for a favour we are using up our capital with him. So how she could have got anyone to make any kind of commitment I don't know.'

But Cornelia was still frowning. 'How could Fiscilia have made that contact anyway? Could she have been planning to visit some great man's house among his clients, do you think? But whose?'

'Well, women do occasionally come to ask a favour. Not women like Fiscilia: they might be freedwomen of mine or my father's, perhaps. A lady like Fiscilia would send me a letter, asking if I could call on her, or if she might call on me.'

'An unmarried girl?'

Torquatus laughed. 'No. An unmarried girl wouldn't do either. And certainly not late in the evening.'

There was a silence while they all digested this. Then Cornelia said thoughtfully, 'Of course, we don't know that she did have a contact with Octavian.'

'I thought we'd decided that she must have had one?'

'No. We decided she must have thought she did.'

'Yes: perhaps she wasn't being cheated, just misled,' Torquatus agreed. 'Someone may have thought they could help her. Someone who didn't know as much as he thought he did. Someone she trusted enough to meet alone. She left Calliste behind, after all.'

'That didn't work, though,' Manlia pointed out with a dark look. 'Calliste ran away.'

'Whoever she was meeting was pretty incompetent, wasn't he?' Cornelia said quietly. 'We can deduce a good deal about him. He didn't know what he was doing. He didn't know Octavian was out of town. He didn't even know enough to realise that the shrine on the Velia, while it might be quiet enough for most of the year, wasn't going to be a good meeting-place on the Ides of May. Which makes me wonder whether perhaps he wasn't even a Roman? Someone from Mevania perhaps?'

She turned to Fiscilius, smiling, then cried out: 'Are you all right?'

The young man was white and shaking. For a moment he seemed unable to speak, then pulled himself together with an obvious effort. 'Yes. It was just - thinking of Fiscilia going into that dark place to meet a cheat, a liar - ,' He shook his head. 'I'm sorry. You asked about people from Mevania who might have helped her. I've been thinking about that, and it's true that there are plenty of dissatisfied people there just now. Whether any of them are in Rome I don't know. But I don't believe a word of all this. What I want to know is what went so terribly wrong for my sister, what turned her into a criminal. Calliste should be able to explain that. I have to find her. '

Cornelia selected a handful of raisins from the silver bowl. Torquatus offered her more wine but she waved the jug away. She turned to Fiscilius. 'We need to consider every possibility, Fiscilius. She might have already agreed to meet someone in Rome before she set off. It would make her journey a bit less of a lost cause, wouldn't it? Say she and - whoever - intended to plead their cause together, not just for their families, but for Mevania as a whole?'

'It would make more sense, I suppose,' Fiscilius agreed. 'But who? And then who burned the shrines? Did they do it together? Or was the arsonist someone else altogether?'

'I think Fiscilius is right. All of this has as many holes in it as a municipal fountain,' Manlia complained. 'Too complicated, relies on too many people being just where they ought to be. The answer must be simpler.'

Cornelia smiled. 'I do agree. In fact I think the whole idea that she meant to try and get the settlement revoked is just nonsense. Just like it's nonsense that she would skip round Rome setting shrines on fire.'

Torquatus was smiling at her. 'Very down to earth. And you're right; this is all a bit improbable.'

Cornelia smiled warmly back at him before turning to Fiscilius. 'Perhaps she went to the shrine for some quite different reason. Was she in love with anyone?' she asked him. Torquatus had been wondering that himself, and trying to find a way to frame the question tactfully: trust Cornelia, he thought, to ask straight out.

Manlia laughed. 'That's a much better explanation.'

'It's possible isn't it, if we put the arson to one side. The meeting in the shrine had nothing whatever to do with Octavian, Mevania, or anything like that.'

Fiscilius was scowling slightly.

Cornelia said gently, 'It wouldn't be surprising. She was a young girl, beautiful, from a good family. And she was eighteen, I think you said. She must have been thinking of marriage: a lot of girls are married already by that age.'

'Of course. I'm sorry if I seemed rude: I was just surprised at the rather personal question. But yes, her marriage was all arranged. I had found a good husband for her, a friend of my own, the only son of another of Mevania's leading families. She certainly wasn't in Rome meeting him.'

Manlia glanced up at him, puzzled.

Torquatus responded to his face rather than his words: 'She wasn't happy with your choice.'

Fiscilius smiled and met his eye. 'Oh no, she was perfectly happy. She was just annoyed that I hadn't got on and arranged the wedding sooner. You'll have gathered that patience wasn't her strong point.'

'Well, that seems to leave us with no credible explanation at all,' Torquatus said. 'And if we know anything we know that only one body was found in the shrine.'

Fiscilius put his cup down. 'The only way to find out is to trace the slaves. Calliste will know what my sister was doing, and when I catch her I'll get it out of the little bitch, by whatever means necessary. I'll be off tomorrow.'

'I can see that you have to trace them,' Torquatus told him quietly. 'Tell me, Fiscilius, how trustworthy did they seem, those men? Had they been in your family long?'

'One of them had: Nestor was born on one of our farms. But the other man, Tiro, was quite new. I bought him a couple of years back, in Rome. It was when the proscriptions were at their height, and I was afraid to go to the city without more protection. You think - ?'

'I don't think anything, except that a new slave might be easier to bribe, not having the sense of connection to the family you often find with home-born slaves. And maybe someone put Fiscilia up to what she did.'

Fiscilius stood up and stretched. 'I don't think Nestor would have taken a bribe,' he said. 'And Calliste wouldn't do anything against Fiscilia. But I can't swear to Tiro. Oh, my head's going round. I can't make sense of any of it. I'm for bed. It's been an exhausting couple of days, but without your help it would have been far, far worse. Maybe I'd never have known for certain whether Fiscilia was alive or dead.' He shivered. 'I'll be off in the morning.'

Torquatus hesitated a moment before saying, 'Shouldn't you go to Mevania first? Canidia will be needing you.'

'No. I have to know about Fiscilia. And Canidia has an excellent freedman who'll see she's all right.'

He nodded a casual goodnight to them all and walked off.

'Sleep well,' Cornelia called after him.

After he'd gone, Torquatus stood watching him for a moment, noting how quickly Fiscilius had turned the subject away from his sister's marriage. Then he turned to Manlia and Cornelia, saying, 'Canidia's the one person who can help us understand all this. I'm quite worried about her, actually. Has Fiscilius even written to her?'

'Not that I know of,' Cornelia told him. 'And we would know if he'd sent one of his slaves with a message.'

'Well, why isn't he more worried about her? As I understand it, the settlement at Hispellum will be getting under way. It will be no place for a middle-aged lady to be living on her own, but if I write to her, invite her here, will she listen? She doesn't know me, after all'

'I'll go and persuade her,' Manlia said, getting up and shaking out her skirts.

'You?' Why should you go,' Torquatus asked, horrified.

'Why not?' she countered. 'It occurred to me at dinner. Sempronia was saying that Fiscilius should bring her here. He isn't going to, for whatever reason. You can't: Octavian could call on you at any moment. You don't have anyone to send whom Canidia would be sure to trust - except me.'

'Or me, I suppose,' Cornelia said thoughtfully.

'You!' Torquatus looked horrified. 'I have enough trouble with your father as it is. He's always convinced I don't look after you properly, and he could order you back to his house if he wanted to.'

'No, Cornelia, I don't think you could do that,' Manlia agreed. 'But I haven't got anything much to do, and it could be useful. And if Canidia has anywhere else to go when she loses her home I might be able to find out what she knows about Fiscilia without dragging the poor woman to Rome. At the very least I'll be able to help her pack up and get out.'

'I still don't like it,' Torquatus objected.

'There's something else,' Manlia went on. 'Fiscilius has just told us that a friend of his from Mevania was Fiscilia's intended. But Sempronia thought she was going to marry a man called Marcus Ampudius, from Formiae. At least, that was her assumption. So maybe I'll get a chance, while I'm up in Mevania, of finding out the truth about all that. Do you know if he's written to this friend of his?'

'I don't think he has. Though I suppose he's been so overwhelmed by his sister's death that's understandable. Did you say Ampudius? That's a name I seem to know.' Torquatus shook his head. 'No, I can't place it. Anyway, Fiscilius is bound to be back in Mevania soon: the final mourning banquet is supposed to take place nine days after the funeral. That isn't going to be possible, but he can't delay it for long.' He looked at her with concern. 'But none of that really matters. The point is that I hate the idea of your going up there, with Italy in turmoil. '

Manlia was laughing at him. 'And I love you for it, Aulus. But I'm going anyway.' Seeing that that he looked worried, she patted his head in a kindly way, saying, 'I'll take my bodyguard with me.'

'Bodyguard! If you insist on this mad journey you'll go in the family carriage, with my personal groom driving and Becco and Pulex in the cart with you and a couple of other men riding alongside.'

'Oh, I don't want all those men! You know how troublesome slaves can be on a journey, always belly-aching about their blisters: we'd take for ever.' She looked up into his anxious face.

'We could send one of our own slaves,' Cornelia pointed out. 'A trusted slave. It's not really our problem, and I hate the thought of your going.'

'I won't do anything silly, I promise you. I'll even take all those heavies, if you think I should.' Manlia looked up at her brother seriously. 'I get dreadfully bored, you know - no, it's not your fault, you know it isn't, but I do. I ought to have a household to run and a family of my own to bully, but I only have a brother. I'd enjoy being independent for a bit. It's not as if I was proposing a trip to Britannia or something: Mevania's less than a hundred miles away. And now if I'm going to make an early start tomorrow I'd better go to bed.' She dropped a kiss on her brother's head and walked off, calling for Trofimus, and leaving Torquatus and Cornelia looking at each other in the flickering lamplight.

Chapter 7

The following morning, Trofimus told Torquatus that Fiscilius had left, in pursuit of the runaway slaves, after a breakfast of rolls and honey. It seemed typical of him that he hadn't waited long enough to thank his hosts. Manlia had gone even earlier, quietly and without fuss, as was her habit. Torquatus had tossed and turned half the night, trying to think of a way to stop her, but she was her own mistress. Their father, while he lived, could have compelled her obedience, but since his death she had been independent. She had a guardian, of course, in her husband's absence: a pallid little freedman of their father's around whom Manlia had been running rings for years. Even her husband, had he not been commanding a navy somewhere in the Adriatic, might have found it hard to get her to stay at home, though he would no doubt have methods of persuasion not open to a mere brother.

The last of Torquatus' clients were just leaving when Fiscilius unexpectedly hurried into the reception hall.

'I thought you'd be half-way to Sicily by now,' Torquatus exclaimed.

'I've found out what happened, Torquatus. I thought you ought to know. My sister was murdered, just as you suggested last night, and by her own slaves too.'

For all his own doubts, Torquatus was astonished by this bald statement.

'Murdered? What makes you so sure? How did you find out?'

'Well, I was going through the Appian Gate, heading southwards, and I thought maybe I'd just ask again at the stables there. No luck, though. I didn't find out anything new. A couple of the stable lads saw the girl get into the carriage, but that's all.'

'We already knew they'd picked up Calliste.'

'That was just the beginning, though.' Fiscilius was triumphant. 'I got them to show me where the carriage had stopped when the slaves were having their argument, and there was a bar right there, so I went in and ordered some wine and olives and got chatting to the barman, and it turned out that he'd heard them talking. In fact, just about everyone in the bar had heard them begin to quarrel, but when they realised they were attracting attention they'd dropped their voices. All most people heard was that one man wanted to go to Rhegium and the other disagreed.'

'Rhegium! They'd be hoping to get to Sextus Pompeius in Sicily from there.'

'But that's not all.' The reception hall was empty now and Fiscilius, obviously enjoying having Torquatus' undivided attention, took his time to seat himself on the marble bench at the head of the pool. Torquatus shrugged and joined him. 'The barman took the opportunity to go over to the pavement tables, to wipe them or something, and he heard one of them say, When you've killed the mistress, there's nothing else to do. We have to get out. Then they all seemed to panic and they drove off at top speed.'

'Well, that seems pretty conclusive, I agree. If that man was sure he'd heard correctly. Did you come all the way back here to tell me that?' He was frowning.

'Oh, he was quite sure,' Fiscilius insisted. He looked uncertainly at his host. 'It seems to me the problem's solved.'

'Is it? Why should the slaves murder Fiscilia?' Torquatus said. 'And why there? And what about the arson? Which, officially, is the reason I am interested in this affair at all.'

'I wonder if perhaps it wasn't Fiscilia who did that, but perhaps the slaves themselves. No, Torquatus, I know it's an odd idea, but what if someone bribed them? Maybe someone who wanted to make trouble for Octavian? But I found out something else, as well. Not proof, but it makes you wonder. After I'd been to the bar I went back to the stables and asked a lot more questions. I found out that when those men arrived at the stables, the evening before the Ides, another man came in just after them with a group of his friends: a man called Spurius Malens.'

One of the slaves behind them gave a muffled exclamation and Torquatus turned to see that several of them were looking at each other in consternation.

'Who is Spurius Malens?' he asked them. For a moment they hesitated. Then Trofimus stepped forward. 'I haven't heard of this particular individual, lord, but the whole Malens clan are well-known in the criminal underworld, I believe. Protection rackets and blackmail are their speciality. And they organise gangs of pickpockets at festival times. Of course they don't dare attack Us,' he stated, his nose in the air. 'But I have heard of people paying to have their houses left alone.'

'That's what one of the stable-hands told me. Not that he was keen to speak,' Fiscilius said. 'And apparently my slaves and Malens and his friends all went off from the stables at the same time.'

'Together?'

'I can't say that, but it seems quite likely, doesn't it?'

'I suppose so,' Torquatus agreed, frowning.

'It all hangs together, and makes much more sense than Fiscilia committing sacrilege.' Fiscilius leaned forward eagerly. 'Those two men could easily have fired the shrines on the Palatine and the Caelian, before hiding out on the Velia to wait for Fiscilia. Before we bought Tiro he was in a household on the Palatine.'

'You didn't tell me that before,' Torquatus said.

'It didn't seem relevant. But just think! If you wanted to do something bad like that, how sensible to choose two slaves who have transport and no connections to Rome. You pay them well, they do their job and off they go.'

'What about Calliste? Was she in this plot too?'

Fiscilius thought about this before shaking his head. 'I think not. No. I think what must have happened is that after the slaves were bribed they told Calliste to come to the shrine in the morning. We know she went out in the evening after they'd arrived, to buy food. Perhaps they spoke to her then, and told her to come to the shrine in the morning. She would never have agreed to anything that would harm Fiscilia. So she had to be eliminated. One of them waited for her there and killed the woman who arrived, thinking it was Calliste. He got out without being seen. They would imagine that Fiscilia, finding all her slaves gone, would simply go home, or perhaps take refuge with Acutius or something. But obviously they realised, once she was dead, that it was Fiscilia they'd killed, and they panicked.'

'I wonder why they waited around all day, though? And why they picked up Calliste in the evening. How did she know where to go?'

'Maybe they had to wait to be paid. And I suppose they could have told Calliste Fiscilia would meet them at the stables in the evening as originally planned. She might wonder at that but she wouldn't worry. And that would explain why they had a row when she turned up outside the stables and told them Fiscilia was dead: she'd been in Rome all day and she'd have heard people talking, no doubt. She must have been terrified.'

'That makes sense, I suppose.' Torquatus got up, preparing to go out. 'Case closed'

'Yes.' Fiscilius was fretting to be off, but Torquatus hadn't finished. 'I presume you will be back in Mevania for the banquet at the end of the mourning period? If Manlia's still there, I want you to make sure she comes home after that, whatever Canidia decides. You'll have to break the news to the bridegroom, too, if Manlia hasn't seen him. Marcus Ampudius, I gathered his name was?'

Fiscilius, who'd been shuffling his feet on the floor impatiently, stopped as if an arrow had hit him between the shoulder-blades. 'What? Who told you that?' His face was as ghostly-white as it had been when he first saw his sister's body.

Torquatus was watching him carefully. 'What have I said? That's what Sempronia told Manlia at the funeral dinner, or so I thought. Obviously I was wrong. Come into the garden and tell me about it.'

'But what about the slaves? I can't stop now.'

'You are so far behind them that a few moments more won't make a difference.' Torquatus used all his authority, and it worked. Fiscilius turned back towards him, and Torquatus led the way through his business-room to where an archway led out into the colonnade. In the garden they found Cornelia, scrolls scattered round her feet, and a set of wax tablets in her hand. She could see at once that Fiscilius had something to tell, and sat up straighter in her chair. A slave padded out behind them with wine and cups. She was pale, Torquatus thought, with a stab of concern, but she smiled and told him she was well.

'I was a bit sick, that's all. I think probably one of those mussels wasn't quite fresh.' She shrugged, and waved aside the wine jug with a shudder. 'But you have some news?'

'Yes. Fiscilius has discovered that the slaves were overheard saying that they'd murdered Fiscilia.'

'Really? That's extraordinary.'

'It is. And Fiscilius is about to tell us,' Torquatus said, sitting down on the marble bench facing her, 'that Fiscilia was not going to marry Marcus Ampudius, as we supposed.'

'We must have misunderstood,' she said with a reassuring smile. 'I'm sure that's what Sempronia said.'

Fiscilius' colour had returned to normal. 'I had arranged a marriage for her with a friend of my own, the only son of a family we've had ties to for generations. All arranged years ago, and quite a settled thing till last year.'

'She refused to go ahead with it?'

'She was being very stupid. She'd have grown out of it, no

doubt, but she was making my life pretty uncomfortable.'

Torquatus gestured to the slave, who poured wine and stepped back.

'Did she just object to the man you'd chosen? Or did she have ideas of her own?' Cornelia asked.

'Of course she had ideas of her own: did you ever know a woman who didn't?' Fiscilius took a gulp of his wine. 'It was all going fine until she met another man the last time she and my aunt were in Rome.' He clenched his jaws together so hard the others could hear his teeth grinding. 'I blame Aunt Canidia: she's supposed to be caring for Fiscilia. How did she come to allow her to talk to any young man?'

Torquatus' eyes were bright with interest. 'And that man would be this Marcus Ampudius?'

'Yes, as bloody Sempronia told you. Marcus Ampudius, from Formiae. Formiae! What do I know about Formiae? More importantly: who do I know there? Nobody, that's who.'

Cornelia and Torquatus both stared at his sudden fury. Cornelia smiled. 'I can see this would leave you in a difficult situation.'

'Difficult! If I let her marry this Ampudius, it would be a gross insult to our friends in Mevania; men we've worked with for generations. And what use would a brother-in-law in Formiae be to me? Or I to him, for that matter. And all Fiscilia would say is oh, but I love him.' The last words came out in a squeaky falsetto which made Torquatus want to giggle. He felt rather than heard Cornelia give a tiny gasp, and her voice was a little muffled as she asked where Fiscilia had met the young man.

'As I said, it was on her last visit to Rome, just before the flat was sold: early in the year Pansa and Hirtius were consuls, just over two years ago. She and Canidia dined with Quintus Acutius, who was here at the banquet. I don't know why Acutius had to ask them to dinner: in the old days women didn't go to banquets, and certainly not without their menfolk, and even then they sat on chairs, they didn't recline like men.' He fell silent, clearly brooding over the general decay of manners.

'And this Ampudius, he was there too?'

Fiscilius took another gulp of wine and seemed to calm down. 'Apparently. Not that I knew anything about it until I got a letter a few months later, asking for Fiscilia. I was surprised, to say the least. I'd never heard of the man, and I discovered that they'd only met that once. When I looked into the matter, though, it turned out they'd been writing to each other. One of my slaves - one I trusted enough to send to Rome on business - had been carrying letters between them, apparently.'

'So what did you do?'

'What do you think? Sold the slave, and told Fiscilia to behave herself. I said she could forget Ampudius. I had her engagement to Titus Fulvus made known: the wedding would have taken place next month.'

'So that's why it was so long delayed. The bride was unwilling, and now she is dead,' Cornelia said quietly. There was an awkward silence.

'There's a good deal to work on here.' Torquatus was being cautious. 'Ampudius, for a start. I wish I'd known all this before: fancy having Acutius here in the house and never asking him anything.'

'But why bother?' Fiscilius said angrily. 'We know what happened now.'

Torquatus turned back to Fiscilius, frowning. 'There are some loose ends he could tie up for us.' His face lightened suddenly into a smile. 'I do hate loose ends. Why did you tell me Fiscilia was happy with your marriage-plans, Fiscilius?'

Fiscilius looked embarrassed, but answered easily enough. 'Sheer awkwardness, Torquatus. I suppose I hoped that none of that stupid story would have to come out. It doesn't make my sister look good. And it didn't seem relevant.'

Torquatus gave him a long, steady look. 'You must have known I'd want to know everything about Fiscilia, and you haven't been frank at all.'

'I've given you all the evidence you need,' Fiscilius insisted. 'And now I have those murderers to catch.' He stalked off, offence in every movement, and Torquatus and Cornelia watched him go.

'That young man will need watching,' Torquatus said. 'Have you noticed how his story keeps changing? He would never have mentioned Ampudius to us if Sempronia hadn't mentioned him, would he?'

'If Fiscilius is right then this love story is irrelevant, just as he said,' Cornelia said slowly.

'Well, yes. Though of course if Fiscilia really was murdered - and we still have the problem that we've no idea how - we don't have to conclude that the slaves necessarily did it. If it wasn't them, we still have the attacks on the shrines to explain. I admit that I can't see where Ampudius fits in. He might conceivably have wanted to kill Fiscilius but why he would want to get rid of Fiscilia I can't see.'

'Really? I can think of circumstances in which Fiscilia's arrival might have been highly unwelcome. Let's suppose that Ampudius has recovered from his temporary infatuation with Fiscilia. Perhaps the love was always more on her side than on his. Suppose he's not all that wealthy, and he's just negotiated a marriage with someone else. Someone very rich. Perhaps someone jealous and quick to take offence. For a certain type of man, a threat like that would have to be dealt with ruthlessly. We don't know anything about this Ampudius, after all.'

Torquatus looked at her gravely. 'What a depressing idea.'

She met his gaze candidly. 'People don't often marry for love, do they?'

Chapter 8

There was nothing Torquatus enjoyed more, on a fine morning in early summer, than sitting in his house waiting for his morning guests to be shown in. There'd been a time, during the dark days of the proscriptions, when he'd thought he would be ruined, the last of a fine old family extinguished in shame and dishonour. But Fortune had smiled on him, and here he sat, the old bronze-bound money-chest ready by his side, looking out at the reflections from the central pool sliding softly over pillars and walls. The morning after Fiscilius had left it seemed especially peaceful. And when he had attended to his clients he would go and visit Octavian: he had told Trofimus to make sure everyone knew.

The scene pleased all his senses. An early ray of sunshine picked out the sharp black key-pattern border of the floor, while a pleasant smell of woodsmoke rose from the clean hearth. Torquatus' household gods were not Cornelia's - they were married, as most modern couples were, in a form which left her legally still a member of Balbus' family - but she ignored that and always tended the altar respectfully, and this morning she had placed a pot of flowers on the household shrine: two or three slender blue iris, still dripping with dew. Incense burned on the altar, the smoke twisting up lazily into the rafters. The wax masks of his ancestors looked out from their well-polished wooden houses, just below his chair: the fancy came into his mind that they approved the scene just as he did. Cornelia had ordered them to be moved from their old place to the right of the great doors. To her way of thinking, he wasn't making the best use of them: if you're lucky enough to have the right to display your ancestors' funeral-masks, she said, you should put them where no-one can miss them.

There was a sense of subdued energy. The slaves stood ready, talking softly among themselves. He could smell new bread: one of them had a large basket of rolls on his arm. Another had jugs of wine and water, and was attended by the boy Felix with a tray of cups. Offering food and drink to his morning visitors was an innovation of Torquatus', a good one in a time of hardship. Trofimus sailed through, signing to the doorman to open up. The great doors swung smoothly inwards. The crowd outside begin to press forwards, but Trofimus held up an imperative hand, looking the crowd over and beckoning one or two men forward. The first of them came in, his boots loud on the mosaic. He and Torquatus exchanged the kiss of greeting, and so the morning began.

A steady stream of men came before him, none of them especially distinguished or interesting, and none of them likely to be able to help him in his search for Fiscilia's killer. It spoke volumes for the state of the city, he thought, that so many of his clients were simply hunting for food to feed their families, or any small coins that would help them buy it. A quick, embarrassed greeting, the gift tucked away in a fold of the toga, and the man would slip off, perhaps to some other great house where he might receive a similar gift. Torquatus listened patiently to the man before him, who had got bogged down in an interminable story about his ailing wife and bedridden father and three children. Harassed, Torquatus agreed to whatever it was the man wanted, and Felix reached into the open money-chest. The crowd began to die down, but then there was a bustle, a noticeable surge, and the sea of male heads parted before a headdress Torquatus recognised with a sinking heart. Laid over hair stiffly curled, a comb adorned with large half-pearls held a veil in place. Not the light floaty kind of veil pretty women wear to attract attention but a repellent widowy thing, dun-coloured and prickly-looking. Torquatus' mother had come to call, something she seldom did except to complain of some failing of her son's, and never as early as this. What would it be this time? Since they were under scrutiny Torquatus played the part of the virtuous son, embracing his mother, putting back her veil and kissing her cheek. Cornelia, who'd been sitting in one of the side-rooms, appeared in its doorway. Without apparent effort she whisked Vibia away.

Torquatus brought his attention back to his clients with a sense of foreboding. But he didn't have to wonder for long why his mother had come. One moment the reception hall was so full of visitors it was a wonder no-one ended up in the pool, the next Torquatus looked around and the hall was empty except for the group of clients who would walk with him to the Palatine and the slaves, sweeping up crumbs, tidying papers away, joking with each other in the rough Greek which was their common language. He got up, stretched, and approached the side-room, squaring his shoulders, but as he did so the curtain was drawn back and his mother came out, the stately veil once more drawn down.

'Oh, are you going?' he asked, trying to sound regretful.

'Yes, dear. I think I've said all I wanted to say.' Torquatus glanced at Cornelia, casting up his eyes, and received one of her sparkling looks back.

'Before you go, though, it's just occurred to me that you might be able to help me.'

'Really? I shouldn't think so, dear.' She began to sound much more cheerful. There are men who find the shrewd advice and family connections of their mothers help them in the development of their careers: Torquatus was not one of them. His father, a stalwart on the republican side in the civil war, had died shortly after they had fallen out and Torquatus himself had left to join Julius Caesar. His mother, he knew, had always blamed him for his father's death. Sometimes, he thought she was right. Murmuring a word of excuse, Cornelia left them together.

'As you know, Mother - oh, really, this is too ridiculous. Do put your veil up and let's sit down again. That's better. Now, as I said, this unfortunate girl whose death I'm looking into -'

'Yes, dear, and I can't imagine why. What business is it of yours? So typical of you to get involved with something shady.'

'I'm not sure that's what it is,' he said mildly.

'What else should I call it? These people - the Fiscilii, I mean. Who are they? Some rubbishing little municipal family from Mevania. Mevania! Hardly the centre of the world, is it? Then this girl goes mad and does her best to burn Rome down and anger her gods.' She wrinkled her snub nose, and narrowed her eyes.

'I'm not quite sure she did.'

'That's absurd. Everyone knows her body was found in the shrine.'

'I need to know why, though. And there are some puzzling details which I want to clear up.'

'What a fuss to make about a common criminal.' Vibia sniffed. 'So what did you think I might know about these vulgar people?'

'I need to find out about a man from Formiae. I was only a boy at the time, and my memories are rather hazy, but didn't Father have a friend there? He might have known these Ampudius people.'

'Why, your father's friend was Ampudius.'

Torquatus stared at her. 'Do you mean to say you actually know the man?'

'Well, I did. I haven't seen them for years, and of course the Ampudius your father knew might not be still alive.'

'No, and even if he were it would be his grandson I'm interested in, I suppose. Tell me about the family.'

'They're very rich, or they were anyway: merchants with a substantial shipping interest. Ship-building, I mean, as well as maintenance and repair, with sheds at Puteoli. And marine insurance, and an importing business too. The Egyptian trade, papyrus, linen. All very profitable, and so well-organised.'

Vibia's face had lightened; she'd lost her habitual look of grievance. It struck Torquatus, and not for the first time, that it had been her misfortune to have been born a woman. Had she been a man, she would have filled a respected position in Ancona, would have been a magistrate, no doubt, a powerful citizen and a potential benefactor. She wouldn't have needed to channel her energies through her husband and son: he recalled how his father had often said that she had a better business head than most men. He smiled at her. 'And do you remember where they live?'

'You've been there, when you were a child: a big villa just outside the town. We stopped there, sometimes, on the way to our place at Cumae. I suppose they must have had a place in Rome too, but I don't remember ever visiting them there. Offices and warehouses too, of course, at Puteoli and Formiae, and ship-sheds nearer to Neapolis.'

'That's why the name would be familiar, I suppose. I thought I recognised it.'

'Why do you need to know all this -' she began, and then her disgust-face came back and she fell silent. Torquatus followed her gaze to the doorway, where Felix was standing. Nar was there too, head cocked, eyes bright, tail gently waving as if waiting for an introduction.

'I thought I said - no, I'm quite sure I said - that he was to be kept out of the house?' Torquatus began.

'Only for a moment.' Felix gave him a pained look. 'He badly needs to go out for a walk, and Trofimus told me to ask you if you have any errands, and if you have perhaps Nar could come with me. Trofimus says only if you say he can.' He put on the face of one begging for mercy for an oppressed animal. 'Please! He was getting bored in the gardens.'

Nar showed no signs of boredom that Torquatus could see. He trotted round the room, snuffing at the pool, and carefully smelling the feet of each of them in turn. Cornelia, re-entering the reception hall with a box in her hands, stopped short.

'Yes, very well. You can take a message to Quintus Acutius. I want to see him. And I need to know whether Ampudius has a place in Rome. Acutius will know that. I want to see Ampudius too, if he's here, so you can go on to his house once you know where it is. I'll write the letters now. You know where Acutius lives?'

Felix nodded. Torquatus snapped his fingers and a slave came forward with wax tablets, in which Torquatus wrote a brief message. As he did so, the dog continued his exploration.

'Really, Aulus.' Vibia pulled her skirts closer round her ankles as Nar approached. 'What in the name of all the gods is that?'

'He's a dog. I'm surprised you didn't see that,' Torquatus said cheerfully, and handed the tablets to Felix. Cornelia frowned at him.

'He belongs to Fiscilius,' Cornelia told her, 'and he definitely isn't staying.'

'I should hope not. Hardly the kind of animal one would expect to find in a senator's house.'

Vibia's disapproval seemed to convey itself to Nar. He had been happily sniffing at her feet - perhaps her skirts reminded him of Fiscilia - but he looked up at this, growling. Apparently pleased with the sound, he then tried out a few short barks.

Trofimus appeared from nowhere. 'I beg your pardon, lord. I heard the animal, and wondered how it came to be in the house.'

'Felix is about to take him out of the house, to Quintus Acutius' place,' Torquatus observed. 'Apparently he needs to go for a walk.'

Too late. Moving on from Vibia's feet - for which Torquatus offered up thanks to all the gods - Nar found himself at the base of a large lampstand. Perhaps it reminded him of a tree: he lifted his leg, and with an expression of profound relief on his face released a stream of urine onto the bronze. There was a moment's silence, then Vibia thundered, 'Aulus!', luckily covering Torquatus' own expletive, and Trofimus took Felix's shoulder in one large, capable hand and led the boy, and the dog on his piece of rope, still dribbling out a few last drops, across the reception hall to the main doors. The puddle, yellow and smelly, spread quietly across the floor.

Vibia got up and twitched her stola back into position. 'I shall never understand you, Aulus,' she said. 'How you can prefer these poor little municipal men, bankers and fixers, with no sense of taste or decency - ,' She broke off, looking rather embarrassed:

Cornelia was after all the daughter of Balbus, the richest fixer of them all. Torquatus, glancing at Cornelia, was relieved to see that she looked rather amused. She put the box she'd been holding into Vibia's hand: Torquatus saw his mother's expression change from contempt to profound embarrassment.

'Thank you so much for helping us with Ampudius,' Cornelia said, and Vibia nodded grandly and swept out.

'I don't know what you've given my mother, but it seems to have worked,' Torquatus said, relaxing.

'Some of my pearls,' Cornelia told him, smiling. 'She's going to a grand party, and I've lent them to her.' She glanced up at him. 'I'm so pleased she took them. I do try to get on with her, but she hasn't - well, she hasn't been easy with me, ever since I came.'

Torquatus nodded. Vibia's way of dealing with a daughter-in-law had alternated between treating Cornelia with exaggerated respect as the new mistress of her son's house and ignoring her completely in a vain attempt to assert her authority over her son.

'Did she come to borrow jewellery? She's got plenty of her own, though it's not up to your standard. I don't suppose you put it like that.'

She was chuckling. They moved aside to allow slaves with mops to clean up Nar's little accident.

'If I'd said anything like that, of course she wouldn't have touched my things, and I wouldn't blame her. No, she actually came with some rather bad news.'

'Really? Is it urgent? I am supposed to be with Octavian, you know.'

'I do. But this is important, I think. It's about the settlements.'

'Oh gods, not more trouble!'

'I'm afraid so. You know how Lucius Antonius has been running round telling Antonius' veterans they aren't getting a fair share of the land? According to him, all the best places have been kept for Octavian's troops? Whipped up of course by Antonius' wife?'

'Of course I do.'

'According to Vibia, he's changed tack. Now, instead of complaining that Antonius' soldiers are being short-changed, he's begun to speak out for all those poor people who are having their land taken from them. She told me he'd made a big speech about it here yesterday, and he and Fulvia are planning a tour of the cities, to drum up support. Even though Fulvia is Antonius' wife, which you'd think would put her firmly on the soldiers' side. I wonder whether her husband knows what she's up to? With such a lot of people suffering, Lucius' message is going down very well.'

'Damn him to Hades! Does he have anything to say about where the land for the soldiers should come from, I wonder?'

'Oh yes. He says there's lots of public land, and more in Asia province.'

'Does he have any other bright ideas?'

'Well, yes; he also says that some senators whose lands have been protected should lose their estates too.'

'As you say, the big question is whether big brother Marcus is behind this.'

Torquatus thought he understood now why his mother had been so keen to bring him news of these worrying developments. She was always the first with bad news. It wasn't hard to see where any confrontation between Lucius Antonius and Octavian would end. War was the last thing Rome needed, but could it still be prevented?

'And Vibia had another piece of news as well,' Cornelia told him. 'Apparently Octavian is about to divorce his wife. Interesting, don't you think, given that she's Fulvia's daughter?'

Torquatus shrugged. 'Octavian never liked her. Gossip is that he's never even slept with her. I suppose now he's decided that if war is inevitable between him - us - and the awful Lucius and Fulvia there's no need to keep Claudia any longer.'

'Poor girl. What a sad thing for her. Just sitting around like an unused piece of furniture, waiting for a future that isn't going to happen.'

Torquatus smiled. 'She's rich and well-connected. No doubt somebody else will snap her up. And now I really must go.'

Once out of the house, Nar wanted to explore every interesting smell, and Felix let him do so, enjoying his freedom. He sometimes felt as if he were under constant supervision: by Trofimus, the master, the schoolmaster, and just about every adult human being. Still, he knew he was lucky, being well-fed, and cared-for, and very rarely beaten. And the schoolmaster, disagreeable though he might be, was teaching Felix not only to read and do numbers, but also what the old man called 'systems':

accounting techniques, ways of managing document archives, the correct way to write letters to people of different ranks. But he was lonely; he still missed his fellow-slave Iucundus, even though it was over a year since his friend died. The master had mistakenly suspected Iucundus of involvement in a plot against his life and the boy had died under torture, something Felix still had nightmares about. Now there weren't any other slaves his age in his master's house. Torquatus was a bit old-fashioned and didn't give the kind of parties where the wine was served by pretty boys who could perform other services later, so he was the only young slave. But he was also the only slave whose father was the old master, so he was treated differently: better than most, he knew. In most households a thirteen-year old would be expected to carry as much work as an adult.

He liked Nar very much. The dog was enjoying exploring these strange new streets, with their rich layers of scent. He was especially attracted to the smell of frying sausages which drifted across from a stall perched precariously and illegally on the slope of the Argentarius, and he whined at Felix and tried to drag him across the road to investigate. Felix had some money: tips he'd been given, rewards for special services for his master. Every little coin he got went into an old leather purse which Torquatus kept for him in the family money-chest and one day, he hoped, there would be enough there to buy his freedom, or, better still, to set him up in business if his master decided to free him as a gift. He never carried money with him, as he wouldn't waste it on street food, and he pulled determinedly on Nar's rope, dragging him away from the smells which he himself found just as enticing. When he was free and rich, as he intended to be one day, he would stop at any food stall or eating-place he fancied and he'd buy pies and sausage, or cakes and pastries filled with nuts and dripping with honey, and he'd eat them right there in the street, dropping crumbs and licking his fingers. Pleased with this fantasy, he decided he'd have a dog, too, and he'd buy the dog sausages, though probably not cakes. He pulled Nar closer as a sad-looking donkey pushed past, loaded with what looked like a whole family's belongings.

Whatever attention he had to spare from minding Nar and watching the scene around him he gave to the murder. Why would anyone kill a woman? Murders happened all the time, but in his mind killings were to do with politics, intrigue, ambition; men's things. He didn't have much time for speculation, however: the

Forum was extremely busy, and he needed all his wits to get himself and Nar safely through the crowd. If he'd had time, he could have listened to a herald announcing from the rostra the date of the elections for the next year's praetors. Or he could have joined the crowd listening to a court case in front of Castor's temple; an important one, from the size of the crowd. A laugh rippled through it as he passed. As usual there were fortune-tellers hovering on the margins, and the scribes who will write you a love letter or a complaint to your landlord. Today the weather was hot so on every corner stood a man selling wide-brimmed straw hats. Felix hardly noticed them. They were always there: had it been wet they would have been out with hooded cloaks. There were men with trays of lucky charms or eye-lotions or clay figurines, as well as snack merchants selling packets of nuts and raisins, and the hot food which attracted Nar's ever-ready nose. He pulled the dog away from the tantalising smells and headed up the Velia, just as he had on the day Fiscilia's body had been found in the shrine of the Argei. He cast the shrine a curious look as he passed, but it looked empty, just as it would be on all but two days in the year. He trotted on, Nar capering in front of him, down past the eastern slope of the Palatine, and under the arch of the Aqua Claudia, a cool shadow in the tremendous heat of the day. Immediately they'd passed under the aqueduct he tugged Nar into the quiet side street where Quintus Acutius had his house.

'My master has sent me with a message for the lord Quintus Acutius,' he told the doorman.

The slave looked doubtfully at Nar. 'Your master being?'

'Aulus Manlius Torquatus.'

The doorman let him in, and nodded his head towards a couple of well-dressed slaves talking quietly. One of the men had already noticed the boy, and was walking over, still smiling at something. He held out an imperative hand, but Felix hesitated. 'This is to go to Quintus Acutius, from my master.'

'So it shall, child.'

'And you are?' Seeing the slave's haughty look, he added, 'My master will want to know who I gave it to.'

'My name is Meton, Quintus Acutius' secretary.'

'Thank you.' On his dignity, Felix handed over the sealed tablets with a courteous inclination of the head, such as he'd seen his master use. Meton's smile broadened, but Felix luckily didn't have time to notice, as Nar, bored by these social niceties, decided it was time to leave. If he was my dog, Felix thought, I'd have trained him to be more obedient.

'I'm to wait for an answer. And my master would like to know, please, where Marcus Ampudius lives when he is in Rome. I have to take a letter to him as well.'

Meton's eyebrows rose a little at this, but he went away with the tablets, and came back a few moments later, the tablets sealed shut with a blob of wax this time, as if either Meton or his master supposed Felix might read the message on the way home. Felix carefully kept his face from expressing his annoyance at the implied insult.

'My master says to tell you that Marcus Ampudius lives on the Caelian Hill, close to the temple of Minerva Capta,' Meton was telling him. 'Do you know where that is?'

Felix nodded. 'My master was at the shrine of the Argei there a few days ago. I'm sure I can find it.'

'Of course. It's your master who is investigating the burning of those shrines.' The slaves who were in the hall all turned and stared at him. Obviously public interest in the affair hadn't yet died away.

Outside the house Felix dragged the dog away from some small dead creature in the gutter, which he'd unaccountably missed on the way up the road, and which he seemed to feel an accountable need to roll in. With a sneeze and a regretful backward glance, Nar began to trot along beside him.

It was too hot to run, Felix told himself as he set off along one of the roads that ran parallel to the Aqua Claudia. At the end of that road he passed under the aqueduct again before cutting through a tangle of narrow streets and climbing at last onto the Caelian hill. Along its gentle slopes, the crowded blocks of city flats give way to a greener space where more expensive houses sit among gardens and Felix, slowing to a walk in the heat, couldn't help taking a moment to notice the apple trees overhanging one wall, and to listen to the splashing of a fountain behind another, and to imagine being rich enough to live in a nice quiet place like this. He climbed higher, Nar panting beside him, until he wasn't far from Minerva's temple high among its grove of trees. He stopped, out of breath, wishing he'd asked for a drink of water at Acutius' house and looking around for someone to ask for directions. These were not senators' houses, so they didn't have tall doors like his master's, standing open from dawn till dusk. But as he looked around, the door of one house opened and a couple of slaves came out. His hopes rose, but he was out of luck; neither of them had heard of Ampudius.

Felix thanked them and moved on, intending to ask higher up the hill, closer to the temple. He was thirsty and tired, and hoped he was offered some refreshment when he finally reached Ampudius' house.

Twice more he asked the way, and each time he drew a blank. He was beginning to wonder if Quintus Acutius had told him wrong when he was almost knocked flying by a boy who came running out of a door at top speed. The boy swerved aside and screeched to a halt. 'Sorry!' he called out, and Felix smiled. The boy's face was the sort you couldn't help smiling at: gap-toothed, freckled, with red-brown hair and red-brown eyes, and rather large ears.

'Never mind that,' Felix replied. 'But if you know where Marcus Ampudius lives I wish you'd tell me.'

The boy laughed. 'This is it.' He jerked his thumb back at the doorway he'd just come through. 'Not that he lives here exactly, but this is his Roman house.'

No doubt if Ampudius was only an occasional resident that would explain why the neighbours didn't know him. 'Well, I have a letter for him.'

'Give it to Strato, our doorkeeper. He'll pass it on.'

'No doubt he would, in his own good time. No, it's urgent, see. I have to give it into your master's hands.'

'Tell Strato that, then. I can't stop. I've been sent out to get something the master needs to take with him. They'll kill me if I'm not back before dawn.'

Felix looked around doubtfully at the sunlit street.

'Dawn today, idiot,' said the other boy, rolling his eyes, before jogging off down the road. Felix approached the big front door, closed now, but with a window from which a pair of rheumy old eyes watched suspiciously.

'I have an urgent letter for your master from mine: Aulus Manlius Torquatus,' he said politely. 'I have to give it to him myself.'

The doorkeeper raised his eyebrows at the venerable name, but made no move to open the door. 'Oh you do, do you?'

'Yes. And it's urgent, like I said. You'll get into trouble if you don't let me in.'

'I will, will I? And what about the dog?' He stared again, then his watery eyes turned away. For a moment Felix wanted to shout after him, until he realised that the old man had gone to seek advice. He looked around for somewhere he could leave Nar, but there wasn't anything to tie him to. At last he heard the latch lift and the door opened. A trim, close-bearded man with cold dark eyes looked him over. 'I gather you have a letter for my master. You may give it to me.'

'It's personal. I have to give it to him myself.' This wasn't true, but Felix thought he might as well get a look at this Ampudius if he could. All the slaves knew that he was supposed to have had something to do with the strange death of Fiscilius' sister: no conversation in a house like Torquatus' was ever truly private, and Felix had been serving wine after dinner last night. The steward hesitated, then said, 'Wait here,' and walked off into the interior of the house. A very nice house, too, Felix thought. There was a reception hall, much smaller than his master's but beautifully decorated in the new style, with the effect of a garden full of trees and birds vivid against a warm blue sky. Light poured in through high windows, and one or two statues, judiciously placed, seemed to bring the fantastic garden right into the room. Nar seemed happy to sit at his feet for once, and Felix was busy identifying all the birds perching among the painted bushes when the steward returned, a tall man behind him.

'You have a letter from Quintus Fiscilius.' It wasn't a question. There was something forceful about this tight-lipped, close-cropped man that suggested he was not to be argued with. Felix politely handed over the writing-tablets and watched as Ampudius read their message. When he looked up, Felix wondered if he was ill, his face was so pale.

'Your master is Aulus Manlius Torquatus,' Ampudius stated in a hard, clipped voice and Felix realised that he wasn't ill but angry. Instinctively his eyes fell and he stepped back a pace, almost tripping over the dog. 'I understand Quintus Fiscilius is staying in his house.'

'My master found the lady Fiscilia's body when he was conducting the rites of the Argei, and took the body to our house. Fiscilius was my master's house-guest, but he's left us now.'

Ampudius stood looking into the distance, tapping his fingernails against the closed tablets unheedingly.

'I suppose I'd better answer this.'

He turned away, to a table at the back of the room. The reply didn't take him long, and then Felix was out of the house. He hadn't dared ask for a drink. He waited round the corner for the freckly boy to come back. He had grasped that Torquatus wanted to know whether Ampudius was there, and to see him if he was, but the boy had said he was going to get something the master wanted to take with him on a journey. Felix decided not to go home till he had found out where and when Ampudius was going: the man wasn't the sort a slave could question directly, and he'd seen Felix off the premises himself. He didn't have long to wait: he heard the boy's running feet, and stepped out to intercept him.

'Oh, you still here?'

'Yes. Can I ask you a few questions?'

'Depends what they are, I suppose.' The boy shrugged. 'And why you want to know. But anyway I must take this to my master first,' and he hoisted the box he was carrying a little higher.

'What is it?'

'Poetry, I think.' He shrugged again. 'Or maybe it's philosophy. He's borrowing it. Look, there's a door at the top of this lane. I'll meet you there as soon as I can.' He hurried inside.

Felix had already explored the lane and discovered the door, so he had nothing to do but wait with mounting impatience for the freckly boy's return. Nar seemed happy enough snuffling about, or sitting panting in the shade of the wall. At last the door opened, with a little creak, and the boy slipped through, pulling it to behind him.

'You'll have to be quick. I've got ever so much to do.'

'You're going away?'

'Home,' the boy nodded.

'Today?'

'What is all this? Why do you want to know?'

Felix had anticipated this question and his reply was ready. 'Only that my master intended to ask yours to dinner. I should have asked him - your master, I mean - when would be convenient, but I forgot, and if I go home without finding out when he's leaving I'll lose my tip, I know.'

It was an excuse any slave could understand and the boy nodded. 'Oh well, no harm, I suppose. But I was puzzled because you're not the first person to have asked when we were leaving.'

'Really? Someone else has been up here today?' Felix supposed another of Torquatus' slaves had also been sent on the same errand.

'Not today, no. It was yesterday. A weedy-looking slave came up and started asking the doorkeeper all sorts of odd questions.'

'What sort of questions?' This couldn't have been anyone from Torquatus' house.

'Oh, when we were going, and where, just like you did. But the doorkeeper really got suspicious when the man wanted to know if the master was married.'

'What an odd question,' Felix agreed.

'Strato told him the master isn't married, and doesn't have any plans to be, as far as anyone knows, and shut his little window, refusing to answer any more questions.'

'What did he look like?' Felix asked. 'And when did he come?'

'Some time late in the morning, I think it was. And it's hard to describe him because he was so very ordinary: medium height, brownish hair, a bit pigeon-toed. And weedy, as I said.'

'Not one of ours. But about my master's dinner-party - ?'

The boy shrugged. 'He can forget it: we're going in an hour or two, as soon as we're packed up. As to when we'll be back, I've no idea. The master lives in Formiae pretty much all the time, doesn't like Rome much, so I don't suppose he'll come back till he needs to.'

'Thanks. If it takes so long to pack you must be taking a load of stuff with you?'

The boy laughed. 'It's the mistress, Ampudius' mother. She takes practically everything whenever she goes anywhere: her bed, her favourite comfy chair, her pet talking bird, plus Jupiter knows how many slaves, some of them almost as old as she is. The master will lose patience any time now and say he's not waiting for her. She's got plenty of slaves to guard her, and she likes to go at the speed of the big ox-wagon carrying all her gear; worried that something gets pinched wherever she stops for the night, I suppose. The master prefers to travel fast, so you see - ? If that's all, I must get back.'

'Thanks. What's your name, by the way? Mine's Felix.'

'Epaphroditus.' He made a face. 'That's what they call me, anyway.'

Felix understood: the masters liked to burden slaves with a hefty chunk of Greek. No doubt this boy had a real name, but he would only find that out if they became friends. The boys clasped hands briefly, and Felix jogged back down into the stuffy heat of Rome, regretting that he wouldn't see Epaphroditus again. Something about him reminded Felix of his dead friend, Iucundus.

Lost in these thoughts, he let his feet choose the quickest way home, cutting across the Fagutal to the Vicus Sandalarius. The Fagutal is a pleasant place, where a few of the ancient beech trees that gave it its name still stand, casting a welcome dappled shade. But there are many houses here now, too, smaller than Ampudius', but very respectable places. Just as Felix crossed a quiet side-street there was a shout behind him, and he jumped out of the way of the litter that was coming up the road behind him. Carried by two brawny men, it was the narrow, plain kind one can hire at any of Rome's gates, and throughout the city. The boy watched, idly entertained, as the men came to a standstill, panting, outside the front door of a neat house. The litter's curtains opened, and a lady stepped down onto the pavement.

Felix stopped abruptly, his heart pounding in his chest as he watched the woman shaking out her skirts, and mounting the steps to the house-door. In a moment she was gone, and the spell was broken. Felix pelted down the street, Nar galloping beside him, barking with excitement. A man had come out of the house to pay the litter-men. He was about to go back in as the men trotted away, but hearing Nar's barks he turned to look doubtfully up the road. The boy ran up to him, his heart still feeling as if it would choke him, the hot afternoon air rasping in his chest.

'Who was that?' he demanded.

'Who was what?'

'That lady, the lady who just went into your house.'

The man looked contemptuously at Felix down his long nose. 'That was my mistress, though I fail to see what concern it is of yours.'

'Does she live here?'

'When she is not at her estate on the Clitumnus she does.'

Her estate! Felix was so astonished and so breathless that for a moment he couldn't speak, and before he was able to ask another question the pompous slave turned and went up the steps. Ignoring Felix's anguished cry he stepped in and the door shut with a snap. His haste to get home forgotten, Felix lingered uncertainly, wiping away tears with the back of his hand while Nar tugged energetically at his lead, then headed down to the crossroads at the bottom of the street. As he suspected, there were shops, and - oh gods, thank you! - a fountain. On the lower side, a wide basin collected water that flowed steadily down from a wide mouth, and on the higher women were drawing water from narrow spouts. Felix joined the queue waiting to get a drink. The women stopped their talk and turned to him, asking him where he came from.

'My master lives on the Quirinal,' he told them. 'He's a senator.'

'Is he, now? I could see you came from a rich household, by your tunic,' said one of the women. She turned away, pushing her jug into the flow of water.

'Tell me,' Felix asked the other women. 'That house just up there. With the black front door and the bay trees beside it. Whose house is it?'

They hesitated, as if unsure whether they should speak, but after all this was only a slave-boy. 'It belongs to Faberius,' one of them began.

'No, no, Flavia, Faberius is dead now, isn't he?'

'Oh, you're right. I was forgetting: a couple of years ago, wasn't it? His widow, then. I suppose she still lives there?'

'Yes, she does. And a stuck-up piece she is.' The woman who'd been filling her jugs turned round, dumping them on the ground. 'You don't see her, or even her slaves, down here.'

'Probably has her own water-supply,' the first woman agreed.

'Nereis, is that what she's called?' Felix managed, with a supreme effort, to make himself sound as if he was asking out of mere idle interest.

'That's her name, yes.'

'Iulia Nereis,' the second said, sniffing.

And then it was Felix's turn, and he could bury his flushed face in the cool stream of water.

Chapter 9

Torquatus was still on the Palatine when Felix got home. For a moment he was tempted just to go and hide in the stables. His long walk in the sun had given him a headache, and he had a lot to think about. But he knew the lady Cornelia would be in the garden, and that she would be waiting to hear what he had to say, so he turned to make his way out there. At that moment, however, Torquatus swept back into the reception hall with his followers, stripping his toga off and throwing it to Victor. All too soon he found himself hurried along into the gardens with the master's troop, to find, as he'd expected, Cornelia sitting in the shade with a book-scroll in her hand.

'You've done what you were told?' You've discovered Ampudius?'

For a moment Felix looked as if the name meant nothing to him, then he seemed to shake himself. 'Oh, him. He's probably left Rome now, going home to Formiae. They were packing up: the master was going first, and the mistress was going to follow him, in an ox-carriage. I couldn't find out when he's coming back: apparently he doesn't come to Rome very often. I gave him your note, lord, and here's his reply.' And Felix handed Torquatus the small set of wax tablets, blank except for one page. He read aloud: *'I hope you won't find it uncivil if I say I can't meet you yet, Torquatus. I am struggling to understand what can have made Fiscilia behave as she did. I ought to hate her, I suppose, but I can only think she must have been suffering from some temporary madness. And I understand from your slave that Fiscilius has been staying with you. Perhaps you are friends? If you are, my warnings will no doubt go unheeded. But if you are simply offering hospitality out of a sense of duty I will advise you not to believe everything he says. He is not a man with a deep concern for the truth. The double loss, of the woman I loved and of my respect for her, is stunning, and I am going to see if the peace and quiet of Formiae will help me to regain my strength. Later, perhaps, there'll be a time when we can talk, but not yet. Ampudius.*

'There's nothing there,' Torquatus said slowly, 'to suggest that Ampudius was planning an elopement with Fiscilia.'

'No,' Cornelia agreed, and added, 'though she may have been running away to him all the same.'

Torquatus said, 'Did you find out anything else, Felix?'

Again it seemed as if Felix was having to drag his attention back to the present time and place. He told them what

Epaphroditus had said about the slave who had come asking questions about Ampudius.

'And you said that was in the late morning yesterday?' Torquatus said, his brows meeting in a frown over his nose.

'Yes, lord. And the description he gave of the slave seemed to me to match Fiscilius' man. He's pretty nondescript. Epaphroditus said he was pigeon-toed, too, which Fiscilius' man is.'

'I can't say I noticed his slave. But if it was his man, that would fit with when Fiscilius left here. And he asked when Ampudius was leaving and where he was going, and if he was married? Can you make anything of that?' he asked Cornelia.

She laughed. 'No. The whole thing's completely mad, and it gets madder by the moment.'

Torquatus nodded to Felix, who took it to mean he could go.

Torquatus sat down. He was still frowning. 'Octavian wasn't best pleased that he'd had to send for me: obviously I should have been calling on him daily.' He stopped, looking sour, and Cornelia nodded. A daily visit would make him look more like a client than a friend. Octavian must be very hard-pressed if he'd forgotten that.

'He wants you to do something?'

Torquatus nodded. 'I'll be off the day after tomorrow. To Ancona.'

'Ancona? Whatever for?'

'There are two legions there. They were Antonius' men, but Octavian's going to need them if - when - war breaks out. I'm to go and persuade them they love Octavian, and bring them to Rome.'

Cornelia smiled. 'Of course. Ancona's your mother's home and you're the chief patron of the city. You're just the man to send.'

They were sitting in their favourite seat in the dappled shade of a vine. Trofimus had followed them with a small table, and slaves now poured out wine for Torquatus. Cornelia waved the jug away.

'That's better,' he said. 'I always think better with a wine-cup in my hand.' He lifted it to her. 'Here's to Ancona. Oh, and Trofimus - ,'

'Lord?' The steward turned back.

'Did Fiscilius take everything with him when he left?'

'I believe so, lord, but I will enquire.' He padded off.

'Is there going to be war?' Cornelia's face was serious.

'If Lucius doesn't change his tune, yes.' He sighed and drank. 'I don't know where my mother gets her information, but she was quite right. Our esteemed consul has thrown in his lot with the dispossessed. Very shrewd, not to say unprincipled. The soldiers are used to being bribed, and won't be satisfied whatever they're given. Whereas people who've lost everything will love Lucius for supporting them, and blame Octavian for stealing what was theirs.'

'That's not fair, though: Antonius' soldiers are being settled too.'

'Human nature, I'm afraid.'

'So you have to help raise an army?'

'And make sure we don't lose the one we've got. By bribing if necessary. While carefully preserving the façade, of course: armies are just there to fight barbarians, the three men who rule the state being a happy and harmonious team.' He snorted and buried his nose in his cup again.

Trofimus reappeared as silently as ever. 'Fiscilius took all his own belongings with him, lord, but he left two boxes of clothes which I understand had been the property of the lady Fiscilia. The other thing he left behind being the dog.' Cornelia thought the faintest glimmer of a smile crossed his plump face.

'Did he say anything about the boxes?'

'Only that he would arrange to have them collected, lord. In the meantime I had them placed in one of the old store-rooms.'

'Very well.'

Trofimus bowed and withdrew.

'That dog was his sister's dog. If he was such a devoted brother why not take Nar along with him?'

'On horseback?'

'Oh, well, I suppose not.' He shuffled about uncomfortably, and when Cornelia raised an eyebrow at him he said, 'I know there was something about that flat that bothered me. The broken window-fastening? No. I'm sure it was something to do with those clothes.'

Cornelia sat up and told a slave they wanted the boxes. 'Let's look through Fiscilia's things. Maybe that will jog your memory.'

'Good idea,' Torquatus agreed, and when sweating slaves

had unearthed the boxes and brought them down, he pulled out the contents one by one.

'A fine linen tunic, in a sort of cream-colour. A shawl, very soft wool, green. A pink tunic. A soft blue one, tangled up with a pair of shoes. Ah!'

Torquatus stopped, the shoe in his hand. Cornelia waited patiently. 'I think it's these. But what's wrong with them?' He turned the shoe over. 'Heavy, clumsy things. Not new. They've been mended. They're the sort a slave would wear.'

'Calliste's, then?'

'Must have been. I can't see any significance in that, can you?'

Cornelia shrugged. 'Not really. Calliste took a spare pair of shoes with her, and then left them in the flat in her hurry to get away. Is that so odd?'

'I suppose not.'

'What about the clothes?'

'All these tunics are good ones which must have been Fiscilia's. But this one - ' he held up a gown of dark green, rather crumpled now - 'this one's been pulled out of the box so violently it's got caught on a nail and torn. And yet it's expensive. You'd handle it gently, wouldn't you?'

Cornelia looked out unseeing across the garden pool, while her fingers unconsciously pleated a fold of her gown. 'I'm wondering if we shall ever know the full truth about how Fiscilia died.'

'Fiscilius told us first that she burnt the shrines in revenge for the settlements. Then that the slaves killed her. Or Ampudius. I'd like to know why he keeps changing his story. But I certainly haven't got time to find out. 'There's one thing I can still do, though. Octavian wants me to go with him to the theatre tomorrow, which is why I'm not going to Ancona till the day after. Before I do that I'll talk to Acutius. I didn't get the chance to ask him much during the funeral dinner, and maybe he'll have more to tell us, now Fiscilius isn't here to listen.'

'The theatre? Oh, of course, it's Rosalia tomorrow. But that's a festival for soldiers and surely honouring the soldiers isn't going to go down well? The people of Rome are up to here with soldiers.'

'Which is one reason why all Octavian's friends are going with him. It's the theatre that's the dangerous part: nothing's going to happen at dawn when the soldiers make sacrifice and deck the standards with roses as usual. Nor later I think, when Octavian sacrifices to Venus, as she is the family goddess, after all, and a lady who just loves roses. But after that there's always theatre. Not Sophocles, that's for sure, but a bit of lewd entertainment never goes amiss. If assassins are planning anything, that's where they'll do it.'

Cornelia stared at him, her hands clasped tightly in her lap, an image in her mind of a theatre full of baying soldiers, men used to killing, angry and greedy, and in the centre a group of distinguished men in their purple-bordered togas, unarmed. She swallowed hard and dragged her mind back from that dark place, saying lightly, 'Roses are a bit Dionysiac, I'd have thought. Octavian doesn't usually go for that kind of thing.'

Torquatus looked at her in mock-horror. 'Don't mention Greek cults in Octavian's hearing, please. He wants it all very Roman, all about honouring the military; and Rosalia's as traditional as Rome itself. But as I said, while I wait for the fun to begin I'll see what old Acutius has to say.'

'Oh yes, good idea.'

Torquatus had got up, calling for his steward and toga-slave.

'Trofimus, where's that boy Felix gone? He should have brought me a note from Quintus Acutius.'

Cornelia's eyes met Trofimus' briefly. 'Get that reply, could you?' she asked, and the steward went off. 'You're worried about Fiscilius, aren't you,' she asked her husband.

'I'm worried about war. I'm worried about the safety of this city. I'm worried about what Lucius Antonius might be up to. I'm worried about Manlia. After all that I'm worried about what Fiscilius might do, yes. I'm sure he hasn't told us everything. And his behaviour has been impulsive, let's say.'

'Shock. The shock of losing his sister - so unexpectedly and in such a brutal, senseless way - on top of losing his land, and with it his rank and power. No-one would be quite normal after all that.'

'You may be right.' He looked down at her, smiling. 'You're a very fair-minded woman.'

'I don't know. But I wouldn't want to judge him on the basis of these few days.'

At first it seemed as though Acutius wouldn't or couldn't help them. He hobbled in briskly, a politely neutral expression on his face, kissed Cornelia politely on the cheek, congratulated Torquatus on the funeral banquet and his consideration for Fiscilius, but seemed disinclined to go further. 'I don't know the boy all that well,' he explained. 'My friendship was mainly with his father, one of the most level-headed, reasonable men you could hope to meet.'

'In contrast to his son?'

Acutius' lips tightened. 'I didn't say that.'

Torquatus sighed. 'You didn't need to. We've had the man living here for the last few days, so we know that whatever good qualities he has he certainly isn't level-headed.'

Acutius gave him a thin smile, and folded his hands over the top of his walking cane. They sat in silence for a few minutes.

'Tell us about Fiscilius' father, then,' Torquatus suggested.

'Of course.' The old man seemed to relax. 'I first met him when we were both young men, junior officers under Sulla. Those were wonderful days: Sulla was our hero.'

Torquatus reflected that Sulla also invented the proscription, and killed large numbers of people. 'Yes, he was my father's, too.'

'Of course, I'd forgotten: your father was one of his generals, far senior to us, and a good man. He was Crassus' legate in Sulla's second invasion of Rome, if I remember rightly, and what a fight that was!' The old man stopped, shaking his head. Torquatus was restless. This invasion story had been one of his father's favourite anecdotes, and he really didn't need to hear it again.

'The younger Fiscilius, he's about twenty, isn't he, so he must have seen quite a bit of military service, I suppose?

Acutius brought his mind back to the present with an obvious effort.

'He served under Caesar. It was his first posting.' His voice was quiet. Cornelia could almost feel his reluctance.

'Under Julius? Really? I served with him myself for several years, but I'm sure I'd never met Fiscilius before the night he came here, or even heard his name, that I can remember.'

'No. He wasn't on Julius' staff for long.' Acutius was now looking deeply uncomfortable. Torquatus thought before speaking again: no need to distress the old man needlessly.

'Well, Julius had his likes and dislikes, especially during the last couple of years or so,' he said at last. 'I don't think it would be wrong to call him capricious. And he could get rid of men quickly if they didn't suit. Was that how it was?'

'Oh, I couldn't blame Caesar.'

Torquatus said nothing, just sat and waited, and at last Acutius said, as if the silence was unbearable: 'Fiscilius got drunk and picked a quarrel with another officer. Who died.'

'I do seem to recall hearing about some scandal of that sort,' Torquatus said thoughtfully. 'It must have been just after I'd left Spain, if I remember.'

Torquatus was thinking back to the time when Julius Caesar had just conquered the last of the great Republican armies at Munda. Julius himself had stayed on after his victory for several months, subduing pockets of resistance and settling soldiers in new colonies, while some of his trusted legates, Torquatus among them, had been sent back to Rome ahead of him, to prepare his triumphal procession.

'Julius certainly wouldn't have been happy about that,' he continued. 'How did Fiscilius come to be with him? Everyone was after positions on his staff: fathers because their boys could come in for some rich pickings, and the boys because Caesar was the most exciting general Rome had ever produced. How did he do it?'

'I got it for him,' said Acutius, with a sour face. 'I had long-standing business associations with Julius' brother-in-law Atius, and I was able to help Caesar himself once or twice while he was in Gaul. I have weapons workshops.'

'If you got Fiscilius his place you can't have been very pleased when he messed up like that,' Cornelia said, and Acutius smiled at her.

'I was appalled. He'd only been with Julius for a couple of months. Can't say I was all that surprised, though.'

'And the man he killed?'

Acutius seemed for a moment so overwhelmed with embarrassment that he couldn't speak. Torquatus waited. Then the old man said quietly, 'His name was Quintus Ampudius.'

'What? Ampudius?'

'Related to Marcus Ampudius, no doubt.'

Acutius nodded. 'His brother.'

Torquatus and Cornelia stared at each other.

Torquatus exclaimed, 'Of course: that's where I knew the name. I knew I'd heard it before.' He was thinking. 'The Ampudii must be the grandsons of the man my father knew.'

'And Ampudius must have been referring to the killing when he said in his letter that he had his own reasons for hating Fiscilius,' she agreed. 'But what an extraordinary coincidence that Fiscilia should fall in love with Quintus' brother.'

'No coincidence at all, really,' Acutius said. 'They met through me. I had connections with the Ampudii as well as the Fiscilii, and they each had an army-mad boy to place, so I did what I could to help. It cost me, too. Julius was absolutely furious when Quintus died. I never asked him for any favours, after that. And then, early last year, Fiscilia wrote to me that she was coming to Rome with her aunt and hoped to see me. I'd always been very fond of Fiscilia, so I asked them to dinner: she said they were staying at the family flat. I'd never have done it, though, if I'd known that Marcus Ampudius would turn up at my door that very day. I couldn't help asking him to dine with me, though I warned him Fiscilia would be there too. He said he wouldn't hold the girl responsible for her brother's misdeeds; and then, the moment they met, it was obvious that they were drawn to each other. I've never seen a clearer case. I tried to warn Ampudius that Fiscilius wouldn't hear of it, but he was so sure of himself, he wouldn't take no for an answer. And when you come to think of it, it was Fiscilius who owed him an apology, not the other way round. But that was him all over.'

'You think it's typical of Fiscilius to cherish a grudge against a man he's injured?'

'Yes, I'm afraid I do.'

'I don't suppose you saw much of Fiscilius after his disgrace?'

'I certainly didn't. I went to the funeral when his father died last year, and that's all. I'd heard Fiscilius was drinking and gambling too much - well, perhaps that's just me just being old-fashioned. I think he got in with the wrong crowd: I certainly didn't like the only one of his friends I met at old Fiscilius' funeral - a man by the name of Titus Fulvus.'

'The man Fiscilia was about to marry,' Torquatus said.

'I suppose that's why the name's familiar,' Cornelia agreed. 'Tell me: did Fiscilia know that her brother had killed Quintus Ampudius?' The old man started and stared at her. 'Do you know, I've no idea. I mean I'd have thought Marcus would have told her, but I don't know. I'm sure Fiscilius wouldn't.'

They all sat in silence for a moment. Then Cornelia turned

to Acutius again. 'Can you think of anyone who might have wanted to kill Fiscilia? Had she made some powerful enemy? Was anyone going to get rich by killing her?'

'I believe she is Canidia's heiress. But in any case she wasn't murdered, was she? She died in the fire she'd set.' Acutius seemed to Torquatus to have closed up again.

"I'm just checking all possibilities. There are some discrepancies in the official narrative, and I want to be sure they aren't significant. Anyway, I don't suppose a maiden aunt's fortune would be much of a motive for murder.' Torquatus was dismissive, but Acutius smiled.

'Not a maiden aunt. Canidia's a widow, has been for many years. She was married to Sisenna, who died, oh, about the time you were born, I suppose.'

'Sisenna? You don't mean Cornelius Sisenna the historian, do you? Well, fancy that. My father used to admire his writing very much. We've got the whole of his Histories in the library somewhere. Has Canidia any family?'

'None that I know of.' Acutius was looking more and more uncomfortable. 'But even if she did, that wouldn't be a motive for killing Fiscilia. Not while Canidia lives.'

'So can you think of anyone who might have wanted to kill her?'

'Certainly not.' The old gentleman was very stiff now. 'I think these questions are tasteless and quite off the point. I've heard nothing to make me think there's any doubt at all about what happened.'

'I think there is. If this was sacrilege, how did Fiscilia know where the shrines were? How did she know reed men would be in them, ready to be sacrificed that day? Why didn't she leave the shrine on the Velia when she set light to it, as she had done with the others? Why did she attack the one on the Palatine after the reed man had gone? How did her neck get broken?'

Acutius was looking shocked. 'I hadn't thought. I see now why you gave the girl a decent burial. If she didn't burn the shrines, though, who did? Interfering with the rites is always dangerous. And what a time to choose, when Rome seems to be drifting into yet another civil war!'

The two men sat in silence for a while. Then Acutius roused himself from his reverie. 'A word of warning, Torquatus. You seem to have got most of your information from Fiscilius. I'm not sure you should trust him to tell you the truth.'

Torquatus' face was grim. 'No, in the light of what you've told me, I'm beginning to think so too, but I can't see what he can have had to gain from deceiving me.'

By the time Acutius left, the afternoon was well-advanced. Wafts of aromatic smoke from the bath-suite suggested that the slaves had been busy there. A bath, Torquatus thought, would be very pleasant, and then a few drinks and a quiet meal with Cornelia in the gardens. Fiscilius' presence had always been unsettling, and the house felt deliciously calm without him. There had been altogether too much excitement and there was war ahead. What a good time, then, to enjoy a quiet evening with his wife. If only Manlia had been with them, the household would have been complete. As he headed across the gardens, with his slaves behind him carrying clean clothes, bath-oil, and razors, a small bundle of fur bounced out from under a rosemary bush and trotted over to greet him, tail wagging energetically.

Torquatus bent to fondle the dog's ears a moment, but couldn't help saying: 'I just hope that forgetful master of yours comes back for you. If he doesn't - well, I seem to remember Fortunatus' suggestion that slaves could eat dog?'

After Acutius left, Cornelia went back into the side-room where they'd been sitting, at a loose end. She had taken her bath earlier. Unlike Manlia, she didn't care for weaving. Nor was she in the mood for study. She tidied a few papers away, and picked up the scroll she'd been reading and rolled it up neatly, before becoming aware of Felix standing silent in the doorway. She realised she hadn't seen as much of him as usual.

'That was well done of you to find out about Fiscilius' slave.' she said cheerfully, then getting no answer, she turned to look at him. For a moment she hesitated, before asking quietly, 'There's something else, Felix, isn't there?'

The boy was looking as if he might burst into tears, and she held out her hands to him.

Felix looked as if he'd hardly heard her. Then he nodded. Tears began to stream down his face.

'What is it, Felix? Something's happened, hasn't it?'

Chapter 10

Going to the play the next day took Felix's mind off his troubles, since he'd never visited any theatre, let alone the magnificent one built by Pompey the Great. It was also the first time he'd accompanied Torquatus to a formal public event. He walked at his master's heels in a dignified way, feeling very grown-up in a grand new tunic with a border of leaves woven into the hem. As soon as they left the house they could hear the gathering crowd, like a swarm of bees, and as they walked down the slope of the Quirinal it grew louder till it was a swelling roar. The little party left the city through the Porta Sanqualis - the broken shutter had been mended, Torquatus noted as he passed - and merged into a throng of others crossing the Campus Martius and making their way through the dusty grounds of the Villa Publica.

Torquatus turned aside from the crowd and headed for the entrance set aside for the senators, a spacious tunnel that passed right underneath the high tiers of seating to come out close to the stage. Emerging from the cool darkness of the tunnel, Felix gasped. Behind the stage something like the front wall of a block of flats rose high into the air: a great cliff of colonnades and balconies and doorways on three levels. Facing this in a semicircle were tiers upon tiers of seating filling up with spectators. The brilliant light of early afternoon was filtered through coloured linen awnings hung from masts all around the top of the curved colonnades at the top of the building. The masts creaked and the awnings rippled gently in the hot breeze, and there was also the welcome sound of water. Looking around, Felix saw that between the blocks of seating there were channels filled with constantly tumbling water, cooling the air. Far away up at the very top of the curve was the famous temple with which Pompey the Great had crowned his great precinct. Returning his gaze to ground level Felix realized he'd been left behind as Torquatus made his way over to a group of senators and he hurried across to him. The senators stood talking, smiling and at ease, apparently unaware of the crowd's attention.

The senators' seats were being set up for them by the slaves on the flat area in front of the stage. At the back of this was a low semi-circular wall, now decorated with garlands of roses. The first tiers of seating behind this were of marble and reserved for the equites, and Felix noted old Acutius being helped into one of the seats by an attentive slave. He thought the theatre couldn't get much fuller, but people were still pouring in like water, more and more of them coming round the covered way at the top of the building and streaming down the steps, turning off to right and left to find a seat. At the very top slaves and women squashed together onto hot, uncomfortable benches. Below them, schoolboys with their tutors, soldiers and freedmen all had their proper places.

Felix's attention was distracted by the arrival of Octavian at the head of a large group of supporters. The empty space in which Torquatus and his colleagues had grouped themselves suddenly filled with white-robed men, brilliant in the soft light. The two groups merged into one around that small, fair man, and at sight of him applause rose from one or two places in the crowd. Felix remembered what his master had said, that all the great men had their supporters, whose job it was to cheer them. They listened carefully, Torquatus said, to gauge their popularity. If that was true, Octavian couldn't be very happy now: the sound wasn't spreading out at all. After a minute or two, Octavian held up his hand for silence and sat down. The cheering died away, and was replaced by an anticipatory buzz, but before the actors could begin a wave of shouts and catcalls burst out behind them. Octavian's bodyguards leapt to their feet and swung round, their hands on their weapons.

Octavian himself stood up at and turned to see what was happening. It seemed that a soldier had come down and settled himself on one of the benches allocated to the equites, now almost half full, just a few seats from Acutius. Acutius himself was making angry gestures, and the crowd was beginning to pick up a chant. 'Get out! Get out!' they were calling, and every repetition brought more voices. Felix knew that most of the people hated and feared the soldiers, who were lounging about in every street and taking food that was scarce enough already. Worst of all they were armed and arrogant, and no-one dared challenge them.

The chant grew stronger. Octavian pointed at the soldier, smirking in his seat. Then he pointed up to the crowded banks of seats allocated to soldiers, now filled with angry faces shouting abuse. For a long moment the man hesitated, and Octavian looked at his bodyguard. A little jerk of the head, and they were over the seats and surrounding the man, hustling him away towards the dark mouth of the tunnel. The crowd laughed and cheered, but Felix, squinting up at the soldiers in their crowded rows, noted their angry looks and gestures. Their shouts of disapproval quietened down to a sullen muttering once the man was out of sight, however, and the attention of the crowd turned back to the stage.

And then Felix forgot everything: Octavian, his master, the soldier, the angry crowd, because sudden deafening blasts from horns were bouncing and braying off the walls of the theatre and men in satyr-costumes and women in very little indeed were running onto the stage. The play seemed to have a simple plot: there was an old man who tottered about after a pretty girl, and a fat man who got stuck in doorways. There was a clever slave and a lot of chasing about, and people unexpectedly popping up on balconies above the stage. There was singing and dancing and some wonderfully lewd jokes made by a chorus of men as they waved their huge phalluses at the women, whose tiny outfits seemed designed to fall off at the slightest touch. The crowd roared its approval. Felix sat open-mouthed till the last blast of music had faded, and the last naked girl had scampered off the stage. Then came a break, when dozens of men with trays of nuts and skins full of wine came round, selling refreshments, then another play, very much the same as the first. Felix began to come out of his trance only when the show was over and the crowd was beginning to make its way to the exits. It was still immensely hot but shadows had fallen across some of the seats now.

Octavian had almost reached the tunnel which would take him back into the world when a group of soldiers burst through it towards him, shouting. For a moment everyone froze. Then the bodyguards, in a silence even more menacing than the shouts, leapt forward. But more soldiers were pouring through the dark mouth of the tunnel, and Octavian's party were pushed back by the pressure of numbers. They moved awkwardly, hampered by the chairs which still littered the senators' area, until at last the low wall blocked their way. With an oath, Octavian grasped the shoulders of the men on each side of him, and scrambled up onto it. His sudden action brought a moment's silence, and he seized that moment to shout out, 'What's all this? '

His voice was cold and steady, and he looked poised and calm, though his toga was a little rumpled and stirring at its edges in the hot breeze. Felix saw that the audience, realising that the entertainment wasn't over, were no longer streaming out but turning and staring down at the strange scene.

'Where's our man Strabo,' one of the soldiers called out.

'You've killed him! All because he sat in the wrong seat!' A great confused chorus of voices broke out.

Octavian lifted a hand, and, to Felix's surprise and relief, the soldiers quietened down, watching him out of suspicious eyes. 'I have done no such thing,' he told them, in a chilly, even voice. 'I simply directed him back to the seats allocated to the military. When he refused to go to those seats - as you saw - he was thrown out of the theatre. He is not dead. But the law gives the front rows of seats to the equites, and I will not have the law broken: not by the soldiers, not by anyone.'

'No, because it's your law,' someone shouted down from the soldiers' seats, and a ragged laugh echoed round the half-empty theatre.

There was a moment of uncertainty. Everyone went very quiet: then Octavian jumped down from the wall, raising a growl from the soldiers which Felix thought sounded like the noise a guard-dog makes when you go too close, and walked steadily to where a flight of shallow steps allowed him to mount the stage, ignoring the rising chorus of curses and catcalls. Once on the stage he turned to face the soldiers and what was left of the crowd. Torquatus and the rest of Octavian's group followed him. Felix told himself that only a little boy would hold onto Torquatus' toga, but it felt hideously exposed up here. And if that was so for him, what must it be like for Octavian himself? Whatever he was feeling Octavian looked calm, quietly directing them to stand away from him so he could be seen. He turned through a half circle, looking up at the faces in the half-empty auditorium, now gaping down in fascinated horror: Felix thought they looked as if they were expecting to see a massacre.

'I am accused of killing a soldier who defied the law and took one of the seats allotted to his betters. The soldiers are already granted the right to sit in better seats than many citizens: there seems no reason why they should take over the entire theatre.' Now Octavian was on the stage, the people could hear him clearly and there was a chorus of agreement from the stands. 'I am going to send some of my men to find this soldier, to prove that he has not been killed.' The soldiers growled contemptuously, but Octavian nodded at a group of his bodyguards, who set off at the run towards the group still standing against the dark mouth of the tunnel. But before they got there, it broke up, and a man came sauntering through. There was laughter, and some of the soldiers slapped him on the back. He paraded round in front of the rows of benches, bowing ironically to right and left. The crowd began to laugh and applaud, recognising the man Octavian was accused of having killed. His movements brought him at last to the foot of the stage, where he looked up at his supposed killer, standing very still, the image of the Roman magistrate. Felix watched as the man slowed down and stopped, seeming uncertain what to do next. Then Octavian lifted a hand and with a gesture of great authority dismissed the soldier from his presence. Octavian watched the man hesitate, then run back to his friends, before himself walking calmly down the steps and setting off steadily towards the exit without looking back, his entourage swirling into a stream behind him. Felix and Torquatus were a small part of that stream.

'What did you think of that, Felix?' Torquatus asked, under the cover of the burst of chatter which signalled everyone's relief.

'Don't the soldiers like Octavian?' the boy asked. 'I thought he was their leader.'

Torquatus smiled. 'So he is, up to a point. But things are pretty bad: Lucius Antonius wants soldiers too, so the men can change sides if they get offered a bigger bribe. That makes them pretty powerful, and they know it.'

Felix thought about this for a bit.

'It would have been bad if he'd panicked, wouldn't it?'

Torquatus shivered. 'It would. And, do you know, I don't believe I've ever seen Octavian panic. Not once.'

It was while Torquatus was at the theatre that Cornelia received a visitor. Nothing unusual in that, of course, but this lady wasn't one of Cornelia's circle of friends, and she declined to give her name, saying simply that the lady Cornelia had asked her to call. Cornelia herself, hearing that a nameless lady was awaiting her in the reception hall, nodded in a satisfied way and told the slave to bring the visitor into one of the side-rooms. As soon as honeyed wine and little cakes were arranged in front of the two women, every single one of the slaves was sent away and the door firmly closed behind them.

For a moment the ladies took stock of each other. Cornelia was surprised and impressed by the visitor: not a girl but a woman in her full beauty, her gown was simple but made of a finely-woven mix of silk and wool, of a soft green which flattered her creamy, well-kept skin and honey-brown hair. The visitor was scrutinising Cornelia intently in her turn. Her eyebrows rose. 'You are Balbus' daughter? You don't look like him.'

Cornelia laughed. 'No. I favour my mother. Nor do you look as I expected Iulia Nereis would. Do please sit down.'

Gracefully the woman took her seat. Cornelia, in the absence of slaves, poured a little sweet wine into their glasses. Her visitor sat back in her chair, calmly waiting to hear what was wanted of her.

'My husband is looking into the death of a young woman. Fiscilia, from Mevania.'

'Fiscilia? Fiscilia from Mevania? She's dead?'

Cornelia raised her eyebrows at this and the visitor blushed. 'I've been out of town for a couple of weeks, so I wasn't aware -. Can you tell me how she died?'

'She burned down three shrines and died in the third fire,' Cornelia said, brutally honest.

'No!' Nereis' shock was palpable. 'How could she do a thing like that? Are you sure?'

'The shrines were burned down and her body was discovered in one of them,' Cornelia told her.

'Well, I wouldn't have believed it.'

Nereis sat silently for a moment or two.

'How well did you know her?'

'A little. We weren't close friends.'

Cornelia sat patiently, saying nothing, and after a few moments, Nereis went on. 'There were reasons why my family and hers weren't - well, weren't close. But I met her socially in Mevania, of course, and I liked what I knew of her. She was a straightforward person, even a little blunt.' She shivered a little. 'And now she's dead. What made you think I might be able to help you?'

'When Felix told me you had an estate on the Clitumnus, I thought - are you all right?'

All colour had drained out of the visitor's face, and looked as if she might faint.

'Felix? There's someone here called Felix?'

Cornelia nodded.

'Not - my son?' She whispered the last word, her face white.

Cornelia pushed Nereis' untasted wine towards her. 'Here, have some of this. And yes, I mean your son, Felix. You are surprised that he is here? I can't think why you should be, since he's lived here all his life.'

'I am more than surprised. I am - oh, sweet Venus and Juno - so astonished I can hardly speak.'

'And yet you could have found out where he was at any time, had you wished.'

'No. No, I couldn't.' Nereis took a deep breath, and clasped her hands tight together in her lap. 'Oh, are you thinking I just abandoned him? I'd better tell you how we were separated.' She gave Cornelia a tight little smile. 'Not something I like to think about. It's a common enough story: I was one of your mother-in-law's weaving women. Your father-in-law took a fancy to me and made me his mistress.'

She laughed without much amusement. 'Mistress isn't quite the right word, of course: I had no choice in the matter. I had a child by him. Felix. Felix, who is here, now, in this house,' she said softly, as if she still couldn't believe what she was saying. 'That situation continued for several years. But six years ago, Julius Caesar visited the master at his villa on the Bay. The master was keen to please Caesar and sent me to his room that night. I did please him and the next day the master made him a gift of me.'

Nereis was looking down at her clenched hands now. She paused for a moment gathering her energies. 'I had to leave the villa with Caesar. Felix stayed. I couldn't even say goodbye to him, couldn't explain.' She stopped a moment and Cornelia saw her make her hands relax. As if those had been the hardest words she went on more easily. 'For some time I went everywhere with Caesar. Then newer, younger girls came along and he ceased to send for me. I was still part of his household, of course, and Caesar was always a generous master. Had it not been for the loss of my child, those would have been good years. At all events they ended four years ago, when Caesar decided to free his chief secretary, Faberius. He freed me, too. He thought I'd make a good wife for Faberius.'

Cornelia said gently, 'You must have been pleased to get your freedom.'

Nereis looked up at that, flushing. 'I wasn't the woman Faberius should have married,' she said angrily. 'He already had a relationship with another slave, whom he'd promised to marry if it were ever possible. He had a child with her, a child who'd always be a slave, unless Caesar freed him. And it wasn't only that he'd promised Briseis. He didn't know whether he'd be able to have children with me, and that's what he wanted more than anything of course: children born into full citizenship. But no-one argued with the dictator. He could only accept and look pleasant.'

'You didn't try to contact Felix?' Cornelia couldn't help sounding critical.

'I did. Of course I did.' Nereis stopped and relaxed her hands again. 'When I was first free and married I wrote to your husband. I got a reply saying that he was away - with Caesar in Spain, I think - and I should contact him again when he came home.'

'And did you?'

'No.' Nereis pulled her gown more closely round her, as if on this broiling afternoon she could possibly be cold. 'Faberius found the letter. He was furious. I was pregnant at the time; I think if I hadn't been he might have killed me. I didn't know him so well then, or realise how violent he was. He didn't want my boy, passionately hated the very thought of him. I was Caesar's leavings, he said, and before that I'd been Lucius' whore. My child was nothing but slave rubbish. I can't tell you how much that hurt me. I didn't dare to write again. And then I heard - I heard that a slave had died, under torture, in this house, a young slave, a boy, and I thought it must be Felix.' Nereis turned her face away. 'I don't know how I lived through those months. So you see that finding out that he isn't dead, that he is here.' She looked around as if Felix might be standing quietly, as slaves do, in the corner of the room awaiting orders.

'No.' Cornelia took her hand. 'I'm afraid he isn't here just at the moment. He's at the theatre with my husband. I judged you harshly before, and I see I was wrong. You have another child, then?'

Nereis smiled and gently withdrew her hand. 'No. I lost it. But you didn't invite me here to talk about myself?'

'No. As I was saying, Felix mentioned where your estate was, which led me to ask you here, since my husband needs to know about the Fiscilii. And also, of course - ,' She broke off, and Nereis gave her a clear look.

'To see if I was the kind of woman who would simply forget her child.' She smiled. 'I'll tell you what I know of the Fiscilii, then. They are major landowners around Mevania. Obviously they - and one or two other families - run Mevania too. But now they've lost land and influence, and they hate it.'

She sat for a moment, reflecting, then went on, picking her words with care, Cornelia thought. 'The Fiscilii are neighbours, as I said, but not friends. You see, when Caesar gave Faberius his freedom, and a wife, he also gave him enough money to raise him to the equestrian class. As an eques he needed land, and the estate he bought with some of Caesar's money was on the Clitumnus near Mevania. He had it from a lady called Canidia, who lived with the Fiscilii. Some people thought she didn't get a good deal.'

'Canidia!'

'Yes. You didn't know that?'

'So Faberius actually bought your estate from Canidia? I'd no idea. Did you think Canidia was fairly treated? Perhaps it's not quite fair of me to ask you?'

Nereis' smile was tight. 'I can't really say. I'd moved so long in Caesar's circle, and all the men around him were the same: out for everything they could get. Caesar, too, I suppose, except that he was more sophisticated. He loved to be seen as generous, judicious in his use of power, forgiving to his enemies. That stopped him being quite as openly grasping as the others. Or maybe it was simply that in his position he could lay hands on the best of everything without having to exert himself at all. He had people to do that for him. It distorts your idea of what fairness is, when you're with people like that. And Faberius was a hard man. He'd been a slave, and he was determined never to be weak or poor again. He wanted to get a really first-class estate as cheaply as possible, and he pulled every lever he could find to do so. I still have his files, so I can have a look for the papers concerning the estate, if the sale's of interest to you. Apart from the contracts and so on there may be something among the letters too. They all wrote to each other all the time: my husband, Oppius, Balbus, Pansa, Hirtius. All Caesar's friends. I do remember him being very pleased, saying that he'd got it for an excellent price.'

The two women's eyes met. They sat in silence for a moment. Then Nereis picked up a cake at last and nibbled at a corner of it. 'I don't know that I can do any more.'

'Not if you don't know the Fiscilii well.'

Nereis was choosing her words carefully. 'Faberius always knew they resented him, and he hated them right back. They were angry with Canidia for selling the estate: they put pressure on her guardian Epictetus, who had been her husband's freedman, to get her to rewrite her will. They even tried to bring a lawsuit. They went to the praetor, claiming that Epictetus was an inefficient guardian, and that old Fiscilius should take over. Canidia wouldn't support them and the praetor threw the case out. They are by far the most powerful family in Mevania, you see, and they weren't used to being thwarted.'

'But what power could they have over Canidia? From her name she must have been Fiscilia's maternal aunt, not one of the Fiscilius family?'

Nereis nodded.

'Then they'd have had no claim whatsoever in law to her estate, and no right to interfere in her guardianship.'

Nereis shrugged. 'Well, they certainly felt they had a moral right. And now, of course, neither I nor they will have that land: it's part of the area that will be cut up and given to the soldiers.'

'What will you do?'

'I have a house in Rome,' Nereis pointed out. 'I was always an outsider in Mevania, and I have other property. Faberius died a rich man. I shall survive.'

Looking at her Cornelia didn't doubt it. Here was a woman who had survived slavery, forced sexual relations, an abusive husband and separation from her child. And yet she sat meeting Cornelia's eyes candidly, self-contained and confident. Nereis smiled and leant forward slightly.

'And now I want to talk to you about my son.'

After Nereis had left her Cornelia sat for a while turning over in her mind how to pursue her enquiries into the Fiscilii. So many of the people Nereis had named were dead: Faberius himself, old Fiscilius, Caesar and his friends Hirtius and Pansa. Canidia, if she was willing to do so, could help them better than anyone, of course. She could explain, for instance, how Faberius had known about her property. There seemed to be no obvious connection between those two. Cornelia wandered about the reception hall, unconsciously tidying the shrine which was already immaculate, and straightening a bench which wasn't out of place. Suddenly a thought popped into her head: there was one person who might very well be able to inform her about Canidia and her dealings with Faberius. She called for her litter and was carried out into the baking heat of the late afternoon.

Evening was falling as Torquatus got home. He had come right up to his house before he realised something was wrong. The tall black doors were standing open, light spilling out across the shadowed street. Even before he went inside he could hear urgent voices, shrill with anxiety. He strode into the great hall.

'What's going on?'

Silence fell. There was quite a group gathered there: the steward Trofimus, the toga-slave Victor and about a dozen others. Even Fortunatus had left his kitchen. They were all standing around Torquatus' litter, which was empty. What in the name of the gods were they all doing there? His sense of foreboding deepened. Trofimus came toward him, and in the flickering light of the lamps he was as pale as death.

'It's the mistress.'

For a moment the room seemed to swing around Torquatus. His throat tightened. 'What about her?'

'She hasn't come home.'

He put out a hand to steady himself: the sun-warmed marble of the pillar brought a sharp memory: his father, looking sour as Cicero told him it was wrong to have such pillars in a private house, a sign of degeneracy, a nation gone soft. Cicero's booming laughter, his admonitory finger wagging in his old friend's face, flared in Torquatus' mind, then died to dust. He took a breath.

'What happened?' There was a babble of self-justification. He pointed to Trofimus. 'You. You tell me.'

'Yes, lord. The mistress was at home when you left, as you'll remember. She was alone for a while. Then a lady called. A lady who didn't want to give her name, but the mistress seemed to be expecting her, and she was shown in. All the slaves were sent away.' Trofimus cleared his throat. 'Shortly after the lady left, the mistress ordered the litter and went out. She said she was going to visit the lord Balbus.'

'You should have stopped her.'

At the sight of Torquatus' angry face, Trofimus seemed to become smaller. But he met Torquatus' eye firmly. 'I had no right, lord. And she had Rachel with her.'

He bit back angry words. 'Very well. So what happened?'

'Just before you arrived, lord, the litter-men came back, very distressed. They had waited and waited, expecting their mistress at any moment. In the end the lord Balbus' steward came out and told them to go home. They said the lady Cornelia was staying at her father's house.'

Torquatus felt as though he'd been hit in the wind. He turned to the litter-bearers, whose black bodies were gleaming with sweat.

'You. What did you do when you were told to go home?'

One of the men stepped up. 'We said we couldn't go home without the mistress.' He spoke slowly, his Latin unsure. 'Then the lady's father came to us and told us she was not coming home again.'

'Not ever?'

The man looked at him seriously. 'I think, not ever.'

'He didn't say why?'

'No, lord. He told us to go away.'

Suddenly the hesitation cleared from Torquatus' mind. He had seldom been so angry, so alive with rage. From paralysis, he flew into a restless state, where he wanted to be doing something, anything. He pushed himself away from the pillar. 'I'll take the litter. And my bodyguard, of course. I'm going straight to Balbus.'

Just as he was about to step into the litter, Torquatus thought of something.

'I presume there's some connection between the visitor you mentioned and Cornelia's visit to her father. Someone must know who she was.'

'No, lord. She wasn't a lady any of us had seen before. Not a senator's wife, I could see.'

Torquatus was puzzled. 'What then? A slave? A freedwoman?'

Trofimus spoke confidently. 'Definitely not a slave. And if she was a freedwoman she'd done well for herself, married a wealthy man. She was very well-dressed. A quiet, confident sort of person.'

Torquatus reflected. 'You said my wife was talking to Felix before this visitor arrived. Is this anything to do with him? Where is he?'

The boy pushed his way through the crowd of slaves, and looked up at his master, his eyes heavy and reddened with weeping. Torquatus glanced round. 'Go away,' he said, and the subdued slaves moved off in small groups, murmuring quietly. He moved across to the marble bench at the head of the reception hall pool, and sat down heavily, his sudden burst of energy dissolved into weariness and fear. The boy followed and stood in front of him, not meeting his eyes.

'Did your mistress go off because of something you'd told her after we left?'

Felix's face was troubled. 'I don't know, lord.'

'Well, what did you talk about? Come on, boy, you'll have to tell me.'

Felix hesitated, glancing up doubtfully. 'I told her I'd seen my mother.'

'You saw your mother? Is that all?'

Felix's face was red, his eyes full of tears. 'I dare say it doesn't seem important to you, lord, but - ,'

'Not at the moment, no. And what's important to me has to be important to you. Remember that.'

The boy seemed to shrink into his tunic. 'Yes, lord. But that was what we talked about. I told the lady Cornelia I'd seen her - my mother - and she wanted to know more, and asked all sorts of questions, and then she sent me away and said she had to write a letter.'

'Questions about your mother?'

'Yes, lord.'

'And nothing else?'

'No, lord.'

Torquatus ran a hand over his neatly barbered hair, exasperated and deeply disappointed.

As the litter-men ran off down the street, Torquatus braced himself for a confrontation with his father-in-law. Balbus had never wanted his daughter to marry into the Roman aristocracy, arguing that such a marriage would put her in danger. The murderous proscriptions carried out by the Three had been in his mind, but he knew that Balbus would think his meddling in crimes that were none of his business had put her in harm's way just as effectively. Especially if, as Manlia had suggested, there was a political dimension to them. He was cold with fear for Cornelia. And for himself. Balbus was a ruthless and powerful man who wouldn't think twice about commanding his daughter to return home if that suited his interests. His fear dissolved in a burst of anger: if Cornelia had kept her nose out of this unpleasant crime she'd have been safe now. And then his anger faded into regret that he'd been so harsh with Felix: everything he'd said to the boy had been true, of course, but he needn't have been so sharp with him. And he hadn't tried to stop Cornelia interesting herself in the crime, had he? He wasn't sorry when the litter drew up outside Balbus' house.

Inside, the usual sense of quiet and order prevailed. Torquatus paced restlessly up and down the immaculate mosaic of his father-in-law's reception hall, his stomach churning. What was he going to say to Balbus? Surely Cornelia couldn't have agreed to leave him without a word? - and then a well-known step behind him made him spin round. Balbus was standing there. Torquatus swallowed hard.

'Cornelia. My slaves said she's here.' He stopped, unable to say any more for a moment. Balbus just went on staring with those big dark mournful eyes. Torquatus forced himself to use a reasonable tone. 'What is going on?'

Balbus smiled, a grim little smile.

'You'd better come into my study,' he said at last.

Silently, Torquatus followed his father-in-law, the usual troop of slaves following after, bringing wine and setting chairs as if this were a social visit. Torquatus kept his temper with some difficulty. At last they were alone, the line of slaves backed against the wall.

'I gather that Cornelia came here to see you this afternoon.'

'She did.' Balbus picked up his wine cup in one plump hand and turned it as if studying the chased pattern on the silver.

Torquatus waited, but Balbus said nothing more.

'And - ?' Torquatus prompted.

Balbus put the wine cup down with a snap. 'And I put it to Cornelia that she would be better off staying here with me.'

'She couldn't have agreed to that?' Torquatus was incredulous.

'Not initially, no. But once we'd talked for a while I persuaded her that it would be in her own best interests.'

'How did you do that?' Torquatus' mouth was dry and he took a slug of wine.

Balbus' plump face was suddenly tight with fury.

'You haven't even noticed, have you?'

'Noticed what?'

'How unwell Cornelia is looking. She told me she's been sick ever since that funeral dinner: the funeral dinner you put on for a criminal. And you didn't know anything about it.'

Torquatus stared at him. 'She said, the morning after, that the mussels hadn't agreed with her,' he said slowly.

'And you were satisfied with that? You didn't wonder why she still didn't look well, why she wasn't eating? Did you even notice she wasn't?'

Torquatus hardly knew what to say. 'Cornelia would always tell me anything I ought to know,' he came out with. It sounded lame in his own ears. 'And is that all? That you think Cornelia isn't well? If so, my own doctor will care for her, of course. There's no need for all this drama. And if you've forced her to stay here - ?'

'I haven't needed to.' Balbus' smile was complacent. 'And there isn't any drama. I intend to keep Cornelia here for a while. If she gets better and wants to come home, and if I can see that you have dropped this ridiculous enquiry into that girl and her crimes, well, then we'll see if perhaps Cornelia can come back to you.'

Torquatus' gave him a stern look. 'That sounds like blackmail to me. You know very well that as a priest I have to discover what lay behind those crimes.'

'I don't agree at all. The woman died in the fire she'd set. The sacrifices went well after that and there have been no ill effects. The whole thing is over, the gods are content. Leave it, Torquatus.'

'I want to hear from Cornelia's own lips that she is willing to stay here.'

'You don't trust me?'

Torquatus' smile was grim. He crossed his arms on his chest. 'Not an inch. Where is she? I have to see her.'

'She's asleep.'

'Asleep?'

'You heard me. She was tired out. Frightened too. I don't even know that I'll keep her in Rome: she told me that she'd been scared, just the other day, when a mob started running about the Forum, demanding cheap bread. I don't want her here. So I might send her down to Neapolis.'

'And she agreed to that?'

Balbus' smile was smug. 'Oh yes. She agreed. And now she's quite comfortable. Asleep, as I say.'

Torquatus towered over his father-in-law, all his frustration and anger loosed. A couple of slaves moved closer. 'How dare you? You can't keep my wife from me!'

'I can, of course.' Balbus' voice was calm, amused. 'Think about it, my dear boy. You aren't married in the old way, so Cornelia never passed from my control to yours. People don't seem to marry like that, these days, and as a father I can quite see why. It's really very convenient .' His face suddenly became stern. 'I can divorce you from my daughter. I don't need her permission for that, but in fact she agreed with me that she doesn't feel safe in your house. You know I've never really approved of your way of life - too prominent, too dangerous - but Octavian approved the marriage so I gave way. But there's nothing I won't do to keep Cornelia safe, even risking his friendship if it comes to that.'

Torquatus glared at his father-in-law speechlessly. He was glad to see the man step back, glancing around for the slaves.

'I don't believe you,' Torquatus insisted. 'Cornelia's never said one word to me of being afraid.'

'Didn't want to worry you, no doubt. Or knew you wouldn't be interested.'

'If this is true - if she really wants to leave me - she'll have to tell me so herself. I'm not taking your word for it. But I don't believe she does, and if not I'll get her back. I'll find a way.'

'There isn't a way,' Balbus said, quite kindly. 'Don't you worry about her. I can take care of her, if you can't.'

Chapter 11

There was nothing for Torquatus to do but go home with what dignity he could muster.

Since Manlia was still away Torquatus had no-one to discuss the situation with. The house felt sad, empty, utterly bereft of everything that gave it life. He ate, alone at a small table, served by a silent Felix: the clatter when the boy dropped a serving spoon rang through the place like a trumpet blast. Unable to think of anything that might cheer him up, he went to bed. The heat was intense once again, in spite of occasional rumbles of distant thunder, and the walls of his bedroom seemed to be closing in on him. He shifted around in his bed, seeking a cool spot, then threw the covers off and wandered across the colonnade into the moonlit garden. The marble bench where he and Cornelia liked to sit was cool against his heated skin, though the column behind his back still held the day's warmth. He called for a slave, and when the sleepy-eyed man appeared, Torquatus sent him for wine. For what felt a long time he sat, wine-cup in hand, watching the moon-shadows slide across the garden. He was both exhausted and sharply, hideously awake, but at last the regular splash of the dolphin-pool began to soothe his nerves. His rage at his father-in-law died away into a miserable feeling of defeat. He sat up straighter, telling himself this wouldn't do, and resolving to pay Balbus back one day.

He was contemplating going back to bed when he first heard the noise. It was just a rustle, like some creature in the foliage, but there shouldn't be any animal out in his garden during the night. He thought of Nar, but the dog would have been far noisier: there was nothing surreptitious about Nar. He sat quietly waiting, his empty wine cup in his hand, and almost dropped off to sleep before it came again, a rustling, then a stony scrabble, followed by the rattle of falling mortar or stone fragments. Torquatus called softly to the slave to rouse the house, though by the time lights and slaves arrived, whatever it was would probably have gone. If he wanted to catch the intruder he'd need to do it himself, he knew, though his guts churned at the realisation that the assassin - if that was what he was - must be desperate if he was planning to attack Torquatus in the heart of his own household. He stood up and slipped as quietly as he could through the moonlit garden towards the place the sound seemed to come from, his heart beating a little faster. There was silence for a minute or two. Torquatus' eyes strained against the dark, but nothing moved. Then the shuffling sounds began again, followed by a heavy thud from over by the wall. Torquatus pushed his way through the bushes towards the place where groans indicated that the intruder had landed.

It wasn't easy to find the assassin among the tangle of lilac and rosemary. Torquatus cursed himself for not having picked up at least a knife before rushing across the garden, whose dense foliage seemed to both hold him up and advertise his presence. He stopped to disentangle a bramble from round his ankle, and heard, once again, surreptitious movement. And then a small shadow raced into the gardens through the archway that led to the stable yard, barking, a high and hysterical sound. Since there was now no chance of catching the intruder unawares Torquatus plunged straight for the place the groans were coming from, pushing his way through some young fruit trees. As he approached the wall the moon, emerging again from a bank of cloud, threw a long line of silver right along it. There, under the wall, something was lying. A dead body, he thought. Torquatus finally got free of the shrubbery and was running towards it when it got up rather awkwardly and hobbled along the wall, groaning and muttering to itself, turning to look towards where the dog was barking, and apparently unaware of his presence. It was coming towards him, an indeterminate shape in a cloak and hood, reassuringly smaller than himself. He braced himself, but the hooded figure still came on. Behind him the dog was still crashing about in the bushes. He was holding his breath, and when the figure came near enough he let out a shout, and seized it by the shoulder. The hooded figure almost fell against him, and he caught it in a tight grip, pinning its arms to its sides as it screamed. Then, suddenly, he burst out laughing, freed one hand and pushed back the intruder's hood. With a sigh of relief he pulled Cornelia against him; she sobbed, turning her face against his breast. For a moment they stood silent, aware of their pounding hearts and ragged breathing. Then, just as the first of the slaves broke through the shrubs towards them, Cornelia raised her head with an uncertain smile, before screaming again, harder this time, as Nar sank his teeth into her leg.

It was some time before the household was quiet again. Cornelia's ankle had been badly sprained in her fall, and by the time it had been wrapped in a cold poultice and then strapped up, and

Nar's bite washed, both she and Torquatus discovered that they were hungry: he because he had been too miserable to eat much, and she, as she explained, because she had been afraid.

'My father tried to kidnap me,' she said baldly. 'He ought to have known I'd never leave you like that.'

'I didn't think you would. But how could he force you to stay?'

'He tricked me, saying there were some things I'd left in my old rooms that I should take a look at so that he could either send them here or get rid of them. I went to my rooms, and when I tried to leave I couldn't. There were guards on the door.'

'So you made a fuss?' he guessed.

'A huge fuss,' she agreed. 'But he was adamant. I was going nowhere. So I pretended to be exhausted, and said I needed some sleep. He sent up a drink which I pretended to drink - I was pretty sure it was spiked - and then I pretended to sleep. And once the house was quiet I climbed out of my window and down the fig tree into the garden. My only worry is for Rachel. If my father found out she'd stolen the key of the garden gate for me he'd punish her dreadfully. But no-one will think anything of it if she goes out shopping first thing in the morning, and she'll be home before anyone knows I've gone.'

Torquatus nodded. 'And had you ever climbed down the fig tree before, I wonder?'

Cornelia snorted with laughter. 'Only once. Papa wouldn't let me go to a friend's party, and I climbed out and went anyway. He never found out. I was younger then, of course,' she pointed out.

'Of course you were,' he agreed.

Torquatus watched Cornelia as she took another handful of nuts from the bowl. He could see now what Balbus had meant when he said his daughter wasn't well. Why hadn't he noticed before that her skin, which normally had a rich healthy glow, looked a little dull and pasty, and her eyes seemed too large for her face? He watched Cornelia eating, as he'd never watched before, but if there was anything wrong with her it hadn't affected her appetite. She tucked into all the dishes Trofimus had conjured up with every sign of pleasure. Catching Torquatus' eye she said, 'Well, it is very late, isn't it? And I missed my dinner.' This made his eyes crinkle with laughter.

'It's good to see you eating well. Your father kept saying

you were ill, or unhappy.'

'I'm fine,' she said quickly. 'You know what he's like: the world's biggest fusspot.'

'Are you sure? You are a little pale. I could get my doctor to look at you.'

'Ugh! No thanks. I'm perfectly all right. If I'm pale I expect it's rage.'

'But you were frightened the other day?

'Did my father tell you that too? Really he is the most awful old woman sometimes. Though that's hardly fair to old women.' Seeing that Torquatus eyes were fixed steadily on her she blushed a little and said, 'Well, yes, as it happens I got caught up in a bread riot. It was the riot Octavian sent you to put down. Not that I was in it, really: just that my litter was obstructed by some of the men running down to the Forum. I was in no danger, and my slaves brought me safely home.'

'He said you felt unsafe in this house.'

She flushed angrily. 'Now that's pure invention on his part. He tried to persuade me of that, and I told him it was nonsense. Let's say no more about it.'

'If that's what you want? And if you can assure me that you really need nothing?'

Cornelia was laughing. 'I could do with a good sleep. Not one induced by my father's sleeping-draught, though.'

'You don't use them yourself, then?' Torquatus reflected that she might have any sort of drugs in her rooms and he wouldn't necessarily know.

'Venus, no. I'm far too healthy to need them. My father, now, he's a terrible old insomniac, and takes them all the time.'

'Probably lies awake worrying about his money being stolen,' Torquatus said crossly. 'But, Cornelia, this isn't a joke. I mean, he's just tried to kidnap you. Do you know why?'

'Interesting, isn't it? He's tried to persuade me I'm in danger before now, but never done anything as outrageous as this.'

'Did you upset him, do you think? What did you ask him? Did you go there because of something your visitor said? Who was she, anyway?'

Cornelia sighed. 'Yes, I owe you an explanation. It was Felix who started it.'

'That boy! I knew he was involved somehow or other.'

'Not intentionally, Aulus. He's had a shock.' And she told

him how Felix had seen his mother, and how it had become clear that Felix's mother might have known the Fiscilii.

'So she was your anonymous visitor?'

'She was. She told me that Faberius, her husband, had bought his estate from Canidia.'

'Well, that's an odd coincidence. But I don't see why you needed to pursue it. I'm presuming that's what you did?'

'Of course. Faberius, Balbus, Oppius, that whole group, were all devoted to Caesar, and were well rewarded.' Seeing that Torquatus still looked puzzled she said, 'I was wondering who might have wanted to murder Fiscilia, of course. I've never really managed to convince myself that she burned those shrines. And now Fiscilius tells us she was murdered by the slaves. But I just thought it was worth looking to see if Fiscilia had money, the sort of money it would be worth killing her for. Or enemies. Just as a matter of curiosity, you might say.'

'So you went to Balbus to ask about Canidia's fortune?'

'That's right.' Cornelia helped herself to more nuts. 'Felix, could you get me some of that nice fruit juice? Trofimus knows what I mean. I don't seem to fancy wine.'

Torquatus glanced up quickly.

'Is that because - ?'

'No, it isn't.' Her voice and face told Torquatus she didn't want to say more, but after a moment she relented and gave him a rather tight smile. 'Do you imagine that if I'd been pregnant I'd have been climbing over walls?'

'I suppose not.'

There was an awkward little silence. To break it Torquatus asked smiling, 'Did you really did need to climb in over the garden wall?'

'Of course. The doorman doesn't sleep anywhere near the doors. I'd have had to raise the house before anyone heard me. Far too embarrassing.'

'I didn't know he didn't sleep in his little room,' Torquatus admitted.

'He's old,' Cornelia pointed out. 'Once the doors are shut for the night he sleeps in one of the store-rooms. It's not as if anyone could get in, and there are plenty of slaves all over the house.'

Torquatus let it go. Typical of Cornelia that she should know such a detail about his household, he thought. And that he hadn't.

'What was it you said that sent your father into such a panic that he tried to kidnap you?' he asked.

'I don't really know,' she said slowly. 'I asked about Faberius, and he clammed up, so I let that go and talked about Canidia. That didn't go down any better.'

'What were you asking him?'

'Well, let me think. He knew, of course, that Faberius got his estate from Canidia, but claimed not to remember any of the details.'

'Well that's quite believable, isn't it? It was a few years ago, and he wasn't either buying or selling.'

Cornelia gave him a doubtful look. 'Possible, I suppose. But if you knew how encyclopaedic his memory is - it's been one of his great strengths, that he holds onto details like that about everyone he knows. Anyway, when he claimed to know nothing about Canidia either I asked about Sisenna's fortune. If she was rich her money must have come from her husband. My father was quite expansive about that. You know how he absolutely venerates money. He can't help admiring anyone who's got it. Then I pointed out that Canidia couldn't have inherited all that much and he got a bit cautious. I didn't notice at the time but I can see now that we ended up having quite an academic discussion about the Voconian law, and how you can get round it so that wives and sisters and daughters can get their fair share. He steered me away from Canidia there.'

She paused, brooding. Trofimus had come in with the jug of fruit juice and was pouring it for her. She smiled at him and took a sip.

'Ah, that's good. For some reason my father seemed quite offended when I asked if Canidia might have had a fideicommissum. He told me I couldn't know anything about such things. Really most unlike him: he knows very well that I run my own affairs perfectly competently.'

Torquatus nodded. Cornelia was a business-like woman, and it was a reasonable question. One way round the Voconian law and its restrictions on what women could inherit was to add to your will a fideicommissum. This was a letter which had no legal validity but which was morally powerful. In it, you requested a named man, a relative or close friend, to hold a large inheritance on behalf of a child during his minority, or of a woman until her death or a date specified. It was an onerous responsibility, and a proof of friendship, and any man who took on such a charge would be aware that any failure to carry out the testator's wishes would be judged very harshly.

'And did she?'

'I never found out. Papa got very cross, wondered what we were doing talking such nonsense about people who could mean nothing to us, and immediately turned the conversation back to me and my health. I couldn't get anything further out of him.'

'I'm worried, Cornelia. What if your father tries to get you away again?'

She scanned his exhausted face in concern. 'There's no chance of that. There are far too many slaves here, and visitors coming and going all the time, clients, messengers, soldiers. He'd never risk it.'

'I don't know. If he'd try to take you hostage once - ,'

'I won't go to him again.' Cornelia was firm. 'If he comes here and wants to see me I'll sit with him in the reception hall, where one is never alone for a moment; and I promise I won't go to his house again. Not until you're back and can come with me. It'll upset him, but I can't help that. The most frightening thought is that because we aren't married in the old patrician way he still has power over me, and could make me go back to him if he wanted to.'

'We could get married again, with a patrician wedding, if you like,' he offered, smiling, his arms round her.

'But then I'd be legally your daughter instead of his,' she pointed out with a sniff.

'True. And you wouldn't be able to inherit from Balbus, because you wouldn't be part of his family any more. Instead of becoming completely independent when Balbus dies, you'd have to wait for me to die, which will probably take a lot longer.'

Torquatus was laughing, but she pulled back, looking up at him anxiously. 'Don't talk like that. And no, of course I don't want to get married again, and I'd be furious if I didn't inherit from Papa. What, all that lovely money to go to my horrible cousin Lucius! You've never met him, have you? He's truly appalling. Like Papa but without the charm.'

He yawned. 'Well, you're back. We should go to bed and celebrate while there's still some night left. Because I have to go to Ancona in the morning.'

She was laughing too now. 'Of course. Let's go to bed.'

Suddenly she became serious again. 'The trouble with my father is that he always wants to be in control. And I don't like the thought that, as far as our marriage is concerned, he is.'

Next morning, as Cornelia said goodbye to her husband in the reception hall, a small, quiet slave-woman walked in without fuss.

'Rachel! You're safe,' Cornelia cried, hurrying to the door. The two women hugged briefly. It was reassuring that Cornelia now had her own maid with her, as well as Trofimus and all the other slaves to guard her. As long as she stuck to her word, he thought, and stayed at home, where Balbus wouldn't be able to harm her, she would be safe.

So Torquatus rode off, with a small escort of his own slaves, to Ancona. In spite of the reassurances he'd given himself, he still felt a little anxious about what Balbus might do. Who would have thought that he would try to entice Cornelia away, or try to drug her when persuasion failed? He noted that she herself had been neither shocked nor especially alarmed at her father's actions. Well, she obviously knew Balbus far better than he did. But it troubled him that he hadn't known all of Cornelia's fears: she hadn't told him that she'd been alarmed by a bread-riot in the Forum. Why not? His feelings seemed to have changed without his noticing, and now the idea that Balbus might take her away was not just humiliating, but a blow over his very heart. What would he do if Balbus ordered her back to him? If he would never again see her walk into his reception hall with that quick, confident stride and the clear-eyed glance that showed her everything from an untended hearth-fire to a weepy slave-boy?

The ride to Ancona was tiring, dusty and hot. His own horse Bucephalus had gone lame, and he was riding a hired brute, which had been given the name Celer by some cynic, and which had a hard mouth, no turn of speed and a slightly lop-sided gait that left him aching and sore by the evening. Each day felt like a battle between his own need to cover as many miles as possible and Celer's preference for a slow but steady pace. Or preferably a nice quiet stable with a manger full of hay. But at least when he arrived at Ancona the task itself turned out to be easier than he'd feared. He had to listen as patiently as he could to the men's complaints that Octavian and Lucius ought to be working together, and to the officers who told him they simply didn't know what Marcus Antonius wanted them to do. The mood in the camp was febrile: rumours swirled, and everywhere men were giving each other suspicious looks and muttering in corners. For two days he did nothing but listen and talk and listen again. And hint that money was available for troops that served Octavian faithfully.

Whether it was due to his powers of persuasion, or whether the report that these two legions had been on the brink of declaring for Lucius Antonius was simply wrong, Torquatus never knew, but at the end of the two days he was assured of their loyalty, and he began to lead them back to Rome, this time riding a spare cavalry mount. His unlucky groom, Catus, had the task of leading Celer. The horse seemed as unwilling to hurry back to Rome as he had been to leave.

At last the city became visible on the horizon: a flash of light on a golden pinnacle, a pall of smoke and dust hanging over the Tiber valley. Here he left the legions beginning to set up camp on the Campus Martius, the great field outside the walls given over to military exercises, and the closest armies could come to the city. He himself went on ahead: his mind ran beyond the report he'd give Octavian to what he might expect to find at home. Would there be a letter from Balbus, telling him he was now a divorced man? Would his house have lost the one person who made it a home?

But when he finally arrived, there was Cornelia, walking though from the garden into the reception hall, her hands held out in greeting. Manlia was still away, as he noted with a stir of anxiety. Otherwise his house felt quiet, at peace with itself. Torquatus felt himself relax.

All through Torquatus' morning greetings next day, he half-expected a visit from Balbus. He somehow couldn't believe that the man was going to accept defeat so quietly. But nothing happened. Trofimus carried out his duties with his usual imperturbable competence, Felix assisted him without fuss, and at the end, when the reception hall was quiet again, Torquatus stood for a moment, irresolute. He needed to go to the Palatine, to call on Octavian, but realised he was hesitating to leave the house out of anxiety for Cornelia.

This was like that quiet period of a war, he thought, when the two sides are preparing for battle, but days pass and nothing happens. He wondered uneasily what Balbus could be planning: he was sure there would be something. He told himself that Cornelia was safe, or at least as safe as he could make her. He dismissed his litter, saying he'd walk, and turned his mind back to politics. He had brought the legions from Ancona to Rome. Now he needed to pass on to Octavian what they had told him: that they wanted, not money, but peace. They were unhappy at the division between Lucius Antonius and Octavian. Octavian was Julius Caesar's heir, and they respected him for Caesar's sake. Marcus Antonius was a charismatic and talented general as well, and one of Caesar's right-hand men. Many of the soldiers had fought under him. None of them wanted to see Caesar's favourites at each other's throats. There must be some misunderstanding, they said. How had it come about that Lucius Antonius was unable to go about his business as consul in the traditional way? Why was it proving so hard to create the veterans' settlements the men had been promised? The officers who were coming to Octavian would demand that the two men meet and find a way they could work together.

Octavian sighed. 'Oh, don't say they want me to meet Lucius, and pretend to be brothers: shaking hands, kissing, gazing deeply into each others' eyes, swearing eternal friendship? Surely even they must know that's nonsense?'

'They don't seem to. The delegation will suggest staging the meeting at Gabii, since Lucius Antonius is at Praeneste and you're in Rome. Not too far for either of you.'

Octavian sighed again, and shrugged. 'Staging's the right word. Oh, well. If it gives us a little longer for re-arming, I suppose it's worth it.'

Chapter 12

On the evening of the day on which Torquatus had left for Ancona, Manlia arrived at Mevania. Even before the ox-carriage ground to a halt outside the closed front door of the Fiscilius house she was wishing she hadn't made that rash decision to come here.

Everything about the journey had gone wrong. She had expected to be able to stay at the houses of one or two friends along the way, as normal. If the friends were there, they would welcome her; if they were not, their slaves would make her comfortable. But these were not normal times. The first house she'd expected to stay in had been left locked up and completely unstaffed, and at the second the single, elderly slave who'd been left in charge had been unwilling even to open the door to her. She had stood outside the front door in the rain, arguing with the old man through the merest crack in it. At last he had accepted that she was indeed a friend of the family, and had let her in, but there had been little food in the house and they had almost had to camp that night. She could see that on the return journey she would need to rely on public inns for accommodation. She couldn't help grimacing to herself as she thought of what her brother would have to say to that.

The Fiscilius house looked as if it too might have been abandoned. The track leading off the road to it had been rutted and almost overgrown, and her driver, now looking over his shoulder at her in enquiry, had complained loudly about the damage it must be doing to the carriage. The house was a typical country villa, with a comfortable square block at the front for the master and his family and the necessary barns, outhouses and mills for grain and wine and olives clustering under a muddle of pantiled roofs behind. She could neither hear nor see any livestock, only the evening sounds of birds roosting in the trees around the house. The front door, she could see, was not adorned with the cypress branches that announced a death. It was also very firmly closed.

Manlia's heart sank. Perhaps Canidia had already left? The land around the house would go with it, but all the territory Manlia had just passed through had been a chaos of new boundaries with markers, posts, ropes, piles of stone for walls and freshly dug ditches everywhere. She could hardly blame the old lady if she'd fled already. She jumped down from the carriage, shaking out her skirts briskly. Her maid was already at the door, and at Manlia's nod she knocked on it. She had to do so twice before anyone came, and Manlia was already wondering where they could get shelter for the night if this house, too, had been abandoned.

But she was in luck. The door was opened at last, however reluctantly. Manlia stepped in decisively, before the slave could change his mind. He was a freedman, not a slave, a small man with bright dark eyes, reflected in the little flame of the lamp in his hand. He looked at her curiously, but said nothing. Manlia smiled.

'You won't know who I am,' she began. 'My brother is Aulus Manlius Torquatus.' The little man inclined his head politely.

'He is investigating the death of the lady Fiscilia in Rome.'

The man's eyes widened, and even in the gloom Fiscilia could see the shock in his face.

'You didn't know? Fiscilius hasn't written?'

'No. Oh, my poor mistress! How will she survive this blow?' He seemed for a moment sunk in his own thoughts, before turning to Manlia again with an apologetic smile. 'I'm sorry. I must take you to my mistress. I am Epictetus, by the way; her freedman. You will break it to her gently, I'm sure? And there are your slaves?' He peered into the semi-darkness beyond Manlia, taking in the maid and the two great bodyguards. 'And you have a carriage outside?'

'Yes. There's the driver and his assistant, too.'

'Oh dear, oh dear. No, no, I don't mean that, of course, but we haven't much left in the house. However, we'll do the best we can.'

'I'm grateful to you. I was afraid you might have left already.'

Epictetus was leading her out of the gloomy entrance hall towards a range of rooms that opened into a courtyard garden at the back of the house. In the first of these rooms a lady was sitting. Various lamps hanging on chains threw a dim light across the room. Another at the lady's elbow showed that she was not reading or sewing, but appeared lost in thought. She looked up as Manlia came in, and rose to her feet with a slightly bewildered look.

'The lady Manlia,' Epictetus announced simply, and went away.

The old lady shot a her a shrewd glance. 'You'll be one of the Manlius Torquatus family, I suppose? Ah, I can see you're surprised that I should place you so quickly, but your father was a friend of my husband's years ago. I don't suppose you were even born then. How can I help you? Do you need accommodation for the night? I haven't much in the house, I'm afraid, but we'll do the best we can.'

'Thank you for welcoming me so graciously,' Manlia replied smiling. She took a breath. 'As it happens I'm not just a passing stranger. I think you must be Canidia?'

'That's right. You've come to see me?'

'I have.' Manlia paused, wondering how she was going to break her dreadful news to this unsuspecting woman, and astonished too that Fiscilius had apparently not written a word of what had happened.

'Well, let's sit down and talk,' Canidia suggested, glancing around for another chair. Following her gaze, Manlia saw that there was very little furniture in the room, and no slaves. She saw a stool against the far wall and carried it herself to a position next to Canidia's chair. She sat herself down, and gestured to Canidia to sit too.

'I have something painful to tell you,' she began softly, and saw Canidia's face tense.

'Quintus? Or Fiscilia?' Canidia asked.

'Fiscilia,' Manlia told her. 'There's nothing wrong with her brother.'

'She's hurt?'

Manlia shook her head.

'Not dead?' The voice was little more than a whisper in the half-dark.

Manlia nodded and took her hand. 'I'm afraid so.'

Canidia drew her hand away and covered her face, rocking backwards and forwards silently. Then she lifted her hands away from her face and Manlia saw it wet with tears. She let her cry for a while, and when the old lady's hands dropped, said softly, 'I'm so sorry to have to bring you such news.'

'Tell me all about it. What happened? She was well - she never was ill in her life - how could she be dead?'

Manlia said nothing.

Canidia sighed, saying, 'You know she ran away to Rome? She pretended she was going to friends. Why couldn't she have told me the truth? And then I found a letter she'd left for me. A dreadful letter, threatening to do such things - !'

'I know,' Manlia told her. 'I've seen the letter.'

'How could you have seen it?' Canidia cried out, and Manlia

told her how Fiscilia had attacked the three shrines and been trapped and burned in the last one, how Torquatus had become involved, and how Fiscilius had followed his sister to Rome and searched for her.

'So your brother took her to his house and arranged her funeral? That was extraordinary, given what she'd done.'

Manlia didn't tell her about the men with their hooks at the ready. At least she could be spared that. 'And the slaves all ran away. Fiscilius has gone after them, because they're the only people who can explain what Fiscilia did. We think they were probably heading for Sicily.'

'Yes. They'd be frightened to come home with a such a story as that.' Canidia lay back in her chair for a few moments, and Manlia watched her curiously. She was probably in her fifties, a neat, small woman with tidily arranged brown hair and a face set into lines of worry, well but simply dressed. Manlia noted that Canidia had said nothing about Fiscilius' failure to write to her.

After a few moments Canidia sat up decisively. 'Well, my dear, you've given me a shock. A dreadful shock. I'd have said Fiscilia was simply incapable of what you say she did. I can't begin to understand it.' She got up and picked up the lamp from the table next to her with a trembling hand. 'But here you are, and you'll need something to eat and somewhere to sleep. Let's go and find Epictetus.'

Looking back, Manlia later thought those few days one of the strangest parts of her life. Their presence in the house felt wrong, as if it had already been given to its new owner, and they were simply awaiting eviction. One hot day succeeded another, as she could see through the unshuttered windows, but the inside of the house felt melancholy, shadowed. From outside she heard the shouts of the surveyors as they moved about, the rumbling of carts, occasional arguments or bursts of laughter. There was a whole world coming into being out there, a new city with which they had nothing to do.

They talked. Manlia had been lucky to find Canidia still in the house. Most of her belongings had been sent away already.

'I have a comfortable house in Perusia,' she said, as they sorted through the blankets in a couple of old chests. 'I've been looking forward to going back to it, once Fiscilia was married.' She picked up a dark old rug, then dropped it into the pile of rejects. 'I don't think I need this one; it's so coarse and hairy.'

'And Fiscilia was going to be married, I believe? To a man called Marcus Ampudius? Tell me about him.'

Canidia put the blanket down, frowning. 'No, dear, you've got that wrong. Titus Fulvus was the man she was engaged to marry. Now, what about this stripy one? Shall I take it, or not.'

'Is that right? Sempronia said - ,'

'Oh, Sempronia! I've no doubt she did.' Canidia's face flushed, her lips gripped together angrily. 'But Quintus had arranged the wedding, and it was far too late to change the plans without causing an immense amount of upset.'

'So how did Sempronia get it so wrong?' Manlia demanded, and Canidia told her how she and Fiscilia had gone to Rome and met Ampudius.

'I could see they were attracted to each other, but I told her to forget it. Quintus would have been humiliated if he'd had to draw back. Fiscilia was a high-spirited girl, but I never knew her to be downright disobedient to me. Or to her brother, who after all was her head of household. I was horrified when Quintus discovered they'd been writing to each other. Such behaviour! I told Quintus he'd better bring the wedding forward, because who knew what she might do next.'

Canidia's face was inflexible, and Manlia could see why Fiscilia hadn't wasted time trying to get her aunt's support. As if she'd read Manlia's mind, Canidia gave a short laugh.

'Oh, she tried to get me to help her, but I wouldn't, of course.'

'No, I see. And what did you say the bridegroom's name was?'

'Titus Fulvus: his place is over towards Trebiae. He and Quintus have been friends all their lives. And now I think that's all those blankets sorted. I shall leave the rest. If the new man doesn't want them, that's his problem. Let's look at the food stores next, shall we? There's a lot of preserves there and I don't see why he should have them.'

Manlia could see that Canidia wasn't going to tell her any more about Fiscilia's love affair, and that from her point of view it had been a simple error of judgment and best forgotten. Canidia was a very self-contained woman, she thought; she wasn't going to be caught out or trapped into saying more than she chose. She was happy to talk at length about Fiscilia's childhood; she would describe her house at Perusia and the quiet comfortable life she planned to live there; she would even, cautiously, admit that her nephew had caused her a good deal of heartache through his impulsive and sometimes selfish behaviour. But it was clear that his position as head of the family outweighed all the rest.

Every now and then, as they worked, Canidia would uncover something and put it on one side, before directing a slave to put it in 'the little side-room.' At last, when almost every room was cleared, Canidia took Manlia to one they hadn't entered before, a shabby little place with paint peeling from its walls. Here was a pile of all those items Canidia had put aside. There were three or four strong wooden boxes filled with clothes, a fishing rod, a bag of books, a saddle and some harness, gaming pieces and one or two handsome silver wine cups. On a small table at one side stood a small but beautiful statue of Mercury, cast in bronze.

'All this is to go to Titus Fulvus,' Canidia told Epictetus. 'Is he at home, do you know?'

'I think so.'

'Then I think when you take these over there you should invite him to dinner. Tell him it won't be a grand banquet. He'll understand, I'm sure.'

Epictetus looked disapproving. 'He won't mind, as long as there's enough wine,' he said. 'I don't see what you want to invite him for, madam.'

'It's what my nephew would want, I'm sure,' Canidia said firmly, and with another disapproving sniff, the freedman went away.

'You want to say goodbye to Fulvus?' Manlia suggested, when Canidia turned away.

'It's what Quintus would want,' she said firmly. Then her lips quivered. 'I don't know whether he even knows that Fiscilia's dead. I've put off sending for him as long as I can, because I don't want to have to tell him. But if Quintus didn't write to me, I don't suppose he's let him know either. I can't go without a word.'

'No,' Manlia agreed. 'I can see that you can't.'

That evening the strangest party Manlia had ever attended took place. The house, which Manlia had found half empty, was now stripped of everything except the basic furnishings, which Canidia would not be needing in her own well-appointed house. There were still three dining couches, but so little in the way of cushions and linen that Canidia decided they would all sit in chairs, around the square table from Canidia's sitting room.

Titus Fulvus, when he appeared, was a bulky young man, his rather thick neck and short legs unsuited to the toga which he had chosen to wear in honour of the occasion. As soon as he arrived, Canidia went up to him, and took his hands in hers.

'I have some bad news, about Fiscilia,' she said quietly. Fulvus' scowl deepened.

'What's she done now?'

Manlia could almost feel Canidia bracing herself.

'She's dead, Titus.'

He stared at her. Not in grief, Manlia thought, but in surprise. And there was a kind of calculation in his eyes too. But about what?

'Did you know she'd gone to Rome?' Canidia asked.

'I didn't know anything. Who bothers to tell me? I haven't heard from Quintus for a bit. I just assumed he was getting ready to move out of the house.' He looked round the gloomy room, as if assessing where furniture or pictures had been removed. 'So what happened?'

Manlia waited to hear what Canidia would say, and wasn't greatly surprised that she chose to answer very briefly. 'Her body was found in a burned-out shrine on the Velia. Nothing else is really clear.'

Fulvus whistled. Manlia, who had taken an instant dislike to him, observed that he wasn't even pretending to grieve. That didn't greatly surprise her: his lack of shock did. 'In a shrine? What in the name of all the gods was she doing there?'

'As I said, we don't know. And you haven't seen or heard from Fiscilius?'

'Not a word. As I said, I thought he was here. I'd have thought he might have had the decency to let me know.'

He was quite quiet for the rest of the meal, apparently lost in thought. Manlia could see why Epictetus had commented about his drinking. The freedman had obviously prepared well, opening an amphora of wine, of which the ladies drank a glass each. There wasn't going to be much wasted when they moved out next day.

The only time Titus Fulvus seemed to be about to say something about Fiscilia's death was at the very end of the evening. Canidia had gone off to tell Epictetus something about the journey and Manlia seized her moment. She told him that Fiscilia was thought to have committed arson, which Canidia had not mentioned. 'Would you have any idea what would make her do that?'

He seemed to consider within himself. Then he gave her a bleary look and said, 'No idea. But I'm interested that she was found in the Argei shrine on the Velia. Because - ,' he hesitated, and at that moment Canidia came back into the room.

'Because - ?' Manlia prompted him.

Fulvus hesitated, before shrugging and saying, 'You need to ask Fiscilius, not me. He was there.' He wouldn't say any more. He was half-drunk, she thought with disgust, and probably didn't mean anything. If she ever saw Fiscilius again she would ask him what Fulvus had meant. And that might never happen.

Manlia was greatly relieved that it was Rome they were heading for. Canidia had intended to go straight to Perusia, but when Manlia put it to her that it would be immensely helpful to her brother if Canidia would come to Rome first, she could only give way. She owed, she said, the Manlius Torquatus family that at least.

The journey down to Rome was, if anything, even worse than Manlia's trip north. The big roads were mainly clear of refugees, because they were military roads, and in what was clearly the build-up to another outbreak of war legions were on the move. They took no account of civilians, especially poor and unprotected civilians, shoving them rudely out of the way where they impeded their line of march, and helping themselves to anything the poor people might have with them in the way of food or livestock. So the refugees preferred to walk on the smaller roads, and wherever Manlia's carriage had to turn onto these roads it almost immediately was slowed down by the press of traffic.

There were groups travelling together, whole families including grandparents and babies. There were old men and women, stumping along as best they could on their own. There were women with babies and small children. A lucky few had brought with them some possessions wrapped up in a cloth. One or two had even managed to bring away a mule or a goat or a small handcart. But most had nothing.

'Think what it must be, Manlia said, 'to work so hard and then have to leave tools you've saved for or made yourself, ground you've cleared and tilled, animals you've bred. To have to take to the road, to go who knows where, with nothing but a little bundle of clothes and food. What brought tears to Manlia's eyes was the sight of children walking alone: she felt she couldn't have borne it without Canidia's company.

Whenever their carriage was forced to a stop in the crowds people clustered round. Here were rich women travelling with bodyguards and slaves in a big comfortable carriage: surely they could help? The little money Manlia had was soon given away. In one or two places they gave lifts to a group of children going to the next town, but even that was dangerous: Becco and Pulex had to fend off a rush of shoving, shouting, desperate people who had seen the children climb into the cart. Why shouldn't they go too?

And the inns Manlia had depended on to house them were shut. At some her slaves were told that they had run out of fodder for the horses, bread, wine, everything. Produce wasn't getting to the markets, with the roads cluttered up with marching soldiers and fleeing refugees. They hoped they would be able to open again next week. At others the doors were locked and barred as if the owners had simply abandoned them. On the first night of their journey Manlia persuaded the old slave at the house where she'd camped out before to let them in again, and they slept rolled up in rugs and blankets after a meal of stale bread and cheese. On the second the moon was full and Manlia insisted that the driver keep on going through the night. At dawn they were at the gates of Rome, and never had she been happier to see them. She didn't think she would ever forget the nightmarish scenes, the desperate people she'd seen. And where would they all go? What would happen to them?

So when Torquatus got home, there was a pleasant surprise awaiting him. As he walked through the great doors and into the entrance to his house, he caught sight of a woman in the reception hall, sitting in a lady's chair, her skirt falling in graceful folds about her feet, a cloud of dark hair escaping from its pins so that one or two tendrils fell on her cheek. She was absorbed in the scroll she was reading, quite still except for one hand which gently twisted one of those errant strands of hair. Then the clatter of his party's booted feet attracted her attention, and she jumped up, the scroll thrown onto her seat.

'Manlia!' As he spoke, a small dark shape bounced out from under the chair. 'I thought I said - ,'

Manlia was on her feet, her hands in his; slaves hurried in from the back of the house.

'The Animal came in with Felix,' he heard Trofimus say, at the same moment as Manlia murmured, 'Well, he's no trouble, really.'

They both stopped, which gave Torquatus the chance to continue, quite loudly and clearly: 'The lady Cornelia does not care for dogs in the house.'

'No, lord.' Trofimus' expression was bland and inscrutable as ever. Clearly feeling that the expulsion of dogs was beneath him, he clicked his fingers imperiously at one of his underlings, who picked the little dog up bodily and carried him off in a diminishing fusillade of barks. Torquatus hardly noticed: he was holding Manlia away from him so he could scan her face.

'You've had a hard time.' It wasn't a question. 'I shouldn't have let you go to Mevania. When did you get back?'

'Just a few hours ago, and I've got lots to tell you. I've brought Canidia with me. But the journey back was dreadfully slow. Weren't the roads you came on the same? Choked with people who've been kicked off their land? We travelled through the night last night, because there was nowhere to stay. Our friends' houses are empty, and the inns are shut.'

'No. I don't think I passed through any of the new settlement areas. Why wouldn't the inns be open?'

'They can't cope, Aulus. Some of the innkeepers are afraid of the soldiers, who don't pay, but just take what they want, and there are soldiers everywhere around Mevania. They'd started to cut up the Fiscilius estate when I got there. And then there's no food getting to the markets. And some of them were just shut. Abandoned.' Her eyes were full of tears. 'But that wasn't the worst. It was the tenants who've been thrown off their land, the landowners who've lost estates; all ruined and mostly heading for Rome. So many of them, Aulus. They are very angry, and quite helpless. And children on their own.' She swallowed hard. 'What in the gods' names will happen to them? We helped a few where we could, but there were hundreds of them.'

'I'm thankful you were safe, anyway.' Torquatus could find nothing to say. He knew that the refugees were simply more of the innumerable casualties of war. 'And Canidia's here?' He looked round, as if she might be sitting in some corner.

'She is. She's having a rest. She found the journey even more tiring than I did.'

The house was fully alive again, with Manlia and Cornelia at home. Torquatus thanked all the gods for sending her back to him safely, and for Cornelia's continued presence. Manlia ought by rights to be living in a house of her own: when and if the day ever came for her husband to give up fighting and come home, Torquatus would relinquish this beloved sister with a pang. But that would be a legitimate loss, as it were, the right and proper development of her story. If Cornelia were taken away from him, that would be a very different kind of loss, and one he felt unable to contemplate. But whatever Balbus had hinted, Cornelia herself had said nothing to suggest she was anything other than committed to their marriage.

Torquatus' first impression of Canidia was that everything about her was designed not to attract attention. He had taken her hands in his when they had met, saying, 'I am so sorry we've had to meet in such sad circumstances,' and her eyes had immediately filled with tears.

'Thank you,' she murmured. 'Manlia was so kind. When she could see I hadn't heard of Fiscilia's death she broke it to me as gently as she could.'

'Manlia broke it to you?' he asked, startled. 'Hadn't Fiscilius told you what had happened? He went off hunting for the slaves, but I assumed he'd at least have written.'

'No. I haven't heard from him.'

Torquatus couldn't understand this. It had been twelve days since Fiscilius had left; surely he could have traced the slaves and still got home before this?

Manlia said, 'We've been three days on the road, of course, so perhaps he's there now. But if he doesn't go back to Mevania soon, he won't be able to go at all. The house has already been allocated to one of the centurions: the man's just waiting for the commission to establish the boundaries before he moves in.'

Torquatus couldn't quite meet his sister's overbright eyes. He glanced down at his cup, saying, 'It's to be hoped he's taken away any personal belongings of his own, then.'

Canidia put in quietly, 'I sent some of his things to his friend, Titus Fulvus, to look after.'

'He's missed his chance to put on the banquet for the end of mourning for Fiscilia, then? I assumed that he'd simply forgotten to invite me.'

'Yes,' Canidia agreed. 'It should have happened days ago.'

There was an awkward silence.

Cornelia turned to Canidia and asked, 'I hope our people have made you comfortable?'

Canidia smiled. 'Very comfortable indeed, my dear. And most welcome after that rather distressing journey.'

'You will have had to remove your own belongings from the Mevania house?' she asked. 'Trofimus said you hadn't brought much with you. And only the one slave.'

'No. There was no need to impose on you. My maid can do everything for me that I need. I sent most of my things to Perusia as soon as the settlement was announced, and I'll go there myself in a little while.'

'Perusia?' Torquatus pushed a dish of crab patties nearer to her.

Canidia helped herself to a patty, but shook her head at the offer of bread rolls. 'I have a house there. It was my husband's: he was from an old Perusine family, you know.'

'Sisenna, the historian, I believe? My father was a great admirer of his.'

'That's right,' Canidia agreed, then busied herself with taking a stuffed egg from a silver dish. Torquatus waited for her to say more, but she seemed interested only in what was on her plate.

He waited a moment before prompting her. 'I've been looking forward to finding out from you all the things, family details, that Fiscilius didn't tell us. About Fiscilia in particular, of course.'

Canidia met his eyes as if bracing herself for some ordeal, dreaded if not unforeseen.

'I looked after her for six years,' Canidia said quietly. 'Long enough to see her grow from a wild girl who would fight with her brother and ride any horse in the stables to a young woman, still energetic and courageous, but also thoughtful and kind.'

'And Fiscilius?'

She shook her head. 'He grew from a wild boy to a wild young man,' she said. 'I don't know what he'll do now. I do know that the loss of his home and his land will hit him very hard.' She paused, as if gathering her strength, then looked Torquatus in the eye. 'I want to tell you that Fiscilia simply couldn't have burned down those shrines. Whatever the evidence.'

'You knew her better than anyone, Canidia,' he said gently. 'So I have to respect what you say.'

He sat back and thought for a moment, then turned to her again. 'Tell me. Did you know why Quintus left Caesar so suddenly.'

'No,' she said sharply. 'I never did. My brother-in-law didn't want to talk about it. I always assumed he'd simply crossed Julius in some way. Even when I knew the man that would have been a mistake.'

'You knew Caesar?' Cornelia asked.

'Oh yes. Only when he was a young man, of course.' She smiled faintly. 'We were all young then. I hadn't seen him for years when he died.'

Before Torquatus could speak again, a strange slave was ushered in by Trofimus. For a moment Torquatus' heart seemed to contract. Then he realised that the man was too dusty and travel-stained to have come from Balbus' house and he let his breath out in a sigh of relief.

'I recognise you, don't I? You're one of my nephew's people?' Canidia was asking.

The man nodded. 'My master sent me with this.' He held out a pair of sealed tablets.

Torquatus took them. 'Are you to wait for an answer?'

'My master didn't say.'

'Very well then. Go to the kitchens: I'll send for you later to give you any answer I may have.'

The man bowed and left, and Canidia said, 'Now at least we shall know where he is.'

Torquatus watched the man walking away. Yes, he was pigeon-toed just as Felix had said. He broke the seal and read, then threw down the tablets onto the couch beside him. 'He says he's going to Mevania - or he was when he wrote this. He's probably there by now.'

'Does he say where he's been?' Manlia asked.

'Oh yes.' Torquatus turned to Canidia. 'You don't believe Fiscilia burned down those shrines. Neither do I. There were always things about the case - where her body was found, and how she died - that made me doubt it was quite so simple. And then Fiscilius discovered that the slaves, who'd run away, had been overheard admitting that they'd killed their mistress.'

Manlia stared at him. 'Really? That's extraordinary.'

'Yes. He came rushing in, full of excitement, to tell me about it, the morning you left.'

He told them how the slaves seemed to have been in contact with a notorious family of criminals, how Tiro would have known about the Argei shrine on the Palatine, and how Fiscilia was probably murdered in mistake for Calliste. 'It all hangs together,' he concluded. 'Fiscilius had witnesses to what the slaves had said. And now in the letter he says he's traced them as far as an inn at Tempsa, where they were overheard discussing how to get to Sicily.'

'Where's Tempsa?' Canidia asked.

'If it's where I think it is it's far south, a little place on the way to Rhegium. No doubt the slaves reckoned that was as near to Sicily as they could get if they wanted to cross. Everyone knows that Rhegium has made a deal with Octavian: they don't get any soldiers settled there, and in return they block the flood of refugees to Sextus Pompeius in Sicily. I've heard that it's pretty much impossible to get a boat for Sicily from there now. It seems as if the three slaves set off from Tempsa: he's tracked down the man whose boat took them across. If all that's true there's no need to look any further. Oh, and Fiscilius says he called on Ampudius on the way there and said he obviously knew nothing about the murder.'

'Does he say when?' Cornelia asked at once.

'No. I suppose he could just about have managed to do that, if Ampudius had travelled fast.'

'You don't sound convinced,' Manlia said.

'I am, I think, though what Acutius told us made me doubtful of Fiscilius. And his story has changed, though maybe that's understandable enough. Can you believe that Fiscilia's slaves killed her, Canidia?'

'I suppose they must have done.' Canidia looked troubled. 'We hadn't had Tiro very long, and I never liked him much. He had a sly face, I thought, and I caught him pilfering once.' Canidia shook her head firmly. 'But I can't imagine that even he would have taken a bribe from a stranger to burn down shrines. He didn't like Calliste, that I do know. I heard him once calling her a nasty little arse-licker. Even so, I can't think he'd have murdered Fiscilia. There must be more behind this, mustn't there? The slaves knew Fiscilia well. She'd always treated them kindly and if they were caught, they'd die a hideous death. What could make them risk that?'

'I don't know. But I hope I'll find out.'

Canidia's eyes were bright with tears. 'I'm still struggling to understand that Fiscilia is really dead. I catch myself thinking she'll walk in, laughing at us for believing such an absurd story - ,' She broke off, pressing a hand to her lips. She looked directly at Torquatus for what felt to him like the first time. 'I can't tell you how grateful I am for your hospitality.' Her lips quivered. 'I felt so alone in the house up there, not knowing where Fiscilia had gone, and with no-one to trust except my manager, Cornelius Epictetus. I don't think I realised quite how bad it was till I came away.' Then, as if to herself, she said quietly, 'Now Quintus is the only family I have.'

There was a moment's silence before Cornelia ventured to ask, 'Fiscilia was your heiress?'

'She was.' She closed her lips rather tightly, as if she'd said more than she should. Then she relaxed and yawned. She turned to Torquatus with a smile. 'I hope you won't mind if I go to bed now. I still feel so tired from the jolting of the carriage, and perhaps I'll be more sensible in the morning. You'll understand, I'm sure, that I can hardly bear to talk about Fiscilia's death, and perhaps I don't even need to. Manlia and I discussed it all such a lot while we were alone together; she can probably tell you everything you want to know.'

'And she really didn't know that Fiscilia was dead?' Torquatus asked when Canidia had gone.

'No. I couldn't quite understand what she was feeling. Great grief, of course. But she was in a strange mood, very anxious, and guilty, I think, though what about I don't know. It was to do with not protecting Fiscilia, but it's hard to see what more she could have done. I thought she was feeling upset about leaving Mevania, but then I realised that was quite wrong. She has a huge sense of duty, and had taken on those children because of that. I don't think she ever liked Mevania much, and had been looking forward to her new life in Perusia, once Fiscilia was married. Cornelius Epictetus has gone there already with the rest of her slave household.'

'If his name's Cornelius I assume he's a freedman, freed by her husband?'

'In his will,' Manlia nodded.

'The surprisingly grand husband of Canidia,' said Torquatus. Manlia looked a question. 'Well, her sister married into the Fiscilii, which I would think was probably her social level: provincial equites with some local clout but no wider profile.'

'I think you're wrong.' Manlia helped herself to a handful of raisins. 'If anything, the Canidia who married old Fiscilius married a bit beneath her. Tell me about Sisenna, though. Was he really important? Canidia seems to have been quite devoted to him.'

'Oh yes. He was a big supporter of Pompey's, and a writer. Father admired his histories: I haven't read them but they dealt with the war against the allies, and no doubt praised Sulla to the skies, if they pleased Father. And he was seriously rich, I believe, with a famous collection of silverware: I remember Father drooling over his memories of a pair of tripod tables Sisenna commissioned, made of solid silver. If he didn't have any family - and I've never heard of another Cornelius Sisenna - Canidia might have inherited quite a bit, but it must have all gone by now. I mean, the man died twenty-five years ago.'

'Women aren't supposed to be able to inherit very much, of course,' Manlia agreed.

Cornelia nodded. 'But there are ways round that. I want to ask Canidia if Sisenna left a fideicommissum.'

Torquatus frowned at her. 'Better not. I don't want your father cutting up rough again.'

Manlia cocked an enquiring eyebrow at them but Cornelia laughed and lay back among her cushions, while Torquatus simply frowned, so she went on. 'She told me he'd died over twenty years ago,' she went on. 'She was only a wife for such a short time, poor woman. He was much older than she, was in public life, and then died just after he'd been one of Pompey's generals against the pirates. His loot from that would be substantial, wouldn't it?'

'I'm not sure he lived long enough to collect it. If I remember rightly he died before that campaign was really over,' Torquatus said thoughtfully.

'We should find out. If there was a lot to leave he might well have set up a fideicommissum for her. What does it matter, anyway? The slaves didn't kill Fiscilia for her money. Oh, and I must tell you, Aulus,' Manlia went on. 'You'll never guess who came to dinner, just before we left for Rome: Titus Fulvus. Fiscilius' friend, and Fiscilia's betrothed.'

Torquatus caught her expression. 'That must have been fun,' he said politely, and Manlia snorted. 'I'm not a bit surprised Fiscilia ran away: anyone would. His manners are horrible and he drinks too much. Mind you, that was quite helpful, because he let out something I'm pretty sure he wasn't supposed to. He was interested that Fiscilia had died on the Velia, because, in his words, Fiscilius was there. I wondered if it was his flat in Rome that

Fiscilius borrowed when he followed Fiscilia here. Interesting?'

Torquatus whistled gently. 'Now I wonder why Fiscilius never told us that?'

Cornelia had been sitting upright, staring at her sister-in-law. 'Of course! Titus Fulvus! The man's a tenant of mine - at least if it's the same one. I knew the name was familiar. He has a flat almost opposite the shrine. I've never seen Fulvus myself: he's not there all the time, but I'm told he's regular with the rent.'

'Things don't look good for Fiscilius,' Torquatus said, frowning.

Manlia nodded. 'I suppose that's what gave him the idea of the arson attacks: there were people rushing about, getting ready for the festival.'

'Fiscilia probably wouldn't even know about the shrine on the Velia, would she?' Torquatus pointed out.

Cornelia had been thinking. 'Do you think that if Fiscilius knew Canidia would have no-one else to leave her money to once Fiscilia was dead, that would give him a motive for killing her?' she asked.

Torquatus shook his head. 'A bit far-fetched, I'd say. Canidia doesn't have to leave whatever money she has to anyone. She must have friends? Relatives of Sisenna's? Or she could just make a friend her heir. People often do.'

Manlia said, 'I don't believe Sisenna had any relatives, or none near enough to know about. And she has none: she told me that.'

They sat in silence for a few moments, aware of the sounds of the house: slaves moving around, a voice raised to call someone, a laugh. Cornelia sat up and swung her legs off her couch. 'Like Canidia I'm unaccountably tired. Perhaps it's just the prospect of having to keep Nar until Fiscilius condescends to come for him? For a devoted brother he seems pretty offhand about his sister's beloved dog. At all events, I'm off to bed as well.'

When she'd gone, Manlia looked curiously at Torquatus, saying, 'Just what did happen to Cornelia? She didn't seem to want to talk about it.'

Torquatus told her.

'But she escaped? Came back?'

He couldn't help laughing. 'She remembered that there was a branch hanging over the garden wall, which she'd meant to have the gardeners cut back but had forgotten: it wasn't strong enough to bear a man's weight, she thought, so it wasn't urgent. Rachel stole the key of Balbus' garden gate while Cornelia climbed down the fig tree outside her room. Rachel let her out and put the key back. Cornelia then walked home, climbed the garden wall and fell into the garden.'

'That's how she sprained her ankle?' They were both smiling.

'Yes. She was right; the branch wasn't strong enough to bear her weight.'

'You know, when she dies no-one's going to put up a monument to her saying she never did anything but mind her household and work wool.'

Torquatus threw back his head and laughed. 'Shouldn't think so. Mind, there are moments when I wish she would do a bit of weaving. But I admit I'm worried. I can't quite believe her ghastly father will leave it at that. He could force a divorce at any time.'

'He could. What made Balbus suddenly want to take her from you?'

'He said she'd been frightened, and mentioned a bread riot. But she told me one thing that was odd. Cornelia asked Balbus about Faberius, she said, and she thought that was what upset him. When I saw him he never mentioned Faberius, though he warned me off investigating Fiscilia's death. You know who I mean? Julius Caesar's secretary?' Manlia nodded. 'Well, I've been puzzling over that. Cornelia said she'd met his widow, and that Faberius had bought land from Canidia, up near Mevania.'

'Oh, so that's it.'

'That's what?'

'Well, Canidia told me she'd had sold an estate on the Clitumnus river. She didn't tell me who the buyer was, only that the Fiscilii had never let her hear the last of it.'

'Really? Do you know when?'

'Not sure, but I got the impression it was when Julius was settling scores with some of his old enemies.'

Torquatus looked sceptical. 'Canidia can never have been his enemy, can she? And Sisenna had been dead for years and years.'

'No, I think someone's just thought she would be easy to bully, perhaps. Someone who'd realised she had this very desirable piece of real estate, and thought they'd get their hands on it. And then went and told Faberius about it.'

'So why was Balbus so unwilling to discuss Faberius with me?'

'I can't imagine. But there must have been a reason.'

Chapter 13

Instead of setting out for the Forum with a retinue of friends and clients the next morning, Torquatus walked alone, but for Felix, Becco and Pulex, to the shrine of the Argei on the Velia. He needed to look at it again, and had sent a message to the local magistrate ordering him to meet him there. Now that he knew Fiscilius hadn't told him the whole truth, but had been staying close to the shrine at the time of Fiscilia's death, the whole affair took on a different hue. Something Cornelia had told him had stuck in his mind. Was it possible that the building itself could give him a clue?

He had only just left the house when a litter drew up outside it. Its discreet curtains were drawn back and a small, plump, swarthy man descended from it in a leisurely way.

'Tell my daughter I'd like to see her,' he told Trofimus, and the steward bowed, leaving one of the house-slaves to settle the visitor on the bench at the head of the reception hall pool. This was the mistress's father, and Trofimus hesitated. He knew perfectly well that all the ladies were sitting in the garden, and would normally have simply accompanied Balbus to his mistress. But he also knew that something had happened between the lady and her father, and that the master had been furiously angry. It was all most mysterious. Rachel, who must know all about it, had been annoyingly tight-lipped. So he was playing safe.

As he had half-suspected she would, the lady Cornelia stopped the other ladies from leaving the garden, and instead accompanied Trofimus silently back into the house. She didn't even take Balbus into another room, but instead sat down beside him on his bench. Trofimus could only gesture to the slaves that they were to stand well back, out of earshot.

Balbus looked up with a smile as Cornelia approached, saying, 'My dear, you still don't look well.'

'I told you I'd had a mild stomach upset. I still haven't really got my appetite back. Nothing to worry about. Let's not discuss my health, Papa. This is rather a public place for that.'

Balbus looked round, dissatisfied. 'Yes. Well, why don't we go somewhere more private? Don't tell me this house has no quiet spaces where we can talk in comfort.'

'I'm more comfortable here, thank you.' Cornelia met his eye firmly. 'What can I do for you?'

'Well, my dear, if you insist on talking out here - I've been thinking and worrying about you a lot, you know.'

'So you told me before you tried to trick me into leaving my husband. I'm well cared-for here and you've no need to worry.'

Balbus looked discomfited, but only for a moment. 'But are you well-cared for? I don't think you quite realise what a delicate situation yours is. That husband of yours - ,'

'Excuse me, Papa. I can't talk about Aulus to you.'

'But we must talk about him. I've already told you, when you were at my house, that I'd heard he was thinking of divorce.'

'Yes, you told me that. I've seen no signs that it's true, though. And he's said nothing about it to me.'

'No, well, he wouldn't, would he? If he wanted to marry someone else he'd get all those arrangements in place before telling you your marriage was over. It would be most uncomfortable for both of you, otherwise.'

'Uncomfortable for him, I suppose you mean,' she said bitterly.

'Now come, Cornelia, you know perfectly well that men like Torquatus never marry for love. Of course not. They marry for advantage, for money, to forge political alliances. Torquatus never pretended it was a love-match when he asked for you. It was all Octavian's doing.'

'I know,' Cornelia said quietly, looking down at the hands clasped in her lap.

'And of course they marry for children. When you said you'd been sick I thought, perhaps - ?'

Cornelia said nothing, and Balbus shrugged. 'He's the last of his family, you know. Of course Torquatus needs children.'

Cornelia took a deep breath. 'The other day you told me that you thought Torquatus was regretting his marriage. I want to know why you thought that. What evidence you have. Has he spoken to you about it?'

'No,' Balbus agreed. 'No, he hasn't. He's never discussed his marriage with me: it's not likely that he would, is it? But I've heard things.'

'Gossip, you mean?'

'Well, call it gossip if you like. But gossip isn't always wrong, you know.'

Cornelia managed a smile. 'Not always, no. But it isn't always right either. So what exactly is it that you heard?'

Balbus seemed most uncharacteristically unwilling to come

to the point. 'You know how it is. You overhear half a conversation. You aren't sure you've understood who's being spoken about. You wonder whether these people really know what they're talking about.' He shrugged.

'Well, what are they talking about?'

'I've heard the name of Octavia mentioned?'

'Octavian's sister? What about her?'

'I've heard a suggestion that Torquatus might be negotiating to marry her.'

Cornelia stared at him. 'She's married already. Has been for years, and she and Marcellus have children. Three, I think.'

'Marcellus is ill. No-one expects him to live much longer. And in that case - ,'

'I see. She would be a most desirable bride, I can see that.'

'And it would be a great honour, you know.' Balbus spoke as gently as he could. 'You see how difficult it would be to turn down such an offer?'

'I need to talk to Torquatus about this. As soon as he comes home.'

She began to get up but Balbus put out a hand to stop her. 'Oh, no,' he said. 'I really don't think you should do that.'

'But why not? How else can I find out whether this is true or just a load of old men with time on their hands gossiping in the baths?'

'Leave it with me. I'll find out. If it's true he wouldn't tell you anyway. And if it is - well, maybe it'll be Torquatus facing the divorce, rather than you. At least that's the more dignified way to do it.'

Cornelia got up and walked restlessly about, before coming back to him again, her face troubled. 'I know you love me, Papa, and want what you think is best for me. I respect that. But I've seen you intriguing against other people often enough, and I can't help wondering if this is just another of your games. What do you hope to gain by this? If you separate me from Torquatus, what's in it for you?'

Balbus looked pained. 'You misunderstand me, my dear. I'm only concerned for your welfare. I can't and won't stand by and see you put in danger - and don't tell me you aren't in danger. That man of yours will be off fighting any moment now: then what will happen? Who will guard you?'

'Trofimus and the other slaves are more than capable, I

assure you. I won't be bullied into leaving my husband, whatever you say. And now if that's all, I'll leave you.'

She turned on her heel and walked into the back of the house again nodding to Trofimus as she passed. Balbus, a heavy scowl on his face, stood up, staring after her. His attention was distracted by someone's passing through the garden colonnade behind the business-room, and he glanced across to the archway which led out into it. Canidia came quietly through it. Both of them stopped, silently staring at each other, then Canidia lowered her eyes and walked quickly to one of the staircases that led to the upper storey. Balbus stared after her for a moment, then allowed Trofimus to usher him courteously out of the house and climbed into his litter without a backward glance at the slaves following him.

Down on the Velia Marcus Claudius Erotes was just as Torquatus had found him previously: obsequious and anxious to please.

'Oh yes!' - with a sour face - 'I know Titus Fulvus. He's not here all that often, but he still objected very strongly to our plans for moving the shrine.'

'I remember my wife telling me about that. It's a pretty unusual thing to do, isn't it, moving a shrine?'

'Not that uncommon, though Fulvus seemed to think so. You know what Rome is, just one big building site, and when a rich man wants to build a temple or a block of flats, sometimes the architect will work round something like a local shrine, sometimes not.' The magistrate shrugged. 'Cuts into their profits, doesn't it, if they have to do anything complicated? Costs a lot less to make a donation towards moving the building, and then they get a nice plaque calling them generous benefactors.'

'Was that what happened here? Where's the new development?'

'The little shops built onto the front of that block over there.' The man pointed to a smart block of flats, next to the one Cornelia owned. The entrance was flanked by two shops: a dealer in tunics on one side of the entrance and on the other racks of knives and colanders and spoons flashed in the sunshine. Neither establishment was much bigger than a cupboard which could be closed up for the night with shutters. 'Gave the owner the chance to squeeze out a bit more rent. And it was an opportunity for us: we'd been wanting to move the shrine for years.'

'Why? Where was it before you moved it?'

'Only about fifteen feet away. Much nearer to the corner.'

Erotes went back towards the corner of the Porticus Margaritaria. 'You can see from the marks in the road where it stood. Being so close to the corner it used to get damaged by carts and wagons coming round, which is why we'd always wanted to move it. But we could never get the aediles to agree, because of the sewers.'

'Sewers?' Torquatus swung round and stared at him.

'Yes, lord.'

Torquatus sighed. 'I wish you'd just tell me this from the beginning. You wanted to move the shrine. The aediles wouldn't let you because of the drains. A property-owner wanted to extend his block of flats. Sounds like nonsense to me. So what actually happened?'

'Well, I'd say some money changed hands, somewhere.' The magistrate smiled and laid a finger against his nose. 'After all those years, you see, suddenly we got permission to put the shrine where it is now. And the flats were extended. That's all, really.'

'The shrine must have cost a lot: it's a fine building.'

The magistrate swelled with pride. 'The man who owns the flats paid us compensation, of course, and several of the wealthy residents offered money, too.'

'Was Titus Fulvus one them?'

'He was not, although he could have afforded it. But these provincials, you know, they don't understand about the city cults. Anyway, the job turned out, as these things will, a bit more expensive than we'd thought and we needed to ask more of the local residents to help.'

'And Fulvus refused?'

As they spoke, the two men had been threading their way through the crowded street back to the new shrine. The sandal-maker stopped abruptly, and stared at Torquatus out of round brown eyes.

'Refused? He wouldn't even let me in.'

'But you managed to get the funds you needed?'

'Oh yes. This is quite a wealthy area, and several people gave us substantial amounts. Their names are on the side of the shrine.'

And indeed a brilliantly white tablet proclaimed in sharp red lettering that the shrine had been restored by L. Calvus (in very large letters) and two or three others in much smaller ones. Including, Torquatus noted, Cornelia Balbi.

'That wasn't there on the Ides of May.'

'No. We'd hoped to have it put up, but the stonemasons couldn't finish it in time. Calvus wasn't best pleased. It looks good, doesn't it?'

'Fine,' Torquatus agreed. 'And nothing else has changed since then?'

'No, it's all just as it was.'

'I still don't see what this has to do with the drains,' Torquatus said impatiently.

'I'm sorry, lord. There's nothing to see, because the manhole cover's inside the shrine now.'

'Inside the shrine?'

'Yes. That was our problem with the aediles' office: the access point for the drains was right where we wanted the shrine. The trouble it caused us, you wouldn't believe. We had to go to them to get approval, and show them our plans, and then the aediles got the idea that we ought to build another manhole further up the street. And it was when we were faced with doing that that I had my little run-in with Titus Fulvus.'

'I can't see another manhole.'

'No, lord, you wouldn't. We were able to persuade the aediles in the end that if we changed the orientation of the shrine very slightly the manhole cover would be accessible from inside the building.'

'I don't remember seeing it in the shrine.'

'You wouldn't notice it. It's just an ordinary slab of stone, with a mark on it to identify it. We had to get the priests to come and inspect it all and agree that the shrine would work just as well if it faced a little bit more to the north. The letters we had to write! The meetings! The money we had to raise! Well, I suppose these officials have nothing better to do than - but I'll say no more.'

Torquatus was smiling. His friend Aurelius Cotta was patrician aedile that year: he was going to enjoy explaining to him that he really hadn't enough to do. 'You'd better show me this drain. I can't think why you didn't tell me this before.'

The sandal-maker stopped so abruptly that a woman walking past with a basket of fish on her arm nearly bumped into him. She swerved to avoid him, muttering something that sounded decidedly uncomplimentary. He didn't seem to notice. 'Why, lord, you don't think - I mean, it was the girl who burned the shrine down, and she walked in. '

Torquatus had forgotten that Erotes wouldn't have known the turn events had taken. 'I don't know what to think,' he said, 'but if I'd known there was another way in - or out - well, let's go and look at it.'

They were back beside the little shrine. No-one was paying any attention to them. People were too busy looking for food in the small shops that had been built against the back wall of the Porticus Margaritaria and the stalls wedged in wherever there was a gap. One or two of the shops were locked and looked abandoned: the baker's had no more than a few loaves left, and the price, according to the sign on the back wall, was twice what it should have been.

Telling the slaves to wait outside, Torquatus turned and went into the hot darkness of the shrine, the magistrate close behind him. Felix lit the lamp, throwing strange wavering shadows gliding over the walls. The shrine was simply an empty space now, smelling of warm wood and new stone. There was nothing to tell what had happened here. The magistrate pointed to a stone slab, rather longer than the others. 'That's the manhole,' he said.

'How do we open it? Does it need tools?'

'No, lord. All the manhole covers are made the same way. The far edge is made so you can - ,' and he knelt down and reached for the narrow end of the slab - 'slide your fingers underneath.' With a grunt he lifted the end of the stone, then forced it upright till he could lean it back against the wall with a slight grating sound. The noise of running water and an unpleasant smell seeped into the shrine. The opening, Torquatus thought, looking down into it, was as dark as the mouth of the underworld. The rectangular shaft was solidly built of brick, with footholds on one of the short sides. He guessed it must be fifteen feet or so to the water, from which occasional glints flashed out as it hurried away to join the great drain in the Forum. He knelt down and looked carefully at the edges of the hole, which were as clean as he'd expected, since they were relatively new. Felix, behind him, exclaimed, 'Can you go down there?'

'Slaves do, to clear the sewers,' Torquatus told him. 'And you'd know if anyone had used this since the Ides?' he asked, looking up sharply into the magistrate's face.

'I would. To my knowledge, lord, no-one's ever used it at

all. What a fuss about nothing.'

'Someone has. Look!' Torquatus held up a small fragment of something in his fingers, something pale, and soft enough to have shaped itself round the edge of the stone slab. 'I can't see it properly in here, but I'd lay money on this being a bit of reed. Here's some more. A burnt bit.'

'Reed!'

'Yes.' Torquatus bent over the opening again, then stood up with a grunt. 'I don't think there's anything more to see here. The sewer here goes down to join the Cloaca Maxima, the great drain under the Forum? And presumably you can walk along the bottom of it? I know they take a boat along the Cloaca from time to time to inspect it. '

'Oh yes, lord. But are you suggesting that the girl wasn't guilty after all?'

'Well, think about it. For the unburnt reed to have become trapped like this the stone must have been standing open before the fire started, and then the burnt piece fell in too, during it. It wasn't open when those men came in to clear up, I presume? If not someone shut it again.'

'Let's ask the men. It seems dreadful to think - ,' and Erotes shrugged and turned to replace the slab. Torquatus watched him, reflecting that it didn't seem to be as heavy as it looked, since the stone had been cut quite thin.

They came out blinking into the dust and heat of the street, and Erotes hurried off, coming back a few moments later with the two building workers whom Torquatus had first seen clearing the rubble from the shrine. They stared at the question. Certainly there had been no slab of stone loose in the shrine when they'd been working in there.

Torquatus nodded, unsurprised, and handed the tiny pieces of reed to Felix. 'Take these, will you, and mind you keep them safe.' He smiled. 'Evidence! I do like evidence, and we haven't had much so far.'

Erotes was fussing at his elbow, just as he had been on the day of Fiscilia's death. He was looking rather pale.

'How fortunate, lord, that you took that young lady's body away for a decent funeral. Because I don't suppose she would have been planning to get out that way. How would she even know the drain was there? In which case she must have been murdered, I suppose. I wouldn't have liked to think of her being dragged about and thrown in the river, not if she was innocent. ' He said goodbye to Torquatus and went off shaking his head and muttering.

Torquatus glanced down at Felix, saying, 'Why do you think the murderer didn't put Fiscilia's body into the sewer, I wonder. I mean, there it was, open and ready.'

They were crossing the Forum now, but ignored the bustle and noise around them.

Felix considered this. 'I think he wanted the body to be found. Perhaps he needed someone to know that Fiscilia was dead.'

'Not just dead, but guilty, too. I wonder who.'

'Couldn't it have just been everybody? I mean, if you wanted to do something, or - I know - if you were going to inherit something, everyone would have to know the person was dead, wouldn't they?'

'They would. But Fiscilia had nothing to leave, unfortunately.'

'Some of the slaves said that she was the lady Canidia's heiress,' Felix suggested.

'True. But as Canidia's still alive that wouldn't mean much.'

Felix couldn't think of anything else, so he walked on in silence.

Torquatus must have stopped thinking about Fiscilia, because after a moment or two he turned his head and looked at Felix seriously.

'I'm going away pretty soon,' he told the boy. 'This meeting at Gabii, and then I'll be off down to Capua, recruiting. Catus goes with me, of course, but I'm not sure whether to take you too, or whether it would be better to leave you here to continue studying. Hermes tells me you're doing well - though not always as hard-working as he'd like.' A smile glimmered in his eyes.

'Oh, do take me!' Felix grasped his arm. 'Please take me! I could do all the things you need. And I can ride a horse: Catus has been teaching me.'

Torquatus looked at the boy, realising that he was on the cusp of adulthood. He must be thirteen or fourteen; quite old enough to be trusted with a responsible job. If he'd been freeborn, they would have been discussing when he would be given the plain toga of a man. Neither of them mentioned Iucundus, the boy Torquatus had bought to be his armour-bearer and body-slave, and who had died horribly in his house.

'Very well, I'll take you. I suppose it'll be useful experience for you, even if it isn't the kind of work you'll end up doing. Trofimus can help to prepare you: he knows everything.'

Manlia was as quick to see the implications of the sad little scraps of blackened reed as Torquatus had been, but thought that there might be a simpler explanation for why the body hadn't been tipped into the sewer.

'If you've set fire to a little place and you're inside, in the heat and smoke, you haven't got much time. And he had to get the slab arranged so he could drop it back down after him.'

'Possible,' Torquatus agreed. 'But I think he wanted Fiscilia guilty.'

Canidia had come out as they spoke, and they heard her gasp. 'Are you seriously suggesting Fiscilia could have been murdered?' She asked, sitting down rather quickly onto a bench.

'It's shocking, isn't it,' Manlia agreed, sitting down next to her and taking her hand.

'It is.' Canidia considered. 'But if that means she didn't burn the shrines it would almost be a relief. Who would have murdered her?'

No-one wanted to say Fiscilius' name. She looked from one face to the other, before saying quietly, 'It's Quintus you're thinking of, isn't it?'

Torquatus nodded. 'There's quite a bit of evidence against him, you see. The problem is that we've only had the story as your nephew chose to tell it. And he's changed it as he's gone along. When I didn't believe in the sacrilege he 'found out' that the slaves had killed her. When I expressed doubts about that too, he suggested that they had been hand in glove with a notorious criminal gang.'

'But why?' Canidia asked.

Torquatus was about to answer when Cornelia came quietly out of the colonnade and sat beside Manlia. She picked up one of the fragments of reed. 'Is this what you found? I heard Felix telling one of the other slaves about it.'

'Yes. And I think this changes everything.' Torquatus was about to say more, but his mouth snapped shut as Nar appeared from behind a large rosemary bush, his tail wagging, and something bulky and awkward in his mouth.

'What on earth's that?' Manlia asked. She snapped her

fingers at Nar, who at once came over and dropped his treasure at her feet. It was a clumsy and well-worn shoe, made of a single piece of leather to form a sole and a series of flaps which could be drawn up around the foot and fastened with a leather thong. Manlia bent to pick it up, but Nar took this as an invitation, and leapt on the shoe, growling and wagging his tail furiously. This was a game he was very fond of.

Catus appeared, looking hot and cross. 'It's an old shoe he's found somewhere, lord. He keeps it in the stable. I didn't mean him to bother you with it.'

'I know what it is,' Torquatus said. 'It must have dropped out of one of those baskets we found in Lollia's flat. It was Calliste's, I suppose. It's the kind of shoe a slave would wear.'

'Oh, of course,' Manlia agreed. 'Though I can't see why Calliste would have burdened herself with extra shoes.'

'Of course!' Torquatus exclaimed, staring at her. 'Of course she wouldn't.'

'But what of it?' Manlia began, when Trofimus appeared with a slave carrying a set of wax tablets.

'From the Palatine,' he announced, and Torquatus took the tablets in silence, broke the seal on the cord that sealed them and read the message. 'Tell your master I'll be ready at dawn tomorrow,' he said, and the man bowed and walked out.

'I told you the soldiers had demanded Octavian meet Lucius Antonius at Gabii,' Torquatus told Manlia. 'Octavian called it play-acting. And now it's going to happen: who knows how long it'll all take, or even what the result will be? But before we go, he wants us both to see him.'

For a moment Manlia's anxiety was evident. Then she schooled her face into indifference. 'I wonder what for?' she asked. 'Or can I guess?'

'Do you know what Ahenobarbus is doing?' Torquatus asked.

She nodded, her face pale. 'I suppose that's it. Octavian wants to know what my husband's up to. I do know where he is. I had a letter from him about a week ago, as it happens. He's still somewhere around Sicily, or maybe North Africa. But he did say he might see me soon.'

'Do you think Antonius might be planning a return to Italy? Coming to support his brother? You don't think your Gnaeus might have gone over to his side, do you?'

'I'm sure he'd tell me if he had, and he's never said any such thing.' Manlia was emphatic. 'As far as I know he's still independent. And I shan't believe he's gone over to Antonius until he does tell me, himself. Oh, I do hope he hasn't - Octavian's been very good to me, so far, but even his courtesy might be a bit challenged if my husband becomes a sworn enemy.'

'Of course he knows you can't make Ahenobarbus change his mind,' Torquatus told her. 'He wants to see both of us, remember. I know he's concerned about the implications of the Fiscilia case. An attack on Rome is an attack on him. We'd better go now, I think. He turned and looked searchingly at Cornelia, taking her hand in his. 'Are you sure you're well?

Cornelia summoned up a smile. 'I'm just feeling a bit tired. That stomach upset has left me feeling rather weak, too. I think I'll have a nap if you don't need me.'

As they walked away down the hill, Manlia said, 'Balbus came to call. They haven't met since she came back. She wouldn't let him in but went and talked to him in the entrance hall. It must have been a little difficult.'

'Oh, did he? I wonder what he wanted?'

'He's her father,' Manlia said, smiling. 'Perhaps he just wanted to see her.

'He's her father, who wanted to kidnap her. I don't trust that man.'

Octavian was in one of his most sphinx-like moods that afternoon, saying very little, questioning Manlia non-commitally about her husband's movements, and making it clear that she was always under scrutiny. It had been most unsettling, but there had been nothing to suggest that Manlia was under any greater threat than usual. It wasn't until they were about to leave that Octavian asked about Fiscilia's death. Told that she had probably been murdered after being set up as the arsonist, he visibly relaxed.

'Some family feud, after all,' he suggested with a shrug.

It had been Manlia who told Torquatus of Balbus' visit, and he wondered uneasily why Cornelia didn't mention it, but as they settled down to dinner, she told him of it. Scanning her face, Torquatus could see nothing in it but a slight irritation.

'He doesn't understand that trying to kidnap me makes me feel differently about him. It really is all fair in love and war where he's concerned.' She shrugged. 'Don't look so worried, my dear.

As I said, I can't stop him coming here, but I shan't go anywhere unguarded, I promise.' She smiled comfortingly at him.

Torquatus could only accept her reassurances. And, in any case, the next day he rode away to pick up his military career again. The two ladies, alone in the big house, never quite settled back into their old intimacy. Manlia, watching her sister-in-law anxiously, thought Cornelia seemed to be a little better, though her usually glowing complexion was still rather pasty, and she was quieter than usual. She spent less time in her own rooms and went back to her favourite seat in the garden. She wouldn't talk about her health, saying with a snap that she knew perfectly well that she needed to eat but hated to be fussed over. In her own mind what she needed even more was to think about her father's warnings: how much should she trust him? Might his affection for her have misled him?

Twelve days had passed since Torquatus had ridden away and Cornelia was sitting toying with some little pieces of bread and honey, and considering what she had better do. She had never been so unhappy. Nothing Torquatus had said before he went had truly reassured her, or dispelled the notions her father had put into her head. She knew Torquatus hadn't married her for love, and now it seemed that he didn't want her as his wife. He had always been very kind to her; but then, she thought miserably, that was probably just because he had very nice manners and was the sort of man any woman would want to be married to. She wiped her eyes and picked up another bit of bread.

Perhaps, when he came back, they would have a proper talk, have time to understand each other, but then again, perhaps they wouldn't. She hadn't missed the excitement in his face as he hurried away. He was obviously looking forward with great pleasure to campaigning, to the company of Octavian and the other officers, to living the active life of a soldier. First he was to accompany Octavian to the meeting with Lucius Antonius at Gabii. Then he would be down in Campania for however long it took to recruit (or bribe) soldiers. She wasn't stupid, and she could see that for the foreseeable future Torquatus might be able (if he wished) to find any number of excuses for not sitting down to talk to his wife.

Cornelia gave up on the bread, and sipped at the cup of grape-must syrup in water that Trofimus had suggested she might like. When she first started suffering from this horrid sickness she had hoped that she might be pregnant. But she wasn't; it had been nothing but the tainted mussels after all. She had longed to be able to tell Torquatus she was carrying his child, and the disappointment when her period had come as usual had been terrible. But now, perhaps that was a good thing? If Torquatus divorced her, any child of theirs would be his, not hers, legally speaking. He could take it from her at birth, find a nurse for it, bring it up in his household, deny her all contact with it, if he chose. She took another bit of bread, hoping that it was true that one couldn't eat and cry at the same time. Perhaps she should take Manlia into her confidence. She longed to have someone to talk to, someone who would understand how she was feeling. But Manlia was so close to Torquatus. Suppose she already knew, as Cornelia herself did not, that he was planning to end their marriage? Would she be, she wondered with a flash of anger, the last one to hear?

It was a relief when one of the slaves brought her a set of wax tablets. The message was from Nereis, whom Cornelia had invited to visit again. Nereis was unwilling to do so, for two reasons: until she could come to the house as Felix's mother to talk to Torquatus about freeing him and adopting him she preferred not to disturb the boy. Cornelia could easily understand that, and applauded Nereis for her self-restraint. The second reason was that she felt she had already given Cornelia all the information she had on the Fiscilii, and could therefore see no point in any further meeting. This seemed odd. On her previous visit Nereis had seemed very open. Cornelia thought she remembered her saying that if she came across any further information in her husband's files she would share it. So why this sudden clamming up?

But perhaps if what Nereis had told her had sent her father into such a panic that he had tried to abduct her, it was a good thing if she kept away? She considered Balbus yet again. How well did she really know him? His motive for what he had done could only be concern for her. She thought back over her life, trying to understand him. She hadn't seen much of her father until she was fourteen. Her mother had died and Balbus had left Spain for good when she was a baby: all her earliest memories were of the grandparents who had brought her up. It had been a secure and comfortable childhood. A thought caught her unawares: Balbus had only come back into her life when she was approaching marriageable age. Perhaps she had then acquired a value for him which she hadn't had before, as a pawn in his political manoeuvres?

She pushed the thought away, reminding herself how kind he'd been to her, how attentive to her comfort, wrapping her round with concern. And he hadn't used her as a pawn, she told herself. He hadn't - as he might well have done - married her off to some elderly aristocrat she'd barely met. Instead, he'd betrothed her to a wealthy young merchant in Neapolis, though the young man had died in an epidemic before they could marry. Again that alien inner voice suggested to her that by planning a marriage for her with a relatively powerless man Balbus had been intending to keep control over her. And in the end he had agreed to her marriage to Torquatus reluctantly, and only to please Octavian. And - another unpleasant new thought - could you really be driven by love to try and break up a happy marriage? Was that love? She stood up suddenly, and a slave came and took the cup she handed him. This was getting her nowhere. She was making herself unhappy, and all on account of something that might never happen. There were properties of hers here in Rome she hadn't visited for a while: nor had she seen her agent. She needed to occupy herself. She told a slave to send for her agent, and tell him to bring his accounts.

But however hard she worked, whatever distractions she found, she always had in the back of her mind her fear that she was about to be abandoned. She could hardly bear to meet Torquatus - whenever he returned - pretending that there was nothing wrong. The more she considered, the more she realised that she did believe her father. What he'd said had made perfect sense, was all too likely to be true. If such a grand marriage was being prepared for her husband, what chance did she have of interfering? Would she even be right to do so, if she loved Torquatus? Brushing away sudden bitter tears she hoped he would not come home for a while. Who could have imagined she would ever wish that?

Her wish was not granted. That very evening, as Manlia, Cornelia and Canidia were sitting in the garden before dinner, a sudden trampling of boots from inside the house announced the master's return. Slaves ran here and there, voices were raised in enquiry and command. And then Torquatus himself strode out through the shadowy colonnade, to where the women of his household were standing, smiling, with cups in their hands. He hugged and kissed them all as they exclaimed at his sunburnt face, before slumping onto a couch.

They were all asking how the mission had gone, and he laughed at them. 'One at a time, please!' He looked around at them, noting with a pang of anxiety that Cornelia still wasn't looking well. Manlia was her usual self, composed, her feet tucked under her neatly on a lounging chair. Canidia still looked as if she was trying to make herself invisible. He took a mouthful of wine and rolled it around appreciatively. 'Oh, I feel as if I've been away for far longer than a couple of weeks,' he said with a sigh of satisfaction. 'But I'm afraid I have to report complete failure, ladies,' he told them lightly.

'Oh, surely not?' This was Manlia, her eyes laughing at him.

'I'm afraid so.'

'Did Lucius not show up in Gabii, then?'

'Better than that. Neither of them did.'

There was an outcry at this. Torquatus raised a hand for silence. 'What happened was this. You know how I had to go south first, to check on the strength of some of our legions? And then I was to meet Octavian at Gabii for this famous meeting with Lucius where we were all going to swear undying friendship? Peace and love all round?' He took another mouthful of wine, enjoying their intent faces around him. 'But when I got near Gabii I thought things seemed remarkably quiet. A message had been left there for me. Apparently Lucius, coming from Praeneste, had sent out scouts, fearing that Octavian might have set a trap for him. Octavian, of course, had done the same as he approached from Rome. Two of the scouting parties met, there was a skirmish, both sides called in reinforcements, the whole thing escalated into a minor battle, and Lucius called the whole thing off. He claimed he was afraid he would be assassinated, and went back to Praeneste.

'So what now?' Cornelia asked.

'War. Can't be put off any longer. In fact I'm only here for one night.'

The women nodded, their faces serious. If war was inevitable, no military commander could expect to see much of his home until it was over.

'I'm off to Capua again, to bring up more legions. I might see you again after that, but I don't know. Lucius is bound to head north: his brother's main supporters are in Gaul, and will presumably come and fight with him. They have eleven legions between them: this isn't going to be easy.' He grinned suddenly. 'Octavian's obviously decided he needs all his generals here: Salvidienus is the most senior, and he was on his way to fight Sextus Pompeius' supporters in Spain, as you know. Apparently Octavian decided a few weeks ago that he was going to be needed here - and his six legions even more so - and quietly sent messengers after him. He should already be turning back. I hope so, anyway. Even with his forces Lucius will outnumber us. Though Octavian's gone off to Alba Longa, in the hope of bringing over two legions which are stationed there. They've mutinied, apparently, so he might be able to - ,'

'Bribe them?' Cornelia asked with a smile.

'Offer them a bonus,' Torquatus corrected her.

All that evening, the four of them sat, discussing where the women would be safest if there was war, and what Torquatus needed to do before setting out on what might be a lengthy absence. He and Cornelia went off with Trofimus at one point, to discuss a long-planned meeting with Torquatus' agent for his estates in Greece. These estates had been bought by Torquatus' father after his governorship there, and the agent should be arriving in Rome shortly. Cornelia could handle that, once Torquatus told her what he wanted done. The household itself would continue as normal, except that Torquatus intended to take the boy Felix with him, as well as Catus. Trofimus was charged with a message to Torquatus' clients and friends: the morning greeting was to be suspended, but they should continue to call at the house, where he would send news as he had it. It was late when Torquatus and Cornelia returned to the garden, a thick warm darkness heavy with roses, but Manlia and Canidia still reclined on their couches, chatting like the friends they had become.

'I think I will leave here before you come back,' Canidia told Torquatus. 'I have been so well cared-far, and I've so much enjoyed Manlia's and Cornelia's company, that I've put off going to my new life. But I have stayed far longer than I ever intended, and my household needs me. Even Epictetus, who's always encouraging me to take things easy, has written that it's time to go home. I shall be quite safe in Perusia. The city hasn't had any land taken for settlements, so it hasn't any reason to get involved in this civil war. In fact it has every reason not to.'

'I think you're right,' Torquatus told her, 'But of course you are welcome to come back here at any time if you need to. We regard you as a friend now, and a friend can always claim hospitality. And I will send you home in my own carriage, with my slaves to guard you.'

'Oh, you need not - ,' she began, but Torquatus stopped her.

'You only brought a couple of slaves with you when you

came, I can't allow you to travel unguarded. Believe me, things could get very messy now.'

It was only when they finally went to bed that Cornelia was able to talk privately with Torquatus. For all she had agreed with Balbus not to try to discover her husband's plans, her heart was too full for her not to speak at all. They made love with pleasure, as they always did. Nothing seemed to change that. And then afterwards, as she struggled to think how to frame her question, Torquatus suddenly opened a way for her. They were lying comfortably entwined on his bed. Torquatus yawned, stretched and said: 'I just hope you'll all be comfortable: I suppose with Lepidus in charge of the city it will be safe enough. It's easy for Octavian. His mother's dead, and he hasn't any family to worry about. Not even a wife now. Where my mother gets her information from I don't know, but she was right, too: Octavian has divorced Claudia, packed her off to Fulvia, wherever she may be.'

Cornelia rolled towards him and put her arm over his chest. She took a deep breath. 'Octavia? He's close to his sister, isn't he?'

'Oh, well, but she's married. He loves her, loves her dearly, but she's not his responsibility any more.'

'Marcellus is ill, so I heard?' Cornelia could hardly breathe for anxiety.

'I believe he is.'

'If he dies, she'll be a tremendous catch, won't she?' Cornelia asked lightly.

'Oh, terrific. She's a delightful woman, as well as being Octavian's beloved sister. Beautiful, too. What more could any man ask?'

Cornelia made a neutral noise. Torquatus grunted, turned over, and in a moment or two fell asleep.

Chapter 14

Ten days had passed since Torquatus had hurried away again, and Cornelia was still unwell. She said nothing about it, unwilling to have Manlia and Canidia asking after her, fussing over her. Even less did she want her father getting to hear that she wasn't well. Torquatus had taken his doctor with him among his attendants, so there was no-one to ask awkward questions, and she was able to settle into a routine agreed with Rachel, whose discretion she knew was absolute. She would get up a little later than usual, attended only by Rachel, who would bring her the grape-must drink Trofimus had invented for her. She would stay there until she had finished vomiting, which was generally about mid-morning, and then join the other ladies or attend to her household duties in her usual quiet way.

Manlia, seeing her usually lively sister-in-law so pale and silent, and getting no response to her hints, asked her outright one day.

'I am a little worried about you. You still aren't quite yourself. And I've noticed that you aren't about in the mornings in your usual way.' She looked directly at Cornelia. 'Are you pregnant, my dear?'

'Oh, no.' Cornelia kept her voice light. 'It's that stupid stomach trouble. I haven't quite been able to shake it off.' Knowing that the man wasn't there she felt quite safe in adding, 'If Aulus' doctor was here I think I'd get him to have a look at me.'

Manlia smiled. 'Don't tell me Balbus doesn't have a doctor of his own?'

Cornelia couldn't help laughing. 'He has, he has. Not just one, either. He would hate you to know this, but he is a terrible hypochondriac. There is no disease known to man that my father hasn't thought he was suffering from at one time or another.'

'Really?' Manlia put down the scroll she'd been reading.' 'It doesn't seem to fit with his image.'

'Not at all. Balbus, the ruthless climber, loyal attendant of the great, always energetic and active in their interests. Don't tell anyone: he's half ashamed of it himself, and would hate it to be known.'

'So don't you think perhaps - ?' Manlia hinted.

'That one of his tame doctors might examine me. No thank you.' She swallowed hard, on the verge of sudden tears. 'My father is bad enough already.'

She longed to be able to tell Manlia that she thought now that she really might be pregnant, but couldn't bring herself to do it. The comfort, the support, of this much-loved sister-in-law would make all the difference to her. And yet she remembered what Balbus had said, and she knew she couldn't risk it. If Torquatus was about to abandon her, Manlia too would be cut off from her. She could depend on no-one but herself.

Almost overcome, she got up quickly from the bench, and hurried out into the reception hall, murmuring that there was something she'd forgotten to tell Trofimus to do. She almost bumped into Canidia, coming in from a visit to friends. She smiled automatically. saying, 'I hope you've had a pleasant morning? It must be so good to pick up the threads of friendships from long ago.'

Canidia seemed flustered. She ignored what Cornelia had just said, and after a moment asked her if they could go somewhere private to talk.

'I've just heard something which upset me very much. I think you ought to know,' she said.

Cornelia felt her heart pounding in her chest, but she said calmly, 'Of course.' She turned and led the way to her own suite of rooms. Once slaves had placed two chairs, she braced herself and turned to Canidia.

'What is troubling you?' she asked, as calmly as if she had no fears for herself at all.

'It isn't about me,' Canidia began anxiously. She seemed unwilling to speak, but when Cornelia moved sharply she smiled faintly and said, 'My friends were talking about what's going on in Rome. Gossiping, I suppose you'd have to say. And I heard a rumour about your husband that upset me very much.'

Cornelia gripped her hands together. 'Go on,' she said.

'Yes, my dear. But I don't want to hurt you.' Cornelia said nothing, but looked a little paler than usual. 'Well, then. I heard that when Marcellus dies, Torquatus might be offered the chance to marry Octavia. I don't know if it can possibly be true. I hope it isn't.'

Cornelia managed to laugh. 'I wonder if there are gossips anywhere to equal Rome's?' she asked lightly. 'It's the silliest thing I ever heard. So let's not say any more about it. I hope you told them they were talking nonsense?'

'Oh, of course, my dear.' Canidia was looking nervous, and as if she didn't know quite what to say next. Cornelia thought about Canidia's friends; the elderly wives of elderly senators, for the most part. She knew what their attitude would be. They would have instinctive respect for her husband as the head of one of Rome's oldest patrician families, and an equally instinctive dislike of his abandonment of his father's republican principles in favour of Octavian. As for Octavian himself, they would respect his connections to Julius Caesar, and the way he had grasped the opportunities offered to him by Caesar's death. But they would fear the sort of Rome he would create if he ever had the power. And not one of them would blame Torquatus if he were offered the chance to become even closer to Octavian's power than he already was.

'I hope I haven't spoken out of turn? Canidia was asking anxiously.

'Not at all. It's always better to know what people are thinking. However nonsensical it may be. But now we won't speak of this again, please.'

Canidia could only agree, wondering anxiously if she had done more harm than good.

While the three women were waiting to hear from Torquatus how his campaign was going, the situation in Rome changed yet again. As they sat in the garden one day at the end of July, enjoying the turn from the boiling heat of afternoon to the gentle gold of evening, Trofimus came hurrying in, looking, for him, rather discomposed.

'I am sorry to interrupt you, ladies,' he began. 'But one of the slaves has just brought in some disconcerting news.'

They turned anxious faces to him. 'My husband?' Cornelia asked faintly.

'No, mistress. It concerns the city, not the master.'

'Very well. What then?'

'I gather that Lucius Antonius has ridden into the city and is now controlling it.'

'What? That's impossible!' Manlia exclaimed.

'Lepidus is in charge, and he has troops, surely?' Cornelia agreed.

'So we understood,' Trofimus said. 'I've sent out slaves to find out the truth, because I'd have thought we must have heard if the city had fallen.'

The three women looked at each other, stunned. 'What do you think will happen, if it's true?' Canidia asked, pulling her gown around her as if she were cold.

'No harm will come to us,' Manlia said firmly. 'Why should it? We are causing Antonius no problems, and we have plenty of slaves here to guard us. Becco and Pulex alone should be quite enough.'

Cornelia nodded. 'Besides, if they have taken the city, they'll be too busy running it, setting up guards, hunting through the temples for any hidden cash reserves and so on, to worry about us.'

They stared at each other, hoping what they'd said was true.

None of them had much appetite for dinner. Trofimus came in and out with news. The rumours were true: the city, placed under the guard of Lepidus and a legion of troops, had fallen. Lepidus had fled without a fight.

Later he heard that the soldiers were all over the city, quartered at all the gates. He suggested that the ladies stay indoors until it became clear what Lucius intended to do, and seemed very relieved when none of them expressed any desire to go out into the city.

The next day, a slave sent down to the Forum reported that Lucius had made a speech in the Senate. He had described himself as the upholder of the best republican traditions, a man steeped in Rome's ancient ways; and he reminded them that it had been Antonius, not Octavian, who had displayed his military virtues on the battlefield at Philippi. With the backing of the Senate, he said, he and all the many legions who owed allegiance to his brother Marcus would restore Italy to prosperity and calm.

Manlia laughed at this. 'Marcus Antonius being such an exemplar of ancient virtue,' she mocked. 'But I bet the Senate bought it?'

'I believe the speech was very well received, madam,' Trofimus agreed calmly.

For the rest of that day, the ladies stayed quietly at home. Manlia, as was her custom when she was restless, went away to her weaving-room, and worked steadily. She was making a length of cloth of the finest wool, into which she was weaving a border of flowers and fruit. The intricacy of the pattern and the fineness of the thread kept her mind occupied. Cornelia rather envied her.

She had never cared for weaving. Her way of passing the time was to visit the kitchens and discuss with Fortunatus how the household would manage if markets were interrupted and supplies became difficult. She was afraid there might be a siege: Octavian could hardly cede Rome without a blow, though as news came in it became clear that this was precisely what Lepidus had done. Canidia sat in her room writing a long letter to Epictetus, her freedman, about the preparations he should make for her arrival in Perusia.

Cornelia half-expected Balbus to visit her again, but nothing was seen of him. She remembered how he and the Antonii had fallen out over Balbus' support for Octavian and wondered if he had fled the city, or was simply holed up in his house, just as she was in hers. But wherever he was he was keeping quiet.

Three days went by, and Rome remained in an uneasy peace. Normal life carried on, Trofimus said. Markets were open, people went down to the Forum, drank in bars, chatted on street corners. Manlia herself, on the second day, walked down into the city, saying she couldn't bear to be cooped up indoors any more. Not that she had anything to report: a kind of normality continued, though when a market stall had been tipped over with a crash by a passing donkey everyone had jumped and run for cover.

On the third day Cornelia discovered that her father was still in Rome. A slave of his appeared with a letter, which with a word of excuse she took away to her own rooms. With trembling fingers she opened it.

My dearest Cornelia, he began. *This present situation is quite intolerable. I intend to leave Rome and I want to take you with me. I have organised passage on one of my ships for myself and for you.*

I know what you will say, but before you act impulsively, I would ask you to think. You can do nothing for Torquatus by staying here. He needs nothing from you. But you may be putting yourself into danger.

You can see that war, which I'm sure everyone deplores, and no-one more than myself, has in fact now broken out. There will be no more peace in Rome until it has been fought to the finish. What that finish will be I don't pretend to say. What I do know, however, is that I am not prepared to leave my only daughter to the mercy of whatever armies hold Rome. I intend to take you to my villa in Neapolis, where I am going for safety. I am not asking you to come to me: I am demanding your obedience as my daughter. I am sure that Torquatus himself would prefer to think of you living comfortably and safely at Neapolis than exposed to the fortunes of war in Rome.

I shall be leaving tomorrow. I shall come to your house and expect you to be ready to accompany me.

Your loving Papa.

Cornelia sat for a moment with the tablets open on her knee. She was shaking, and biting back tears. It felt as if her whole life, everything she loved and valued, was crashing into ruins around her.

Then she made herself read the letter again. For all that her father pretended to know what Torquatus would want, he hadn't claimed that he had any kind of agreement from him. Nor did he say that Torquatus had decided on divorce. There was nothing in the letter but her father's own panic and desire to get her back under his control.

She smoothed out the wax with the back of her stylus, wiping away her father's neat writing. Then, without thinking too much, she wrote a brief reply. She felt as if she had committed herself now to whatever might come, and took a shaky breath. Forcing herself into at least an outward calm she tied up the tablets and gave them to a slave.

'To go to my father, please,' she said, and the man hurried off. She got up, steadying her knees. She went to find Trofimus, who was luckily on his own.

'Tomorrow,' she told him, 'my father will come here and demand to see me. You will tell him that my explicit orders were that he was not to be let in. You will make sure you have sufficient slaves to deny him entry, by force if necessary. He is not to come into the house, whatever he says or does. Is that clear?'

Trofimus smiled at her as if this were all perfectly normal. 'Perfectly, mistress.'

She nodded, still feeling shaky, and the man sailed away. Writing the letter had been easy. But what on earth was she going to do? She couldn't go with Balbus, and yet his leaving felt like a loss. She was stuck here in Torquatus' house, with these two women she couldn't confide in. What on earth was she going to do?

That same evening one of the slaves came running in with news which threw them all into confusion. Lucius Antonius had departed as suddenly as he'd arrived, hurrying north on the via Cassia. His intention was to join forces with Antonius' legions which should be marching hotfoot from Gaul under the command of Ventidius and Pollio.

These two men were stalwart supporters of Antonius. When Octavian had returned to Rome after the battle at Philippi, he had brought with him Antonius' time-expired veterans as well as his own. It was his job to settle all of them equally on the land they'd been promised. The original agreement among the Three Men had envisaged a division of the empire into three. Antonius was to hold all the eastern parts, and he had stayed on after Philippi to rule them. But he had also been allocated Gaul, from the river Po to the far northern coast. He had put the trusted Ventidius and Pollio in charge there so that if Octavian failed in his task or tried to cheat his colleague, the eleven legions of experienced men stationed in Gaul would force him back into line. These legions would no doubt march into Italy on the via Flaminia. But Octavian, who would almost certainly come back to Rome after Lepidus' flight, was already on that road. And although Lucius had more legions than Octavian, he was anxious to avoid a battle with him until he, Ventidius and Pollio had amassed such overwhelming power that the outcome would be in no doubt. So Lucius chose to use the other road north, the via Cassia, from which he could cross to the via Flaminia at various points once Octavian had passed on his way south.

The situation was grim for Octavian. His own most experienced military commander was Salvidienus Rufus. Salvidienus had been allocated six legions with which he was to fight against Sextus Pompeius in Spain, but when war seemed about to break out Octavian sent off messengers at top speed after him, telling him to turn round and come back as fast as possible. With those six legions and his own four based at Capua Octavian desperately needed to stop Lucius Antonius' forces from joining up. It was all he could do, and if he failed his situation would be disastrous. As it was, Octavian's chances of victory were slim, since he was heavily outnumbered, and had too many raw recruits in his legions. If the enemy's armies were joined against him it would take a miracle to win.

The slaves who had brought this news told them that the soldiers had all gone. Not all, Manlia exclaimed; they must have left some to guard the city. But no, it seemed that no forces at all had been left in the city: it was open to whoever might decide to take it. The three women stared at each other in consternation.

'I must go home,' Canidia said. 'I should have gone days ago.'

'But you can't go up the Flaminia,' Cornelia pointed out.

'Oh no. But I don't need to. I can just as well go up the Cassia, and then there's a decent road across below Lake Trasimenus,' Canidia said.

'But Lucius has just gone that way!' Manlia exclaimed.

'He'll be far ahead of me, from the sound of it, and won't cross to the via Flaminia till he's much further north. Now don't try and dissuade me, please. I shall be safe at home, well away from the fighting: Perusia is wonderfully well-fortified, it hasn't lost any land for settlements, and the Perusines won't want to involve themselves in a war. To tell you the truth, I shall feel a lot safer there. This house makes me nervous. It's too open; anyone can walk in. Doesn't it frighten you?'

'No, not really. The doorman can turn people away,' Cornelia pointed out.

'And there are slaves all over the place,' Manlia agreed.

'I just don't feel comfortable with those great open doors,' Canidia said. 'Sisenna lived like your husband, of course, but I must be getting old, or maybe it's just that I've lived more modestly for years now, and I'm not used to the public life of houses like this. I'll be happier in my own house. I did just wonder, though - could I persuade you to come with me? You'd be well looked after and Perusia is a pleasant city. Then, when it's all over, you could come home in safety.'

'I'd rather wait here for my brother to come home,' Manlia said at once, assuming that Cornelia too would stay in Rome, but at that moment Trofimus came back, escorting a visitor. Late as it was, he announced the lady as if she was paying a late-morning visit for gossip and spiced wine.

'The lady Nereis.'

Cornelia jumped up, surprised. 'Oh, what brings you here?' she asked.

'I've come to ask you to help me,' Nereis told them, clutching at the rather large bag in her arms.

'Oh, Manlia, Canidia, this is Iulia Nereis, Faberius' widow,' Cornelia said quickly, and Manlia stared at her, astonished.

'But I know you,' she said at once. 'You are Felix's mother, aren't you? You used to be - ?'

'One of your slaves,' Nereis agreed. 'But I'm free now, and I'm frightened. The lady Cornelia knows all about me. Canidia, too: we knew each other at Mevania. I want to know - I wondered if - I could come and stay here for a little while, with you?'

'Of course you can,' Cornelia said at once. 'But why? Is something wrong?'

'It's your father,' Nereis told her, dropping her eyes and clinging even more tightly to that bag.

'My father? What's he doing? Oh!' Cornelia exclaimed. 'I told him you knew the Fiscilii. I told him Faberius had bought Canidia's estate.'

Nereis nodded. 'Yes. And he's furious with me. He's threatened me, told me to get out of Rome if I know what's good for me. But I don't know what to do, or even if it's safe to have told you that.' She looked close to tears.

Canidia said, more drily than Cornelia had ever heard her speak: 'You need to get away from Balbus if that's the mood he's in.' She laughed. 'Come with me to Perusia. He won't find you there.'

Nereis was staring at her. 'To Perusia? But - ,'

'Just for a while, until Torquatus comes back. He'll sort this awful muddle out, I'm sure. And in the meantime, you'll be out of Balbus' reach, and safe with me.'

Nereis said, 'I don't know. I hadn't thought of leaving Rome. I thought - ,' she paused and asked rather timidly, 'Is Felix here?'

Cornelia said gently, 'No. He's with Torquatus, somewhere on the way to Nursia, we think.'

'Oh.' Nereis' head drooped. Then she seemed to shake herself. 'Are you really sure I won't be in your way?'

'Of course not,' Canidia said smiling.

'Then I will come, with pleasure. I'll write a message to my staff here in Rome: I won't say where I'm going, just that I'm staying with a friend.'

'You must have brought some of your slaves with you? Manlia asked.

Nereis shook her head. 'I thought that they'd be safe in my house. And I know how terrifying it is for a slave to be whisked off somewhere, not knowing whether it's safe, or whether your owner will be killed or harmed and you'll be blamed for it. So I didn't even tell them where I was going. I thought Balbus might try to force them to tell him where I was. He might catch up with me, and then - ,' She laughed with a little self-consciousness. 'I was very frightened and I panicked.'

'You ran from my father,' Cornelia said thoughtfully. 'What I can't understand is quite why he was so upset about the Fiscilius estate? What's it got to do with him?'

'Who knows? But I think we should all go to Perusia,' Canidia was smiling 'It would be so comfortable.'

Manlia had opened her mouth to repeat that she wouldn't leave Rome when she was astonished to hear Cornelia say, 'I'd like that very much. But have you got room for such a big party?' Manlia stared at her in dismay. Could she really be thinking of leaving her husband's house?

'Of course, my dear,' Canidia was saying. 'It's Sisenna's old family home. I shall be delighted to have you with me: the place will be livelier than it's felt for years.' She turned to Manlia again. 'Are you quite sure you won't come with us? I can't see what you can do to help Torquatus by remaining here, you know.'

'I suppose that's true. But thank you for asking me.' She couldn't help adding, 'I'd feel like a traitor if I left my brother's house now.' As soon as she'd spoken she regretted it, thinking that Cornelia might take her words as a criticism of her. But Cornelia was smiling and looking relieved.

Canidia took her hand. 'He would never think that, would he? And you'd be safe in Perusia.'

Chapter 15

When Torquatus left Rome late in June it had been to dash down to Capua as fast as Bucephalus could carry him, with Felix and Catus and his other slaves keeping up as best they could. The time for drilling and preparation was over, and all Octavian's thoughts were on stopping Ventidius and Pollio from sweeping down into Italy from Gaul. Arriving in Capua, he'd been relieved to see that the four legions based there were ready for action, well-exercised and fit. Not that he was surprised: Agrippa had been working with these men for weeks. Agrippa hurried off northwards with three of the legions, intending to leave two with Lepidus in Rome, for the defence of the city. Torquatus led the last of them south to Brundisium: Octavian had no desire to find that Marcus Antonius had sailed in to rescue his little brother.

July was drawing to an end by the time the men were settled and the summer heat was intense.

'Do we just stay here?' Felix asked, fanning himself wearily. He was longing to go back to Rome where he would be able to visit his mother.

Torquatus smiled. 'I know. It's boring not to be where the fighting is.'

They were just passing through the cavalry lines as they spoke. Slaves and soldiers worked side by side, cleaning up the ground, carrying off the waste to dungheaps which were already substantial and already smelly. Torquatus broke off to speak to one of the centurions, who had come to ask about supplies.

'I hope we shan't be staying here,' he told Felix. 'But we have to wait and see.' And in fact he received a letter from Octavian a couple of days later, telling him to go to Rome. Reading between the lines, Torquatus suspected that Octavian had little faith in Lepidus, and wanted someone he trusted to support him in the defence of Rome. The legion at Brundisium could be left under the care of junior officers for the moment.

With a light heart he and Felix headed back to Rome.

'You'll be sore tonight,' Catus told Felix, as their little party approached the city.

Felix's head ached in the harsh afternoon sunlight, and his eyes were dazzled, but he said firmly, 'Not me. I can ride all day now and not get sore at all.'

They were close to the Capena Gate now. Torquatus hadn't

thought about Fiscilius for weeks, but the sight of the gate reminded him of the case, and he wondered vaguely where that violent young man had gone.

Felix must have had the same thought, because he said, 'I wonder which bar it was that Fiscilius went to?'

Torquatus wasn't listening. He pulled his horse up hard. 'Those aren't our men.' He sat for a moment, watching the gate, his slaves around him. 'There's something wrong here,' he said. 'Felix, just go and ask at the gate, will you. See whose troops those are.'

Felix quietly got down from Firefly, passing the reins to Catus. His legs were stiff but he was very conscious of the groom watching him as he followed Torquatus back down the road and out of sight. After a moment he forgot about his legs because the men on guard at the gate had seen him and were watching him out of hard, hostile eyes. Felix walked up to them briskly.

'Where are you off to?' the men asked.

'I've a message to go to the house of Marcus Ampudius,' he replied in a bored voice, thinking that it was highly unlikely they would have heard of him. 'It's urgent.'

The men grunted approval, and let him through, and Felix breathed a sigh of relief. Once inside, he ran to the nearest bar - probably the very one where Fiscilius had claimed to have found evidence of the slaves' guilt. He looked around. There was a slave leaning against a shady patch of wall, very obviously waiting for his master. Felix sidled up to him. The man seemed to come out of his doze with a start.

'Didn't see you there,' he admitted.

Felix leaned alongside him. 'It doesn't matter, does it, as long as they don't see. It's too hot to stay awake.'

'Too right. Your master's like mine, then? Too mean to buy a drink for the slave.'

Felix sighed. 'That's right. Doesn't think we need it.'

They passed a few moments in comfortable silence, before Felix felt it was safe to say casually, 'Load of soldiers around today.'

'That's right. Ever since Lucius Antonius came in yesterday they've been all over the place.'

'Yesterday? Really? There must have been a battle? Sorry I missed that.'

'No, there wasn't any fighting at all. Not that I saw, anyway. He's gone, Lepidus has.'

Felix's heart beat so hard he had to steady his breath.

'Really? Well, one master, another master, doesn't make much difference, I suppose. Oh, and there's my man, had his drink and ready to go.'

He nodded and slipped away from the wall, quietly attaching himself to a group who looked as if they might be street performers of some sort. They had a hand-cart full of clothes, musical instruments, masks, pots and pans, shoes, tattered book-rolls and food. The soldiers cast a cursory eye over the group and waved them through impatiently, Felix with them. Once through the gate, he sauntered off casually in the direction Torquatus had taken, and he found the little party waiting anxiously behind a large round tomb. The road was lined with such tombs, and in the welcome shade of the cypress trees around it the tired horses swished their tails against the flies.

'It's Lucius Antonius,' Felix said, running up to Torquatus. 'He's taken Rome!'

'What!' Torquatus stared down at him. 'What happened?'

'Yesterday. Apparently there wasn't a fight, or anything. Lepidus has run away.'

'Gods! Octavian will love this!' Torquatus muttered. He thought for a moment, then turned his horse, saying, 'Let's go.'

Felix was busy mounting his pony Firefly again. As soon as he had he trotted after Torquatus, saying, 'But aren't we going into Rome, then? No, I suppose we can't, can we?' His shoulders sagged with disappointment.

'No. We certainly can't,' Torquatus told him. 'Lucius would just love to get his hands on one of Octavian's senior officers. We'll have to go round, as fast as we can, and then head north. Where the devil is Lepidus, I wonder? And what in Hades has become of his legions?'

Felix, who had hoped that if they were going back to Rome he might have a chance to see his mother, choked back tears of frustration.

If he had thought they were travelling fast before, he quickly realised he'd been wrong. Torquatus pressed the horses as hard as he could once they were free of the city. Wherever there were stables he stopped and changed to new ones: the first time he did this, one of the slaves was told to take the exhausted Bucephalus and Firefly home, gently and quietly. They went on, galloping wherever there was a broad swathe of green beside the road, keeping to shade where there was any. Felix lay down that night on the grass beside a fire. They'd eaten little but some rather stale bread and some dried fruit all day, and his legs felt as if they were on fire. He would never get to sleep.

And then it was the next morning, and he woke, stiff and cold, and they were on the move again. They hadn't gone far before Torquatus told everyone to be silent. He had led them off the road and through a wood; Felix wondered why as they picked their way carefully and quietly through the trees. Then he saw. On the road, frighteningly close to them, columns of soldiers were marching by, the tramp of their boots threatening, the sunlight glinting off their helmets. The smells Felix had grown used to floated across through the trees: unwashed bodies, the sharp scent of horses, hot leather. They waited quietly, the horses flicking their tails and stamping from time to time. The soldiers didn't seem to be setting any kind of watch, and the crash of their boots drowned out the noises from the horses.

'That's one of Lepidus' legions, or part of it,' Torquatus told Felix quietly. As he spoke, Lepidus himself rode past, a tall figure cantering up the line of soldiers, so close to them they could easily have called out to him.

They waited in silence till the soldiers were gone, leaving nothing but a cloud of dust behind them. Torquatus waved his group onwards, and they picked their way as fast as they could through the rest of the wood. When they finally scrambled down onto the road again, a mile or two further on, the tramp of the soldiers' boots was close behind them. They had managed to get ahead of the retreating troops.

'Quickly, now,' Torquatus urged them, and they all kicked their horses into a gallop. This was the hardest ride Felix had endured so far, and he had to grit his teeth not to cry out from the pain in his legs. The August sun beat down on them relentlessly, the road was desperately dry and the dust seemed to stick in his throat: Torquatus wouldn't allow a stop for a while, but at last they came to a place where a fresh stream ran beside the verge, and he let them all dismount and water themselves and the horses.

Felix felt much better after this. So much so that when Torquatus told them to mount once again and ride on he was able to smile and obey at once.

'We'll be there before Lepidus,' Torquatus told him. 'Octavian needs to be warned of this.'

'What will happen now?' Felix asked.

'We'll go back to Rome. Octavian won't want to leave it in enemy hands.'

'Enemies,' Felix said thoughtfully. 'But they looked just like our men.'

'They are just like our men,' Torquatus agreed. 'Most of them have fought for Antonius, so they are attached to him. Most of ours - except the new, young ones - fought for Julius Caesar, and they support Caesar's heir. But none of them want to fight each other.'

Felix considered this. 'But when you told the men the war was beginning, they were happy, weren't they? I heard them cheering.'

'They were. It's an odd thing with soldiers: you'd think they'd be pleased to have a clever commander who gets what he wants without a fight, but they don't. They really like battles.' He smiled down into the boy's brown, intelligent face. 'Never forget that.'

Felix wondered why he said that. Even if he was freed, Felix would never be an army officer like Torquatus.

He hadn't long to ponder, however. They arrived outside Sentinum at dusk, and Felix gasped. He'd never seen siege works before, and he could hardly believe his eyes. Piles of logs and stones lay everywhere. Men were running about, working to complete as much of the siege wall as they could before the light went. A line of cavalry horses was being led in from the pasture where they'd been feeding. The noise and dust were unbearable. Torquatus hurried to the command tent, and Felix stopped gaping and pushed his pony into a trot for one last time.

He was thoroughly glad that as Torquatus' personal attendant he had the right to hand his reins to Catus at the tent door and run in to join his master. But on this occasion at least he wasn't welcome. A very pale Octavian jerked a thumb at him, and Torquatus nodded curtly, so he had nothing to do but back out again, feeling foolish.

He went to where the officers' quarters were, but the other slaves had already made sure there was accommodation for them. There didn't seem to be anything for him to do. Even Catus had gone down to the cavalry lines to talk to the other grooms about where Torquatus' horse could be fed and cared for. So since no-one seemed to need him he went to the top of a little hill which would allow him to get a good view of the walls. Men were beginning to come back into the camp as the shadows lengthened. The wall - or rather fence, because it was made of logs, not stone, and raised on a bank of earth - wound round out of sight far away. Towers had been built into it at regular intervals, allowing a sight of the plain and the city itself.

He stayed watching the men, coming in now as the shadows lengthened, each little group going quickly and confidently to the right place in the camp. After a while he felt cold, and hurried back to the officers' accommodation, thinking about how familiar he'd found the camp. He remembered thinking, when they'd first left home, that he would never get used to long days in the saddle, or to the noise and smells of the camp, the haste and the shouted orders, but he knew very well now which trumpet calls summoned the men to the parade ground, where the cavalrymen would take their strings of horses to feed, and when his master was likely to need his weapons.

It was mid-afternoon the next day before anything else happened: Felix wondered why the news Torquatus had brought hadn't got out. Torquatus was on the parade ground, drilling some new recruits under a scorching sun, when the look-outs called out that they could see a party of horsemen approaching. Some wag commented audibly that perhaps Lucius was suing for peace, and they'd all be back home before autumn. Torquatus called the men to order sharply, and set them to a difficult manoeuvre, handing over command to one of the centurions before hurrying off. Felix, who'd been polishing the bridle of Torquatus' horse, laid it down along with the polishing rag and quietly slipped away. He arrived at the main gate just as the little party, the horses stumbling with fatigue and streaked with sweat, came trotting in. The group opened out once it was inside the camp, and the tall horseman at its centre was revealed as Lepidus. An anxious silence held for a moment, then the soldiers came forward, offering help, asking questions.

Lepidus looked as arrogant as Felix remembered him on that day in May when he'd come to advise about the disturbed ritual on the Velia. He looked around disdainfully.

'Where's the general?' he asked.

Felix slipped away and joined a stream of men making their way into Octavian's tent: it seemed everyone had heard about Lepidus' sudden arrival. It was easy enough for him to get in:

slaves were hurrying this way and that, bringing orders, messages, information. He slipped down along the side-wall until he could get a good view of the general's table and chair. Octavian was standing, looking rather pale - but then, he always did - and accompanied only by a couple of his commanders. Torquatus joined them, his dark face severe, those black brows drawn together forbiddingly. A bustle announced Lepidus' arrival, and soldiers made a way for him. His look of arrogance was slipping, and he held his hands clasped before him as if he'd forgotten what he ought to do with them. Octavian looked at him coldly.

'Why are you here?'

'Lucius has taken the city,' Lepidus said, his gaze falling before that blue, cold stare.

'The city of Rome? And how did you allow that to happen? You had, if I remember rightly, two legions to defend the city? Isn't that correct?'

'It is.' Lepidus' voice was very quiet now. 'But the man in charge of the city's gates handed over the command of his legion without a fight. And Lucius had sent men into the city in small groups: when these heard that Nonius' legion had changed sides, they drew their swords and made a disturbance, and the other legion, thinking the battle was lost, gave up too.'

'So the gate commander was disloyal - why didn't you know that?' Lepidus opened his mouth, but Octavian swept on. 'And Lucius was able to send infiltrators into the city - why didn't you notice that? And when the soldiers were uncertain, the commander - apparently - wasn't there to rally them, to lead them against the intruder. Why was that, Lepidus?'

There was an uncomfortable silence. Lepidus didn't attempt a reply but stood, looking at his feet. Apparently satisfied that the man had nothing further to say, Octavian continued. 'So now I have lost two badly-needed legions.'

Lepidus looked up. 'No, I persuaded some units to follow me. They'll be here as soon as they can. I've left some of them watching the roads north. We'll know what Lucius means to do soon enough.'

'Do you imagine I hadn't set scouts already? Or do you suppose we are all as irresponsible as you?'

Lepidus suddenly burst out, 'What would have happened to the city if I'd stayed and fought to the end? I was outnumbered. Rome would have been destroyed. And for what? Lucius isn't likely to stay in Rome, is he? He'll be heading this way soon enough and we'll get our revenge.'

'You betrayed your trust. I shall now have to go south again: I cannot leave Rome in enemy hands. But what a dilemma that presents me with. What am I to do, Lepidus? Advise me.' The voice was soft and even and cold. 'Ventidius and Pollio - men loyal to their commander, Antonius - are on their way here from Gaul intending to wipe me out. I am here besieging this city because it controls the road they'll come on. I dare not leave the road unguarded. But Rome needs me too. Which way should I go, Lepidus? Shall I risk being stabbed in the back by Antonius' faithful generals? Or should I go to the rescue of the city which should never have been lost?'

The silence was painful Lepidus still hadn't replied when there was a stir among the men watching, and a travel-stained man came forward. 'The city has fallen, sir. Lepidus fled almost before the enemy arrived and there was no battle. I believe Lepidus may be on his way.' He stopped, red-faced, as Lepidus stepped into the lamp-light. There was a silence.

Octavian smiled. 'Thank you,' he said to the messenger, and the man bowed and went out.

'I suppose you'd better stay with me,' Octavian said, and turned away. Felix almost gasped: it was the way a master might dismiss a slave but Lepidus took it without open resentment.

'Torquatus: dismiss your men quietly. We break camp at dawn. Sulpicius: get your cavalrymen back in camp well before nightfall. Send all the centurions here for their orders.'

The men scattered on the various tasks, Felix following his master as Torquatus walked quickly back to the exercise ground, and suddenly remembering the job he'd abandoned when Lepidus arrived. Torquatus came out of his own thoughts to see Felix beside him and smiled. 'What did you make of that, Felix?'

'When we saw Lepidus that day - the day of the murder I mean, he seemed so - so tall and cold. As if no-one could touch him. And Octavian dismissed him like a slave,' Felix blurted out, but then realised that he had another, more pressing concern. 'But what about Rome, master? Will everyone there be safe?'

'I should think so. There was no battle. So I daresay everything is quite normal.'

'But our household, lord - everyone at home -'

'They'll be fine. And you need to have all my gear ready to

move. We are off at first light.'

'To Rome?'

Torquatus looked down at him, surprised. 'To Rome, of course. And if Lucius Antonius is still there you'll see your first battle.'

Next day they slipped away in the dew of dawn, leaving their fortifications half-built. For as long as possible they made it look as if nothing unusual was happening, but at last they were all gone, marching fast, hearing continual news from Octavian's scouts and spies. One said that Lucius had made a speech about how his brother Marcus Antonius only wanted legitimate power, and longed to restore law and order, and the senators had cheered him to the rafters, supposing that the rule of the Three was over. They hurried on, and at the end of the fourth day they reached Rome to find it open and undefended. Lucius Antonius had gone. The legions marched onto the Campus Martius and set up camp there. Agrippa had arrived already, and he hurried to greet Octavian, his heavy face alight with satisfaction. Torquatus knew that Agrippa longed even more than he did himself for military command, and as he watched that radiant face he knew he was seeing a man who has found his vocation.

Octavian was sitting on a stool, neat as a cat, reading military reports, when Torquatus and Agrippa found him.

'So Lucius has gone north, up the via Cassia, no doubt hoping to avoid Salvidienus,' Agrippa said, striding round the room restlessly. 'I have to get after him, before he can meet up with the legions from Gaul. But there's Salvidienus to consider. Where the hell is he?'

'Delayed by a mutiny, so his last letter said. But he's on the via Flaminia, and I heard just before you came in that he'd snatched Sentinum while the garrison was busy chasing me, and he's taken Nursia too.'

'Good man.' Agrippa's face was full of admiration.

'And he goes on to say that he has seen nothing of Ventidius or Pollio. They chased him to the borders of Gaul, but seem to have stopped at the river Po. He says that rumour has it that they are quarrelling over which of them has precedence, and are also uncertain whether Antonius wants them to fight us or not.'

'Let's hope all our enemies are as clever,' Agrippa said with a grin.

'Yes indeed. As you say, it's crucial to stop Lucius before he meets those eleven legions - eleven! When I think what I could do with eleven more legions! We must keep them away from Lucius at all costs. And in the meantime the defence of Rome really needs to be in capable hands. Torquatus will do that job. I want to go back up the Flaminia: I'm haunted by the thought of those eleven legions getting through. You can follow Lucius up the Cassia. I'm making offerings daily to my dear deified father to help us a little, and with luck you and Salvidienus will catch him between you.'

Agrippa pressed his finger and thumb together. 'We'll crack his nuts for him. If I need to give Salvidienus more time I'll distract Lucius, draw him off.'

'How can you do that? Surely nothing's going to distract him from meeting Ventidius and Pollio, is it? He must put that before everything else. I would, I know.'

'Yes, well, he doesn't think like you.' Agrippa's smile was warm. 'You wouldn't have left Rome undefended, for a start.'

Torquatus hardly knew whether to be pleased or sorry to be left in charge of the city. It was a great honour, and a sign of Octavian's trust in him. On the other hand, the events of the last few weeks had fired Torquatus with a desire for the chase. Administering the city, while vital, would not be exciting. He watched Octavian and Agrippa march their armies away northwards two days later with genuine regret.

It wasn't until they'd gone that Torquatus found the time to leave the Palatine and go to his own house. He longed to hear Manlia's laughter, to see Cornelia quietly setting flowers on the family altar. But when he and Felix clattered into the familiar reception hall it seemed unusually quiet, the soft cooing of pigeons on the roof only emphasising the emptiness of the wide space. Felix stared round, dismayed, at the corners filling with shadow as the afternoon melted into evening. When Trofimus hurried out of those shadows to greet them it appeared that Torquatus was doomed to disappointment: the ladies had gone with Canidia to Perusia.

'What in Hades did they do that for? Though I suppose they'll be as safe there as anywhere,' Torquatus said doubtfully, running a hand over his dusty hair. 'So there's no-one here? Did Balbus send me any message?'

'I'm sorry, lord: I have misled you. The lady Manlia - ,'

He was interrupted by hasty footsteps, and Manlia hurried into the room. Torquatus cried out with pleasure at seeing her, and held out his hands to her.

'The lady Manlia,' Trofimus continued sedately, 'is here, as you see. And the lady Cornelia did receive a letter from her father, but there has been nothing for you, lord. When I mentioned the ladies, I was referring to the lady Cornelia and Nereis.'

Felix, beside him, gave an inarticulate cry.

'Nereis?' Torquatus stared at the steward. 'What's she got to do with this?'

'She came here, lord, just as the ladies were discussing their plans. She seemed very shaken, if I may say so, though I don't know why.'

'She must have come to talk to Cornelia?'

'She did,' Manlia agreed. 'She'd also had a letter from Balbus, telling her to keep quiet and leave Rome if she knew what was good for her. She showed it to us. And then they said they would all go to Perusia, but I preferred to stay here.'

He hugged her again. 'Thank goodness you stayed. I couldn't have borne to find you both gone. But I don't understand why Balbus should write to her. Why in the name of all the gods should he threaten her.'

'She wouldn't say. Perhaps it was something to do with Faberius buying Canidia's estate? I think Nereis knew something about that, but she wouldn't say what.'

He hadn't even thought about the Fiscilia case for weeks, and now here it was again. Well, he couldn't think about it now.

'But you said Cornelia had a letter from Balbus, too? What was he wanting?'

'She didn't say.'

He looked down at Felix, standing silently beside him. The boy was very pale under his sunburn. Before Torquatus could speak, he burst out, 'So now my mother's gone again. When we came back last time there wasn't time for me to go to her house. And now she's gone to Perusia. Am I ever going to see her? Does she even want to?' His face crumpled and he turned away, struggling against sobs.

Torquatus put an arm round the boy's shoulders. 'Felix, she was frightened. She didn't go because she didn't want to see you.'

'No,' Manlia agreed. 'She asked for you while she was here, and was very disappointed when you weren't. I'm sorry she's not here for you.'

Felix nodded rather brusquely and shrugged them off, wiping his eyes.

Torquatus let him go, turning to Trofimus. 'Gods, I'm so hot. I'd like a bath. But I suppose there isn't any hot water?'

'Oh, yes, lord.' Trofimus gave him a superior smile. 'The bath suite's been prepared every day, in case you should arrive at short notice.'

'Well, Jupiter be praised for that.' Torquatus let out his breath in a long sigh. 'Come on, Felix: time to get clean.'

Manlia watched him go, noting that Torquatus had said almost nothing about Cornelia.

Not that he wasn't thinking of her. As he and Felix bathed, he had a hard time talking normally to the boy, asking himself again and again why she had chosen to go off with Canidia rather than wait for him. It was horribly unsettling. And he felt sure Balbus must have something to do with it. He'd write to Cornelia. And he'd go round to Balbus' house and find out what the man had done to make Cornelia run away like that.

Their dinner was a quiet affair. The slave Torquatus had sent round to make an appointment with Balbus had come back saying he was in Neapolis. Torquatus would have to write to him too: more frustrating delays. They ate in the shade in the garden, enjoying the little breeze that stirred the hot, sluggish air of August. Felix waited on them looking as if he might fall asleep on his feet, and as soon as the second course was set out Torquatus said, smiling, 'Oh, go to bed, Felix, before you fall in the salad.'

The boy rubbed his eyes, muttered a word of thanks and hurried out.

'And now I want you to tell me the truth about Cornelia,' Torquatus told his sister. 'Why did she go running off to Perusia?'

'I don't think I quite know what to tell you,' Manlia began. 'I don't understand her. She wouldn't tell me why she wanted to go.'

'She wasn't well,' Torquatus said.

'No. I thought she might be pregnant, but she said not.'

'Pregnant?'

Torquatus sounded astonished, and Manlia said tartly,

'It does happen, you know.'

At this most awkward moment, Trofimus came along the colonnade leading a man in a dusty travelling cloak. He came past the steward with something of a swagger and put back his hood. Torquatus saw a complete stranger, but Manlia exclaimed, 'Titus Fulvus! What can you be doing here?' Torquatus had a moment to pull himself together as Trofimus welcomed the guest with offers of wine and food. Fulvus' face, he guessed, was naturally truculent, but tonight the man seemed hardly to be able to bear the steward's courtesies or Manlia's introduction of her brother, so big with news was he. At last they were alone but for slaves standing quietly against the walls.

'Is there any way I can help you?' Torquatus began.

Fulvus sneered. 'I shouldn't think so. You've just passed through my homeland, I believe, so you'll have seen what you and your master are doing to us.'

'Octavian is not my master.'

'You say that, do you?' Fulvus snorted derisively, then took a gulp of his wine.

'I suppose you've come here because you have something to tell me.' Torquatus was resolved not to lose his temper with this man. He tried to remember everything Manlia and Quintus Acutius had said about him.

Fulvus swept on. 'I thought you might like to know that Fiscilius is with Lucius now.'

'It makes no odds to me where he may be,' Torquatus replied coldly. 'I haven't seen him since he left my house in my absence, dashing off to confront Marcus Ampudius. Or he said that was what he was doing.'

'Really?' Fulvus' bloodshot eyes opened wide: Torquatus thought he was genuinely surprised.

'I'd have thought you'd have known that better than me,' Torquatus suggested. 'He can't have been at Formiae all this time? When did he join Lucius Antonius?'

'He stayed in the south for a couple of weeks, I think. No idea what he was doing there. Then he came back to Mevania, and decided to pick on me. Well, it takes a bigger man than Quintus Fiscilius to do that.'

Torquatus wanted to laugh. 'So what did he have against you?' he asked, in a carefully neutral tone.

'He was trying to make me tell lies,' Fulvus said with a virtuous look that taxed Torquatus even more.

'Lies about what?'

'About what happened in Rome, that time when Fiscilia

died.'

All desire to laugh left Torquatus. 'And what did happen? I know Fiscilius used your flat.'

'Oh, you do, do you? He spun me some tale about how she'd gone to try and persuade your - Octavian, then - not to settle troops around our city. Not sure I ever believed that, but he was insistent he must follow her. He went to my flat as soon as he arrived in Rome, but I don't know if he ever found her. It shouldn't have been that hard: they didn't know anyone much in the city. So what was he doing there? I mean, he talks me into lending him my flat, using the services of my slaves, eating my food, and then he just disappears without a word. What sort of a friend is that?'

'Disappearing without a word seems to be a habit of his,' Torquatus agreed. 'But wait a moment. 'When did he ask for the use of your flat? Had he just been to Spoletium?'

Fulvus stared. 'Spoletium? What the hell's Spoletium got to do with it? Of course he didn't. He was going to Rome.'

'He told us that he went first to Spoletium, because Fiscilia had told her aunt she was going to visit friends there. What were the lies he wanted you to tell? And who did he want you to tell them to?'

'Why, you, of course.' Fulvus looked surprised at the question. 'He seemed very worried about what you might ask. He wanted me to tell my slaves to say I'd been with him in Rome, and when I said I wouldn't, he threatened me. Me! A man he's known all his life, a man he wanted as a brother-in-law.'

'So would you tell me, in detail, just what he wanted the slaves to say?'

Fulvus helped himself to more wine, slopping it into the cup so that some splashed onto the table. When a slave came forward to wipe it up, he gestured the man away as if he'd been in his own home. Torquatus said nothing.

'Well, he got to Rome in the evening of the day before the Ides, as you know, with a group of my slaves in a carriage of mine. He couldn't bring the carriage into the city, so he left them outside at some stables, and got a litter.'

'Which gate? Do you remember the name of the stables?'

'The Fontinalis Gate, I suppose; that's the one we always use. And no, I've no idea which stables.' He shrugged. 'I can't see why you want to know.'

'I don't suppose it matters. I expect that's all true, don't you? Go on, anyway. He took a litter to your flat.'

'Yes, and of course there wasn't anything ready for him, he'd set out in such a hurry. Fiscilius got into a temper about that, though what he expected I don't know. Anyway, while the slaves were making beds and buying food and all that he went out, and didn't come back till late. He ordered the slaves to find food for him, they said, just as if it was his place, not mine. The next morning he must have gone out very early and been really quiet, because the slaves said they hadn't heard him.'

'And then?'

'Then nothing. The slaves waited a few days, hanging around doing nothing, but he never came back. So in the end they came home; and I waited for him to come back and explain himself.'

Manlia leant forward into the light. 'I expect you'd told Fiscilius about the shrine, hadn't you?'

'Well, yes, and afterwards, I wondered - ,'

'You wondered?' Torquatus prompted.

'Well, the girl was found in there, and I'd told him about the way they'd kept badgering me for money, and -'

'And no doubt you told him about the manhole cover in the shrine?'

'Gods! How did you know about that? Well, yes, I did tell him how the magistrate had gone on and on and on about the bloody manhole cover. And I began to wonder whether Fiscilius might have - but why should he want to kill his sister? Doesn't make any sense, does it?

Torquatus was watching him keenly, his empty cup forgotten in his hand. 'Go on.'

'When Fiscilius did come home, he wouldn't say anything about where he'd been. Not even to me. Not until he came round and started telling me he wanted me to say we'd been together in Rome, like I said.'

'I see. And are you trying to tell me that you didn't get some reason for this out of him?'

'Of course I asked, but he wouldn't tell me.'

'What does the name Ampudius mean to you?' Torquatus asked, and Fulvus jumped up, dropping his wine cup with a clang. It rolled away noisily under Fulvus' chair. The young man seemed to pull himself together with an effort. 'That was the officer

Fiscilius killed, wasn't it?'

'That's all you know ?'

'What else is there to know? He messed up, lost his temper - again! - killed this guy and got chucked out by old Julius. What's that got to do with this?'

'You didn't know that Fiscilia was in love with his brother?'

Fulvus' face answered his question. It went red, then white with fury. 'That bastard! Another lie! Is that why he was rushing off to Rome, to drag the bitch back and get me married to her to save the family name? So I was to be sacrificed, was I?

'I take it that you wouldn't have been willing to marry Fiscilia if you'd known she had run off to another man?' Manlia asked quietly.

'That's not a question, is it? I don't care how much money she had - no, of course I wouldn't.' Fulvus sat down again.

Torquatus sat very still. His dark, severe face was expressionless.

'And did she have a great deal of money?' he asked quietly.

'She was supposed to be inheriting a lot, yes, when the old woman died.'

'I see. I presume you mean Canidia? And yet she doesn't seem a very rich woman.'

'No. But Fiscilius persuaded me Fiscilia'd be in for a load of money when the old woman goes: he told me she - Canidia, I mean - was married to a very rich man, had plenty of cash salted away. He said once Fiscilia inherited we could all be comfortable together. More of his lies, I wouldn't wonder.'

'Perhaps. Well, this is all very interesting, though I'm not sure why you've come to tell me all this?'

'Why? Because I'm never speaking to Fiscilius again as long as I live. There's nothing for us now in Mevania. I shan't be going back. And nor will he. He's with Lucius Antonius, and the last thing he said to me - well, shouted at me, actually - was that he would get even with me, and you, and everyone. So I'm warning you, Torquatus, when this war's over, to watch your back.'

Torquatus wondered where Fulvus was going. 'You will be watching yours, no doubt?'

'You can bet I will. He's a nasty character, and has killed before. He wouldn't think twice, you know.'

'And you? Where are you going?'

But it seemed that Fulvus had come to the end of his

revelations. He muttered something, stood up, snapped his fingers for his slaves, and hurried off. Torquatus, left alone with Manlia in the soft lamplight, turned over what he'd heard. He was sure now that Fiscilius had got up and fired the three shrines, creeping into the one on the Velia at dawn, killing his sister and escaping via the sewer. But how to prove it?

'He would only kill Fiscilia if he could be sure she would be blamed for the fires,' Torquatus said. 'Canidia's a woman with an old-fashioned sense of duty. With her niece disgraced and dead, who could she leave her money to but her dear nephew, Fiscilius.'

'But how did he know Fiscilia would be there? How did he arrange the meeting.'

'I don't know,' Torquatus replied. 'But I'm pretty sure of one thing. Fiscilius murdered his sister.'

Manlia stood up. 'Things were looking bad for Fiscilia, weren't they? My impression is that Fulvus was to marry her because he was Fiscilius' follower. That precious pair would have treated her like a slave once she'd inherited. Maybe she's better off dead.'

She thought for a moment.

'But where do you think he was going? He didn't want to tell you, that was clear.'

'No. Which means he's probably joining Sextus Pompey in Sicily.'

Chapter 16

At dawn, a group of centurions clattered into his reception hall, and Torquatus was swept up again into his military duties. It was vitally important to get this right after Lepidus' failure. He knew what he had to do, had heard Octavian's question - why didn't you know your gate commander was disloyal? - and set himself to learn the ways and minds of these men the city must rely on. First, he made it clear that no-one but himself was in overall charge: each gate would have its own cohort, answerable to himself, so that no one man could hand the city over. Then he made it clear that Octavian would reward all those soldiers he could depend on to protect the city, over and above what the other men would get. It stuck in his mouth to bribe the men, but that was what it took now, and he did it.

August was at its scorching height and he had still heard nothing from Balbus when the slave he'd sent to Perusia came in with a reply from Cornelia. Torquatus found his heart beating wildly as he tore open the cords that bound the tablets shut. He read, then threw the tablets down with a clatter onto the table.

'That's from Cornelia? What does she say?' Manlia asked.

'Oh, she's well, she's quite happy and comfortable, thanks for asking,' he said bitterly. 'I'm surprised she doesn't tell me what the weather's been like in Perusia. I wonder if Balbus will have anything more interesting to say?'

Days passed, then weeks. In the absence of real information rumours swirled. Agrippa was said to be somewhere on the via Cassia, pursuing Lucius, while Salvidienus Rufus had been held up by a mutiny among his men. September was passing, and at last the days were becoming cooler. The sense of exhaustion which always bore down on Rome in summer lifted and the city came back to a subdued life. The Senate met. Shops reopened. As he walked about the city Torquatus noted how little shock he now felt at the sight of temples crumbling from want of maintenance, with damp stains on their walls and weeds poking from their roofs, to see bakeries shut and locked because there was no corn to buy, to see roads unmended and water leaking from the aqueducts. There were empty houses too. Such a glut of property had come onto the market during the proscriptions, so many families had been ruined or had fled into exile, that some of the appropriated houses had never found a buyer. Nobody ever counted the population of Rome, but Torquatus felt sure that it was smaller than it had been when he was a boy. He found himself smiling to find himself thinking like some old greybeard, then sobered at the thought that when he was born Rome's terrible troubles had in truth been only just beginning.

Though his was a responsible task, Torquatus felt once again that he was missing all the excitement of the war. Then the rumours began to harden into real news: Agrippa, knowing that Salvidienus was not far ahead now, had been unable to catch Lucius as he hurried north-westwards on the via Cassia. As he had suggested to Octavian, he decided to distract his enemy and let it be known that he intended to seize the city of Sutrium, so as to limit Lucius' access to Rome from the north. This was a brilliant move: the main protectors of Sutrium's interests for many years had been the Antonius family, and for any member of the family to fail to go to its aid would be a dreadful admission of weakness. Sutrium was also one of the most important cities of Etruria, and if Lucius let it go without a fight the leading men of other such cities would waver in their allegiance. For a little Lucius pressed on northwards, then changed his mind and hurried back to Sutrium, in a race with Agrippa. Agrippa won, and when Lucius was forced reluctantly to concede Sutrium's loss, and turned northwards again, he discovered that the game had changed. Salvidienus had not stayed at Sentinum after its fall, but was here, now, and he was caught between them. Where were Ventidius and Pollio, who were supposed to be stopping Salvidienus? Lucius struggled on, hoping from day to day that he would hear from them.

All this Torquatus heard as September slowly passed away in a regular succession of mundane tasks. It seemed that the trap was slowly closing on Lucius Antonius. Like Agrippa, he wondered why it was taking Ventidius and Pollio so long to appear. When they did there would surely be a great battle, a battle Lucius' huge forces ought to win. The thought even came into his mind, briefly, that if Octavian, Agrippa and Salvidienus went down to defeat, he himself would be forced to hand Rome over to the conquerors without a fight. There would be nothing for him then but to take his own life. He put the thought away, and instead remembered that Octavian had told him the Antonian commanders in the north were having difficulties of their own. Surely, though, they couldn't resist such a wonderful opportunity to wipe Octavian out, once and for all?

But whatever Ventidius and Pollio chose to do, it was clear that Italy was in turmoil, and his fears for Cornelia grew stronger by the day. Initially he had thought that she would be quite safe in Perusia. Now it seemed to him that there was nowhere as safe for her as her own house in Rome. Besides, he was missing her more and more every day. Had he made that clear to her, in his letter? He wasn't sure he had: he knew he'd been angry with her for running away. Perhaps she had felt his anger but not his love. He would write again. And this time he would get Felix to take it. 'He's growing up. It'll do him good to be given something responsible to do.'

'He'll be delighted,' Manlia agreed. 'He's been longing to see his mother.'

'Yes. I keep forgetting that she's there too.' He walked about the room, unconsciously stopping by his table and straightening the stylus next to the wax tablets. 'I don't think I really made it clear to her that I want her back.'

'You love her, don't you?' Manlia asked.

'I do. I didn't realise, at the beginning - one doesn't think - or I didn't think, anyway - .'

'No. But as time goes on you do know. And then it's dreadful when they aren't there.' Manlia's own eyes were bright with tears. 'But I always thought she loved you too.'

'Did you? I hope you're right.'

Once Felix had gone Torquatus couldn't settle to his tasks. At the back of his mind, behind everything he had to do, was a constant restless anxiety. He couldn't help counting the days since Felix had left, along with a couple of other slaves. Torquatus knew that they would have to travel carefully, even though as far as he knew the armies of Agrippa and Lucius were well to the west of Rome and Ventidius and Pollio still far in the north. Even though the formation of settlements had stopped now war had broken out there were still refugees coming into Rome, and bands of desperate people on the roads.

It was ten days before Felix came back, and Torquatus hardly recognised the boy. He was dusty and tired, of course, but Torquatus had never seen his face so grim. It was the face, not of a child, but of a young man with adult concerns. Torquatus' heart turned over.

'What's happened, Felix?' Torquatus asked, jumping to his feet.

The boy looked at him sadly. 'Fiscilius is there, lord,' he said quietly.

'Fiscilius? What about it?'

'He's living in the house, and the women are prisoners. He doesn't let them go out at all.'

The world seemed to spin around Torquatus' head. 'What? He can't do that: it's Canidia's house. He has no right.'

'That's not how he sees it.'

'And are you saying you never saw the ladies? Oh, I should have gone myself, I knew it.' He saw the boy's hurt face and sighed. 'Tell me what happened, Felix. And give him something to drink, and a chair.'

'We had quite a good journey,' Felix began, when he'd gulped down a cup of watered wine. 'Better than I expected. We rode into Perusia and asked the way to Canidia's house. It took us a little while to find it, but we got there at last. I could see at once, though, that something was wrong. The doorman didn't let us in, but went off to consult somebody else, which seemed odd. I mean, I was the slave of Canidia's guest, bringing a message from her husband. All very ordinary, you'd think.'

Torquatus nodded. 'But you did get in?'

'Oh, yes. He came back and opened the door, but inside were about six enormous men: you know, like Becco and Pulex. And they wouldn't let us see the ladies. They took your letter. I insisted that you wanted me to give it to the mistress in person, but they wouldn't have it. While we were arguing, Fiscilius appeared. That was a shock. Anyway, he said Canidia was ill, and he said - he said that I couldn't see any of them. I could only give him the letter. I'm so sorry.'

Manlia said gently, 'So you didn't get to see your mother either?' and his lip suddenly trembled. He bit it and managed to say, 'No. I haven't seen her.'

'I have to get her away,' Torquatus was saying, striding angrily about the room. 'I can't leave her there with that murderer. I've got perfectly good junior officers here and the city is quiet. I will send to Octavian to tell him I'm going: it wouldn't do to go off without informing him.'

The very next morning, however, as his clients were leaving, a wiry little man appeared before him. He introduced himself as a centurion from one of Agrippa's legions. For a moment the two men looked each other over, the tough, weather-beaten soldier and the tall, thoughtful-looking officer.

'You have orders for me? Information?' Torquatus asked.

'Yes, orders, sir. Your forces are to move at once. It's all in here.' He held out a set of tablets, on whose seal Torquatus recognised the sphinx of Octavian. He took it, but said quickly, 'Move? Where to?'

'Perusia. Haven't you heard?'

Torquatus felt as if the air was darkening around him. His mouth was dry. He swallowed hard.

'No. I've heard nothing.'

The soldier was beaming. 'It's as neat an ambush as you'd hope to see, sir. Lucius was trying to go north up the Cassia.'

Torquatus nodded impatiently.

'Well, he's no fool, and he realised that between Agrippa and Salvidienus he was making no progress. And you know, sir, how bad it is for morale when the enemy are picking away at you continually, and you can't do anything about it?' Torquatus' dark face was full of impatience and he hurried on. 'So Lucius turned aside, you see.'

'Towards Perusia.' Torquatus said the words slowly.

'He was near Clusium. That's the best place to cut across country to the Flaminia, which I suppose is what he was trying to do, but the forces against him were just too strong. So he ended up cutting and running for Perusia and now Octavian wants all his forces concentrated there. If Lucius is up for it we'll have a battle on the plain, which will maybe settle things. Or it'll be a big siege, if Lucius shuts himself up in the city; perhaps almost as big as Julius' great siege of Alesia.'

The man was beaming, obviously delighted to be taking part in such a grand operation. 'I was at Alesia,' he said. 'That was really something.'

Torquatus turned his attention to the tablets. He was pleased to see that his hand wasn't shaking. The letter told him nothing the messenger hadn't said already: he was to leave no troops in the city but to bring his men to Perusia as soon as possible. There were no longer any troops threatening Rome, so it would be quite safe to leave it unguarded.

Torquatus heard himself asking sensible questions, providing reassuring answers. The soldier went away and Torquatus was left to deal with his own thoughts. Trofimus was standing beside him and they looked at each other in horrified silence.

'I have to get her out,' Torquatus said. 'I've sent that man off with a private note to Octavian asking him to offer any help he can. Of course I don't know what the situation is. From what that said, Lucius settled his troops into camps outside the city at first: maybe he's still outside? Maybe the Senate of Perusia don't want him, won't let him in?'

Trofimus said nothing.

'Well, there's nothing I can do tonight, apart from sending word to the men to be ready to march at first light tomorrow. Where's my sister?'

Torquatus bathed and ate and gave orders, hardly aware of what he was doing, overwhelmed by horror at the thought of Cornelia shut up in a besieged city. He'd taken part in enough sieges himself to know what would happen if he couldn't get them out. The city would run out of food, of course, but even before that happened, it would be rationed. Soldiers first, then the civilians they needed, then the rest. Enemy women might be overlooked, if they were lucky: at worst they'd be put under guard and - . His mind spun away into the darkest of dark imaginings. Felix waited on him, red-eyed and silent, as he ate his solitary dinner. Torquatus remembered that his mother was in Perusia too, and wished he could say something to cheer the boy, but there was nothing he could think of.

He sat long after his meal, the wine-jug on the table before him, thinking about Balbus. The man had been right to object to his daughter's marriage to a politically active man like him. He had thought she would come to harm, and he had been right. He hadn't trusted Torquatus to keep her safe, and he had been right. Balbus hadn't spoken to him once since that night when he'd tried to steal her away, hadn't even replied to his letter. Ought he to tell him what had happened? His pride said no. And yet, Balbus knew everyone, and everyone owed him something. His face darkened. The Antonii might be the one exception: he knew for a fact that Marcus Antonius had fallen out with Balbus when he chose to support Octavian. But it was possible that Lucius might still be on terms with him. Was he adding to his wife's danger by refusing to ask for her father's help? His mind went round and round, and at last he stopped it, with an effort. He would decide in the morning.

'We'll have to get them out, won't we?' he said to Felix as

the boy helped him get ready for bed without any of his usual chatter.

'How can we do that?' Felix's voice was dull, disbelieving.

'Well, we don't even know that there'll be a siege. There may just be a great battle, if Perusia shuts itself up and won't allow either army in. The two armies, fighting it out on the plain. But even if there is a siege, you've seen yourself how long it takes to build walls. So you see, the city might not be completely closed straight away. That centurion was looking forward to a siege like Alesia. And if that's what happens it'll take a long time, because it will mean double walls.'

'What are double walls?' Felix was interested in spite of himself.

'One ring facing inwards to keep Lucius and his army inside, and around that another ring facing outwards to keep Ventidius and Pollio out.'

'And I suppose the ladies may not even be there: if they realised that danger was coming it wouldn't take them long to get out, would it?' Felix absently took the towel his master had finished with, and stood twisting it in his hands.

'No, you're right. We may get to the camp and find them there, safe and sound.'

Torquatus didn't tell Felix that the very first thing Cornelia would have done, if she'd escaped from the city before it was shut, would have been to send a message that she was safe. Then he reflected bitterly that perhaps she had, and that the message had gone to Balbus and not to him.

He was glad to get up in the morning, glad to have work to do. During his sleepless hours, he'd decided what to do. Whatever the cost to his pride, he'd enlist Balbus' help if he could get it. He thought Balbus' love for his daughter was the one true emotion in the man. He'd write to Neapolis again. And after all, what he had told Felix wasn't a lie. His wife was an intelligent and resourceful woman, and might well have fled Perusia when trouble threatened. He had no more time to think: he was on the Campus, giving orders, watching the men march off in the growing heat. Clouds of dust rose behind them, as he saw when he rode back down the line checking that all was well. Felix, trotting along beside him on Firefly, couldn't help being excited at the prospect of his first battle. If only it was a battle, and not a siege, Torquatus thought, he would vow a great bull to Jupiter.

When they arrived at Perusia Felix could hardly take in what he was seeing. He had thought the siege-walls they had been building at Sentinum were large. Now he could see that they were like a child's toy fort compared to what was going up here. Perusia itself impressed him greatly, and he couldn't imagine how it could ever be captured. A splendid stronghold, it sits on a great hill with strong city walls, its lands spread out on the plain below. And now the circuit of stone walls above was mirrored by a chain of banks and walls that were rising on the plain, slung like a necklace around the ancient city. Inside these rising fortifications the plain was busy with thousands of soldiers hurrying this way and that, ordered, purposeful; ox-carts laden with wood or stone or the parts for artillery-engines moved slowly through the dust-laden air; the military camps already had a settled look, and the stink which Felix had come to know well: a compound of stew, shit, sweat, leather and horses. Slowly the city was being cut off from all that sustained its life. He realised suddenly that his master had ridden on, and Catus with him. He kicked his pony into a trot, hurrying after them.

As for Torquatus, he'd seen those rising fortifications with far stronger emotions. There was no enemy army to be seen: Lucius had gone into the city. There would be no pitched battle. Instead, there would be a siege, and unless he could get Cornelia out before the trap was shut, she would stay there until Perusia fell.

At the moment when Torquatus was talking to Agrippa's centurion in his reception hall in Rome, Cornelia was looking thoughtfully out of a high window in Perusia. In the room with her was Nereis, but the two were not talking because there was also a sullen-faced, pigeon-toed slave of Fiscilius' standing just inside the door.

When they had first arrived, Cornelia had been happier than she had felt for a while. She hadn't realised how anxious she had felt over the past few weeks. Not that coming to Perusia had changed anything, of course, but at least, if Torquatus or her father intended to turn her life upside down, she would find out in a more private place. She was glad Manlia hadn't accompanied them. She realised this with a pang, because she had come to love and value Manlia. But she knew how close Torquatus and his sister were, and she was thankful to be able to stop pretending, not to have to evade confidences she'd have loved to make.

It wasn't only Manlia and Torquatus she was happy to leave behind. Her father was going to be a problem, too. Because the truth was that she was now definitely pregnant. There were no dodgy mussels involved this time. Her heart ached: how she would love to be able to tell Aulus about it, how she longed to see his face lighten in that smile she loved, how she would love to direct the household in its preparations for the child that was to come. It ought to be such good news. And for a while Canidia, who had guessed what was happening, had made her feel that this was something joyful. It had been wonderful to bathe in the warmth and support of Nereis and Canidia: her eyes prickled at the recollection of the comfort she had taken from them. But all too soon reality reasserted itself: of course her pregnancy was just the opposite of joyful. She would probably end up losing both her child and her husband, she thought bleakly. It was just as she was forcing herself to face this truth that she had received Torquatus' letter. She had read it twice, the first time with a scarcely-recognised sense of disappointment, the second with anger. She could hardly tell whether he was really missing her: it seemed to her that his most dominant emotion was humiliation. She had gone off without consulting him, and her father threatened to end his marriage. There was no word of love.

She turned away from the window impatiently. The room they were in was not large. Its walls were washed with a faded yellow, and it was furnished only with a small table and two stools and an old unlighted brazier. She thought the only reason the window was left unshuttered was that the drop from it to the ground was too dangerous to attempt, and that Fiscilius was so confident of his grip on the house that he knew any attempt to call for help would fail.

'Tell your master,' she said to the slave, 'that if he is to keep us shut up in this room we shall need something to do. Perhaps we could choose some books from the collection downstairs?'

'I'll have to ask about that,' the slave said reluctantly.

'Obviously,' Cornelia snapped. The man still stood there, looking thoroughly bad-tempered. 'Go on, then,' she told him.

'I can't leave you alone, lady,' he said.

Cornelia and Nereis looked at each other. 'We can't even have a conversation without that man reporting what we say to Fiscilius,' Cornelia said bitterly.

'No,' Nereis agreed. 'Perhaps, if the slave came too, we

could walk in that pretty garden, where we used to sit when we first came.'

'The master said you were to stay in here,' the slave insisted and Cornelia turned back to the window. There was no escape that way. But escape they must, somehow.

Their problems had begun with Fiscilius' arrival, about twelve nights ago, when all the ladies were in bed and asleep. She had been jolted awake by the sounds of doors banging and voices talking, and heavy feet on the stairs. She had thought one of the voices was familiar, and in the morning she had found Fiscilius, very displeased that the house was full, as he put it, of unwanted women.

'These ladies are my guests, Quintus,' Canidia told him with quiet dignity.

'I can see that. But why? I can't see what you need guests for.'

'This is my house, you know. And I can invite my friends to it if I wish.'

Canidia spoke lightly, trying to smile, but they all knew that Fiscilius was very unlikely to accept her mild rebuke.

He helped himself to a thick slice of bread and dribbled honey onto it. 'I just wish you chose your friends with a bit more regard to me,' he said angrily. I'd have thought the Balbus family never ought to be invited. And as for Nereis, she was married to Faberius. Fine friends!'

Cornelia opened her mouth to ask him to explain, but Canidia was before her.

'I am not a member of the Fiscilius family,' she said sharply. There was a little colour in her pale cheeks, and she was sitting up very straight. It was clear that she was seriously annoyed. 'Not that the Fiscilius family have always recognised that. And now I think we all have things to do.' She got up and left the room with Cornelia and Nereis. The women separated: Cornelia and her maid went out to do a little shopping, Nereis sat down to write a letter to her steward and Canidia summoned the cook to discuss what would be needed now the household included Fiscilius and three of his slaves.

And that was the last time Cornelia had seen Canidia. When she and Rachel came home, Fiscilius was waiting for her with two burly slaves. They marched her upstairs, her bag still in her hand, and into the little room where Nereis already sat. Rachel had struggled to go with her mistress, but the men had forced her away: Cornelia didn't even know if she was in the house. The sulky slave guarded them the whole time. Even when they went to the other room they were allowed to use at night, the slaves stood in the doorway while they slept. And when Pigeon-Toes was tired, one of Fiscilius' heavies took over.

Ever since then, Cornelia hadn't thought once about the problem of her pregnancy, but only how they might escape. She wondered where Canidia was. She couldn't even communicate with Nereis at first, although after the first couple of day she discovered that the guards, bored and sullen, paid little attention when she appeared to be reading the book she had brought up in her bag. This was why she had asked to be allowed to choose books from downstairs.

Fiscilius came to see them that evening, and she made the request again. 'I don't know why you're holding us like this,' she said. 'But if we are to be prisoners I don't see why we shouldn't be comfortable at least. Let us have some books, please.'

Fiscilius scowled at her. 'Why should I do anything for you?' He pulled at his lip. 'But I suppose, if it keeps you quiet - ,' he shrugged.

'Good. I'll go down to the study straight away. Your slave can make himself useful carrying the books.'

'I'll stay here with this other one,' Fiscilius nodded, and the slave followed Cornelia down the stairs.

She was lucky enough to find Epictetus in the book-room, looking through some papers. Cornelia was able to tell him they were being allowed some books before the slave gestured for him to leave, and as he went he pushed a book towards Cornelia, saying, 'That's one of the mistress' favourite stories. Maybe you'd like it too.'

The slave picked up the roll suspiciously, shook it loose, gazed at it as if the writing might be some sort of magic, and rolled it up again clumsily. Cornelia took it from him and selected several others, before dumping them all in his arms and setting off up the stairs again.

The following day she read a great deal, and with a little gesture encouraged Nereis to pore over her book too. The slave's look of boredom grew intense. Turning away from him slightly as if to catch the failing afternoon light, Cornelia gently tore a tiny piece off the book-roll. It was quite an old one, the papyrus soft and thin, and to her relief it didn't make a noise. She sat with it in her lap, longing to fish one of the pieces of old charcoal out of the brazier. But how could she, when the man was standing there, looking bored and unsuspicious, but wide awake. Nereis caught her eye.

'I need to relieve myself,' she said to the guard. He looked a little awkward.

'Aren't there any pots in there?' he asked, and Nereis shook her head. The guard looked at then both suspiciously.

Oh, please do hurry up,' Nereis insisted, and the man stuck his head out into the passageway for a moment, calling to the slave who was outside to bring a pot. Quick as a flash Cornelia reached for a piece of charcoal, and wrote We must escape on her little piece of papyrus. She put her hand over it and the charcoal on her lap because now the man had turned back to the room and was eyeing them warily again.

When the man came with the pot, Nereis made a fuss about the men watching her, distracting them for long enough for Cornelia to hide the charcoal in her clothes. As Nereis sat down again she passed her the little note, and saw Nereis read it and give a tiny nod.

Cornelia was triumphant for a moment, before reflecting that passing a scrap of paper in front of their guard was nothing to what she'd need to do to get them out. Still, Nereis seemed just as keen as she was herself to get away. She spent the rest of the day pretending to read and trying to make a plan of escape. In the evening she demanded to be allowed more books, and since Fiscilius had agreed yesterday, the slave took her downstairs, leaving his colleague to guard Nereis. By that time she'd managed to use the charcoal to write a message to Canidia in the book-roll which Epictetus had told him was her favourite, and she left that one lying on the table when she picked some others to take upstairs. She looked around to see if there was any communication from him. There wasn't, but one roll had been left sticking out a little from the row, so she made sure she took that one.

Sure enough, when she got upstairs and found an opportunity to open it she found that something had been added to the very end of the text: a note from Epictetus, saying that Canidia wasn't well. She wanted them to escape if they could, apologised for having put them in danger. She herself wasn't well enough to go anywhere.

The next day was one of mounting frustration. The guards seemed to have been warned against slackness and were watching the ladies with renewed suspicion. Cornelia spent a good deal of the day at the window, despairing at their situation. She could see the steep, narrow street, quiet enough most of the time, and the entrance gate. Inside that, in a paved courtyard in front of the house was a large old fig-tree. As dusk fell she thought she saw someone move behind it, and looked more carefully. For a moment there was nothing. Then came another movement. She couldn't be sure whether the man was in the courtyard or the street. Two other men came whistling up the street side by side. Another man was coming down. Each of them seemed to turn aside into some shady corner or doorway.

And then the door banged. Cornelia saw Fiscilius come out. he looked around almost furtively, and she wondered if he were signalling in some way to the men she'd seen in the shadows. Or perhaps he feared them? Whatever his feelings, after a moment's hesitation he set off up the street. Cornelia noticed, with a pang of alarm, that he was fully armed, but before she had time to think too much about what this might mean she saw one of the men outside detach himself from the shadow of a doorway and quietly cross the street towards the house. He joined the man she could half-see under the tree. Another man came sauntering casually down the street and slipped in beside them. As she watched all the men converged silently on the house.

Torquatus was with Octavian in his command tent, the general perched on a camp stool and surrounded by piles of wax tablets, notes, book rolls and writing materials, Torquatus standing before him. 'Why ever did you send her to Perusia?' Octavian asked. He was looking wonderfully relaxed, Torquatus thought.

'I didn't. She just decided to come here.' Torquatus tried not to sound bitter. 'They went while I was away at Sentinum.' He remembered that he'd thought at the time that she'd be quite safe in Perusia, and admitted as much. 'Who'd have thought the war would end here?'

'Who's to say it will end?' Octavian asked sharply. 'It may, if we are lucky and clever.'

'Do you think there's any chance Lucius might negotiate?' Torquatus said. It was all he could think of, and must be worth a try.

Octavian looked thoughtful, and Torquatus saw with relief that he was giving the question serious consideration. Octavian was a negotiator by nature, he knew, rather than a fighter. Or rather, he hated wasting money on wars when there was so much else that needed doing.

'I take it you're proposing to offer yourself as negotiator? At best, you'd relieve us of this siege, and even if that didn't work, Lucius might be prepared to let your wife go, as a personal favour. Is that it?'

'That's what I thought,' Torquatus agreed. 'I think he'd have to respect me as a close ally of yours. We'd have to give him safe passage, of course. Is Fulvia in there too?'

Octavian nodded. 'She is, and the Perusines are welcome to her. But don't imagine she'll have any pity on your women. She's not good at pity.' He sighed. 'I'd have to give her safe passage too, much as I hate the idea. Maybe I could make it conditional on her going back to her husband.' He laughed. 'Let Marcus Antonius have the pleasure of trying to keep her in order.'

'But if we could get rid of Lucius - ?'

Octavian frowned. 'Yes, That's the nub of it. I'm not interested in a deal unless it gets him out of my hair for good - or for a long time, anyway.' He turned suddenly to the soldiers guarding the doorway. 'Ask Maecenas to come here, would you?'

'Maecenas is here?' Torquatus was surprised: Maecenas was not in the least a military man. On second thoughts he was cheered, as his presence suggested Octavian had always intended to settle peacefully if he could.

When Maecenas bustled in, in armour like everyone else, he pursed his lips over Torquatus' suggestion.

'What exactly will these talks be about?' he asked sharply

'Peace,' Octavian told him with a straight face.

'Very nice too.' He rubbed his nose thoughtfully. 'With all due respect to Torquatus, if we want peace with Lucius we mustn't even mention Cornelia. No, Torquatus, listen. If we get a negotiated peace, your wife will be free to leave anyway, won't she? But if Lucius begins to think that by letting her go he might get a better deal he'll be harder to pin down.'

'What do we offer him?' Octavian said.

Maecenas' plump face creased in a sudden smile. His small black eyes were very bright. 'Oh, I think you've already decided, haven't you?'

Octavian was smiling as well now. 'Spain? Well, Salvidienus never actually made it there, did he, and I'm sure we can find a plum for him somewhere else.'

'Yes.' Maecenas was almost purring. 'We write to Marcus Antonius, telling him - quite truly - that Lucius' military abilities were desperately needed in Spain, if we weren't to lose it to Sextus Pompeius. That's true enough: if Sextus gets to control Spain as well as Sicily there's no end to the harm he could do us. We really needn't say much about what a little shit his brother's been. I'm sure he knows it anyway. As consul Lucius would have been going off to run a province in a few months anyway, so all we're doing is offering him a handsome province, and an early start.'

'Handsome? The Spanish are the most quarrelsome, difficult - !'

'A post where his exceptional talents were genuinely needed, then.' Maecenas waved a hand airily, and the two men laughed. Maecenas sobered first. 'And what we get from him is that he publicly disowns Fulvia and all her works, and that he lets us send her off to join Antonius in the east. Shouldn't be hard to persuade him: he's been having to listen to her for months, and she's put on armour and gone recruiting in Campania now, just as if she were a man. No-one likes that. No, I don't think big brother could object to that, do you?' He turned to Torquatus, suddenly serious. 'Even then, I doubt - however, if you want to try, we've nothing to lose.'

'What if he's not satisfied with Spain?' Torquatus asked.

Octavian and Maecenas looked at each other. 'We could take Africa off Lepidus?' Maecenas suggested.

'Well, Lepidus hasn't done anything to deserve kindness from me,' Octavian said briskly. 'And Marcus Antonius won't object. We can take it if we need to. Besides, there are already two Roman commanders in Africa, fighting over it. He's welcome to it. What do you want, Torquatus? A military escort, I suppose. Anything else?'

'No.' Torquatus was light-headed with relief and excitement. 'I'll play it like this: first, we're all wasting money fighting each other: second, Fulvia's a pain to everyone: third, Sextus Pompey is sitting in Sicily, diverting Rome's grain ships to feed his own troops, which makes him a pain too, and we'd be better off fighting him than each other: fourth, none of our men want to fight other Italians. Final triumphant conclusion: Octavian and Marcus Antonius are colleagues and partners, not enemies.

The sooner we can get the men settled the sooner all our unfortunate citizens can start to get their lives back, and begin to feel grateful to Octavian and Antonius for bringing peace at last. How does that sound?'

'Grand,' Octavian said, smiling. Then he became serious. 'But I don't hold out much hope. If Lucius had wanted peace he could easily have had it long ago.'

The following afternoon Torquatus was riding Bucephalus up the steep and winding road towards the massive Etruscan arch of the main gateway to the city. A thunderstorm had lowered the temperature, and the plain was a mess of mud, puddles, piles of tools and materials behind them. Not that the soldiers seemed to care: they didn't mind digging, took pleasure in the wicked stakes they were embedding in the trenches to impale enemy soldiers and horses if they should attempt to come out and fight, and were looking forward to victory. But Torquatus, leaving them behind, was thinking of the city. He'd been awake half the night planning his speech, trying to make it an offer Lucius couldn't refuse. He'd been hoping the Perusine Senate might already be regretting giving succour to Lucius, but maybe it was too soon for that. On the other hand the city's predicament was dire. It wouldn't have been expecting a siege, wouldn't have laid in supplies or encouraged citizens who could do so to leave the city. Even if the Senate was regretting its decision - especially if it was - he felt sure Lucius would do everything he could to prevent him from finding out. And although he had asked to address the Senate, he had no idea whether he might in fact only meet Lucius in private, which would offer quite different challenges.

The guards at the gate had seen them coming, and heads were beginning to appear above the ramparts. They were expected, of course. Torquatus, wearing a toga to show his peaceful intentions, followed a herald and looked calmer than he felt. Felix trotted behind him as usual, and at the rear a small group of splendidly equipped soldiers showed that Torquatus was not unprotected. Coming close under the tall gate, the herald blew his trumpet and called out: 'Aulus Manlius Torquatus has come to speak with Lucius Antonius, in the name of Caesar Octavian.' There was a brief silence. More and more heads were appearing along the walls, Felix could see. They seemed to wait for ages, with Bucephalus tossing his head impatiently, made skittish by the breeze. At last there was movement. The guards huddled, heads on the ramparts turned, a buzz of talk floated down to the waiting envoy. Then the centurion came forward and saluted smartly. 'I'm to tell you, sir, that I can admit you, but your soldiers must remain at the gate.'

Torquatus had not expected to be allowed to ride in with an armed guard, and he nodded his agreement. The centurion saluted again and stepped back, signing to a couple of his men to escort the visitors. At first they came to take his horse's reins and lead him, but Torquatus wouldn't allow this: he would look too much like a little child on a leading-rein, he thought, and he ordered the men simply to walk in front, nodding to Felix and Catus to follow him. His hopes rose a little as they climbed through the city's narrow, winding streets; perhaps there was some hope for this desperate venture after all. There were soldiers everywhere: there must be camps on every patch of open ground, but with such a huge number of men to accommodate, many must be billeted on Perusine families, and Torquatus knew all too well how quickly relationships between soldier and civilian soured when that became necessary. The thought gave him a glimmer of hope.

Some of the streets consisted simply of wide, shallow steps, dark between tall buildings, where the wind funnelled down. Many windows were shuttered but some were not, and Felix kept close to his master, aware of the faces looking down; curious, silent, hostile. The faces of those in the streets were carefully neutral. At last, after riding silently up street after street, the little party emerged into the grey autumn light of a forum. They were in front of what was obviously the Senate-house, filling one side of the square. No buildings faced it: instead the square was open to an extraordinary view of rolling fields golden with stubble, neat lines of olive trees, their silvery leaves restless in the breeze, miles of dark woodland, and behind all this, blue hills floating against the sky.

Felix turned his eyes away from this view to take in the temples to the city's two patron deities Vulcan and Juno, one on each side of the square. The temple to Vulcan was just like those at home. But Juno's temple, perched on the very edge of the cliff, looked odd to him. Its roof was shallow and came down low over the walls, giving deep eaves below. And on the roof was the most astonishing array of statues, arranged along the roof-ridge and up the slopes of the front and rear edges. Felix realised that he was being left behind and scrambled down from his pony to follow his master into the Senate-house, leaving Catus outside holding both horses.

As he walked into the building Torquatus was thinking about the implications of his negotiation with Lucius taking place in front of the Senate. He would have to turn the presence of the senators to his advantage. They would put pressure on Lucius, if an honourable settlement were on offer. They could hardly want their city to be subjected to the horrors of a siege, after all. He tried to keep out of his mind the thought that the Senate would have no interest in the fate of Torquatus' wife, should Lucius refuse to make peace. And if the worst came to the worst, it would be harder to make an emotional appeal to Lucius in front of hard-bitten city elders, but he would do it if he had to.

The hall was filling rapidly, and Torquatus guessed that news of his embassy had flown around the city. As he watched the senators hurrying to their seats, some still twitching the folds of their togas into position, his hopes rose. He looked round for Lucius Antonius among the white-robed men, then realised with a shock that he was at the far end of the long room, and not in a toga. He was a big, untidy-looking man dressed in full armour and conveying the impression that the comings and goings of the Perusine senators were of no great interest to him. He seemed to be deep in conversation with a knot of his officers also dressed in armour. The message was clear enough: whoever was ready to negotiate, Lucius Antonius was not.

Then Lucius stepped forward into the light, accompanied by two others. It took Torquatus a second glance to realise that one was the redoubtable Fulvia, Antonius' wife and Octavian's bitterest enemy, dressed in full armour and looking implacable. On Lucius' other side was Fiscilius. His heart sank. Here was a man who had probably murdered his own sister, sharing a house with Cornelia. His own powerlessness made him want to scream. He took a couple of deep breaths, and tried to stop his heart from pounding in his breast. He must treat this occasion just as if he were pleading a case in court, something he'd done many times. He'd never lost a case, he reminded himself.

The senators fell silent. An elderly, rather stooped man was on his feet, welcoming Torquatus to the city as its chief magistrate. His smile had genuine warmth. 'You are surprised at my greeting,' he commented. 'But although we have never met, I knew your brother Lucius. He was a good man, and a friend: I attended his wedding - you were only a little boy then, of course - and remember very well the verses which the poet Catullus wrote for the occasion. Catullus wished, as was proper to the occasion, that the children of your brother's marriage should resemble their father both in looks and in eloquence. And I am sure that you too will have your family's gift of persuasive speech and sound counsel, just as you have your father's looks.' And with a smile he sat down on one of the two stools set on a podium above the other senators.

Torquatus had got his balance back. He mustn't hurry. He took a deep breath, and looked carefully around the chamber, noting which men looked hopeful, which sceptical or hostile. He would see if he could win over the Senate first: they might then lean on Lucius to do a deal.

'Thank you for that gracious welcome: the proper greeting from one senator to another, and an auspicious sign, I hope, that we can come to an agreement and our two cities can be at peace. Rome has never sought a war with Perusia; indeed, she recognises Perusia's pre-eminent position among the cities of Etruria. I am here today because Caesar feels - and who could disagree with him? - that the position we're in is harmful to us all. Caesar finds himself obliged to waste time and money and men's lives and health on a siege which may last through winter and beyond. His position is a strong one: he has sufficient troops, control of the supply-route from Rome, and the whole-hearted support of his generals. If the siege is not lifted, a winter of hardship lies ahead of you, surely not what you want for your wives and children, your businesses, your households.' He looked around, saw the thoughtful faces and moved on. 'But this is not what Caesar wants either, not what he's ever wanted. And so he is offering a settlement which would allow us all to compromise without any talk of defeat or victory.'

He sensed the relief in the hall, could see senators glancing at each other. It looked to him as though the Senate hadn't welcomed Lucius in, rather they'd bowed to force majeure, not having sufficient soldiers in the city to keep him out. Then Lucius Antonius, who had been leaning against a pillar at the back of the hall, stepped forward. 'You mean one that would leave Octavian still stealing Italian land, still suborning the legions allocated to me, as consul's legions?'

Torquatus snapped back, 'And aren't your brother's soldiers being settled on that land, as much as Caesar's? Ask him how happy he will be if they don't get that land.'

Some of the senators nodded agreement, and Torquatus offered up thanks to whatever god it was that had spared Perusia any land confiscations. 'Your city is overflowing with soldiers: I could see that for myself as I rode here,' he went on quickly. 'If they are fed, who will go hungry?'

'No one in Perusia,' Lucius said loudly. 'My brother's legions, led by Ventidius and Pollio - eleven legions, I would remind you - will be here very soon. They are full of seasoned soldiers, and led by men with good military records, unlike the boy-general and his baby tribunes opposing us. And the very day they arrive this siege will be broken.'

'You say they will be here soon. How soon? The fact is that they could have been here a long time ago. And where are they, Lucius Antonius? Hanging back in Gaul, their generals bickering over precedence, if what I hear is true.' There was some smothered laughter at this. 'And your brother's never been a great letter-writer, has he? Too many parties, too much drinking and whoring. So his generals don't even know what it is he wants them to do. That's what I've heard.'

Lucius swung round, glaring at the senators. 'They'll be here soon enough. And then we'll fight that pretty boy, and we'll win. Have you forgotten who really won at Philippi? My brother, Marcus Antonius, while your Octavian lay sick in his tent, or hid in the marshes, depending on who you believe. My brother's restoring order to our eastern provinces, and when he's finished there he'll be back. Do you want to have to explain to him why you refused to help his brother?'

Torquatus allowed his face to register surprise. 'But aren't Octavian and Marcus Antonius colleagues? They agreed after Philippi that Antonius would control the east and Caesar the west, where he would settle veterans on the land they'd been promised. Not just soldiers from his own legions, but Marcus Antonius' too. Which is exactly what he's doing. If anyone's breaking the agreement it's you.'

He looked around carefully. 'The land settlement was never going to be easy. But tell me this: is it better to have the men settled and beginning to farm, or to leave discharged soldiers wandering the land, armed and angry, and ready to help themselves to anything they fancy?' Torquatus paused and looked around.

'But I haven't even told you yet how Caesar plans to resolve this unnecessary conflict.'

He could see the interest on the faces of the senators. His heart was pounding, but he forced himself into an appearance of calmness. 'His offer is this: first, the city remains untouched. No soldiers will be allowed to enter it, and the Senate will continue to govern. I want to stress that: no-one will be punished. Whereas you know very well how a city that has held out against a siege is treated: the soldiers expect to be let loose, and will do whatever they want with you and yours.'

That registered with the senators. He could see them giving each other sidelong glances. Unfortunately, so did Lucius.

'If you win,' Lucius reminded him with a sneer.

Torquatus turned again to the senators. 'As to Lucius Antonius, he will become governor of Spain, with command of six legions, and - ,'

He got no further. Lucius left his companions and came up to Torquatus. 'Spain!' He almost spat the word at Torquatus. 'A nest of vipers, not a province. And I'd want more than six legions, if I went there, which I shan't. Oh, and I can assure you that you're wrong about Ventidius and Pollio: they'll be here very soon to drive away that stupid boy playing at sieges out there.' He swung round. 'We have nothing to discuss. The Senate is dismissed.'

The mild-looking gentleman rose to his feet.

'With all due respect to you, Lucius Antonius, it isn't for you to dismiss the Senate of Perusia, of which you are not a member. Instead, I call on - ,'

'The Senate is dismissed.' Lucius was shouting now. 'Or do you want me to summon the soldiers to turn you out?' He looked round belligerently. For a moment there was silence, as man after man dropped his eyes before that angry glare. Then one or two at a time began to stand, twitch their togas straight and walk out with what dignity they could muster. Torquatus, seeing his opportunity going, shouted, 'Wait!' But the senators gave him no more than apologetic glances before filing out in silence. Lucius folded his arms, a contemptuous smile on his lips, and watched them go. When the chamber was empty, he made to follow them, but Torquatus blocked his path. 'Wait,' he said again.

'Well, what?'

'I've something else to ask you.' Torquatus was cursing inwardly. Having to ask a favour under these circumstances wasn't at all what he wanted, but it seemed to be the only chance he had. Lucius said nothing but stood silent, arms still folded across his chest. Torquatus took a deep breath.

'My wife is at present in the city,' he began.

'I know she is.' Lucius was smiling and Torquatus' heart sank.

'I suppose Fiscilius told you? But she can't be of any value to you. Just an useless extra mouth to feed.'

Lucius was smiling, but his eyes were cold. 'I might need to drive a bargain, you never know. And she'd come in handy, perhaps.'

'But having to feed - ?'

'My dear Torquatus, if food supplies run low, none of the 'useless extra mouths', as you so rightly call them, can expect to be fed. You can carry that back to your little Caesar. Maybe it'll make him that bit readier to come to terms.' His smile broadened. 'My terms, that is.'

'And those are?'

'He withdraws. He hands over those six legions of Salvidienus Rufus. And he concentrates his attentions entirely on settling the soldiers: no doubt when he's done that my brother will have more orders for him.'

Lucius' tone was light, contemptuous, and Torquatus could feel a flush of anger and shame rising on his face. He turned away, and Lucius followed him out.

'If you've nothing more to say, I'll see you out of the city.'

The big square was empty now, apart from the waiting soldiers, and their boots echoed on the paving. In silence, the two men mounted and turned their horses back down towards the gate, followed by a well-armed escort. There were still people in the streets, but apart from the soldiers, everyone Torquatus saw was keeping his head down, walking quickly, avoiding the knots of military that gathered everywhere. Lucius looked about him continually with sharp, suspicious eyes. But as they descended one of the winding streets, Lucius suddenly touched Torquatus on the arm. He pointed to a handsome old house set back from the street behind a courtyard, with a fig tree sprawling over its wall. 'That's where your wife is, he said with a smile. 'The lady Canidia's house.'

Felix could hardly bear to look at it. His mother was in there. How could he get her out?

Torquatus stared at it miserably and rode on. There was nothing else he could do.

Chapter 17

Torquatus had never known such despair. His mind dark with horror he would gaze across the plain to the great city walls morning and evening, thinking of Cornelia trapped and threatened. Every night he lay awake, his mind scrabbling after desperate half-formed plans for her rescue. And in the morning, each plan would be looked at and discarded. But there must be, there had to be, some way of crossing that short distance, and bringing her out. Time was short. The walls were rising fast, along with all their elaborations: towers and fences, banks and ditches, lookout posts and embrasures with catapults large and small. Groups were digging complex trenches on the plain, too, and filling the bottoms of them with sharpened stakes and blades, to slow down any attacks from the city. The gates of Perusia were open but soldiers clustered tight round them, while gangs of slaves brought out materials which would block the roads leading up to them. Every day there were sorties, tight-knit groups of Lucius' soldiers running out of the city and attempting to drive Octavian's soldiers back to their walls. Or groups of Octavian's men would approach the city to harass the slaves and soldiers carrying their loads of wood and stone down onto the access roads Once all the traps, walls, ditches and embankments were made even such slender opportunities as still opened themselves would shut down, like the city, and then the suffering would begin.

With every passing day the situation he was dreading came nearer: the walls rose higher, the pits were filled with impaling stakes, the catapults sat in their places. Torquatus was ridiculously relieved when Octavian decreed that the walls encircling Perusia were not long enough: he wanted flanking sections built right down to the river so that no supplies could be brought to the city by water. Yet more fucking digging, the new recruits complained. The veterans laughed at them. Digging was what the army was all about, they said. If you'd been with old Julius, you'd have seen real digging! But while Octavian's men went on building, Lucius' men went on trying to stop them. Clashes happened perpetually, delaying the moment when the gates of the city would shut, and no-one would leave until either Octavian and his army were defeated, or the city surrendered. Treachery, Torquatus thought wearily; it was so often treachery that brought sieges to an end. If only he knew someone in the city who might agree to open the gates in return for leniency. But he didn't. His mind went round and round, uselessly turning over options which the day before he'd dismissed as impractical. He had nothing he could offer Lucius in exchange for the women. He knew no-one in Perusia whom he might employ as a go-between. Lucius had made it quite clear what he thought of diplomacy.

He had to do something. But what? The thought of his beloved Cornelia trapped in a city under siege was horror enough: the knowledge that her fate would depend on the goodwill of Lucius, Fulvia and Fiscilius was material for nightmares such as he hadn't experienced since he was a child.

His camp was to the south of the city, outside the Gate of Mars: to the north was Octavian's much larger camp. One day, as he watched the soldiers arming yet another deep ditch with sharpened stakes, an idea came to him. As he watched, a group of Lucius' men came trotting down the road from the gate. The two groups clashed: it was the sort of petty conflict that happened all the time. Lucius' soldiers too had brought a group of slaves, who helped them to dismantle and take away the trap. The slaves had jumped into the pit, but some of Octavian's slaves were still standing there, uncertain what to do. For a moment the two groups, unarmed, of course, pushed and shoved each other in the narrow space. Then Octavian's men managed to pull their own slaves free and make off. But for a moment the two groups of slaves had mingled, cursing and shoving. Slaves were everywhere, he reflected. They always were, of course - but who notices them? Watching intently, he noted how once the two groups had got free of each other no one paid any attention to them. As long as they did what was wanted, they were invisible.

That evening, as he washed the dust of the camp off himself, he said to Felix, 'I suppose there must be a supply of tunics, somewhere?'

'Soldiers' tunics,' Felix nodded, carefully putting down the big bronze bowl and handing his master a clean towel. 'They're in a big long tent, next to the general's quarters. Boots, too, and weapons. There's a horrible fierce man at the door who takes the chit from you, and practically body-searches you when you come out, to make sure you haven't got anything you shouldn't have.'

'H'm. I'm delighted our systems are so efficient. A bit surprised too, I must say. But that wasn't quite what I had in mind. I mean, those are soldiers' clothes, and I want a slave's tunic.'

'You do?' Felix almost dropped the towel. 'I don't think there's a place for them. I mean, slaves always belong to someone, and they get their clothes from that person, don't they? But maybe I could - what is it you want, exactly?'

'A workman's tunic, dirty and patched: perhaps one of those which only has one shoulder, like builders wear.'

'What size?'

'Oh, big enough for me.'

Felix stared at him. 'You, lord? Whatever do you want it for?'

'I mean to get into Perusia, and rescue our ladies.'

Felix's eyes were sparkling. 'Could you do that, lord?'

'I don't know,' Torquatus said truthfully. 'But I'm going to try.' And he told the boy how he had watched the slaves. 'I always know when there's a sortie planned, so I'll take advantage of that. I reckon Fiscilius can't be there in the daytime much, and he certainly won't be if there's an attack going on. If I can get to the house, Canidia and Epictetus will help. He could get a cart organised so I can smuggle the ladies out under a heap of wood or something.'

Felix put his head on one side, thinking about this. 'Will you tell Octavian?'

Torquatus' smile was tight. 'You do go for the difficult questions, don't you? I haven't decided that yet. All I know is that if I fail I shan't care about anything and if I succeed, Octavian won't care how I did it. You understand now why I say this must be secret, Felix?'

The boy didn't seem to have heard, and Torquatus was just about to repeat his demand when Felix nodded decisively, and said: 'It won't work.'

Torquatus stared at him. 'What do you mean, it won't work?'

'Oh, lots of things. I know you say you wouldn't care, but I don't believe that. Octavian would be furious, wouldn't he, if he found out? And you could never pass for a slave. You don't look right, or walk like a slave, or speak like one. And your hair's too short. Too Roman.'

'Of course I can. I've watched slaves often enough.'

'No.' Felix took a deep breath. 'It's a good idea. But instead of you going, it should be me.'

'You?' Torquatus swung round so quickly the stool creaked.

'Yes, of course. I'm used to being a slave; I won't have to

act the part. And besides, I'm not just a slave, I'm a boy too. So that's two reasons for people not to see me.'

'I understand. But no, Felix. You aren't strong enough to tackle Fiscilius' men. And even if you were - it's too much responsibility. If they caught you they'd kill you.'

'Yes, lord, I know. But if they caught you, they'd make you a hostage, wouldn't they? And then Octavian would be really angry with you, because he seems to hate not being able to trust people, from what I've heard. He's pretty loyal to his friends too, isn't he? He might feel he had to let Lucius go, make a bargain to get you back. That would make him even angrier.'

Once again Torquatus looked into the dark face so like his own, and saw an adult. The soft chin and rounded cheeks of the boy had thinned down: with the same big nose and strongly arched brows as his own he could see that Felix was a Manlius Torquatus like himself.

'No, Felix. It's my responsibility. I can't let you do such a mad thing.'

'No madder for me to do it than you,' Felix muttered, turning to tidy away the towels and oil-flask.

Torquatus sat in silence for a while, Felix watching him hopefully. Then Torquatus laughed. 'You look like Nar when he hears a rat scratching somewhere. Of course it's your mother you're really thinking of, isn't it, Felix?'

'Of course it is. I'd like to rescue her. She'd want to know me then, wouldn't she?'

'I'm sure she wants to know you already, Felix.'

The very next day, Torquatus heard that Octavian's men were to attempt an attack to the north of the city, where his camp was based. It had been especially difficult to build the flanking walls Octavian wanted on that side of the city. The river runs to the east of Perusia, and Torquatus was responsible for building the wall which would run from the southern tip of the siege walls down to the Tiber. On that side, while he had faced a number of attacks, he had been able to fend them off without great loss of life. But the wall running from the northern end of the siege wall had been constantly hampered, and was not yet complete. So there would be an attack, which would, Octavian hoped, scare Lucius off for long enough to allow him to finish the job.

Torquatus' heart was in his mouth as he sat quietly in the

meeting, listening as the centurions got their orders. This was the very chance he'd been looking for. Tomorrow morning his men were to set out for their work in the plain just as usual, with the usual load of sharpened stakes for pits, loads of brushwood to cover up traps and carts full of the tools they'd need. He would go along with them, mingling with the slaves, and with luck there would be a clash with one of the Perusine groups, and he'd be able to slip into the city along with them. He'd need a lot of luck, he knew, but it was the best chance he had.

While he was in the meeting, Felix had gone off to try and find a slave's tunic for Torquatus, and the boy wasn't back when a slave from his household came up with a bag full of letters from Rome. Torquatus, his head full of his plans, opened them with no great expectations. He was right; his agent was wanting to tell him that this year's vintage should be a fine one, and that the olive harvest would shortly begin; Trofimus told him that the bath-house had sprung a leak and asked if he might buy an extra kitchen slave as Fortunatus was complaining endlessly about being short-handed; and Manlia told him that Rome was still quiet, although there had been one or two more bread-riots. Torquatus didn't recognise the last pair of wax tablets. He broke the seal and they opened with a little creak. He read the letter, his eyebrows raised, then sat down rather heavily on his stool and read it again.

When Felix came running back a few moments later, saying, 'Look, lord, I got this. I hope it'll be big enough but I'm not - ,'

He stopped and stared. Torquatus looked up at him as if he'd been far away.

'Thank you, Felix, but we shan't be needing that now.'

'Oh, have you decided it's too dangerous, lord? Will you let me go instead? I'm glad.'

Torquatus' jaw was clenched. He said carefully, 'No, I didn't decide that. But it seems that neither of us need to go.'

'But - ,' Felix began.

'Balbus has rescued the lady Cornelia, and your mother too,' he told the boy. 'Nereis is now in Rome, and Cornelia is in Neapolis.'

Felix began to say, 'Oh but that's wonderful.' He stopped, seeing Torquatus' face. He had never seen his half-brother look like that. It was as if the skin was stretched so tight over his bones that it might rip, and his eyes glittered dark in their sockets. Felix stepped back from him. The look faded from Torquatus' face, and he turned away.

'Yes, it's wonderful news, of course,' he said tonelessly. 'And now I want you to take a message for me to the catapult operators. I want to see their calculations, to be sure they can hit the walls.'

Felix ran off. He'd never been so glad to have an excuse to leave his master.

Torquatus threw himself on his bed wondering what further humiliation Balbus could possibly heap on him. For a moment he'd felt, as Felix had, a surge of relief that Cornelia was not trapped, not subject to Fiscilius, not threatened by starvation or rape or murder. Then a great wave of fury and guilt had rolled over him. Why hadn't he been able to rescue Cornelia? Why had it been her father who had taken the initiative? Then he was angry with Cornelia: how dared she put him in this stupid position? He never wanted to see her again: he wanted to go and see her now, this very minute. At the thought he jumped up off the bed again and strode about the tent, muttering oaths under his breath. He couldn't go and see her. Balbus had taken her to Neapolis, apparently. How had he got her out of that hell-hole, Torquatus wondered, gazing out of his tent at the great city, serene and beautiful on its hill, floating above the mass of men scurrying like ants below.

He read through the letter again. Balbus gave no details of how the rescue had been carried out, but it was clear that it had taken place even before Torquatus' negotiations. His rage flared up again: what a monkey they'd made of him, Cornelia and her father. There he'd been, desperately trying to talk the Senate round, fighting for Cornelia, and Balbus had just paid some colossal sum, or sent in some heavies, and snatched his daughter away. Lucius and Fiscilius must have been furious to lose such a valuable bargaining chip, but how they must have laughed when he'd pleaded for Cornelia's life in the Senate house. And it was very clear that Balbus now meant to keep Cornelia under his control. She needed to be cared for, Balbus said, wasn't well, wanted rest and a good diet. But there was nothing in the letter to say he wasn't to write to her. He'd do that. And this time he'd tell her how much he wanted her and loved her and needed to have her back.

He'd write to Balbus, too, he thought grimly. And that wouldn't be a loving letter at all.

That evening Torquatus sat down to write. What he had to say was important, and it wouldn't fit onto a cramped little wax tablet. He called for a roll of papyrus. It was hard at first; the words didn't seem to want to get themselves out through his pen. He threw it down, exasperated. He sat for a moment, glowering at the sheet with its faltering sentences. Then he picked up the pen and wrote, fast and hard so that the pen sputtered: I love you, Cornelia. I don't know when I began to love you, but I do know that I never want it to end. As if something had broken in him the words began to flow out onto the white surface in a steady stream. He wrote and wrote, square after square of text, until his hand ached. Suddenly, the strip was full. The camp was very quiet: no doubt everyone was asleep, except for those slaves waiting for him to finish his task. He sighed and yawned and stretched, suddenly exhausted. He had said what he needed to say. He rolled up the papyrus neatly, tied it with cord, melted a blob of wax onto the cord and pressed his signet ring down hard onto it. Tomorrow the slave would take that little roll, and all his feelings of love and longing, to Cornelia. The die would be cast.

Felix was relieved that Torquatus said no more about the rescue, though he found it worrying, too. He had stayed up half the night after the letter had arrived, while Torquatus wrote and wrote. And in the morning he had offered to take the small roll and the set of tablets all the way to Neapolis if the master wished, but Torquatus pointed out that the slave who had come up from Rome the day before was still waiting for replies, and gave them to him to carry. Felix watched the man depart looking bored, as if this was just another job for him. How happily would Felix have gone, and made the time too to call on that quiet house on the Fagutal! He held close to his heart what Torquatus had said about his mother. He longed to know more: if she was now in Rome how had she got there? What was she doing? Why had she gone to Perusia in the first place? And, more importantly, when would he get to see her at last?

Torquatus turned back to his duties with a determination that if he was a complete failure as a husband he would at least be beyond criticism as an officer. His slaves got used to having orders snapped at them; his centurions, who already respected him, began to worry if he might be a bit of a martinet. But before anyone could worry too much about Torquatus' changed mood, the news they'd all been waiting for came in. Scouts reported that Ventidius and Pollio were at last) approaching Perusia, though apparently at no great speed. Octavian decided that he and Salvidienus should stay at Perusia, making a push to complete the siege works, while Torquatus and Agrippa set out to meet the threat from the north. It was a relief to have a job to do, a job that took him away from the endless routines of a siege. The short November days were cool, and the men marched with goodwill, pleased to be spared yet more digging. Felix was excited, too. Now, at last, he would see his first battle.

He was disappointed again. After marching so far, neither of Antonius' generals seemed to want to fight. The armies would come face to face with each other, and each time the enemy generals would pull their men back. For Torquatus and Agrippa this was a relief. They couldn't afford to waste lives, they knew. Carefully they drove the two invaders away in different directions. Once they were separated, Torquatus pushed Pollio towards Ravenna, where he finally shut himself up inside the town with his army. Agrippa chased Ventidius into Ariminum. Leaving as few soldiers as they dared to make sure the Antonian forces stayed where they'd been put, Agrippa and Torquatus rode back to Perusia cheerfully together, their soldiers in high spirits.

What they saw when they arrived back at Octavian's camp made Felix gasp. Where there had been a mass of men hurrying here and there, digging, shouting orders, or cutting wood, now there was silence. The plain was empty between the walls the besiegers had built and the steep slopes of Perusia's hill. Ditches zig-zagged across it and pits dotted it here and there, but it was empty. No more carts of wood or stone creaked out through the gates, or teams of oxen dragging catapult beams. The city gates too were shut, and the city apparently silent. Their own camps were overflowing with men, waiting with barely suppressed excitement for one side or the other to make a move. Looking outside their camp, Felix could see a boat on the river, its crew hurrying past the besieged city, and a line of cavalry horses out feeding, attended by their grooms, on the edge of a wood. There was nothing else.

When they got back to their own tents, there were letters waiting. A bag of letters, including two from Neapolis. Felix made an excuse and left the tent: he doubted whether Torquatus even heard him. Behind him, Torquatus was telling a slave to light lamps and go. The short November afternoon was closing in.

Torquatus opened Balbus' letter first, dreading to read that he was now a divorced man.

My Dear Torquatus, he read, *I can quite understand that it must have been unpleasant for you to learn that it was I who rescued Cornelia. Since you seem to want to know how it was done, I will tell you. As soon as it became clear to me that with armies skirmishing about Umbria Perusia was no fit place for my daughter, I decided to act. I have, as I'm sure you're aware, a very wide circle of acquaintances, not all of whom would perhaps be welcomed into polite society. Such men have their uses. I gathered together a group of ten of these men, all most trustworthy and - where necessary - violent. I gave them money, weapons and freedom to act as they saw fit. As I understand it, they forced their way into the house when Fiscilius was absent, disposed of his slaves, and took Cornelia and Nereis away. They brought them to Rome, where Nereis preferred to remain, having for some reason a dislike of the idea of living in my house. Cornelia then came down to Neapolis by ship. She will remain with me here.*

I enclose her reply to your letter.

Torquatus read this through twice, his feelings in turmoil. There was nothing in Balbus' letter to suggest that he saw any future for Torquatus and Cornelia: on the other hand he hadn't forced a divorce. With shaking hands, he opened Cornelia's letter. The first thing he saw, with a sinking heart, was that it was very short.

It had no opening greeting at all.

I have been thinking a lot about how you've behaved to me, and I feel utterly betrayed. I don't want to see you. I don't want you to write to me. There is nothing more to say. Cornelia Balbi.

He dropped the tablets as if they were burning him, and threw himself onto his bed. Then he jumped up again, picked them up and read them again. The words seemed to scorch themselves into his brain. The letter was in her own handwriting. There could be no mistake.

He felt the bile rise in his throat, and pulled out the pot from under his bed, throwing up into it violently. Felix came in carefully, and hurried to help him, wiping his face and putting the pot outside the door-flap.

He understood what this meant without being told: the lady Cornelia had gone for good.

Chapter 18

It was now December, the month of the Saturnalia festival of gift-giving, feasting and relaxation. The soldiers complained that just as they should be preparing for some fun they were camping in the mud and wasting their days in pointless make-work activities. For weeks every day had dragged past without variation or interest; for weeks Torquatus and his fellow officers had looked for something to keep the men occupied; for weeks they had tried to occupy themselves. And now, as the days became shorter and colder, something happened to jolt every one of them out of that mood of irritable frustration. The soldiers stopped moaning about the wretched Saturnalia ahead of them, buffed up their armour with new vigour and joked that at last they could get their feet out of the mud. The officers held real meetings, studied maps, and checked their horses' condition. For a time Torquatus' head was fully occupied with his work, leaving no time to brood on the collapse of his marriage.

The news that had woken up everyone in Octavian's camp was that Ventidius had managed to slip past the troops that were supposed to be guarding him at Ariminum, and was marching towards Perusia as fast as he could go. Unlike Lucius' legions of raw recruits, Ventidius had experienced soldiers in his ranks, and if he could make a determined assault on the besiegers, Lucius' men would stream out of the city and attack the siege walls from inside. This was a chance to end the stalemate: if Ventidius and Lucius between them could overcome the besiegers Octavian might well be finished as a political force. But if Octavian could hold on to the city Ventidius' army might be wiped out and Lucius would have little to look forward to but eventual surrender.

For a few days Torquatus and his fellow officers were anxiously waiting to see if Pollio too was on the move, but it seemed not. Nor had Marcus Antonius' other troops in northern Gaul moved any closer. This was too good a chance to miss. Even the men who'd complained most loudly set about their drills with renewed energy when they heard that they would have the chance to fight. To pounce while Ventidius had no-one to call on for reinforcements, Agrippa and Salvidienus hurried out to offer battle, but Ventidius behaved just as he had when Torquatus and Agrippa had tried to engage him weeks ago. Conscious of his own isolation he refused to fight, withdrawing instead into Fulginium, twenty miles away. Agrippa could only wait to see what he would do.

One night, everyone in the camps around Perusia was puzzled by a glow on the horizon. No-one could say whether Ventidius was taking refuge in Fulginium, or simply making his dispositions there before rushing out in a final burst of energy and enthusiasm. The glow on the horizon was taken as a positive omen inside Perusia: Octavian's soldiers could hear cheering and singing inside the city. The men waited restlessly, all prepared for battle. Word came in from Agrippa that the fires had been started by Ventidius, who must at last be planning to come to Perusia's rescue. For several days the men undertook all their duties in full armour, uncomfortable though that was, because everyone expected to be called out to fight at a moment's notice.

Nothing happened. It seemed that Ventidius was taking no risks. After an inconclusive couple of weeks, he left Fulginium and marched northwards again, Agrippa on his tail. The threat of battle receded. The soldiers went back, grumbling, to the slow business of starving Perusia into surrender. What kind of Saturnalia were they going to have, they complained, stuck here in the back end of nowhere?

But by now Lucius' besieged army was despairing of rescue. The besiegers repulsed increasingly frantic efforts to break out and a number of vicious battles took place under the leaden skies. Octavian's troops had no need to waste men's lives in assaults on those frowning walls: they contented themselves with using their artillery to hurl bolts into the city, many inscribed with obscene messages to the enemy. To bald Lucius was the politest of these; For Fulvia's cunt the one the soldiers liked best. The enemy, too, scrawled messages on their missiles, accusing Octavian of everything from impotence to screwing his sister. A routine was established. A vicious artillery attack from the city would precede a rush down onto the plain to attack the besiegers; but however hard they tried Lucius' men never managed to break through the encircling walls, and once they had returned to the city the besiegers would begin their own artillery barrage, sometimes loading the largest and most powerful catapults with the heads lopped from bodies left behind on the plain. These would be hurled over the walls, and the shooting of severed heads into the city cheered the men almost as much as the shooting of the bolts with their obscene messages.

Even with these entertainments, however, the soldiers'

mood worsened as December wore on. They grumbled at the cold and the mud, at the prospect of not being home for Saturnalia, at the lack of action. Even the attempted breakouts from the city died down until, at last, the lookouts saw the great gates of the city open one dark dawn. They shouted down that an attack was under way: trumpets blared, and the men dropped whatever they were doing, grabbing their weapons and forming themselves with practised speed into their fighting groups, buzzing with excitement. Torquatus, placed where he could get a good view of the gate, peered through the dim light. There was something wrong with the way the men coming out of the city were behaving, and as they came fully into the light he could see why. These were not soldiers. A thin stream of men and some women, raggedly dressed in a motley assortment of dark tunics, came hesitantly down the road. They looked like slaves but they didn't seem to have any orders, just milling uncertainly once they arrived down on the plain. Some of the men turned back, going up to the gate as if to plead, but the heavy doors were already shut. The men came back down, and began uncertainly to pick their way through the traps and pits on the plain.

'So they're running out of food. Good,' Torquatus heard one of the centurions say.

'What shall we do, sir?' another asked him.

'Do? There's nothing we can do.'

The soldiers watched, laughing, as the abandoned slaves tried to find a way around the deep trenches filled with sharpened stakes. One or two did, coming slowly right across the ground between the two sets of defences, only to be turned back by Octavian's sentries. On the brink of starvation already, they could do no more than return to Perusia, sit down outside the walls of the city which had been their home, and wait for the cold wind and rain to finish what hunger had begun. For several days, their moans and prayers to be let back into Perusia drifted across to the besiegers' camp; then gradually they died away.

And now Saturnalia was upon them. Torquatus felt that the darkness of the season must have seeped into his mind. But whatever his feelings, the men must be entertained. As he arranged for extra supplies of wine and food to be brought in, he wondered what Cornelia was doing. Manlia, too. Occasional letters came from her, but once they had both expressed their shock and helplessness at what Balbus had done, her letters had addressed mainly their private domestic concerns: what did Aulus want done with the bath-house, which was really in need of a complete overhaul? Was there any chance that he might be able to spend Saturnalia at home? Her latest letter, though, lifted his mood of despondency. Manlia wondered - although he was probably too busy to even think about this - whether he would like her to see Nereis, since she was apparently back in Rome? She might be able to explain what had happened at Perusia, and she might know more about Cornelia's situation.

Torquatus sat up. Now this was something positive that could be done. He had been so absorbed in his own appalling loss that he hadn't really taken in that Nereis had not gone to Neapolis after she'd been rescued. Didn't he remember something about her going to Perusia because Balbus was bullying her? He thought that was what he'd been told. She had always been a peripheral figure for him, but now he saw that she might be able to give him information he'd need when he saw Cornelia. Until this idea came into his head he hadn't even realised that he'd formed the intention of seeing her. But that was what he was going to do. Another intention formed itself at once.

'Felix,' he called, and the boy came trotting into his master's tent.

'Yes, lord?'

'I want letters carried to Rome,' he said, and saw the boy's face lighten. He stood up and saw that Felix was now close to his own height. He smiled. 'There will be one for the lady Manlia, and I'd like you to take one to Nereis too.'

Felix gasped. 'Yes, lord. Of course I'd be delighted to do that.'

'I should have thought of this before,' he said. 'You need to talk to your mother. That's very natural. And I want you to find out from her as much as you can about how the ladies were rescued, and anything, any detail, however small or apparently irrelevant, about the lady Cornelia.'

Felix was grinning. 'I'll go tomorrow, lord, if the letters are ready.'

Torquatus nodded. 'Yes. Go tomorrow.'

So as Torquatus did his best to look as if he was looking forward to Saturnalia with enthusiasm, Felix rode away on Firefly, laughing and joking with Becco, who had come up with the letters.

'I'm surprised the lady Manlia didn't have to hire an

elephant for you to ride,' he heard Felix say. Becco turned to him, his little blue eyes twinkling.

'She did ask,' he said, 'but they didn't happen to have an elephant available, so I had to make do with this Nabatean horse.'

'He's a nice horse,' Felix agreed.

'Yes.' Becco nodded and grinned. 'I had a little talk with him, and it turned out he didn't like going fast any more than I did. Especially trotting. We agreed we hated that. So we get on just fine.'

Felix was setting his pony prancing, but Becco, just as he'd said, was keeping his horse to a walk. Torquatus hoped the man wasn't intending to go all the way to Rome at that speed, but as the two disappeared round a corner of the road he reflected that Felix would be as anxious as he would have been himself to get to Rome. He could rely on the boy to hurry Becco along.

He wondered why he had been so despondent. Balbus still hadn't sent him notice of his divorce: didn't that suggest that perhaps Cornelia wasn't as compliant with her father's wishes as he'd feared? Perhaps he might still have a hope of saving his marriage.

Saturnalia was well past before Felix came back. Torquatus had had a frustrating day, dealing with centurions grumbling at the lack of action (Caesar is in charge of strategy, you know); soldiers wanting to know how long it would be before they were discharged and got their land (I'm sure Caesar is just as keen as you are to see an end to this farce); and it was bacon and beans again for dinner. He sighed, and looked up to see Felix standing in the doorway of his tent.

'Felix! It's good to see you back. Come and sit down and have some of this while you tell me all about your trip.'

'Me?' He looked surprised at being invited to sit with the master, which was natural enough. Torquatus smiled again. 'Of course. It's bacon and beans, you won't be surprised to hear.'

'Well, I'm hungry enough not to care what it is,' Felix agreed, pulling up a stool and serving himself from the dish.

'You will have seen your mother?' Torquatus began, knowing that this would have been more important to the boy than anything.

'Yes. Oh, yes. Thank you so much for letting me be the one to go to her.' Felix busied himself for a moment with reaching for the salt. Then he looked up. 'It was wonderful to see her again, and to hear what had happened to her when she left our house. She's had a hard time.'

Torquatus nodded. 'But now she's comfortably off. We must make sure she's fully involved in deciding what will happen to you next. I mean to free you, of course, and then you'll need to know what you want to do, as a freedman.'

Felix looked, Torquatus thought, a little startled. Perhaps even troubled. He thought he understood what was troubling the boy and went on, 'Once you're a freedman it wouldn't be appropriate for you to act as a body-slave.'

'I like being with you in the camp,' Felix told him, 'and I like Firefly.'

'Firefly will be your horse, until you grow too tall for her and we have to buy you a larger one. Catus will become my body-slave. I'm very pleased with him and think he will do that well. But I have other plans for you: plans more suitable for your new status.'

Felix sniffed. 'If I don't come with you, where will I go on Firefly, then?'

'Well, to answer that we'll have to decide what kind of work would suit you. What do you want to do?' An odd question between master and slave, though not, of course, between brothers. 'As a freedman.'

It seemed as if Felix had at last really understood what was being offered him. 'Will you really do that? Just give me my freedom? I wouldn't have to buy it? I've been saving, you know.'

Torquatus' smiling look met the large dark eyes, so like his own. 'I'm glad to hear it. But you won't need your savings for this, I promise. My father would have freed you, or my brother Lucius. But they are dead, and it falls to me to do it for them.'

'Thank you.' Felix still seemed a little uneasy. His pushed his plate away. 'But you want to hear all about what my mother told me about how they escaped from Perusia.'

'I do.' Torquatus poured out wine for himself, and some for Felix too, and watched as the boy added water.

Felix told how the men Balbus had sent to Perusia had arrived only a couple of days before the city was closed, had gathered in the street outside Canidia's house, watched Fiscilius go off on his military duties, and gone to the door once he was out of the way.

'Cornelia and my mother were upstairs. They were kept in two rooms, one to sleep in and one for the day, with a guard on them day and night.'

'They were prisoners, then?'

'Yes, they hadn't been free to go anywhere outside since Fiscilius had arrived.'

'And Canidia?'

'They didn't see her, but Epictetus managed to tell Cornelia that she was ill. The lady Cornelia insisted that they must have books, and she saw Epictetus when she went to the book-room. They couldn't speak to each other, but they wrote notes to each other in books, because the slaves couldn't read.'

Torquatus couldn't help smiling. 'She was determined to escape, then.'

'Oh yes. My mother said she'd made up her mind as soon as Fiscilius arrived that they should go. But of course it was a problem that Canidia was ill, because the lady Cornelia couldn't bear to leave her behind.'

Felix sat frowning for a moment. 'When the men came to the house they forced their way in. There were ten of them, so the door man couldn't help it.' He was laughing now. 'I must say, I wish I'd been there. There was a terrific battle, from the sound of it, which Balbus' men won handsomely. Then they took the ladies away. Epictetus told them that Canidia had said they weren't to worry about her, and if they had a chance to escape they should do it. Because they could be used as hostages, but she couldn't, you see.' He grinned suddenly. 'I wish I'd been there: Epictetus is a really quiet, respectable sort of man, my mother said, and he crept round the wall behind one of Fiscilius' slaves as they were all fighting, and hit him over the head with a big silver jug. Oh, and the lady Cornelia, too, she had a bag of books, and she knocked out one of Fiscilius' heavies with that.'

Torquatus was laughing too, and Felix thought that he hadn't seen his half-brother's face so relaxed for a long time. 'Yes, I can see her doing that. So what happened then? These men took Cornelia away?'

'Yes. They didn't want to take my mother, or Rachel, but Cornelia insisted. They kept saying they'd only been paid for one, but the mistress damned them to Hades and said she had plenty of money of her own and would pay them when they got to Rome if they were too mean to do it without being bribed.'

'So how did the men get the ladies out of the city?'

Felix's eyes were sparkling. 'I bet you didn't know there

were underground passages in Perusia?' he said.

'Underground passages? Really? Gods! I wonder if we might use them to get into the city and end this siege once and for all?'

Felix shook his head. 'I asked about that. But they - the ladies, I mean - had discussed that, and they thought not. There's only one way out, they were told. And that was the way they went, which comes out at a place which is well covered from the walls. They were sneaked out after dark, which the men paid a big bribe for, but you'd never get in that way without being seen.'

Torquatus nodded. 'I'll tell Octavian anyway. In case any of our spies can think of a way of using those passages.'

'My mother said after that they had a really comfortable journey. There was a boat to take them all the way down the Tiber to Rome, and then Cornelia took ship to Neapolis. She tried to persuade my mother to go too, but my mother is scared of Balbus, and decided that if he was in Neapolis she would stay in Rome.'

In one respect Felix's report was disappointing. Felix hadn't been able to find out anything much about Cornelia. 'I thought my mother was going to say something at one point, but she said she didn't know and then turned the conversation. So I'm really sorry. I don't think I've found out anything that would help you get the lady Cornelia back.'

Torquatus smiled. 'You've done well. And when we get back to Rome, which surely can't be too long now, we'll talk more about what you will do when you are free. Think about it, won't you? It's a big decision.'

Torquatus was simply thankful now that Cornelia had escaped. But he was no nearer understanding what had gone so wrong between them. He wouldn't be able to find that out until this ghastly siege was over. Then, he promised himself, he'd see her if had to force his way into Balbus' house.

There was nothing to do but throw himself into his work, which offered little to interest him. The walls of the unfortunate city still lowered down at the besiegers. Parties of his men still worked the carefully calibrated artillery pieces every day, lobbing missiles into the city which could do no more than kill the occasional enemy soldier or hapless civilian, but the bombardment at least gave the soldiers something to do. Even the attempts to break out died away. The new year came in; a year in which Balbus was to be consul for at least some months, Torquatus remembered bitterly, and yet everything seemed stuck, dull and flat as the heavy clouds overhead. And to add to the soldiers' displeasure a warning had come from the main camp at the other side of the city: there was to be no New Year celebration in case of an enemy attack. No attack came.

It was another two weeks before what appeared to be Lucius' whole army poured out of the city's gates to the north and the south, and for the first time the entire besieging army were engaged. All the short winter's day the battle raged. All day Torquatus and his fellow commanders galloped here and there, gathering up the soldiers where they seemed to be weakening, receiving streams of messages from the siege-walls warning where the attack was fiercest, moving troops from one spot to another. Lucius' soldiers fought with the desperation of doomed men, but without assistance from outside they were unable to break the siege, and as the early nightfall darkened the plain they retreated in good order back into the city. All night the groans and cries for help of the dying sounded in the ears of the besiegers, and in the morning both sides warily sent out parties to aid those still alive and bury whatever dead men they could reach. Great stinking pyres were built outside the siege-works and columns of smoke were seen above the city. The stench of burning flesh hung over the plain, but Torquatus' men were cheerful, pleased that something was happening at last.

'I just hope that Lucius gives up while he still has an army left,' one of Torquatus' centurions said, when he came for orders the next day, and a couple more red plumes nodded in agreement. 'They're good men, and it's a shame to waste their lives, when they can't win.'

An uneasy quiet fell. Surely Lucius must now capitulate? Instead, a few days later, an even more ferocious assault was launched from the beleaguered city. Again waves of soldiers threw themselves desperately against the weakest points of the siege-walls, sometimes scaling them here and there, but always being repelled again after brief, savage encounters. Again Lucius' depleted army withdrew into the city. There could be no doubt now what the outcome must be.

It might take days or even weeks, but the city would fall.

Chapter 19

It was only when the citizens began to stream down the ramp-like road that it seemed possible to believe that it was all over. A trickle of people at first, then a flood, some running with their cloaks flapping behind them in the dull cold air, some self-importantly jostling their way down; then a solid river of humans moving more slowly, women carrying babies on their hips, men with the anxious look of those who have all their wealth about their person, old men hobbling on sticks, thin children stopping every now and then to check their mothers were behind them. If you wanted to know what famine looks like - real famine - this was it. Dull-eyed, exhausted, when the citizens reached the temporary parade-ground where Octavian sat motionless on his chair they stared at him without interest, as if he could hardly do more harm to them now. He, still crowned with the victor's laurel wreath, stared coldly back. Lucius had been sent off to govern Spain, something he might have done months ago without ruining a city. His soldiers, too, had marched out: whoever had starved in Perusia, they hadn't. Around Octavian stood his commanders, Torquatus among them. Torquatus already knew that he would be going back to Rome to maintain order there and to make sure Fulvia didn't cause any more trouble.

'I don't want to upset Antonius,' Octavian had said wearily. 'So let's get the woman off Italian soil. She can go and make his life a misery, instead of plaguing me. Just see to it that she gets to Brundisium, will you?'

Glancing up at the city, where the human flood had almost stopped, Torquatus could see guards moving in an orderly way around the gates. He wondered where the senators were. The citizens milled about like animals rounded up for milking or slaughter, with no-one to speak for them.

Octavian held up a hand, and the people approached him cautiously. 'Perusia has been my enemy,' he began. The crowd shuffled a little. Everyone hung back, especially the wealthy-looking ones. A tall man, glancing around and seeing no-one willing to take control, stepped forward. He said 'Perusia is not your enemy. But Lucius Antonius arrived here with his legions, marched into the town, and ordered the gates shut. We'd no time to call the men to arms, no power to shut him out. So what were we to do? And as you see, we've suffered.' He gestured back at the townspeople behind him. 'Deaths from hunger and disease, our businesses ruined, our food supplies gone. What could we have done?'

'Are you claiming that Perusia was on my side?' Octavian asked.

'No! Perusia's not on anyone's side, that I know of. Except its own, of course.' There was a murmur from the crowd. 'We're frightened, of course. What city in all Italy isn't? Every city fears for its land. Every city is afraid of receiving a colony of Romans who see us, not as their hosts but as their enemies and underlings. You and Lucius Antonius have both settled soldiers on Italian land, so we're afraid of you both.'

'You've spoken well.' A cold smile. 'But if you know of any other way of discharging soldiers after they've done their duty, I wish you'd tell me.' The man stood silent, and that frosty smile broadened a little. 'Well, I shall pardon Perusia.' There was a murmur from the crowd, but Octavian held up a thin pale hand. 'That pardon does not extend to the senators and priests of the city: they are under guard and will be executed. The city's Senate could have shortened this siege by secretly opening the city to me. They chose not to do so, and now they'll pay the price. All the cities of Italy need to know that the soldiers must be settled, and that resistance will only add to the amount of land they lose.' Silence, as this was digested. In the cold air a baby wailed.

'One more thing. If you wish to return to your homes you may do so, but I warn you: I intend to let my soldiers plunder your city. If you want to avoid them, you must leave today, now, as you are.'

A shocked silence. Then a woman cried out, 'No, you can't do this to us.'

'I am the winner here. I can do as I please. My soldiers have been forced to camp here for many long months. Some have been killed, some have died, all have missed the Saturnalia with their families. I say they enjoy their Saturnalia now.'

He got up and walked away to his commander's tent as angry and despairing voices broke out behind him. As Torquatus left the parade ground, he noticed one of the wealthy-looking men setting off down the road, followed by a group of slaves and looking more pleased with himself than ever. Most of the people had broken into small groups and were discussing what to do: some had already started trudging back up into the city. Already groups of soldiers were heading out of the camp at the run. He found Agrippa beside him.

'I didn't think you were here.'

'I wasn't. Some very interesting news has just come in. Calenus has just died.'

'Calenus? Oh, Antonius' governor of Further Gaul. He's died?'

'He has. And his legions have been left without a commander.'

'I think I see where you're going, Agrippa.'

He threw back his head and laughed. 'I certainly am. As soon as I can safely get out of here. And so's Octavian.'

'Oh. You're not going to stay and watch these idiots destroy a city, then?'

'Of course we are. We can't go without some soldiers, can we? And they can march their hangovers off on the way to Gaul.' He paused, scanning Torquatus' face. 'He had to do it, you know. The guys are wild for some fun. They hate sieges. And in civil wars you don't get the booty, which is what they sign up for.' He looked thoughtful. 'Or rather, the booty comes with complications. You kill some barbarian, take his gold torc, where's the problem? But you break into an Italian house and steal the table silver and rape the wife and daughter, and it all feels a bit too close to home. Makes them think, and they hate that. That's why they need to find the wine first.' His tone was unillusioned and accepting. No wonder his troops loved him. He glanced sharply at Torquatus from under his brows, as if to see whether he'd followed his argument.

Torquatus shrugged. 'I think you're right. But excuse me: I have urgent business in Perusia.'

He took Becco and Pulex up into the city with him: if it were not already too late to rescue Canidia he would need their help. Becco looked as vacant as usual, but Torquatus saw a nasty gleam in Pulex' eye. Killing was what made him happy, and he sensed happiness coming his way. It was noon before they were able to head up the road into the city, all armed.

What he found there made him feel sick. The men were ransacking every building they could smash their way into. They wouldn't find much food, but then they were not hungry. Wherever there was wine, they'd enjoy that, and then, well - Perusia was one of the great cities of the Etruscans, home to powerful and wealthy families, prosperous merchants, temples whose vaults would be piled with treasure, gardens and squares adorned with statues. Little of that would be there tomorrow. The soldiers were smashing down doors and pulling up floors in their hunt for valuables. Women too. Torquatus hurried to Canidia's house, his heart beating faster. The soldiers hadn't got there yet. The street was quiet, the doors and shutters of Canidia's house still fastened neatly. Torquatus hesitated, then knocked gently, hoping the unfortunate people sheltering inside would guess they weren't soldiers. They waited, the moments feeling like hours, the shrieks and cries seeming to come nearer. Then the door creaked open very slightly.

'It's Aulus Manlius Torquatus here. The lady Canidia's friend. Will you let me in?'

Cautiously, the door was opened a little more, and as soon as he could slip through the gap, Torquatus did so. The gloomy hall was much as Felix had described it.

'The lady Canidia? Is she here?'

The old slave seemed hardly to hear him.

'Epictetus? Where's he?'

'I'm here,' said a firm voice in the shadows.

'I was hoping that I might not be too late to save Canidia? Is she here?'

Epictetus stepped into the light, his eyes red with weeping, his face gaunt. That face was all the answer Torquatus needed. He beckoned to the visitors to follow him. They didn't have to go far. In a side room, Canidia had been laid out. She had been a small woman when alive: now, in death, she looked as small and fragile as a clay doll.

'I'm sorry,' was all Torquatus could think of to say.

'Are you? I'm not. It was a blessed release for her. She'd lost everyone she cared for, and the stuff she'd been guarding all these years was quite useless to her. Just a burden, that's what it was, at the end.'

'Stuff? What do you mean?'

'Don't you know? Really? I thought that was why you were interested in her.'

'No. I just wanted to catch the man who killed Fiscilia and dishonoured her memory.'

Epictetus sniffed. 'Not much doubt in my mind who killed her. And my lady,' he said. 'Fiscilius, of course. And Fiscilius has got off. Yes, he's gone to Spain with Lucius, I suppose.' He looked for a moment as if he might spit, then turned away. 'But if you're really interested in catching him, I can show you what his motive might have been.'

He turned away and Torquatus was about to follow him, but thought again.

'Becco and Pulex, you can stay here. Guard the door, will you?'

Epictetus looked surprised, and Torquatus smiled reassuringly.

'There are soldiers swarming all over this town, and your doorman's old,' he pointed out.

Epictetus nodded and walked away, Torquatus close behind him. They went along the passage away from the hall, into a warren of kitchens and store-rooms such as all houses have at the back. But whereas in most houses these quarters would be full of bustle and life, this long, dark passage was as quiet as an entrance to Hades. The thought led Torquatus to wonder if they were to descend to some vaulted cellars. Instead, Epictetus turned aside into a dark little room, coming out a moment later with a lamp and a bunch of keys. Without a word he led them further and further away from the hall. He opened what looked like the door of a small store-room, and began, methodically and neatly, to carry out the large empty wine-jars ranged along one wall and stack them in the passage. Behind the jars was an old wooden door, well-barred and bolted. Epictetus fumbled with the fastenings, and it opened with a creak, releasing so much dust it was clear it had been sealed up for years. Standing beside the open door, Epictetus held up his lamp and in its flickering light Torquatus could see what had been crammed inside.

'Jupiter!' was all he could say. Behind the door was a cupboard about eight feet deep and filled to the ceiling. The torch-light flashed off bright metal everywhere he looked. At the bottom were tables, tripods and lamp-stands of solid silver, stools of chryselephantine and statues in fine bronze. Stacked on the shelves above were mirrors, cups, lamps, vessels for mixing wine and cups for drinking it. There were bowls and jugs for offerings, and baby's teething rings and sets of spoons and knives, all of silver or gold. And there were silver boxes, themselves exquisitely chased, which no doubt contained jewels, coins, medallions, precious cameos.

'The room was made for this, wasn't it?' Torquatus was

whispering, as if in the presence of something sacred.

'That's right. The mistress was always frightened of the responsibility of it. She didn't know what to do with it all. In a time of peace you could have all that on display, I suppose, but not in these days.'

Torquatus was remembering what his father had said: that Sisenna had a collection of silver greater than any other he'd seen.

'No. You wouldn't want it known that you had this kind of thing.' He picked up a hand-mirror with clusters of grapes exquisitely cast all around the edges. Where the handle emerged from the foliage a satyr-face peeped out, menacing. 'A beautiful piece.'

'They all are. The master only ever bought the very best. He'd wait for ever to get exactly what he wanted.'

'And then left your mistress to care for it.'

'Yes. And if it had all gone in the sea, she'd have been a much happier woman.'

'What are you going to do with it?' Torquatus asked.

Epictetus gave a small dry laugh. 'I hoped you'd be able to tell me that, Torquatus.'

Somewhere not far away there was a small sound. A foot slipping on the dusty floor, perhaps. The hair on Torquatus' neck stood up.

'I didn't ask you who else was left in the house,' he said softly.

'There are only slaves, lord,' Epictetus said. 'No-one else.'

'I think you're wrong.' Torquatus moved quickly towards the door, but he was too late. Fiscilius was standing there, scowling at Epictetus.

'So you did know where the silver was! I always thought you were lying when you told me you didn't. But of course while Canidia was alive I didn't dare force you to let me in on the secret. And now you've shown me without my even having to ask. Isn't that nice?' He seemed to become aware of the other man, and glanced round. 'I thought I'd find you here, Torquatus! I saw those heavies of yours on the door and let myself in through a back window. I suppose you thought you might as well get your hands on the treasure, now the old girl's dead. Well, that's where you're going to be disappointed.'

He was swaying slightly, rolling up onto the balls of his feet as if getting ready to attack. The long cavalry sword in his hand looked hideously sharp. Torquatus thought he'd been drinking. He looked ready for a fight. Torquatus himself was in full armour, of course, like Fiscilius, though his sword was the short stabbing kind. But Epictetus was not, and in this tiny room it would be impossible not to hurt him.

'Becco! Pulex!' he shouted at the top of his voice, though he had no idea whether the guards would hear him. Fiscilius didn't wait to find out but sprang into the room and rushed at Torquatus. His sword flashed in the lamplight, stabbing at Torquatus, who snatched with his left hand at anything that might serve as a shield. To his surprise and relief it closed on a tripod, a light and elegant piece of silverware such a priest might use. It wouldn't cover his body, but he swung it round and at once Fiscilius' sword tangled in it. He caught a glimpse of Epictetus' intent face and realised that the tripod had been his doing. Encouraged, he dived at Fiscilius, who backed out into the corridor to avoid his thrust.

The bodyguards had heard, and they were now thudding down the passage. Fiscilius saw them coming and darted aside into the kitchens. Becco was hot on Fiscilius' heels, and Torquatus, stopping only to tell Pulex to guard the house, rushed after them. He heard a door open, felt the sudden inrush of cold air, and raced out into an alley which led to the street. For a moment he paused, listening in the quiet street, wondering which way the man would have gone. He could hear running feet: some below him, some above. He guessed that Becco had gone the wrong way. Which was the right way? He thought the sounds below him were of large and heavy feet. Trusting to his luck, and calling to Becco to follow, he ran up the stepped street, smoke catching in his throat. Up and up the seemingly endless street he went, until suddenly he was at the top of it, in the square where the Senate-house overlooked the magnificent view.

Where would Fiscilius have gone? He ran to the Senate-house, but the door was locked and bolted. The temple of Juno, then? The doors of the temple were open as usual, though no priests were going about their business: Octavian said they were to be executed, he remembered. He climbed up the narrow, ancient steps and went in. The great statue, made of terracotta like everything here, gazed down upon the empty space. Her gilded hair and jewelled robes gleamed dully in the shadowed space. This was Juno the queen of heaven, not Juno the mother, and for a moment Torquatus felt a prickle of fear at rushing into her sacred space. She smiled down at him with her ancient half-smile, and as he stood irresolute, he heard behind the statue a sound which put all thoughts of sacrilege out of his mind. Someone was moving around stealthily.

He ran towards the sounds, his army boots clashing and slippery on the marble floor. There was a doorway to each side of the statue, and behind it in a room used only by the priests he found Fiscilius collecting together torn-up cloths and broken pieces of incense. Beside him, a lamp had been unhooked from its chains. His sword lay on the ground at his feet. He looked up as Torquatus thudded in, and nodded as if they had just chanced to meet in the street.

'No bodyguards again?' he asked. 'That's careless.'

'You can't escape.' Torquatus was grim. 'And burning the temple down won't help. Always supposing you could.'

'The statue has robes. And this temple is old, all fired clay and wood: the roof-beams will burn pretty well. It'll make a nice funeral pyre for you, and everyone will think your soldiers did it. How appropriate.'

'I think not.'

Fiscilius looked up, alarmed, as Torquatus moved but when he saw that his sword was still in its scabbard went back to what he was doing. A moment later Torquatus was back, carrying a large bronze jug.

'A bit more oil? Good idea.' Fiscilius was getting to his feet, sprinkling oil from a small pot over his pile of kindling. Torquatus swung the jug and the water in it hit Fiscilius, before swamping the pile at his feet and putting out the lamp. The young man gasped and swore in the sudden dark, and Torquatus heard rather than saw him jumping to his feet, heard the rasp of the sword's blade on the stone floor.

Fiscilius faced Torquatus almost crouching in the half-dark, and slashed in front of him, making the sword sing. Torquatus too had his sword in his hand but he knew he must be careful: it was shorter than Fiscilius' and he needed to find some way of disarming the man, or at least throwing him off balance, before it would be of any use. The two men prowled round each other like a pair of cats.

Suddenly, Fiscilius jumped forward, bringing his sword down across Torquatus' arm. He didn't have to think: instinctively his other hand came up, still holding the water-jug. The long sword clanged on the jug which flew out of Torquatus' hand and bounced unheeded across the floor. He jumped sideways, and put his foot into some of the water with which he'd put out Fiscilius' fire, sliding across the marble. Somehow he managed to retain his balance. Fiscilius, following him, was not so lucky. He lurched and crashed into Torquatus, dropping his sword which skated across the marble floor to the curtain at the back of the room. But by the time Torquatus had regained his balance and was ready to tackle him again, he'd rolled after the sword, grabbed it and jumped to his feet, hurling himself through the curtain. Puzzled, Torquatus dashed after him. Suddenly he realised where Fiscilius had gone, and with an oath crashed after his enemy up the narrow little staircase behind it. It had tight turns in it, which Torquatus took as carefully as he could for fear of ambush, his knees aching, his breath coming in gasps.

He came out suddenly into grey daylight that made him blink. He was on the roof. Ahead of him the ridge stretched out like a narrow road, one great beam covered with lead, and on either side the long slopes of the roof looked far steeper than they had from the ground. For a moment Torquatus waited, getting his breath and looking around him. There seemed to his startled gaze to be people everywhere. A row of statues had been arranged along the roof ridge at intervals, standing gesticulating into the wind with their backs to him. Behind him another row adorned the slopes of the rear gable, to match the set placed at intervals down the edge of the front of the roof. Along the sides of the roof terracotta antefixes in the form of peacocks announced whose temple this was, and more filled the gaps between the statues at the front and rear. Fiscilius, he saw, had got past the figures on the ridge, but was now trapped, standing sword in hand at the far end in the shadow of a huge terracotta group, which Torquatus took in merely as a great number of spears, helmets, waving arms, and possibly a chariot.

This was a venerable old Etruscan temple, whose roof was wider and shallower than the Roman temples he was used to, but for anyone falling from it, there was not much chance of survival. One front corner of the temple touched the edge of the cliff and a plunge from there would probably mean there would be little left to be laid out on the funeral bier. Falling off anywhere else one would simply drop onto the paving of the great square, which might possibly lead to a slower death. But possibly not.

Fiscilius had been able to get himself to the far end of the roof ridge without difficulty: for Torquatus it was going to be far harder. Even as he set foot on it he saw Fiscilius move out from the shadow of the statue-group, sword in hand, and run lightly along the ridge towards him. Moving quickly, Torquatus was able to squeeze past the first of the statues in his way, then the second, though his boots felt large and clumsy on their little plinths. Fiscilius was waiting for him behind the third, and for a moment they both stood still, some demurely robed ancient worthy between them. Torquatus feinted to the right, dodged left, then darted out to the right grabbing hold of the worthy's terracotta hand to steady himself. Fiscilius, cursing, had swung left. Torquatus, his feet slipping terrifyingly down onto the ancient roof-tiles, clung desperately to the statue's hand, using it to haul himself back onto the ridge. He ran towards the great group at the front of the temple roof, scrambling past two more statues on the way. Twice a gust of wind snatched at him, and he wobbled. The second gust so nearly blew him away that he could taste the sour vomit in his mouth. Behind him, Fiscilius followed closely.

Torquatus steadied himself on the wider plinth behind Juno's throne, as he now saw it was. His anger, long forgotten during the war, flared up again as he remembered the golden hair tumbled on the dirty floor of the shrine, Canidia's doll-like figure lying on the bier, Cornelia's sad and wasted face. He turned to face Fiscilius who had jumped to face him on the platform. Now they were both trapped, he thought, and one of them must die. The luck was with Torquatus, who being on the platform already was able to position himself so that he had his back to the side of the roof that hung over the square: Fiscilius, if he fell, would plunge straight down the cliff. On the other hand, Fiscilius could use his sword unhampered, since the smooth back of Juno's throne was on his left. Torquatus, facing him, was pressed against it on his right and would find it hard, standing on this narrow ledge, to manage anything but a straight stab forwards. The roof sloped away on either side behind them, with nothing but some ancient pottery to help them avoid a hideous death if they slipped.

For a few tense moments the two men eyed each other, unsure how to attack without danger to themselves. It was Fiscilius who moved first, lunging viciously. His blade sliced through the cold air and Torquatus instinctively stepped back so far he almost fell off the edge of the plinth. Only the tip of the sword reached him, slicing through his cloak and into his arm. Red bubbled up at once, brighter than the crimson cloth. But Fiscilius had put so much energy into his mighty swing that he lost his balance. He scrabbled desperately with his left hand at the smooth back of the throne. There was nothing there to save him and he tumbled off the plinth and slithered awkwardly down the slope of the roof. He clutched at the tiles, his abandoned sword clattering down faster and faster till it bounced off one of the peacocks at the edge of the roof and flew arcing out, a brief bright flash against the grey sky. Fiscilius himself did not. He spread himself out against the tiles, and the weight and drag of his body gradually brought him to a halt. Cautiously he raised himself onto his hands and knees and worked his way to the front edge of the roof, where he could seize hold of one of the statues by its leg. For a moment he huddled there, gasping.

Torquatus himself couldn't move but stood above Fiscilius waiting to see what he would do, aware all of a sudden that it had started to rain. The blood was still dripping from his arm and it was throbbing with pain. After a few moments Fiscilius pulled himself laboriously into a crawling position, and began to drag himself back up the roof. But his position was hopeless. Torquatus, grim-faced, was waiting above him on the platform, his sword in his hand. The wind was still tugging at him fitfully, though here behind the statue-group he was a little sheltered. Fiscilius edged closer, slipping and sliding on the wet tiles.

With a great scraping and creaking from his boots Fiscilius suddenly launched himself up the roof and made a grab for the edge of the platform. Torquatus jumped forward, stabbing down at the man's hands, but his constricted position made it impossible for him to strike hard enough, and his sword scraped on the edge of the plinth a second after Fiscilius had pulled his hands back and slipped a little further down before coming to rest as he had before.

The two men froze, watching each other. Neither could move without risking his life.

'Let's talk,' Torquatus suggested.

'Talk?'

'You could tell me why you killed Fiscilia.'

He heard Fiscilius' dry little gasp. 'You haven't a clue, have you? After all this time, you haven't figured out one thing!' Fiscilius spat, and even laughed a little, sprawled on the roof as he was, and his laughter blew away on the cold wind.

He raised his face to Torquatus again. 'We could do a deal.

I'll let you have the silver if you let me live. That's fair, isn't it?'

Torquatus' face hardened. 'So you're a coward as well as a murderer?'

Fiscilius' wet face was pale with rage . Torquatus jumped to the very edge of the platform, instinctively realising that the other man was, just for a moment, not concentrating on him. Almost overbalancing himself he slashed downwards. Fiscilius saw him coming and let himself slither back down the roof-tiles, but as he fell back he grasped at the edge of Torquatus' cloak, forcing Torquatus in turn to let go of his sword and scrabble for a handhold on the statues beside him.

For an agonizing moment the two men balanced each other. Then Torquatus threw himself backwards in an attempt to break free but the cloak held, tightening round his neck and dragging him closer and closer to the edge. He was on his knees now, his head back as far as he could get it, his left hand gripping the edge of the plinth, his right scrabbling furiously for a handhold on the smooth terracotta of Juno's throne. He was dragged to the very edge of the little platform before his desperate hand caught onto the heel of an attendant warrior. He braced himself against the dragging cloth. For a moment he thought the stranglehold on his neck would kill him or that he would be pulled over. Then the cloth ripped noisily, and Fiscilius, with nothing to hold onto but the now useless cloak, slithered down and down, crying out and cursing. Torquatus watched, frozen, as the man slipped to the very corner of the roof. He saw Fiscilius grasp frantically at the square plinth of the statue that stood there, but seem unable to get any purchase on it. Then his slide was halted as his flailing foot found one of the terracotta peacocks, and Torquatus saw him push himself back up a little.

Torquatus jumped as a hoarse voice shouted somewhere close by. He looked up to see Becco standing horrified at the far end of the roof ridge. 'Shall I come over to you, master?'

'No,' Torquatus shouted back. 'We're finished here.'

'But your arm's wounded.'

There was a loud crack. Torquatus looked back and Fiscilius had gone. The peacock on which he'd put his foot had gone too. For a moment Torquatus stared around expecting to see the man, unable to quite take in what had happened. He stood up, shaken and cold. Peering out into the distance from behind Juno's attendant warrior across the city's rooftops, now partially obscured by the smoke of several fires, there was only a view of immense calm and beauty. It was over. Turning, Torquatus felt his own exhaustion and stiffness. His arm was aching badly, but the wound had stopped bleeding. He saw that Becco was still staring at him from the other end of the roof-ridge.

'Are you sure you don't want me to come to you, master?' he asked again.

Torquatus shook his head, finding nothing to say. He put his foot on the narrow roof-ridge.

Walking back along it was the hardest thing he'd ever had to do. He wasn't angry now or excited, but tired, sad and cold. And his slaves were watching him: he could see Pulex's eyes glittering in the doorway behind Becco. He took a deep breath, held his head up and forced his shaking knees to carry him across to safety.

He forgot his aches and pains when the little party hurried out into the great square again. The place was quiet. Far off, they could hear the shouts of soldiers, and gusts of wind blew smoke across the square. Torquatus' cloak lay in a tangle of red on the very edge of the cliff below the temple roof. Fiscilius' sword, too, lay bent on the stones, though Torquatus' seemed to have disappeared over the edge. There was no body. Torquatus stared around him. He looked up at the temple roof, trying to work out where Fiscilius must have fallen. Could he have plunged right down the cliff? From the position of his cloak he thought so. His own sword could have gone the same way. He scanned the roof, which now seemed hideously high and far away. They had been just there, behind the statues, now so small and distant. Yes, Fiscilius must have gone straight over the edge of the cliff.

Pulex and Becco were already standing as close as they could to the cliff edge, and Pulex had the torn and bloodstained cloak in his hand. They were looking down at the steeply sloping rock-face, broken here and there by straggling trees: at the very top, just below them, there was lower growth, a belt of hazel and gorse and brambles. Below, thick woodland clothed the lower slopes.

'Shall we go down, lord?' Pulex asked. 'Finish him off, like?'

Torquatus shook his head. 'No time,' he told them. 'We need to get out of the city before those fires get out of hand. And there's no chance anyone falling from that great height and then plunging down the cliff could have survived. Leave it.'

As they walked down into the city they could see that it was being destroyed all around them. For several days the dry, bitter wind that had tried to lift Torquatus off the roof of Juno's temple had been blowing night and day, and now it carried roiling smoke and the smell of burning. Becco told him that Epictetus had led the other slaves out of Canidia's house and they should now be safe in the camp. Down in the city streets their feet began to crunch on broken pots and to slip in pools they didn't stop to investigate. The smell of wine hung in the air, cut through with wafts of acrid smoke. The dark streets looked close and menacing in the fading day. Over to one side a sudden burst of sparks against a dull glow told where the fire had taken hold. To get to the gate they would have to pass much closer to it than Torquatus would have wished. He tried not to look at the smashed shop-fronts, the house-doors hanging off their hinges, the little dark piles in odd corners which might be anything from a bundle of abandoned clothes to a dead child, and to avoid stepping into the slicks of blood or wine or vomit that lay in their path.

They ran round a corner into an open square, and here the fire was raging unchecked. It was a vision of Hades, Torquatus thought. The fire had taken hold on three of its sides. Flames leapt against the dark sky from the roofs of the houses, and burning shutters framed dancing fires inside. A small group of citizens were milling about as if unsure what to do, overwhelmed by the catastrophe. As he watched, they melted away, and he turned to go back, find another way to the gate, but as he turned, his attention was caught. The houses were tall, their upper floors gabled out over the street. It was the sort of place which in Rome would be filled with the poor of all kinds, living several to a room. And as in Rome, upper floors of wood and plaster had been added to the brick lower storeys where the foundations wouldn't take the weight of any more brick. Black smoke gushed from the windows on every floor, oily, and lit with flashes of bright flame. The heat was ferocious. What had caught his eye was a small handcart, loaded with a collection of odds and ends, pans, some bedding, a cloak. Behind it, a man had already lifted the handles to wheel it away, when a woman ran to him out of the burning house, coughing and rubbing her eyes. She threw something else onto the cart, and they began to move off when a scream from an upper window stopped them again. Torquatus and the couple all looked up together, to see a girl, her hair loose, some bundle in her arms, hanging over the edge of a spindly wooden balcony. The room behind her was alight, and she was a dark figure against the shifting red.

The woman in the street cried out and turned back. The man called out something urgent, but she ran right under the rickety balcony and held out her arms. The girl seemed to understand, held out the bundle and let it fall: it partially unravelled as it came down, a white stream of cloth trailing behind. The woman caught it neatly, and it was only as she held it gently to her breast and he heard its thin cry that Torquatus realised it was a baby. He caught a glimpse of her face, glistening with sweat, smeared with smoke, and transfigured by a gentle sadness and love. And as she stood rejoicing in the saving of this child, he glanced up to see the little balcony lean outwards and then come sliding slowly down, riding on a mass of fiery debris. The girl on it came down too, her hair a halo of flame. The whole front of the house had given way, bulged, and burst. The pots of herbs rolled down like toys as the struts of balcony shattered like twigs, a clatter of roof-tiles following behind. When he remembered it later, he saw it as silent as a dream. That great mass of materials cascading down must have made a great roar, but he never remembered that. Simply, he saw again the two women, the baby, the man, the handcart, all eaten up in the collapse. He turned, shaking, and fled, his slaves at his side.

Many years later, when Torquatus' nose suddenly caught the hot dust of a demolition or the smoke of burning wood, his mind jumped back to that moment, as if in his memory the fire burned on with undimmed rage. Sometimes in his quiet bed at night he would wake, hot, terrified, dry-mouthed, revisiting yet again the night he saw Perusia die.

Chapter 20

Torquatus had left the smoking ruins of Perusia behind and was on his way to Rome, alone but for his own slaves. Not even on his gallop to Sentinum with the news of Rome's fall had he pushed himself and Bucephalus so hard. Had the circumstances been different, he would have revelled in a hard ride on verges still showing traces of frost, the rising sun laying pink streaks across the cold sky. But the stink of the burning city lingered in his nostrils as he rode; and he was going to Rome, and then to Neapolis, to discover if his marriage was also ruined. One night he would spend in Rome, and then he would hurry south. Under his breath he muttered a prayer to Venus, a goddess he'd been favouring recently. He was going to see Cornelia again, over Balbus' dead body if necessary. He went over and over in his mind what he needed to say to her.

Behind him Catus rode with the ease and comfort of long experience, keeping his eyes open for danger on the road and obstructions on the ground, and thinking only that he ought to remind the master that Bucephalus would need to rest and drink before long. Behind him again, a couple of other slaves followed. Felix was to see to the sorting of all the clutter Torquatus had acquired during the long campaign, and to accompany the ox-cart that would bring home whatever was needed.

As Torquatus had intended, they arrived in Rome that same evening. It had been a hard ride, but Torquatus forgot his aching legs when he strode into the reception hall of his house and found Manlia sitting by the pool. She had - of course - a book in her hand, which she laid aside and hurried across to greet him.

'I knew you'd be home soon, now that the war is ended,' she said, smiling, but noting with a pang at her heart how much older and more careworn he looked. His face was thinner, with lines at the corners of his mouth she hadn't seen before.

'Ended? Well, for now it is,' he agreed. 'And you've been here all by yourself?'

She laughed at this. 'I think you have about thirty slaves here, don't you? And there's Trofimus, of course, and Fortunatus to cook for me. But yes, I know what you mean. I've seen Nereis only once. She's still a little nervous of Balbus and is lying low. And of course I've seen Mama and Iunia. But we can talk later. Bath first?'

'Wine first.' And Trofimus now appeared, another slave behind him carrying a tray.

'Welcome home, master,' Trofimus said, beaming. 'It's very good to see you home again unharmed.'

And with a slight shock Torquatus saw that the steward meant what he said. 'Thank you. It's good to be home. It feels an age since I was here.' He allowed the man to take the cloak from his shoulders and hand it to Victor, who had come hurrying in with a pair of soft shoes. 'Gods! It'll be wonderful to get these great boots off.'

A small figure had come trotting into the hall behind Victor. Sniffing at the discarded boots, it seemed rather displeased with them, shook its head and sneezed.

'No!' Torquatus exclaimed. 'Don't tell me that creature's still here.'

Manlia chuckled. 'Where else could he be?' she asked.

'I suppose Nereis might like him?' Torquatus asked doubtfully, but seemed unsurprised when Manlia shook her head. 'What's he got to do with her? No, I think the poor little thing's an orphan now, and we're stuck with him.'

The orphan sat looking at Torquatus with his head on one side, as if trying to remember where he'd met him before. Torquatus bent down and gave him a perfunctory pat.

'Fiscilius is never going to come back for him, is he?' she went on, and Torquatus jumped to his feet again. 'Ah, Fiscilius,' he began. 'I've got a lot to tell you, Manlia.'

She read his face at once. 'He's dead, isn't he? And you killed him?'

'I didn't, actually. He fell. But I was trying to kill him at the time.'

She smiled. 'He's no loss,' she said coolly. 'Enjoy your wine and your bath, and then come and tell me all about it.'

Torquatus was only intending to spend one night in Rome. He had already arranged for one of his cohorts to guard Rome's gates, and the other to politely escort Fulvia all the way to Brundisium. Duty done, there was only one thing on his mind, and that was to see Cornelia and Balbus, to mend his marriage if it was humanly possible, to put right whatever it was that had gone so horribly wrong. He didn't even know, he thought in exasperation as the slave scraped the oil off his tired body, what that was. Only that the happy, confident Cornelia he loved had changed into a scared, silent woman. He had pushed away the thought that this was his doing. He'd done something so terrible that all the life had ebbed from his wife. And he had no idea what that was, which was terrifying. It might be something he would continue to do, if she came back to him, and then what?

He shook off the disquieting thought, dressed himself in a comfortable soft tunic and made his way to the room where he knew he'd find Manlia. This was a room where he worked when he didn't want to sit in the public office behind the reception hall. It was painted in a simple style, with blocks of deep yellow and red to resemble panels, and the floor-mosaic was an equally simple geometric pattern in black and white. It held a large table which had been his father's work-table, at present pushed against one wall and piled with documents awaiting his attention, a comfortable reading couch, a couple of stools, and a handsome bronze brazier. On mild days the doors could be opened to give a view across the colonnade into the gardens.

Manlia was in comfortable occupation of his reading-couch, but another one had been brought in and arranged at an angle to it, and he settled himself down on this one with a sigh of relief.

'I've almost forgotten how to recline,' he said, smiling. 'It's only stools in camp, of course.'

'Some officers take couches and beds and all sorts of comforts, don't they? I thought Caesar did? They used to say he had a mosaic that came apart in sections so that he could have a proper floor in his quarters.'

'Officers had better not do that where Octavian can see them. That wouldn't look good and he always thinks of the look of things. As for Caesar, he had some stuff which went to his winter quarters, true. But that doesn't matter.'

'No,' Manlia agreed. 'Your marriage is what matters. What are you going to do? Give it up?'

'Certainly not. I love Cornelia, and unless she tells me herself that she won't - that she can't - ' he broke off and poured himself some wine.

'I see.' Manlia lay for a moment, unthinkingly twisting a strand of hair in her fingers. 'I wish I could help you, but I can't. I offered her the chance to tell me what was wrong, but she wouldn't. I wondered if she might be pregnant, but she said not, and anyway that wouldn't have been a reason to be sad, would it?'

'Not at all. Anyway, off I go tomorrow, and I'll see her if I have to fight my way in. And in the meantime, I'll tell you how Fiscilius died.'

Torquatus slept well, for the first time for weeks, glad to be back in his own home and relieved to have made the decision to confront whatever it was that threatened his marriage. He was up early, took a quick breakfast of bread and some dried fruit and a cup of watered wine, and was riding out of Rome as the gates opened at dawn, with only Catus as escort. Torquatus would use the short winter day to the full. The morning was fine and cold, with fat white clouds chasing each other across a pale sky, and Torquatus and his slave cantered steadily down the grass verges which bordered the via Appia. Had he been travelling on military service the journey could have been completed in two days, using relays of horses, but this was private business, so to avoid exhausting the horses he allowed the party four days, spending the last night at an inn right on the edge of Neapolis.

Soon after dawn the following day Torquatus was standing outside the doors of Balbus' splendid villa, waiting with a pounding heart as the doorman fumbled with the locks. He had left Catus at the gate, fearing that he might have to face the humiliation of being denied admittance to the house. Not that he intended to accept such a snub, if it was offered. If he had to force his way in, he'd do that.

The doors swung back, and Torquatus stepped inside, outwardly calm.

'The master is at breakfast,' the doorman told him. 'I'll go and check if he's ready to see you.'

'No,' Torquatus said. 'I'm the lady Cornelia's husband, and we'll go together.'

The doorman dithered for a moment, but sensing that this large young man intended to have his way he turned and led the way to a large room filled with sunshine streaming in through its high windows.

Balbus, startled, threw down his napkin and rose from his chair. He threw an angry look towards the doorman, and Torquatus laughed.

'Oh, don't blame him. I assure you I was quite determined to see you, whether you wanted to or not. He really couldn't have stopped me.'

'Well, now you're here I suppose you'd better have some breakfast,' Balbus said, not very graciously.

'I don't need breakfast. I need to see my wife.'

Balbus frowned. 'Hasn't she made her feelings clear in her letter? She doesn't want to see you, Torquatus. You're wasting your time coming here.'

'I don't understand any of this,' Torquatus said. 'I don't know what's gone wrong. I only know that I love Cornelia and I want her back, and if she doesn't want me she has to tell me that herself, with her own lips.'

For a moment the two men stared at one another. It was Balbus whose gaze fell first.

'It's over, Torquatus,' he said, resuming his seat at the table, where bread rolls and honey and a jug of watered wine were laid out. 'I wish you'd just accept that. Oh, do sit down. You annoy me, looming like that.'

Torquatus' smile was grim. 'Good. I'm quite happy to annoy you. And I don't accept that it's over, and do you know why? Because after all this long time you've never sent me a notice of divorce. And that suggests to me that Cornelia isn't nearly as compliant with your plans as you'd like. I know you can force a divorce, but would you do that? When you say you love her, what does that mean? Would you really make her unhappy? And would you annoy Octavian, start a scandal? Which is why I'm staying here until I see her.'

Balbus opened his mouth to reply but at that moment the door behind Torquatus opened quietly. He swung round, expecting to see bodyguards mustering to throw him out. For a moment he was absolutely still, shaken into silence. His mouth fell open in disbelief. Then he walked forward, his arms open.

'Cornelia! Oh, Cornelia!'

'Aulus.' She nodded, not coming to meet him, trying to keep her face from crumpling into tears.

'But you're pregnant!'

Her face seemed to close up. 'As you've known for months,' she said coldly. She put out her hands to ward him off as he came up to her. 'And you didn't even bother to reply to my letter.'

Suddenly his frustration and anger boiled over.

'How dare you accuse me of not writing to you when I wrote and told you I loved you and couldn't bear the thought of losing you - and you sent me that hateful reply!'

'That's a lie. I never had any such letter. Are you going to pretend that my letter somehow got lost, the slave ate it, it fell down the back of a reading-couch, whatever? Save your breath. And what about the letter I wrote you?'

They were face to face like two angry cats.

'I've had two letters from you,' Torquatus snapped. 'The first was the sort of thing you might write to anyone: lovely weather, food good, wish you were here.'

'Well, considering that I was just waiting to hear that you were going to divorce me and marry Octavia - !'

'What? I was going to do what?'

They were both shouting now, red-faced. Balbus was on his feet, hovering uncertainly behind them.

'Cornelia! You will harm yourself - and the child.'

Torquatus, grim-faced, and Cornelia, flushed and bright-eyed, turned as one on her father.

'I think you'd better leave us,' Torquatus said coldly, pulling himself together.

'Well, I'm sure if we all calm down and talk this over,' Balbus began.

Torquatus walked over to the door and opened it. 'Out,' he said, and Balbus, after one glance at his thunderous face, went out trying to look dignified. Torquatus glanced round the room. 'And you.' The slaves, their eyes downcast, followed their master and Torquatus closed the door behind them. Turning to face Cornelia and still resting his back against the door, he said coldly, 'You went off to Perusia, and when I wrote to you sent me a cold letter saying you were well.'

She nodded. 'Of course. I needed - ,'

He held up his hand.

'Then when your father had got you out of Perusia I wrote again. And you never sent me one word of answer.'

'Aulus, you must believe me,' she said quietly. 'I never had that letter.'

'What? And I suppose you never sent me that reply, that broke my heart?' His voice quivered for a moment. '"I feel utterly betrayed". That's what you said. And you said you didn't want me to write to you, even. "There is nothing more to say", that's what you wrote. Can you deny it?

She was looking at him, puzzled. Then a flush spread over her face. 'Oh, I see it now! The bastard! The mean, conniving bastard! Just wait till I - ,' She stopped, gasping, and for the first time he thought of her condition and was filled with fear for her.

'Do sit down,' he said. 'It's your father you're talking about, isn't it?'

'How did you guess,' she replied bitterly. 'Of course it is. I wrote those words to him, not to you. It was before we went to Perusia. He wrote telling me that I should go home to him, and that was my answer.'

'And he kept the letter, thinking it might come in handy. I see.' He sat down beside her on the reading couch and took her hand. 'But Cornelia, I still don't understand why you ran away. What had I done?'

She was very pale. 'I should have asked you, I know. But Papa said you would only deny it - and then Canidia had heard the same rumours, and I thought it must be true.'

He was staring at her. 'Dearest Cornelia,' he said very gently. 'What rumours? You said something about Octavia?'

At his gentle words she began to weep, quietly at first, and then in a storm of tears. She couldn't speak, but he put his arms round her and spoke soothing words to her, her swollen body strangely unfamiliar and difficult to hold. After a while she began to gulp her tears back down. 'They said,' she muttered, wiping her eyes, 'that when Marcellus died you'd be offered Octavia.'

He gasped. 'And that was it, was it? My little love, Octavia's a delightful woman, but I don't love her. I couldn't, you see, because all my love is given away already.'

'Is it?' she asked shyly, turning within his arm to look up at him.

'It is. I've come to love you so much. It's been torture to walk into my home and know that you weren't there. I've come to realise that I can't live happily without you.'

'I knew I couldn't live without you the very day we met,' she told him shyly.

'But you didn't tell me you were pregnant,' he pointed out.

'In my letter I did. The one my father never sent to you.' She sat up indignantly, moving out of his arm. 'It was so hard.' She held him off, her lips trembling, her eyes almost spilling tears again. 'I must have started the baby the last night we were together. I only knew I was expecting after you'd gone to the war. And then - well, think of what I was facing, or thought I was: giving birth all alone, and probably losing the baby straight away.' She struggled to speak for a moment. 'How could I bear it? But that's what I thought would happen. My father persuaded me that you had only asked for me at Octavian's bidding, and because you needed children. I knew if we were divorced you'd would never leave the child with me.'

He pulled her back into his arms and held her very close, saying into her hair, 'That's a nightmare you'll never have to face. I promise. And tell me: when is this important baby due?'

She smiled up at him. 'Oh, not until the end of March. And I've been fine, once the sickness was over.'

'You've been sick?' His eyebrows were drawn over his nose in a deep frown. 'I'll get my doctor to see you.'

'Oh, no!' She gave a choke of laughter. 'A doctor's the last thing I need. My father is surrounded by quacks of all descriptions. Living in his house I've been prodded and pushed and dieted on this and that till I almost ran away again. And I'm seven months gone, so there's nothing to worry about just now. Only I didn't know - I didn't think you wanted me.'

He pulled her close into his arms. 'Well, you know now. I'll never leave you, or our child, while there's breath in my body.'

Steps could be heard on the marble floor outside.

'That's Papa,' Cornelia said.

Torquatus looked down at his wife. 'I think, my love, that we're going to have to deal with this together.'

'It's the only way,' she agreed. She was looking lovelier than ever, laughing up at him, relaxed and happy. He kissed her. 'Let's go back to our home, my love. And please never leave it again.'

She didn't have time to reply. Balbus hurried in, looking from one to the other of them. 'I suppose you imagine you can just take Cornelia back to Rome now?'

Torquatus said quietly, 'I don't imagine that, I know it. And there she stays. No, Balbus, listen to me. I don't really understand why you've done everything you could to separate us, but whatever your reasons it hasn't worked. You've even used the letter Cornelia wrote you to try and persuade me she didn't love me. You've failed.'

Balbus looked from one of them to the other. He seemed to deflate suddenly, and looked very much older than Torquatus had ever seen him.

'But she's not far from her time now. Don't you think she ought to stay, just until the baby's born?'

Cornelia exclaimed, but Torquatus put his arm round her,

saying, 'She needs to be in her own house. My house. And travelling to Rome will be perfectly safe for her in a litter. We can take our time, break the journey as often as we want.' There was a glimmer of a smile on his lips. 'Don't tell me you haven't got a litter,' and Cornelia gave an uncertain little laugh.

'You've never seen Papa's litter?' she asked. 'You won't believe it. It's made of exotic woods, cedar of Lebanon and sandalwood, gilded and painted, and it has the softest mattress inside. Filled with feathers and big enough for four people. There are two sets of curtains: fine linen ones for summer, and soft leather ones for the winter or when you want to sleep. It's got eight bearers. It's like travelling in your own bed.'

'I don't think there's a great deal more to say,' Torquatus said. 'Except that I'd like to know how Cornelia was rescued from Perusia, and also how you, my darling, got here.'

Torquatus and Cornelia sat down again side by side on a reading-couch, and Balbus reluctantly went back to his place at the table.

'Oh, Perusia,' said Balbus, discomfited. 'That was just a question of hiring the right men for the job.'

'Felix told me how they broke in and snatched you after a fight with Fiscilius' slaves,' Torquatus told Cornelia. 'And how you did your bit by knocking one of the men out with a bag of books.'

'I did,' she said. 'At last a use for all those old philosophy scrolls. I was afraid at first, because I didn't know they were Papa's men. I was afraid Fiscilius had planned to move us out of the house. But as soon as they said they came from Papa I stopped worrying. They had it all organised. They smuggled us out through some underground passages. You didn't know there were any? Nor did I. They must have bribed somebody very thoroughly because we were whisked away into them, and came out beyond the city and not far from the river. There was a boat there all ready for us. It all went very smoothly though they were a bit put out. They hadn't expected three of us, you see, and they actually seemed to think I'd leave Nereis and Rachel behind.' She sniffed. 'We travelled all the way down to Rome in the boat, where I parted from Nereis, and from Ostia we sailed to Neapolis on one of my father's ships. No storms, nothing.'

'And then?' Torquatus asked.

'Then I discovered that I was essentially a prisoner. Oh, a very well-cared for prisoner, a prisoner allowed every comfort, but a prisoner all the same. I couldn't go out of the house without an escort, and the one time I tried to leave my father's property they made me turn back.'

Balbus said feebly, 'Well, I thought we ought to wait and see whether Torquatus was going to leave you for Octavia.'

'And you didn't give me his letter,' she cried, 'and you sent him the one I'd written to you. I can't forgive that. How could you do such a thing?'

Torquatus took her hand. 'That's all over, my love,' he reminded her.

Cornelia smiled, but insisted, 'I don't like being told what to do.'

Torquatus burst out laughing. 'You know, I had noticed that about you.'

Balbus had subsided, in a most uncharacteristic way, and was sitting tearing a bread roll to shreds. Torquatus thought he really must be very much upset, though whether it was the loss of his control over his daughter or the uncovering of his schemes Torquatus couldn't tell.

Cornelia got up and went across to Balbus, who also stood up. 'You know, don't you, that I won't ever leave Aulus now? Even if you tried to force a divorce between us, I simply wouldn't leave.'

Torquatus too stood up and came to stand with Cornelia. 'And if you did force a divorce what could you do, if Cornelia refused to leave my house? You could reclaim her dowry, of course. The loss of that money would hit us hard, I won't deny that. But it wouldn't alter our decision, you know. And you'd be very unpopular.' His dark face was harsh. 'Scheming and cheating to separate us in a way that would look as if you were only protecting your daughter is one thing; trying to force a loving wife away from her loving husband is quite another. Yes, I know it happens from time to time: Sulla did it to his daughter, didn't he? But you aren't a dictator, you know.'

Balbus nodded. He looked as if he were working out sums in his head, Torquatus thought, and was hardly listening to what was being said. 'Perhaps the best thing is if we just say no more about it?' he suggested. 'I can see I've made a mistake here. But I genuinely thought Cornelia was at risk of being humiliated. I mean, there really was a rumour about you and Octavia.'

'There was,' Cornelia agreed. 'That was what gave Papa's

warnings such force. Canidia told me she'd heard the same thing. But I agree that we should forget this. After all, you'll be a grandfather,' she pointed out to Balbus. 'You won't want to be banned from the house and treated as an enemy, will you?'

'Oh no.' Balbus seemed genuinely horrified.

'Then I think - reluctantly - that we'll put all this behind us,' Torquatus agreed.

They made the journey home so cautiously that Torquatus began to wonder whether the baby might actually be born on the journey. The weather, luckily, was mild for February, and Cornelia seemed perfectly comfortable, suffering only, she said, from a degree of boredom. After two weeks on the road, the bearers finally carried the litter up the slope of the Quirinal to their home.

Torquatus dismounted at the door as the bearers carried the litter inside and set it down in the reception hall. He hurried inside, leaving Catus to take the horses round to the stables.

'Welcome home,' he said cheerfully as Cornelia was helped out of the litter by Rachel and Trofimus.

'Yes, indeed,' Trofimus put in. 'I may say the whole household will be happy to have you home, madam.'

The smile stiffened a little on Torquatus' face when his father-in-law walked out of the shadows towards them. 'You overtook us on the road?'

Balbus saw his face change, and said defensively, 'I just wanted to be sure Cornelia had arrived safely,' he said.

'Of course you did,' Cornelia agreed, laying a hand on his arm. 'Why don't you stay to dinner?'

Balbus looked from his daughter to his son-in-law. Torquatus seconded the invitation, but he wasn't sorry when Balbus decided not to stay. 'You'll want to settle back in, I'm sure. I'll take the litter, now you've finished with it.'

Balbus had hardly left when Manlia came in, embracing Cornelia warmly, and exclaiming at how healthy she looked.

'Aulus wrote and told me you were expecting. You look wonderful, I must say. But I do wish you'd told me about the baby,' she said.

'Yes, I wish that too. But I couldn't. I'll tell you all about it, but not just now.'

To her brother's surprise Manlia just nodded. She was right about Cornelia, he thought. She was golden and serene, in the full ripeness of her beauty and joy. He watched his wife as she wandered round the reception hall, touching the family altar for luck, straightening one of the little wooden houses where the masks of his ancestors lived. He was a lucky man, he thought. He remembered how on the day of his wedding, when he had first seen Cornelia, he had thought that she was a woman any man might be glad to welcome into his home. He still thought that; only now he really knew her and could see beyond her beauty. Yes, he was a lucky man.

He turned to his sister, suddenly conscious that she had fallen silent. To his surprise, her smiles had gone. She was biting her lip.

'Is there something wrong?' he asked.

The face she raised to his was bright-eyed and stormy-faced. 'I'm glad your marriage is thriving,' Manlia said more bitterly than Torquatus had ever heard her. He pulled himself out of his mood of deep content.

'What's wrong? Bad news?'

'Oh, Aulus!' Her face broke up and she burst into a passion of weeping that frightened him. He put his arms round her, and Cornelia hurried across to her. Together they soothed her until she quietened down.

'Come and sit down and tell us what's wrong,' Torquatus suggested.

'Is it Ahenobarbus?' Cornelia asked. 'Your stepson? Manlia, my dear, do tell us what's happened.'

'Of course it's my beastly husband. He's only gone and joined Antonius. It's been bad enough that he was helping Sextus Pompeius, but at least he never officially joined him. I've been writing to him for ages trying to persuade him that Octavian's the man to support. And now that louse Pollio has apparently brought him and Antonius together. He's put all his troops and ships at Antonius' service. Just when I was thinking that at last he might decide for Octavian and come home, and we might have an ordinary life - children - ,' She dissolved again. Over her head, Torquatus' and Cornelia's eyes met. This was serious news. Octavian had accepted Manlia's presence in Torquatus' house even though her husband was an enemy of his, but how would he respond if Ahenobarbus was actively working for Antonius? Anyone could see that it was only a matter of time before the two men left running the state would fall out. They didn't need to speak to know that they both felt almost guilty to be so happy when Manlia was still so far from peace and security. How many more years must she go on, a lodger in her brother's house, childless, husbandless? Torquatus could think of nothing to say to relieve her loneliness.

Cornelia took Manlia's hand and patted it. 'But if he's gone to Antonius, that might be a good thing,' she said. She sounded her usual practical self, and Torquatus smiled to himself. 'He'd have had to be on someone's side sooner or later, there's no such thing as an independent now. It would have been much better if he'd chosen our side. But think. He's had huge naval experience over these last few years. If he had joined Octavian he'd have had to fight against Sextus Pompeius, and you'd still never see him. But Antonius hasn't got any particular naval battles to fight, has he? So maybe he'll end up somewhere on land, somewhere you could join him?'

Manlia blew her nose defiantly, and tucked some strands of hair that had fallen down back behind her ear. 'Well, perhaps he might. Though I think he really likes being at sea. Oh, isn't life dreadful?' She bit her lips, obviously struggling not to cry again.

Torquatus gave her a hug. 'Cornelia's right. The war's over for now. Why don't you go and see your Gnaeus? Where was he writing from?'

'Athens. He's with Antonius there.'

'Easy then. I suppose he'll be there for a while, since Antonius isn't likely to pack him off somewhere straight away. Octavian's expecting to meet Antonius sometime fairly soon, I know. You've always liked Athens, and the seaways will be just about open again. You wouldn't have to wait long.'

Manlia sat up straight and wiped her eyes. She gave him a mischievous look, saying, 'I shan't wait at all. I hope he'll be pleased to see me. He'd better be, after all this time! I'll go at once - tomorrow! Oh, what a wonderful idea. May I leave some of my slaves here? I shan't need them all on the journey, and if - oh Juno, please make it happen! - we actually settle down somewhere together for a while, they can always follow me.'

'Of course. You must do just as you like.'

Manlia jumped up, impatient to be on her way, but as she was about to leave the room she turned. 'Oh, I am selfish! I don't believe I've told you how happy I was to see you back together again. Because it is all right, isn't it?'

'It's absolutely all right,' Cornelia said, laughing. 'Better than all right, whatever my stupid father may think.'

'Good! But I'm so sorry I shan't be here when the baby comes.'

'We'll manage,' Cornelia assured her. 'And when you come back, you'll be Aunt Manlia.'

When Manlia had gone Torquatus opened his arms and Cornelia walked into them. 'My poor darling. You have been through such a horrible time and now it's over.' He thought with a new tremor of fear that she was still not safe. Having the child would be a huge danger. How many women died in childbirth? He didn't know, but he knew it was common enough. He held her closer. 'I wish I'd known about your pregnancy though. I'd have cared for you all through it, not just now, at the end.'

'Do you know, I was almost wishing that the baby would just die before it was even born. Isn't that terrible? But the thought of giving up my child to some nurse, of knowing that he was here in Rome, not far away but separated from me for ever - .'

He pulled her back into his arms again. 'My poor darling, that's all over now. Oh, if we can just have peace! I don't want my son to grow up to fight Romans.'

She chuckled, and murmured, 'Might be a girl.'

'Well, she might. And if she is, I don't want her left alone for years like Manlia, aching for an absent husband and the children she'll never have.'

'No. There's been too much of that.'

The house was alive with activity until about noon the next day when Manlia left. The slaves brought box after box down to add to the growing pile of Manlia's luggage in the reception hall. 'It's as well I'm going, Aulus,' said Manlia as she kissed her brother goodbye. 'I'd be a problem for you if I stayed. Whereas if I'd managed to get Gnaeus to come over to Octavian - oh, well, why talk about it?'

'You know Octavian would never harm you.'

'Let's not say never.' Her voice was very dry. 'But I'm sure he'd prefer not to.'

'Gods! What's in there?' Torquatus exclaimed, as two burly slaves struggled to lift a small but very solid-looking chest into the litter.

'Oh just a few bits of cash and jewellery I managed to save

when Gnaeus was ruined,' she said airily, and they all laughed.

'We shall miss you,' said her brother. 'I suppose you wouldn't like to take Nar with you? He could travel with the ox-wagon, if you like.'

Manlia's long dark eyes laughed out at him from behind the edge of the litter-curtain. 'Still trying to get rid of the poor little thing? Of course I can't take him, when I don't know where I'm going myself.'

'I suppose in the end I'll have to send him to one of my estates. Not sure that's what Fiscilia would have wanted, though.' He sighed. 'I do wish - ,'

'Yes.' Cornelia put her hand on his arm as they watched the litter being carried off down the hill towards the gate where Manlia's hired carriage would be waiting. 'I know what you wish, but you did everything you could have done for Fiscilia. As for Canidia, she died in the siege, like a great many other old people, no doubt. You have to put it behind you, Aulus.'

Chapter 21

It was almost the middle of March, and Torquatus had been busy. Cornelia had settled back into her home quietly and comfortably. It was, thought Torquatus, as if she'd never been away. And she was blooming, her warm complexion and brilliant eyes a proof of health so good that even Balbus, calling every day, had been unable to find an excuse to send in a different doctor to examine her. So intrusive had he been, in fact, that they had found it necessary to limit his visits.

'I really can't have him fussing around like a wasp at a festival,' Cornelia said crossly. 'And I don't need a doctor. I need a good, sensible midwife.'

Torquatus opened his mouth but before he could speak she said, 'Men know absolutely nothing about this. I only had to ask my women friends, and they were able to recommend the very one I need. She came to see me a couple of weeks back, and we agreed everything.'

She shut her mouth with something of a snap, and Torquatus felt bold enough to say only, 'Is she nearby? Can she come quickly when your time comes? Because I don't - ,'

'I told you it's all arranged. She's here already: a small woman, dark hair wound round her head. You may not have noticed her.'

Torquatus was relieved to be able to say, 'Oh, that woman. Yes, I had noticed her. I asked Trofimus who she was the other day and he said you'd hired her.'

Cornelia spluttered with laughter at his air of dignity. 'So you see, there's nothing to worry about.'

The only specific task Octavian had given him was to make sure Antonius' wife went to join him without delay. It had been almost absurdly easy. A volunteer group of men from the Antonian legions took upon themselves the task of escorting her. Before they had all left Perusia the men sent Torquatus a polite request to let them pass through Rome. Equally courteously, he told them they might do so, but only on conditions, and at night. He didn't want any demonstrations of support for Antonius. Or demonstrations against him either, for that matter. So the lady Fulvia was carried through the city in a closed litter late at night, and the first the citizens knew of it was when news came that she had reached Brundisium and set out on one of the five warships

Antonius had sent to escort her.

Settling back in again after his trip to Neapolis Torquatus was glad he'd taken that precaution. The peace was holding, but the city felt as if it might break out at any moment, in bread riots, or riots against the Three, or just riots. Metaphorically shaking the dust of Fulvia from his hands, Torquatus had found he had time, over and above his other duties, to think once more about Fiscilius and his crimes. He still wondered why Fiscilius had laughed at him, up on the temple roof at Perusia, mocking him for his failure to understand. Why had the sight of that pair of old shoes in Lollia's flat made him so worried? What did the pieces of reed stuck under the slab in the shrine mean?

Even more puzzling, just what had got into Nereis that had made her suddenly unwilling to discuss with Cornelia her acquaintanceship with the Fiscilii in Mevania? There had been much coming and going between Torquatus' house and hers as Felix and his mother rebuilt their fractured relationship, but Torquatus felt that Nereis was avoiding him, calling when he would probably be out of the house, or when it would be too busy with visitors for any confidential conversation.

He had settled down to think, and the result of his thinking had been a quiet walk to the Capena Gate where he bought himself a glass of wine and a plate of olives and settled down to chat with the barman. He had written (of course) to Manlia, and had asked her, among other things, what Canidia had told her about Fiscilia's childhood. Another visit to the young musician in the flat above Lollia's too, had helped clear his mind. And now he thought he was ready to close the mystifying business once and for all.

Cornelia, sitting on the bench at the head of the pool in the reception hall, watched her husband as he stood waiting, his slaves busy around him. She thought back to her wedding day: she had been anxious, and angry with her father for high-handedly arranging this marriage without consulting her. And then she had raised her veil and her heart had turned over. This was a man she could be happy with. She had loved his serious dark eyes under those arching brows, but more than that she'd loved his look of competence. A man worth committing to, she'd thought. And she'd been right.

As for Torquatus, unaware of her scrutiny, he was a little annoyed that Ampudius was late. He was suddenly reminded of his own father, a tetchy old consular. What would he have said if he'd seen his son, well embarked on a magisterial career, friend of the powerful, kicking his heels waiting for a mere equestrian? Torquatus had to hide a grin, and acknowledge that he was glad of the absence of that distinguished gentleman. He was just about to share this thought with Cornelia when the sounds of feet on the paving outside, and the murmuring of voices, announced the arrival of his visitor. But it was Felix who first realised that this was not the expected guest at the door, but his mother, Nereis. He ran over to her, Nar capering at his heels with little yelps of joy.

'How many more times must I - ?' Torquatus began wearily, but Felix swung round, his face ablaze with happiness. 'I'm sorry, lord, I forgot. I'll take him away.' He turned back to his mother and Torquatus heard him say in a pleading tone, 'You won't go, will you? I shan't be long,' before tugging the dog away from Nereis' feet and trotting off with him.

Nereis watched her son for a moment, before turning back with a start to Torquatus, who was asking politely, 'How can I help you? I hope you have recovered fully from your ordeal in Perusia? And the rescue was equally hair-raising, from the sound of it?' Nereis looked nervous, he thought. To him she still looked as she had when she had been his mother's weaving-woman and his father's mistress. She had hardly aged and was always very well cared-for, and today seemed especially elegant. The necklace of heavy gold round her neck echoed the red-brown of her hair, and the stola over her plain linen gown had the sheen of real silk. She didn't answer Torquatus straight away but glanced around as if she felt a little unsure of herself in the presence of Trofimus, Cornelia and all the other slaves coming and going.

Cornelia had been sitting comfortably on the bench at the head of the reception-hall pool but had gone to meet Nereis, kissing her on the cheek. She noticed the visitor's unease, and said, with her usual quiet good sense, 'Perhaps you would rather speak to my husband privately?'

'Oh, no! I don't at all mind anyone hearing what I want to ask.' She raised her eyes to Torquatus and gave him a clear, frank look. 'I know what I want is a great favour, lord, and perhaps it's too much. I hope you won't be angry anyway. I can pay a fair price.'

'What in the world is it that you want to buy, Nereis?'

But as she opened her mouth to reply, loud voices in the

street, and the clash of boots on the mosaic floor announced new arrivals. As the party emerged from the entrance corridor into the afternoon light of the reception hall, Torquatus saw a stocky, brown-haired man with a decisive face and steady grey eyes, crinkled with laughter or a life spent out of doors. On his arm was a lady as tall as himself. Beside him, Torquatus heard Cornelia gasp. He himself couldn't tear his eyes away from the lady's rich golden hair. Instinctively he glanced across at Cornelia, shaken by a sudden memory. Then he moved forward, smiling.

'Marcus Ampudius and the lady Fiscilia.' It was not a question.

Ampudius was smiling. 'That's right.'

'Fiscilia!' Cornelia and Nereis exclaimed simultaneously.

'Fiscilia,' Ampudius nodded.

'Who was not murdered by her brother. But whose slave was,' Torquatus agreed.

'That's right,' Fiscilia told him, in a rich, low voice.

'But how - ?' Cornelia began, as Felix exclaimed, 'But wasn't he - ?'

'Come and sit down', Torquatus said. 'We have chairs ready in the garden. Please come with us, Nereis: it's clear you knew the Fiscilii, so this will interest you.' When they were all seated, Felix crouching at his mother's feet, Torquatus sat looking around at them for a moment, as if wondering where to start. 'It was Calliste who died, of course.'

Ampudius nodded.

'I'm delighted to welcome you all here. Especially Fiscilia. I want to know how you escaped, where you've been. And - forgive me - I will get one of my slaves to make notes. The senior aedile is still interested in your death,' he told Fiscilia with a smile. 'I wouldn't exactly say he's investigating it, but he's a thorough, tidy-minded sort of fellow, and I'd like to be able to give him a sensible account of the whole affair.'

Fiscilia glanced at Ampudius. He nodded and she said, 'If you think it really necessary. I must say I would prefer it not to be widely known that my brother tried to kill me, and did kill a harmless slave who'd been part of his family for years.'

'I think that's reasonable. Although, since everyone knew the lady Fiscilia was dead, I don't think you can come back to life without being something of a sensation, you know.'

'I suppose not.'

'But first I think I'll start by saying what I think really happened. Not what Fiscilius told me but what I discovered for myself.'

He looked around. 'First, then, I came to the conclusion that Fiscilia was running away to Ampudius, and not aiming to destroy shrines and commit acts of sacrilege.'

'Of course not,' Fiscilia agreed. 'My brother was pressing me harder and harder to marry Titus Fulvus. I was frightened. I knew that my life wouldn't be worth living once I'd inherited whatever it was from Aunt Canidia.'

'You might not have had to stand it for very long,' Ampudius said grimly.

'No,' Fiscilia agreed with a little shiver.

Torquatus went on. 'Here was a dead girl, who had apparently burned down three shrines, two with the reed men of the Argei in it, and one after the man had been consecrated and taken away. A strange and rather incoherent act of sabotage.

'Next, Fiscilius turned up. He screamed and fainted when he had to identify the body. We put that down to grief, but I should have realised much sooner that it was really because the body wasn't the one he'd been expecting to see. He encouraged me in the belief that it was Fiscilia who had burned the shrines till he could see I doubted it. Then he told me he'd found evidence that the slaves had done the deed. All that time he was simply bursting to get away, wasn't he, Cornelia?'

'He was really anxious, shaky and quite volatile,' she agreed. 'I put it down to his very natural distress.'

'He was desperate to hurry off after the slaves, as he said. In reality he had to find and kill his sister. He couldn't allow her to live. He'd come down to Rome remembering what Fulvus had told him about the shrine, discovered that the festival was on the next day and made his plan. He must have had quite an evening: no wonder Fulvus' slaves said he was out till late. He found out where one or two of the shrines were, hung around Lollia's flat to get hold of Calliste with a message to her mistress to come to the shrine.'

'He did!' Fiscilia exclaimed. 'He pretended that he was from Marcus' house.' She took her husband's hand and smiled at him warmly. 'But we wondered why Marcus, if he was in Rome, would have done such an odd thing. I was very suspicious.'

Torquatus could see Fiscilia was eager to tell what she knew. 'You'd better tell your story, Fiscilia.'

She paused as if not quite sure where to begin. 'You'd better start at the beginning,' Ampudius suggested, with a smile that told Torquatus what a good marriage this was, however strangely entered into. Fiscilia fascinated him. She was like and unlike Fiscilius: her broad brow and pointed chin were just like his, but her hair was a brighter gold. Above all, Torquatus was struck straight away by her quietness. There wasn't a trace of her brother's temper or restlessness. She was blushing a little at being the centre of attention.

'When I arrived in Rome I didn't know Quintus was following me,' she began, but Torquatus held up a hand, laughing. 'You can't start there' he said. 'You came to Rome simply on the way to Formiae, I take it?'

Fiscilia nodded.

'Leaving a misleading letter for Canidia - oh!' He and Cornelia looked at each other, stricken. Fiscilia understood at once. 'She's dead, isn't she?'

Torquatus nodded, and for a moment Fiscilia dropped her face into her hands. 'I feared as much.'

'How did you know she was dead?' Torquatus asked.

'Oh, because Quintus - no, if you want the whole story I really can't start there.' In a low, fierce voice she exclaimed, 'That treasure of hers! I think the gods must have cursed it. She never found it anything other than a responsibility and a burden, I know that. And now I suppose it's mine. I don't want it! I've never wanted it.'

His voice very dry, Torquatus said, 'That's just as well, because it will have - disappeared, let's say, when Perusia was sacked.'

Wiping her eyes, Fiscilia shrugged and said, 'Just tell me how Aunt Canidia died, and then I'll tell you my story.'

'I don't know.' Torquatus face was sombre. 'I saw her when I got into the city after it fell, just after she'd died. She looked peaceful. And she hadn't been hurt.'

'Ah, there's mental torture as well as physical, isn't there? I might have guessed the treasure would be at the bottom of it.' She sighed and shifted on her stool. 'I'd known for years that I was her heir, of course. She'd no family of her own and had lived with us since I was twelve years old. I didn't care about it: I thought she meant I'd get her pretty cameo necklace and maybe a few thousand sesterces I could spend on new dresses when her bank account was cleared. But I suppose I should have guessed it was more than that: she was always very insistent I shouldn't tell Quintus.'

'Always? Wasn't that just from when he left Julius' service after killing another legate?'

Fiscilia stared at him. 'I don't know how you found that out, but you're quite right.'

Torquatus could feel Ampudius' eyes on him. The man had no need to worry: Torquatus had no intention of telling Fiscilia that the victim had been Ampudius' brother. That was a private matter, for him to deal with as he saw fit.

'But your brother did find out, didn't he? How did that happen?'

'I've no idea. This doesn't sound good, but I wouldn't be surprised if he looked into her documents behind her back. Anyway it was about that time my brother started to push for the marriage to Fulvus.'

'That was a new plan?' Torquatus was watching her carefully. She considered.

'No. It had been mentioned before, but only as a possibility. Now suddenly it was a fact, and I realised I had to find a way out of it.'

'You hadn't met Ampudius then?' This was Cornelia, smiling encouragingly. Fiscilia smiled back.

'No. And when I did I knew straight away that this was the man for me. One brief meeting at a supper party, that was all - ,' She shook her head and the pair exchanged a swift, private smile. Torquatus brought their attention back to the present. 'So no doubt Ampudius' offer of marriage drove Fiscilius to extremes?'

'Yes. I suppose he must have been frightened of losing control of me. He knew Fulvus was always going to do what he wanted: Fulvus had been my brother's follower all his life. I was told - told, mind you - that I was going to marry on a certain day. I refused. I knew Ampudius wanted me, and when my brother's bullying became unbearable I decided to run away.'

Fiscilia spoke quite easily, finishing the sentence with a decisive little nod, but Torquatus was only too well aware of the courage it must have taken a girl to run away to a man she barely knew, living in a distant city. It told him more than anything Fiscilia had said about the sort of treatment she'd received. And if she'd been caught before reaching Ampudius' protection, there wasn't a decent citizen or a court that would have hesitated to send her back to her brother.

'Tell me,' Torquatus said, 'Did you ever intend to appeal to Octavian against the settlement of soldiers on Mevania's land?'

Fiscilia threw him a look of amused contempt. 'Of course not. Only my dear aunt could have believed such a silly story. But, oh - ,' her face broke up - 'how guilty I've felt. I tricked her and ran away, and she never knew the truth. I felt I had to: she was very old-fashioned, thought it was a woman's duty to do as her head of household told her, said maybe I would be comfortable enough married to Titus. I couldn't trust her not to tell Quintus where I'd gone.'

'Maybe. But it gave him his chance,' Torquatus pointed out. 'He could chase you and catch you far away in Rome, without his true motivation ever coming out. He expected to be able to round up the slaves easily enough, and have them put to death for not protecting you. But they were too quick for him. They ran away and he had to follow them. He didn't know it was Calliste who'd died, of course. If he had, his hunt for you would have been even more intense.' His face was severe. 'Why did you send her to the shrine?'

Fiscilia jumped up, her fists clenched. 'But I didn't! I never would have done that, and I've wished and wished she hadn't gone. What happened was this. When we arrived there was nothing in the flat and Calliste went out to buy food. On her way back a man stopped her and gave her a note for me, just as you guessed. A stranger, she thought, but she couldn't make his face out because the hood of his cloak was shadowing it. That must have been Fiscilius, but as far as I knew my brother would only just be getting home from Ariminum, and I was sure he'd go to Spoletium next to check I wasn't there. I'd no idea he could be in Rome already. No, the only person who could know I was in Rome was Marcus here. I'd written to him before I set off but I hadn't been able to wait long enough for his answer.'

'What did your brother's note say?' asked Cornelia.

'Oh, only that before making any decisions about my future I should go to the shrine where I would hear something important, something I needed to know. But I was suspicious. I must say I was feeling dreadfully anxious and alone. I'm not sure I even trusted Marcus by then. So I feared it might be someone from his household trying to put me off, or wanting to tell me he was already married to someone else. I don't know. But I told Calliste that if it was from Marcus then why didn't he just come and speak to me? Why all the messing about with hoods and notes? But perhaps he was tired of me? Anyway, I decided to go. Calliste insisted she would do it. She hadn't liked the hooded man, she said, but it was hard to see what harm he could do her, so she would go and pretend to be me. She even persuaded me to lend her my best dress. She was giggling and saying,' - Fiscilia broke off, choking - 'saying that there was no limit to what she would do to get the chance to wear that dress. Oh, I can't explain, but we'd been like sisters. Oh, Calliste!'

She choked back her tears and wiped her eyes, as Cornelia patted her hand. Torquatus said, 'She wore your sandals, too.'

'Of course she did,' said Fiscilia, surprised, but Cornelia exclaimed: 'That old shoe that the dog plays with: it was Calliste's, and not a spare pair.'

'It was the shoes that made me realise it must have been Calliste who died,' Torquatus explained. 'Calliste borrowed Fiscilia's sandals. Those clumpy shoes would have been a complete giveaway. And then when Fiscilia came to leave the flat she found she couldn't wear them, and took another pair of her own shoes. Of course slaves, if they have shoes at all, don't carry a spare pair around with them. Good. What next? We know from Fulvus that Fiscilius went out shortly after he arrived, and then left for good very early the following morning.'

'Fulvus was in Rome?' Fiscilia looked shocked.

'No,' Torquatus said. 'But he lent Fiscilius his flat on the Velia.'

'I suppose that's why Quintus chose that shrine, then?' Fiscilia said thoughtfully. 'I couldn't think what that was about. It wasn't near our old flat or Marcus' house, where he might expect me to be. Anyway, I waited for Calliste to come back, getting more and more anxious. I'd never intended to spend more than one night in Rome, because I was too frightened of Quintus: though even then I'd never have dreamed he would actually kill me. I wouldn't have broken the journey at all if I hadn't had to. Anyway, after a while I went out to see if I could find out what had happened. I put on Calliste's clothes, but her shoes were uncomfortable and I left them behind. I felt safer dressed as a slave, and it wasn't the first time: we'd quite often swapped clothes for a game. This wasn't a game, though.' She shivered. 'I soon heard what had happened; everyone was talking about it. And I couldn't think who except Quintus could have killed Calliste. I dared not go back to the flat. It was the only place I knew in Rome.'

'You'd stolen the key to the flat from Ancilla,' Torquatus said.

'I had,' Fiscilia agreed, unabashed. 'And I slipped it back into the dish on the way out: I think I must have known already that I wouldn't be going back there. I kept out of sight for the rest of the day, feeling terrified, and as if my brother might be hiding behind every fountain or column. At last evening came and I went to meet the slaves at the stables, just as I'd arranged. I had the hood of my cloak up, and they took me for Calliste at first, and I was in the carriage before they realised I wasn't. Then they refused point-blank to go without Calliste. When I told them she was dead and my brother in Rome they flew into such a blind panic that they tried to throw me out of the carriage, but I hung on tight and at last they dashed out of Rome as fast as the mules could go. The worst thing was that I couldn't hold onto my dog, and I lost him.'

Fiscilia's eyes were brimming, but Torquatus, with a slight smile, nodded to Felix and the boy jumped up and hurried off. 'Go on.'

'We went on, down the via Appia, until it got too dark to go any further. The slaves were very nervous with me, and I didn't trust them. They pulled off the road down a little winding track, saying we would camp there for the night. I knew that, incredible as it might seem, Quintus must have killed Calliste. I tried to think what he would do next. I thought if he knew he'd killed Calliste, he'd realise I would hurry down to Formiae as fast as I could, and he'd come after me. But if he thought he'd killed me he'd have no reason to do that. I thought he might chase after the slaves, in which case I needed to leave them as soon as possible, or he might just hang around in Rome pretending to look for me. I was scared, but I tried not to show it, and decided that I'd stay awake all night if need be. One of the slaves had a knife. I took it from him when he was asleep, but then I went to sleep too. The next thing I knew, I was wide awake and they were discussing what to do with me. Nestor, our old groom, was unhappy about abandoning me, but Tiro, the new slave, said their lives were on the line and wanted to kill me. I was glad I'd taken that knife, and thought at least I'd take one of them with me.'

'What were the slaves planning to do? I'd assumed they

would go to Sextus Pompeius in Sicily.'

'That's right. They were arguing about where to sail from: not Rhegium, Tiro said. He thought Tempsa would be better.'

'He was right.'

'Well, Sicily was where they were going. I know that because later - 'Fiscilia broke off, shivering a little. 'Anyway, the light was getting stronger by the minute, and I was worrying about how long I could go on pretending to be asleep. In the end they decided they couldn't wait and galloped off - in my carriage.'

'Terrifying, to be left alone like that,' Cornelia said, patting Fiscilia's hand.

'Well, I was just glad to see the back of them,' Fiscilia told her briskly. 'I waited till I was sure they'd gone, then walked southwards, avoiding the main road as much as I could. I thought it would be best not to get to Formiae too soon, in case Quintus went there.'

Torquatus turned to Ampudius, but before he could speak a scrabbling in the gravel announced the arrival of Felix and Nar. Fiscilia cried out. The dog raced across to her. He was too excited even to stay in her arms, but jumped down and ran round in circles giving little screaming barks, before subsiding at her feet. Torquatus waited patiently, enjoying the look of extreme repulsion on his wife's face. When he could be heard, he went on. 'Your brother brought him here.'

'Quintus brought him? But Quintus doesn't even like him.'

'I gradually realised that. But I can assure you he was deeply moved at finding his dead sister's dog.' He laughed at her face of disgust, but Cornelia pointed out that there had been nothing else Fiscilius could do.

'I wonder when my brother realised I wasn't dead?' Fiscilia wondered.

'I don't think he doubted that he'd killed you until he came here,' Torquatus said. 'As I said, he almost fainted when he saw Calliste's body. I think after he'd murdered her - you, as he thought - he'd sent his slave to hang around outside Ampudius' house, expecting to see Calliste coming to ask after her mistress. She'd have been lured away and killed. I think you were very lucky to escape, Fiscilia, because I suspect Fiscilius realised quite quickly that Calliste wasn't coming, and went down to the Capena Gate to watch for the slaves coming to collect the carriage and horses: he'd have followed them the night before, to see where they were going.

I presume he got his horse and followed you, but by that time you'd turned off the road. I'm curious to know how you survived, Fiscilia?' Torquatus asked.

'I had the most wonderful good fortune,' she said seriously. 'I fell ill.'

Everyone laughed out at this, and Nar took the opportunity to jump into her lap and lick her chin. Fiscilia stared at them. Torquatus suspected that a sense of humour wasn't among her virtues.

'No, really. I must have caught a fever, sleeping in the open that night. By the end of the day I was feeling dreadful: I hadn't eaten all day and I was feverish. I collapsed on the doorstep of a farmhouse. Another stroke of luck: the farmer turned out to be a miserly type who thought Saturnalia had come early bringing him a free slave. He had me put in a cow-byre: if I survived he'd keep me as his house-keeper (and anything else he fancied, of course) and if I died he'd be no worse off. I lived, luckily. And none of the slaves wanted to get too close because of my fever, so they never found the bit of money and the knife in my bundle. I got better after some days, and began to get my strength back though the food the slaves got there was dreadful: coarse bread with grit in it, and a kind of cabbage soup. Finally one evening the farmer came to see me and kindly explained what he had in mind for me, and I reckoned it was time to go.'

'How did you do that?' Cornelia asked.

'It wasn't all that hard. The place was a cowshed not a prison, and although the door was locked and barred the roof was quite rotten in places. Half of the roof had been floored out making extra storage space. There was even a ladder to climb up there. I reckoned I could make a big enough hole to get out. Though I must say that I thought I wasn't going to make it, just at first. The first tile I managed to shift was much heavier than I'd expected and I couldn't hold it. It slid away and crashed on the ground. The shed was away from the house, but the old man's dog heard the noise and barked, and I heard him come out and shout at it to be quiet. I waited and waited, terrified that he would come, but he didn't and at last I was able to go on. It was much easier with one tile out and I quite soon had a hole I could climb through. It wasn't a long drop to the ground, though it felt like it. I didn't worry any more about my brother, but just walked and hitched lifts, turning aside every night to find somewhere safe to sleep. I was in slave's clothes, so no-one challenged me. It seemed to take for ever. I suppose it was really only a couple of weeks. Perhaps a little more. I wasn't counting.'

She paused, her face pale, and took her husband's hand. 'The worst thing - I've never even told Marcus this - was that I found the slaves.'

Cornelia exclaimed, 'You found them? Alive?'

'Why didn't you tell me?' Ampudius asked at the same moment.

'I couldn't. And no, they weren't alive.' Fiscilia shivered. 'I'd turned off the road and walked down a little lane, so quiet and peaceful. I was looking for somewhere to sleep, and thought it was perfect. There were bees humming round the gorse bushes, just as if everything was quite normal. Then I smelt them. I came round a bend in the lane and there they were in a little clearing, in the lovely dappled light under the trees. They must have been dead for some days. I don't know why I didn't just turn and run, why I had to go and look. I think I just needed to know what Quintus had done. They'd had their throats cut. It wasn't only the bees' humming I'd heard, but the flies all around their bodies.' She shuddered. 'The animals and the carriage had gone. Of course, the men might have been set on by robbers, but I was sure in my own mind that Quintus had caught up with them. And that he'd be after me too. I thought then I'd probably never get safely to Formiae.' She shivered again, and held Ampudius' hand more tightly. 'I travelled faster after that. And at last I got to Marcus and was safe.'

'And married,' Torquatus pointed out, smiling. 'That illness probably saved your life. You see, Fiscilius had to give up the search for Calliste. He'd killed the men, but he told me himself that Calliste would never have agreed to anything that would harm you. He had to find her and silence her, but he also had to come back to Rome, to identify you. It was vitally important that you should be known to be dead. He broke into Lollia's flat before coming here, under cover of the noise of the traffic just rolling into Rome at dusk. He needed to make sure you hadn't left anything there which would lead to Ampudius: you had to be trying to see Octavian. When he got here he had a smear of blood on his arm from breaking the shutter: there was blood on the shutter, too. And he left a little lamp, the same as the one Calliste had taken to the shrine.'

'He really wanted to be sure I'd be blamed for the sacrilege,' Fiscilia said sombrely.

'He did. He wanted Canidia to hate you, disinherit you and then turn to him as her last relative. It was only after the funeral that he was able to go back to the hunt for you. No wonder he was agitated. He must have been absolutely desperate to get away, because once you got to Formiae and told Ampudius here what was going on it was all up. But why didn't you let Canidia know where you were, once you were safe? Or me, for that matter?'

'Because I wouldn't let her,' Ampudius interrupted. 'You'll have to forgive me, Torquatus, but I didn't altogether trust you. I knew Fiscilius was staying with you. For all I knew you believed him, were friends with him. I thought the safest thing was for her to stay dead for the time being, since he'd killed once and would do so again if he could. I settled Fiscilia in a flat I have at Puteoli under a false name until I knew it was safe for her to be presented openly as my wife. My steward told me when Fiscilius came sniffing round to try and find out whether his sister was with me, and made sure he was told about the tragic death of the master's intended.

'Fiscilius tried to make me believe you'd been involved in the murder, too,' Torquatus told him.

'That's my brother, I'm afraid,' Fiscilia said sadly. 'He always sees everyone's hand raised against him.'

'And then we heard he'd gone with Lucius Antonius,' Ampudius put in. 'So it was clear he wasn't hunting for Fiscilia any more. And we got married.'

'And that was when I wrote to Canidia at Mevania but the slave came back saying the house was all shut up and no-one knew where she was.' Fiscilia bit her lip and swallowed hard. 'Then I feared she must have gone to Perusia, to look after that horrible treasure. And of course Quintus ended up in Perusia too - nicely placed to bully her into changing her will.'

'She didn't do so, though, as far as we know. Epictetus has gone to see what he can find out about the treasure. As far as I know you're her heir, Fiscilia. For what it's worth.'

'I don't care!' Fiscilia cried. 'The city was sacked, wasn't it, and it'll all be gone, thanks to all the gods. And I don't know what to do with my brother either. What do you think?' She looked round at them all. 'How can I deal with this?'

There was a short, appalled silence. Then, as Torquatus and

Cornelia stared at each other in dismay, Felix broke off his game with Nar and said casually, over his shoulder, 'Oh, he's dead, didn't you know? My master killed him.'

Fiscilia gasped, and Ampudius put his arm round her. The sight of her pinched white face made Torquatus say sharply, 'That's quite enough, Felix.' He turned to Fiscilia and said, 'I'm so sorry. You had to know, but not like this. And I didn't kill him, though it's true that if I hadn't chased him he wouldn't have died.'

Fiscilia's colour was returning, and she sat up briskly. 'Chased him? Don't tell me he wasn't trying to kill you. Well, wasn't he?'

Torquatus nodded. 'Yes.'

'I wouldn't have minded if you had killed him, not really. He had done his best to murder me, after all. And he did murder Calliste and did his best to make Canidia's life a burden to her, at the very least. It was Canidia I loved. She cared for me, and she was the only one who did. I think Quintus was jealous: he knew that Canidia didn't trust him. But he was always my father's favourite, the heir, of course. And anyway my father had no time for women or girls. Once he'd got Canidia to come and look after me he never gave either of us another thought. Until Quintus got into trouble through temper and drink he could do no wrong.' She sighed. 'And he was never going to die of old age in his own bed.'

Torquatus smiled. 'It's good to know what really happened. I suppose you don't know why - ?'

In the reception hall there were sounds of yet another arrival, and everyone's heads turned to the doorway, now deep in shadow. A rather squat elderly lady marched into the garden as if she owned it, and Torquatus felt the welcoming smile freeze on his lips. The visitor halted and stared around her in amazement.

'What's this?' she cried. 'I've come to find out why an important piece of news has been deliberately kept from me, and I find you entertaining strangers.'

Torquatus stood up and kissed the lady on both scented, flabby cheeks. 'I'm delighted to see you, Mother, of course. My visitors are Ampudius and his wife, Fiscilia.'

The look of grievance left the lady's face, replaced by what she no doubt considered a gracious smile. 'I knew your grandfather. A fine man; my husband had the greatest respect for him. I trust your business hasn't been too sadly disrupted by these wretched wars?'

Ampudius tried to look gratified; Torquatus murmured, 'My mother, Vibia. And what is the news I'm supposed to have kept from you, mother?'

'I think I know.' Cornelia's voice was warm. She came forward and took her mother-in-law's hand. 'And indeed it's my fault, not Aulus'. I haven't been home for very long.'

Vibia's eyes seemed to soften as she looked at the glowing, splendid figure of her daughter-in-law. 'I have to say, you're looking very well. When is it due? Very soon now, from the looks of you. Wherever have you been? Why wasn't I told?'

Cornelia, who never blushed, was blushing now. 'Why don't we go into the one of the garden-rooms and have a quiet chat while we wait for dinner?' She shot a rather wild look at Trofimus as she said this, but nothing could disturb the man's calm. 'Of course, mistress. Dinner for six, in - shall we say - an hour?'

'You'll stay, of course?' Cornelia asked Ampudius.

'Thank you; we'd be delighted.'

Cornelia nodded. 'Nereis? I'm sorry, we've neglected you in all the excitement. I know you wanted to ask Torquatus something.'

'Yes, I did.' Nereis stood up from the stool where she'd been sitting almost in the shadows. She smiled, and was about to speak when Vibia seemed suddenly to see her for the first time. She looked the younger woman up and down with unconscious impertinence, then turned to her son again in apparent disbelief.

'I would never have thought it possible that I should be confronted - and in what was once my own house, too, by that creature. I would have thought that even you, with all your faults, would see the impropriety of inviting a - a person who had once been your father's slut!' She stopped, apparently overcome by emotion. Nereis, pale but dignified, stood her ground.

Ignoring Vibia, she spoke to Torquatus. 'If my presence here causes you the least difficulty, I will leave, of course. I daresay what I want can be put into a letter.'

Felix caught hold of Nereis' arm, and seemed about to burst into speech, but Torquatus came over to Nereis and took her hands in his. He spoke in a cool, clear voice, intending to be heard by everyone. 'My dear Nereis,' he said pleasantly, 'your presence here causes me no anxiety whatever. You are welcome here as a friend of the family, and whatever you want of me I shall be happy to grant if it's within my power.' Still apparently speaking to Nereis he went on. 'I am always happy to see members of my family in my house and at my table. But I am the master here and I expect everyone to accept that and to extend their courtesy to anyone I choose to invite here.'

Vibia looked as if she'd been slapped. Red spots of fury appeared on her cheeks. But Cornelia took her arm, saying gently, 'Do come and sit down. I know you want to hear all about the baby.'

For a moment it seemed as though Vibia would stamp out, but after a brief struggle she forced a grim smile and went with Cornelia, the only expression of her true feelings being the poisonous look she shot at Torquatus as she passed him.

Torquatus passed a hand over his hair and sighed. Ampudius, Fiscilia and Nereis all looked at each other uncertainly. It was Felix who broke the silence, saying cheerfully, 'The lady Cornelia will know just what to say to the old mistress, won't she? Thank goodness we've got her back.'

Everyone laughed and sat down again. Trofimus seized the opportunity to place a fresh jug of wine on the table in front of Torquatus, and Felix hurried to Nereis's side.

'You've had to wait a long time to speak to me,' Torquatus observed. 'For which I'm sorry. Tell me now how I can help you.' His tone was civil, but he was at a loss as to what Nereis might need from him. She might be an ex-slave, but she was also the widow of a man who'd acquired very considerable wealth and reached equestrian rank. He took a sip of wine and prepared to listen.

'Before I do that,' Nereis began, glancing round, 'I think I can probably explain something about Canidia's treasure - and why she was so anxious about it.'

'Really?' Torquatus' eyebrows shot up. 'What on earth can you have had to do with that?'

'Oh, nothing. But my husband, Faberius, wanted to - wanted to buy it.' She faltered and looked round hesitantly.

'This would have been after Julius freed him?' Torquatus asked, and Nereis nodded.

'I understand, I think.' Torquatus smiled. 'My father used to enthuse over the wonderful collection of silver Sisenna had collected. I've seen some of it myself. I suppose Faberius had his eye on that as well as Canidia's estate?'

'Yes,' Nereis agreed. 'He found out about the treasure, and

that it was owned by a widow, Canidia, who didn't have a very careful protector.' She stopped again, looking embarrassed.

'How did Faberius hear about this fabled silver?'

'Oh, from Balbus.'

'Balbus?' Torquatus was staring at Nereis in astonishment. 'How does he come into this?'

'He was her fideicommissus. In his will Sisenna had named him as the person to take control of all her wealth, in the interests of Canidia and the child she was expecting at the time.'

'So that's it! Now everything makes sense.' It all fell into place in his head. Balbus must have been in Rome for only a few years at the time of Sisenna's death. Pompey the Great had brought the clever young Spaniard back to Rome with him at the end of a campaign. A useful young man, already wealthy and immensely capable. That would be thirty years ago or more. And Sisenna had been a member of Pompey's intimate circle, so Balbus would have been a good choice of fideicommissus. But it had all gone horribly wrong.

'I didn't know she'd had a child,' he said.

'She didn't,' Fiscilia told him. 'She told me she'd once been pregnant, but Sisenna died during her pregnancy and the child was stillborn. She never remarried.'

'And Sisenna left Balbus to manage affairs for the baby, if it survived, until he or she was of age, and for the rest of Canidia's life?'

'No. If the child died before it came of age he was to hand everything back to Canidia.'

'Gods!' This was much worse than breaking the law. The whole point of a fideicommissum was that it had no legal validity: a man was on his honour to carry out its conditions. There could be no more sacred trust between two Roman men than this, and Balbus had, from the sound of it, broken that trust quite shamelessly. No wonder he'd been so desperate to keep this from Torquatus that he'd even been prepared to kidnap Cornelia when she had happened across Nereis.

Fiscilia jumped up, her face stormy. 'Well, if it was Balbus who told Faberius - or anyone else - about the silver he should be ashamed of himself. He was supposed to be responsible for looking after her, but Faberius bullied her. He never left her alone, that's what she told me. That was before she came to live with us. In fact I think it was one reason why she did come: she needed protection. Who else did she have to turn to? She had no family left of her own. Balbus betrayed her. And in the end my father did help her to fend off Faberius, but only at the cost of a fine estate of Canidia's near our own land in the Clitumnus valley. He persuaded Faberius that the silver was gone, apparently, and that this estate was all Canidia had left. How I wish it had been!' She walked furiously up and down, Nar watching her anxiously from under the bench.

Torquatus was glad Cornelia was out of the room. She was cynical about her father, but knowing that he'd behaved as badly as this would disturb her.

'Go on, Nereis.'

'When Cornelia and I were together at Perusia, we talked a lot, and she told me her father had been distressed when she mentioned Faberius' name. He'd said he was expecting to become a consul, and it would harm his chances if some of the things he'd done when he was younger came out. He didn't tell her any more, but I suppose he felt guilty: he knew he should have protected Canidia, not handed her over to be plundered. My husband's life had been a hard one, and when Julius gave him his freedom he used his power to the full. He was ambitious and determined never to be poor again, which made him hard and unjust sometimes. Not that that's any excuse, I know, but I'm sorry that Canidia suffered by his actions.'

'It wasn't your fault, Nereis,' Fiscilia pointed out. 'But what we need to do now is to discover if any of the silver can be found.'

Torquatus interrupted her. 'No, Fiscilia. What I need to do now is to attend to Nereis. She has been trying to ask me something, and she has still not managed to be heard. Over dinner we can decide what to do about your inheritance, if you have one, but it's nearly dinner-time now. I'll give Nereis whatever she needs first. So what is it you want, Nereis?'

'It's about Felix.' Without a word Felix came and stood next to her, his arm round her.

'Of course: we're both interested in his future, aren't we?' Her smile was a little anxious, he thought.

'I'd like to buy him,' she said quickly. 'He's my son; he should be with me.'

Torquatus' brows shot up. 'I can understand your feelings, Nereis, but he's surely better off here, or he will be when I've freed him, which I was intending to do in a few weeks time. If he stays with me I can see that he gets an excellent education and give him many more opportunities than you can.'

This was so obvious to him that her look of anxiety baffled him.

Nereis bit her lip. Her hands were clenched so hard the knuckles showed white. 'I understand all that. Believe me, I've thought about it, over and over. But you see, if you free him, he still belongs to you, doesn't he? You'll be his patron.'

Torquatus stared at her. 'Is that a problem?'

'Forgive me. I don't want to - but he will still owe obligations to you. For the whole of his life, he'll be yours in some ways.'

For reasons he couldn't himself understand, Nereis' words made Torquatus stubbornly determined not to give way.

'Do you think that what you're asking is really best for the boy? To take him to a small house where he will meet no-one of consequence, where he'll grow up us your freedman?'

'I can't weigh it up coldly like that.' Nereis swallowed hard, and tucked her shaking hands into the sleeves of her gown. 'He's my son. And I lost him. Do you understand what it meant to me when your father gave me as a gift to Julius, all those years ago? No, of course you don't. How could you? I never had a moment to take leave of my child, had no idea where I was going, what would happen to him.' Her voice failed and for a moment she stood, her head bowed, choking down tears. Fiscilia crossed over to her uncertainly, and took her hand, but Torquatus stood silent, at a loss. He had cherished the thought of granting freedom to Felix, had seen in his mind's eye the little procession to the praetor's tribunal, the applause of the people in the Forum, the family party he'd throw afterwards to celebrate the deed.

While he was still lost in thought a new voice was heard. Torquatus wasn't sorry to have been interrupted. 'Oh, it's you, is it?' he said to Epictetus. 'I hope you've got some news from Perusia for us?'

Polite and respectful as always. Epictetus stepped forward, still wrapped in his travelling-cloak. 'I have. But - I hope you won't think me impertinent, lord. I couldn't help hearing what you were saying. And I understand your argument, of course, and all honour to you for wanting to advance the boy. But I'm a freedman myself and I understand Nereis too. She is his mother.'

He turned, swinging the cloak off his shoulders, and caught

sight of Fiscilia. His smile was a little crooked. 'The lord Torquatus told me you were alive,' he said. 'That's why we thought it worthwhile for me to go back to Perusia: to see if you still had an inheritance.'

Fiscilia walked across to him and took his hand. 'Thank you,' she said simply. 'No-one could have been more faithful to my aunt than you were.'

Torquatus was aware of the colonnade echoing with voices: Cornelia and Vibia were rejoining them from the garden-room. He turned back to Nereis.

'If you bring Felix up, who will be his patron? Who will see to his education?' Even to himself his words sounded petulant. He felt humiliated that she hadn't accepted what he was offering. He forced himself to smile, thinking furiously, and suddenly a way of putting himself right came to him. His smile came more easily, and he relaxed. 'I'll give you Felix,' he told Nereis. 'After all, as you reminded us, my father gave you to Julius. Now I can equal him in giving Felix to you.'

For one extraordinary moment, Torquatus feared that Nereis seemed less than pleased. Surely she couldn't be going to refuse such a handsome offer? Then Cornelia walked over to her and whispered something in Nereis' ear. She beckoned Felix, who was watching the scene with anxious eyes. 'Where does Felix want to live?' she asked quietly.

Torquatus was taken aback. This wasn't a question he'd been expecting at all. Felix turned to his mother, beaming, and hugged her close. Nereis blushed and put him aside gently. She stepped forward, a tall, slim, well-cared for woman, with a look of intelligence and dignity. 'I accept with thanks and gratitude.'

And here was Trofimus, coming in to announce dinner. 'And after dinner,' Torquatus told him, 'I intend to draw up a document, a formal deed of gift, handing this slave, Felix, to the lady Nereis as a gift. Make sure everything I need for that is in the business room, would you.'

'As a gift, lord?'

'As a gift. I had intended to free the boy, but his mother wishes to free him herself, you understand.'

Trofimus bowed impassively, but as he walked away Torquatus thought he saw a look of envy on the man's face, a look which shocked him. Then he caught sight of his mother's face, registering disgust, and forgot his steward.

Torquatus had often attended sumptuous banquets at which splendid food and wine were offered to carefully chosen and powerful guests, but he enjoyed this small dinner-party more than any of them. And yet it hardly had the elements necessary for distinction. Any ambitious hostess would have despised the guests as a motley bunch, including two freed slaves and a preponderance of women. There were no garlands of flowers, no flute-players or dancers or poets reciting their work. Nor was the food exceptional. When the order came to the kitchen for dinner for seven within the hour, Fortunatus was torn between walking out and showing his master that even this utterly unreasonable request could be met with style and panache. Having decided on the latter course he had no time to storm out into the garden to find his owners. So it was his underlings who had to listen to his tirade as they chopped and basted and roasted and steamed at top speed. His orders roared out in a constant steam, punctuated by furious complaints. What was the master playing at? Didn't he realise the folly of paying so highly for a chef - and he told his staff several times what he had cost, to the last sestertius - an artist, no less, a man whose dishes were more than mere food, only to break the man's heart by giving dinners that were a disgrace to himself? None of the kitchen staff were stupid enough to attempt to answer these questions, and continued to baste and chop and steam and roast without paying much attention. Only Cornelia really felt for the cook. She noticed that the dinner, though of course well-cooked and beautifully presented, lacked the elaborate creations Fortunatus was famous for. She would go to the kitchens in the morning and sympathise.

At first conversation hardly flourished among the oddly-assorted group. Everyone was hungry, but once the first course was replaced by the second, a general mood of relaxation seemed to steal over the company. Torquatus called on Epictetus to give news of Perusia, and he smiled rather grimly. 'It's as well we've satisfied our hunger first,' he said, looking across at Ampudius and Fiscilia. 'Because the news is bad.'

Ampudius nodded. 'The treasure's gone, no doubt?'

'You're not surprised, I can see.'

'Of course I'm not. The city was given over to the soldiers to sack, wasn't it? There wouldn't be much left after that.'

Fiscilia smiled at him. 'Well, I for one don't care.'

Vibia, who had been on her best behaviour, now looked up,

surprised. 'Oh, but you should. To lose a great deal of wealth, for no good reason, that's a very serious matter, young lady.'

Ampudius' face crinkled in a smile. 'I think I rather agree with you,' he said. 'It's all very well to say it was cursed and so on, but money's money when all's said and done, and I don't like to think of it wasted on soldiers who'll just fritter it away on booze and whores.'

Fiscilia shrugged. 'It's gone. Regretting that won't bring it back. And I mean what I say: it was lusting after that silver that led Quintus to kill Calliste, to try and kill me, to make Canidia's life so miserable at the end. Let it go.'

Ampudius smiled. 'That's all we can do. And to be honest I don't care all that much. I have you, and we have plenty to live on.'

'I'm glad you feel like that,' Epictetus told him, smiling, 'I wasn't nearly so calm when I found every last scrap of it gone, I can tell you.'

'It was worth a lot,' Torquatus agreed.

'More than you realise,' Epictetus told him. 'What you saw was only about a third of it. I didn't know whether I could really trust you to know the whole truth.' He sighed. 'My lady thought that the safest thing would be to build a not terribly well-hidden room, with some of the silver in it, and behind it a very well-hidden one, with all the rest. And as I say, it's all gone. Which troubles me, I have to say.'

Torquatus looked a question, but Epictetus shook his head and shot him a warning look, as if he wanted the subject dropped.

Fiscilia looked relieved. 'I told you I had no dowry to bring you, Marcus, and that turns out to be the exact truth.'

'And I told you I didn't care.' Ampudius returned her smile.

'Well, that ends it all.' Torquatus smiled. 'Who could imagine that a man would murder his own sister?'

Cornelia's mischievous look died away and she gave him a warm smile. She laid a hand on his arm. 'I wonder where Manlia is now?'

Torquatus' face cleared. 'On the sea no doubt, and probably telling the rowers they aren't going fast enough.'

Epictetus laughed with the rest, but shook his head and said, 'My lady loved Manlia. They talked for hours in Mevania, and when my mistress knew she was dying the thought that Manlia at least was safe was a great comfort to her. I never told her that

Cornelia and Nereis had got away. She was so frail by then, she couldn't have taken it in. That was a hard time for her, alone with Fiscilius, who was doing everything he could to hasten her death. And then, I have to admit, I was pressing her to rewrite her will as well.' There was a moment's shocked silence. 'I wanted her to take Fiscilius out.'

'You mean Fiscilius was named in her will? I don't understand. I thought Fiscilia was the heiress?' asked Torquatus.

'She was. She is. But there was a provision for Fiscilius to inherit if Fiscilia were dead. He was her second heir. Yes, you all look shocked: that was as good as putting the lady Fiscilia's name on a proscription list in the Forum, in my view, and I told my lady so. But she wouldn't have it, said that little as she liked Fiscilius, it would be wrong not to name him as second heir.'

'I should have written to her,' Fiscilia said quietly. 'I should have told her Quintus had tried to kill me. I was wrong.'

Torquatus had been thinking. 'Who else knew that Fiscilius was Canidia's heir, after Fiscilia?'

'No-one. No-one at all.' Epictetus was firm.

'The will must have been witnessed, surely?'

'Of course. But all the witnesses did was to confirm that Canidia had signed it, nothing more. They never read the provisions at all.'

'How did Fiscilius know, then?'

Epictetus looked at him sadly. 'She told him herself.'

Torquatus winced. 'Really, if she had wanted to put Fiscilia in danger she couldn't have done it more effectively. She probably put a clause in the will explaining that she hadn't made him her heir because of his bad conduct - am I right? But she still left him in because blood's thicker than water.'

'She thought she was being fair. She had a strong sense of justice.'

'And not much common sense,' Torquatus observed.

Vibia had been subdued all evening, but she spoke up now. 'I think she was wrong. Wrong, I mean, to make Fiscilia her heir at all. Women aren't supposed to take such large inheritances. Fiscilius should have inherited: I'm not surprised he was angry and resentful.'

They were all silent. Then Nereis said quietly, 'She wanted to leave her wealth to the person she loved and trusted. How could that be wrong?'

Vibia cast up her eyes and flopped back onto the couch impatiently, but said nothing more.

The party never really recovered after her scornful intervention. Ampudius and Fiscilia left straight after dinner, taking Nar with them: a parting which was sorrowful on Felix's side, casual on Nar's. As soon as the family were alone Torquatus sat down in the business room behind the reception hall and wrote out the short document he needed to make Felix over to Nereis. He rolled it and sealed it and handed it to Nereis with a kiss on the cheek.

Nereis smiled, her eyes full of tears. 'I'm sure Felix will never be ungrateful. And I hope you'll always be our patron and friend.'

'Of course I shall. And we still need to have that talk about Felix's career.'

Having watched this touching scene with a look of deep cynicism, Vibia did what she could to puncture her son's mood of contentment by reminding him that Balbus was consul this year, and that he should be careful how he criticised him. 'That class of person doesn't always quite know how to behave,' she told him. A moment's reflection led her to tell Cornelia, with a kindly smile, 'Not that I mean anything against you, dear. I've always thought you were a very well-behaved girl.'

'Thank you.' Cornelia's voice was meek, her eyes modestly lowered, but Torquatus was not deceived. As soon as they were alone, she turned an indignant face towards him.

'Really, Aulus, your mother! I think she's even worse than my father.'

'How can you say so? She despises and dislikes me but she's never kept me a prisoner or tried to break our marriage up.' He thought he wouldn't mention what Balbus had done to Canidia.

'Horrid, the pair of them.' She shrugged. 'How wonderful that all this worry and anxiety is over, and we can think of happier things.'

Torquatus laughed. 'I hope you're right. One thing, though: just as they were leaving, Epictetus took me aside and asked if he might have a confidential word with me tomorrow morning. So what do you make of that?'

'It can't be anything important, surely?'

'I suppose he's going to tell me that Fiscilius must have passed the information about the hidden treasure to someone before he died. He must have been the only one except Epictetus who knew about that part of the silver and where it was. But I don't really care. That's not the most important thing. This baby: my mother was pleased about her?'

'Her? I'd love it to be a little Manlia, wouldn't you.'

He drew her into his arms. 'Of course I would. I could never have too many of them. But if it's a boy - ,'

'Lucius,' she nodded.

'You think that's what we should call him?'

'Of course. Your father was, and your older brother. First sons in your family are all Lucius, aren't they?' She looked up at him smiling, and went on deliberately. 'You fell out with your father and your brother: they fought and died for the republic they thought could be saved. Now this little Lucius can heal the family, don't you think?'

'I do love you,' he answered. 'Did I say? And yes, healing the family would be wonderful, though I suspect my mother won't agree.'

'Your mother must do as she sees fit,' Cornelia told him firmly. 'And we should go to bed.'

The next morning, Torquatus found himself searching through the white flow of togas streaming into his reception hall for the insignificant figure of Cornelius Epictetus. He felt both irritated and uneasy at the man's request to speak to him. The Fiscilia case was closed, surely? For some time he thought Epictetus had changed his mind, but then, as the crowds were clearing, he caught a glimpse of the quiet man, patiently waiting, and told a slave to bring him forward.

'Not bad news, I hope?' Torquatus asked, when Epictetus seemed to hesitate.

'No, not at all.'

'Well, what then?'

'Has it ever occurred to you, lord, to wonder whether Fiscilius might still be alive.'

Torquatus stared at him, incredulous. 'No, it hasn't. And if that's what you've come here to suggest you'd better go away.'

Epictetus just stood in front of him, neatly togate, hands folded.

'What makes you think he might be?' Torquatus asked reluctantly, when it was clear that the man wasn't going to take his advice.

'I always wondered. Who but Fiscilius knew the treasure was behind that wall? No-one else could have taken it. And then I knew: I saw him.'

For a moment Torquatus wondered whether the man was mad, but he seemed his usual precise, self-contained self. 'Look, that's simply not possible. He fell from the roof of the temple of Juno in Perusia. He went down the cliff. No-one could have survived such a fall. And as to the treasure, there must have been slaves who knew where it was. The soldiers could have found out from them.'

'Perhaps. But Fiscilius' body was never found,' Epictetus insisted.

'That's true. I didn't have time to conduct a thorough search, though. It hardly seemed the most important thing at the time.' Torquatus didn't try to disguise the scepticism in his voice as he heard again the hoarse shouts and terrified screams and crackling flames of the dying city. He shivered.

'You didn't have time, lord, but I did. I went back when all was quiet again and combed through those woods at the bottom of the cliff. I didn't find his body, nor even any signs that one had fallen there.'

'So where do you imagine that you saw him?'

Epictetus' neat smile rebuked him. 'I didn't imagine it, lord. I've known Fiscilius all his life, and I came almost face to face with him: I couldn't mistake.'

Torquatus sighed. 'Tell me then, where did this happen?'

'In Perusia, just the other day. Please believe me, lord: you're in great danger. I was coming up the hill to Canidia's house. He was coming down. He didn't see me till we were quite close.'

'And when he did?'

'He turned aside, down a narrow lane.'

'Was he hurrying? Startled? Furtive?'

'No, lord. Not that I could see. I ran up to the lane, but he'd gone. There's a maze of courts and alleys and I lost him, I'm afraid.'

Torquatus looked at him quite kindly. 'I don't want you to bother Fiscilia with this story.'

'You don't believe me, do you? But I hope at least you'll take care. There's nothing that man won't do, not now.'

'Thank you. I am always well-guarded.'

Torquatus couldn't believe it. It seemed simply impossible that Fiscilius could have escaped. He supposed that Epictetus had become so obsessed with the man he blamed for his mistress' death that his imagination had run away with him. He shrugged, and forgot about it.

Chapter 22

It wasn't hard to forget about Epictetus and his too-vivid imagination. Two days after his visit Torquatus was woken in the middle of the night by a scared-looking Rachel.

'It's the mistress, lord.'

He didn't need to hear another word. He swung his legs out of the bed, and reached for the day-tunic that had been left folded on the stool. Outside in the colonnade he could hear feet, quiet voices. Trofimus, his voice sharp, said 'Fetch some fruit juice,' which cheered Torquatus up. If Cornelia was drinking fruit juice things couldn't be too serious, surely?

He hurried to Cornelia's suite of rooms. The thin dark woman Cornelia had informed him was her midwife was bustling about. Glancing through the doorway into Cornelia's bedroom he could see a piece of furniture which hadn't been there before, a solid chair, well-used and well-polished, with a hole where the front and centre of the seat should be. For some reason the sight of it threw him into panic. Cornelia, out of his sight, said something to Rachel, and he hurried through to her.

'Oh, Aulus, it's started,' she said at once. 'Thank goodness. I was so sick of carrying this great lump around the whole time.' Her voice was light but her eyes were watchful. He sat down by her bed.

'I suppose you have to sit on that thing?' he asked nervously.

She giggled. 'Scary, isn't it? But that won't be for ages yet. I'm only getting little twinges at the moment.'

The dark woman came through the doorway.

'This is Margarita, the best midwife in the business, so you needn't worry, Aulus.'

The woman bowed her head graciously in acknowledgment of the compliment, but said firmly, 'You shouldn't be in here, lord. Time enough when the baby's born, and that won't be for a long time yet, I daresay. No doubt you have work to do, clients to see?'

She managed to make Torquatus' work seem like nothing of any great significance which, Torquatus thought with unaccustomed humility, it wasn't, compared to this ordinary, everyday drama, which might see him a father at the end of the day. Or a widower. He pushed the thought away, leant over Cornelia and kissed her gently on the lips.

'You'll send Rachel for anything you want? Or if you need me, I'll be here.'

Her eyes scanned his face. Suddenly she took a breath which she seemed to hold for a long time. When it was over she said, 'Yes, of course. And now go, darling, please.'

Margarita already had him by the arm to lead him out. He could only submit.

There were men, Torquatus knew, who went about their ordinary daily routine while their wives were in labour. They would come home at the end of a day in the Forum or the courts, to discover that they had a son or a daughter, or maybe that the child hadn't survived. How did they manage that? He drifted around the house, feeling as if he were in everyone's way. His household were used to his absences in the Forum, over on the Palatine, away on campaign. They clearly had no need of him.

He wandered into his own bedroom, where Victor was sorting through a collection of tunics. A growing pile on the floor suggested that he was planning a serious refurbishment of the master's wardrobe. Victor gave him a disdainful look, as if to suggest that he had no business there at this time of day. Torquatus almost found himself apologising.

It occurred to him that if Cornelia was drinking fruit juice she might also find some broth or soup sustaining, and headed for the kitchens. He might have known better, he thought bitterly. Fortunatus greeted him as one might a well-known marplot, a man to be kept away from knives at all costs.

'No need to worry, lord,' he said, coming quickly across to the kitchen doorway. Behind him Torquatus could see a slave chopping herbs on a scrubbed table-top, and another stirring something in a pan over one of the fires. 'Everything is in hand. There is a chicken stock I've been gently reducing to make a really tasty broth for madam. Also some of her favourite little cakes, the ones with the poppy seeds, to tempt her appetite: I understand that ladies sometimes require that, after these occasions. I shall make those each day, so that fresh ones are always ready to hand, you understand. And I have bought a goat.'

'A goat?' Torquatus was taken aback.

'Certainly, lord. The milk will be an excellent food for the mother, I'm told, and for the child too if it doesn't feed, and if madam doesn't care for the idea of a wet-nurse. You need have no fear, lord.'

Torquatus drifted away again. At least in the library he was disturbing no-one. He pulled out a book-scroll at random and arranged himself on the reading-couch. The book turned out to be Aristotle's analysis of comedy. He sighed. A moment later he thought of something, jumped to his feet, and called for Trofimus.

When the steward came quietly into the room Torquatus was sitting at his writing table closing and sealing a pair of wax tablets.

'Get someone to take those to the lady Vibia's house, will you,' he said, and Trofimus smiled.

'Yes, lord. I was about to suggest that we ought to send to her. I'm sure she'll want to be here. And she might be somewhat displeased if we didn't tell her what was happening.'

Torquatus made a face. 'Just somewhat. The man can offer to escort her back, if she wants to come. I wonder if I ought to ask Balbus, too? No. There have to be some limits. I've told my mother she can stay if she wants.'

She did want. At least it kept him busy to have his mother in the house. Cornelia might be in labour, the household might be waiting for the outcome with quivering nerves, but Vibia still found the time and energy to tell Victor off for wanting to dispose of all those tunics, and to drive Fortunatus out of his kitchen complaining to Torquatus that he wouldn't be answerable for the consequences if Vibia told him once again how to make soup. So he sat down with her in the little garden room where they would be in no-one's way. Hours seemed to have passed since he'd been with Cornelia: looking at the shadows drawing in over the gardens he realised that they had. How much longer would it be?

He and Vibia had never talked. The gulf between them was too wide. He knew what she thought of him. They couldn't talk about his work with Octavian because Torquatus would have to listen to accusations that it was his disobedience that had caused his father's death. They couldn't discuss politics. But to his surprise, just as he was wondering what was left, Vibia took a deep breath, fixed her eyes on his, and came out with something very surprising.

'Well, I didn't think Octavian would defeat Lucius Antonius in the way he has,' she said. 'There's obviously more to him than one might suppose.'

This was a more generous assessment of her son's friend then Torquatus had ever heard. He nodded, and said cautiously, 'He's a survivor.'

'I can see that. But the question is, will he and Antonius be able to work together now? Or will they fight each other?'

'I think they'll work together. For now, at any rate. It's Sextus Pompeius I'm not sure about. If they can't make peace with him he'll go on trying to starve Rome.'

There was a short silence. Torquatus watched his mother, who looked a little uncomfortable. At last she sat up straighter, saying, 'I just wanted to say that perhaps after all you were right.'

Torquatus stared at her, speechless. He wondered if perhaps he was asleep and dreaming.

'Perhaps your father was wrong to think the Republic could be saved. I didn't like Caesar any more than they did, but perhaps by then it was too late. So the side you chose was the right side after all.'

Torquatus went over to her and kissed her cheek. He had never expected this.

But it seemed that his mother hadn't finished. She looked down, apparently intent on rearranging the folds of her stola. 'You know Marcellus died the other day. Poor man, he'd been ill for months. I have heard rumours that Octavia will marry again quite soon.'

Torquatus was smiling. 'I wonder if you heard the ridiculous one about Octavia being given to me?'

She glanced up. 'Well, I did, of course. It would have been a great thing, of course.'

'No, Mother,' he said. 'It would not have been a great thing.'

She shrugged. 'Oh, well, if you say so. I must say Cornelia does seem a dear little thing. And then her dowry was splendid: not that Octavia's wouldn't be; and of course if Cornelia gives you a boy that makes all the difference.'

Torquatus laughed. 'I just want Cornelia to be safe. A daughter will be just as good. A Manlia.'

'I suppose you can always have a son later,' she agreed, though in a grudging voice.

'Oh, how I want this to be over,' he suddenly cried out. 'We've been waiting and waiting. How much longer can it go on?'

'A first labour can go on for a long time. But I'll go and ask,' Vibia said, rising briskly to her feet.

'The women will probably let you in,' he replied bitterly. 'I was told I wasn't welcome in no uncertain terms.'

Vibia patted him on the shoulder and left the room.

Wandering out after her Torquatus sensed a different mood in the house. A bowl of hot water was being carried carefully towards Cornelia's rooms. And as he turned into the colonnade that led to them he could hear moaning. And then came a great yell. He broke into a run, pushing his way into Cornelia's sitting room. There were women everywhere: no-one even noticed that he'd come in.

Cornelia was sitting in the chair, a group of slaves huddled around Margarita at her feet. And as he hurried over to them, the midwife stood up, a horribly bloody thing in her hands. A cry of horror broke from him.

'What is that?' he demanded. 'What's gone wrong? Oh, Cornelia!' Turning his eyes away from the bloody thing he saw that Cornelia's face was convulsing with pain.

Then the bloody thing in the midwife's arms let out a thin cry, and the women all burst out laughing.

'This is your son, lord,' Margarita said smiling. 'And the lady Cornelia's doing very well. Was that the afterbirth come away, girls? Good. Now then, lord, you need to go and assemble your household: there's a very important ceremony you have to perform.'

Torquatus stared at the baby, which was now being gently washed in the bowl of warm water, a process it didn't seem to care for. He was struck dumb by this creature, this thing that he and Cornelia had made. It was ugly, he thought, red and cross-looking. But it was theirs.

A beaming Vibia hurried across and took him by the arm, breaking his trance. 'Isn't she a clever girl,' she said. 'What a fine boy, and with excellent lungs. Now we should go and get the household ready, just as Margarita suggested.'

It seemed as if the whole household had simply been waiting for the summons. Everyone came piling into the hall, smiling and grouping themselves together. The old schoolteacher, almost redundant now since Felix left, came hobbling in from his schoolroom at the back of the house. The women came bustling through from Cornelia's rooms. Even Catus and the outdoor slaves huddled in at the back.

Torquatus, in a clean toga, was standing in the reception hall, his mother beaming beside him, when Rachel and Margarita came bustling through the crowd of slaves. Everyone drew back to let them through. Rachel had brought a fine tasselled cloth which she now folded into a neat square and laid on the floor. When she had made sure it was just as it should be, Margarita stepped forward and laid down on it the little bundle in her arms. Torquatus came forward in his turn, a lump in his throat, and bent to pick up the baby. The child was well swaddled in its blankets, but Torquatus felt it move in his hands. For a moment he felt anxious, awkward, out of place. Then he lifted it into his arms and turned, smiling, so that all the household could see he accepted the child as his. The baby's face was washed and clean now. It was still red and rather crumpled. The eyes gazed around unfocussed. As he held it, one little hand escaped from the layers of blanket and the tiny thumb went straight into the baby's mouth, where Torquatus could see the strong muscles sucking at it.

He smiled, a sense of huge wellbeing flooding over him, and turned to the altar, where Trofimus had already laid a fire for him to light. It would burn until the ninth day, when the boy would receive his name. Another in the long chain of Lucius Manlius Torquatuses, active citizens in Rome for hundreds of years. He watched the flames flicker up from the dry sticks and promised himself that he would do everything in his power to keep this precious child and his beloved wife safe.

Chapter 23

At the end of March it was time for the festival of the Argei to begin once again with the placing of the reed-men in the twenty-seven shrines. Since no new priests had been elected since last year, Torquatus had been allocated the duty again. He supposed that it was as a result of preparations for the festival that he received a note one day from Claudius Erotes, the magistrate on the Velia, telling him that some new evidence in the murder case had been found at the shrine. Since he had been interested in the case, he would be most welcome to join the senior aedile and himself at the shrine at the ninth hour. Torquatus, having nothing in particular to do that afternoon, decided to go. A walk would do him good, and it might be interesting to see what it was the sandal-maker thought he had found. So, accompanied by his bodyguards, Becco and Pulex, he set off down the Alta Semita in the afternoon sunshine. The top of the Forum was quiet now as the day's business drew to a close. On the Velia he saw the door of the little shrine standing open, and tossed a couple of coins to Becco and Pulex. 'There's not room for all of us in there,' he said. 'Go and get yourselves a drink from the bar.' He nodded to where a few pot plants and a couple of rather rickety benches invited the thirsty to take it easy. 'Keep your eyes open. I'll expect to see you there when I come out.'

The big men turned away happily, and Torquatus made his way alone into the little building. The smell took him back to last year at once: warm wooden beams, stone, a hint of incense from offerings that had been made outside. But there was more noise than he remembered, and as his eyes adjusted to the dark he saw why: the manhole had been opened, the slab of stone propped up against the back wall. From the dark hole came the sound of rushing water. He walked over and looked down, but could see nothing in the darkness.

It was as he was standing there that he realised his mistake. Sensing that he was no longer alone he glanced up sharply, to see the entrance blocked by a cloaked figure. The man came in quickly, and threw back the hood that had covered his head. Even before he did so, Torquatus instinct told him that this was Fiscilius. He cursed himself for not taking Epictetus' warning seriously, and even more for having left his guards in the bar: was there any chance that they might realise what had happened and come to the rescue? No.

Those two were good for fighting, but hadn't much initiative, and his orders had been clear.

As were Fiscilius' intentions. The man was coming towards him with a knife in his hand, and Torquatus had no weapon. He swung himself out of his toga and gathered it in his arms. Having a scrap in a space as small as this was a fool's game but unless the magistrate arrived soon he would have no choice. As Fiscilius approached, Torquatus was struck by his changed appearance. No-one would have believed now that this was a man of equestrian rank. His hair was matted and dirty, his eyes glittered with malice or madness, and his cheeks had fallen in, making him look much older than he was. He would keep the man talking if he could.

'I never expected to see you again,' he began. 'How did you escape?'

'Ah!' Fiscilius gave a mirthless laugh. 'Perhaps I flew. And then perhaps I discovered a hiding place. You should have looked more carefully, come down the roof yourself, or got a ladder and climbed up from the square, but I expect you were too frightened to do that. I couldn't believe it when you went away, and left me to pull myself up by Queen Juno's bootstraps. Metaphorically speaking, you know.'

'Where were you?'

'The statue at the corner of the roof was standing on a broken plinth, as it happened. A piece had fallen away. And there must always have been a space between it and those stupid little peacocks on the front of the temple roof. It might have been made for me. And just as I rolled into it I gave one last push at that peacock with my foot and it broke off. I knew then, of course.'

'Knew what?' Torquatus' ears were open for Erotes' arrival. Where was the man?

'Oh, that I'm under the protection of Queen Juno,' Fiscilius said carelessly. 'Not bad, eh?'

Torquatus stared at him.

'No, seriously. If you'd seen me getting back up that roof, you'd know what I mean. It was wet, and I was cold. I couldn't feel a thing in my hands and feet. Never been more frightened in my life,' he added carelessly. 'You see what I'm saying: twice that day I should have been dead. But I'm not. Not a bit of it.'

'And you think Juno did that?' Torquatus stepped back again as Fiscilius crept a little closer, willing the bodyguards to suspect something, willing the magistrate to arrive.

'I can't believe you haven't read the Iliad,' Fiscilius said complacently. 'If you had you'd know the gods have their favourites. I swear Juno herself held on to me.'

'So perhaps it was Juno who helped you take the treasure?' Torquatus spoke sarcastically, and regretted it at once. Keep him sweet, he told himself, keep him talking.

Fiscilius nodded. 'Of course she did. I knew you were so stupid you'd just think the soldiers had looted it. I took it all away, in ox-carts. Three ox-carts to be precise: there was mountains of it in there, silver, gold, art-works, coins, furniture. All packed nicely into the carts and covered up with vegetables for the market. One cart full of carrots, one with cabbages, and one with some really lovely early asparagus. I didn't even have to hurry, you see. Epictetus had gone. They'd all gone. Canidia had gone. Fiscilia, too. All gone.' He shook his head. 'Shall I tell you where it is? Maybe I will. You'll never guess, and I love the thought of you dying knowing exactly where it is and being quite unable to get your hands on it.'

'I've never been interested in the treasure, Fiscilius.'

Fiscilius giggled. 'Yeah, right. And I'm the King of Carthage.'

'In Rome, I suppose?'

'Of course in Rome. Can't one hide any crime in Rome? Or nearly, anyway? And really I can't help telling you - you in particular - where it is. Oh, it's so funny - you'll die.'

Torquatus waited.

Fiscilius frowned and seemed to go off at a tangent. 'I can feel the dead all around me, can't you? I suppose I've killed a few and that's why. But then, who hasn't?' He shook his head. 'I like the thought of your having some unquiet spirits of your very own. Because I think the dead are disturbed by the presence of great wealth, don't you?' He asked this question with an air of great seriousness, and then shook his head. 'I think that's all I'll tell you, after all. I'll leave you to guess, though you aren't very good at guessing, are you, Torquatus?'

Torquatus struggled to keep his anger down. He wondered if Fiscilius was drunk, to speak so insultingly. But then he thought, with a sudden chill, no, not drunk, mad. He made himself speak quietly.

'So now you're here. And so am I? Isn't that an odd coincidence?'

Fiscilius waved his hand in a lordly gesture. 'No coincidence at all, my dear Torquatus. You're here because I invited you.' He giggled like a delighted child.

Torquatus' mouth was dry. He could find nothing to say. He'd been lured here by Fiscilius, his bodyguards were lolling uselessly in the bar, and the magistrate wouldn't come and save him either. No doubt his body would be pushed down into the sewer. Perhaps it would be one of the many fished out of the river Tiber when it finally emerged from the great drain.

'What made you think of escaping through the sewers?' He asked, almost at random. Anything to keep the man talking until perhaps the bodyguards might think to look for him.

'Well, it worked, didn't it? No-one imagined I could have gone that way. I was only just in time, though: I could hear those men walking up to the shrine and I was afraid they might have even seen the trap closing. But they were so concerned about the fire they didn't look. And did you know this is the only drain that feeds into the Cloaca? Luck, or the favour of the gods, Torquatus? What do you think? And down there I found rings you can tie a boat to, and float all the way down to the Cloaca Maxima itself.'

'You went all the way down there?'

'Oh, no. I didn't need to. I knew I couldn't get out the way I came into the shrine: I heard the roof beginning to fall in as I waited down below. But there are other manholes. And you know how it is: a man in a dirty tunic pushes up a manhole and climbs out, and everyone just thinks, some slave going about his business. But enough talking, I think. I owe you several deaths, Torquatus. One for Fiscilia: if you hadn't interfered I'd have found the stupid cow and killed her. One for being Octavian's little helper and losing me everything. One for Canidia who always hated me. Pity I can only kill you once.'

Fiscilius stepped towards Torquatus, his sword lifted.

Torquatus knew this was the end. He saw Cornelia, called to identify a dreadful bloated corpse; he saw her alone with her child. He pulled himself together. There was no way out of here but down: he'd seen iron rungs let into the walls of the shaft on his previous visit. But there was something that might still give him an advantage, something he was sure Fiscilius didn't know.

'You won't be living to enjoy all that treasure, I'm afraid,' he said, shaking his head. 'Epictetus saw you, you see, and Fiscilia knows you're alive too. She's married to Ampudius. Now there's a man who shares your liking for loot, Fiscilius, though he's far more decent about it. So when my body is found there's going to be no doubt at all about who did it.'

With satisfaction he saw Fiscilius' face blanch, and without warning he kicked out at him as hard as he could, aiming his heavy boot for the man's right arm. His foot connected, and he heard the knife go skittering across the stone floor. If he'd only had time to get it, he thought, but knew he hadn't. Torquatus stepped back as Fiscilius sprang at him, and hurled the toga full at him. Loosely crumpled together, it unwound itself as it flew, a fold of it landing on Fiscilius' shoulder and sliding down his sword-arm. The bulk of it flipped right over his head and Fiscilius staggered under it. Torquatus was already lowering himself into the gaping darkness of the manhole. Down he went, as if descending into the underworld, the noise of rushing water louder and louder with every step. His mind was screaming at him to hurry, hurry, but he couldn't: the metal footholds were small and slippery and he had to feel carefully down for each one. Above him he could hear Fiscilius banging around and then he appeared in the pale gap, staring down at him. Why didn't he follow? Even as Torquatus thought this, something whizzed past his cheek and hit his hand. Blood welled up: he could see the darkness spreading against the white skin in the gloom. But he was still there, still holding on; and now Fiscilius had no knife. Probably had no knife. The darkness became complete as Fiscilius too began to descend the grips in the wall.

Torquatus reached the bottom of the handholds so suddenly he almost fell down. He had been expecting to hit water, but instead found himself on a narrow path, above the level of the stream. He turned to his left, and began to make his way along the path, not with any idea in his head, but simply because the alternative was to wait until Fiscilius caught up with him. Fiscilius, the killer. The path narrowed a little and he was forced to go more slowly or risk missing his footing. Torquatus' hands fumbled along the wall as he shuffled along, desperately hoping that there might be some opening, if it was only a crevice, into which he could squeeze himself while Fiscilius passed by. There was no crevice. Instead he continued shuffling along, his heart pounding and his mind racing, for what felt like a lifetime.

The path was getting narrower all the time, so that now he could only shuffle along with his back to the wall. He stopped, listening, but could hear nothing except for the thump of his own heart and his own ragged breathing. Fiscilius might have turned the other way, of course. He wouldn't know which way Torquatus had gone. Perhaps he should take to the water instead of creeping along the path? It might be quicker, but wading along would make a lot of noise, and the water itself smelt horrible. It flowed quickly past, quite close to his feet from the sound of it, much of it simply the overflow of the many fountains and cisterns supplied by the city's aqueducts. He didn't want to think what the rest was. People threw rubbish into the Cloaca Maxima: dead dogs and trash, and sometimes murdered bodies too. And he had no idea what happened to the sewer. The water here flowed down to join the Cloaca Maxima, but what if there were grids or filters? What if he came up against some such obstruction in the dark? He imagined himself struggling against a weight of water, pressed against some grille, and shivered. No, he'd stay on this little path as long as he could.

His heart was quieter now. He still couldn't hear Fiscilius behind him. Now that he was calmer, he realised that if he had come down through a manhole cover, there must be others. It couldn't be far to the next one, surely? If he just kept going he would find it and climb out into the beautiful fresh afternoon sun, leaving Fiscilius down in this stinking underworld. Cheered, he started shuffling along again, as fast as he could along the tiny slippery brick ledge. It was dreadfully slow work in the foul dark. He seemed to go on and on, but without finding any way out. How far apart were these access points? Surely he must soon come across one? Could he possibly have missed one, in his hurry? His eyes ached in their sockets as he strained to see through the thick darkness. And all the time he was carefully feeling forward with his foot, afraid of missing the path and falling into the water. He slipped from time to time on slimy things, scrabbling fruitlessly at the wet bricks of the wall, sobbing prayers to Apollo, god of light.

And then, behind him, he heard a sound. It wasn't the sound he'd been listening for. There was no-one on the path behind him, he was sure. No, the sound he'd heard was the water slapping gently against the side of a boat. He recognised it at once: for a moment he was on his father's yacht, a boy on a sunny morning, with nothing better to do than to hang over the side with a line, the sun hot on his back, imagining he might catch a fish. He heard Fiscilius' voice: there are rings to tie a boat up. Could there really be a boat down here? Again his eyes strained helplessly to see what was happening. He heard the sound again. It was definitely a boat. It was behind him, and it was coming closer. He began to walk faster. Then, without warning, he fell, not far but with a jarring crash into cold, dark, evil-smelling water. The path along the sewer had simply ended. He was on his hands and knees in the dirty water, his face inches from the surface. The drag of it hurrying past almost pulled him over. He stood up carefully, shaking the filth off himself. It was only knee deep, not enough to drown in, he thought. Not accidentally anyway.

And then with a sudden flurry in the water the boat was upon him. It rammed him and he would have fallen again had it not forced him upright against the side wall of the tunnel. He clutched at it, and as it swung away from the tunnel wall and floated off he grabbed the side. Pain exploded in his hands as a heavy oar came crashing down on them. Instinctively he let go, then forced his hands to grab it again before it floated away. He had it now and held tight to the back of it, while Fiscilius flailed at him with the oar. But the roof of the tunnel was lower here, and Torquatus could hear the wood scraping and catching on the bricks. Ignoring the blows he heaved himself over the side, setting it rocking wildly. He tumbled into the bottom of it, banging his head on something as he fell. For a moment he was too winded and dazed to move, then a heavy weight fell on him, crushing him. A furious hoarse voice muttered curses into his ear. The boat was a tiny one, and the two men were tumbled together like lovers in the bottom of it as it rolled about.

Torquatus was aware of the other man's hands feeling - for what? Another knife, perhaps? His will to live responded, before his brain could think. Twisting savagely, he almost overturned the boat, but Fiscilius held on tight and remained sprawled across him. Awkwardly, they were fumbling for each other, but Torquatus' arms were free now and he got his hands on Fiscilius' throat. He gripped and pressed, and as his enemy choked he made a huge effort and forced the man up and over till it was Fiscilius on his back and Torquatus sprawled on top of him. Again the boat rocked and heaved wildly and bumped against the walls. Fiscilius managed to get one hand free, and if he still had a knife - Torquatus' hands squeezed and squeezed as hard as they knew how. But he couldn't stop Fiscilius moving his arm.

Fiscilius seemed to gather his last energies, and Torquatus felt a blow on his back. It wasn't a very hard blow: Fiscilius was weakened by his struggle for breath. Torquatus knew he was bleeding though the pain of the wound hadn't hit him yet. He pressed harder, and harder yet. The boat travelled along smoothly now the two men were still. Fiscilius had stopped struggling, and Torquatus' hands seemed to relax of their own accord. He tried to keep pressing. He knew he had to keep gripping, or he would die. He just had to hold on for a little longer, but the effort was too great, and there seemed to be some light. Perhaps Apollo had heard him after all.

Torquatus came round to see a ring of faces suspended against the blue sky. None of them seemed to be Apollo. They looked instead like the sort of men who work on docks everywhere, tough, weathered, battered. He wondered idly how they could all have piled onto that tiny boat, then realised he wasn't on the boat any more. His back was hurting dreadfully, and he said so. A man of a different sort pushed through the group. He was clean-shaven, with bright dark eyes. 'You look like a doctor,' Torquatus said dreamily.

'I am,' the man agreed.

'In fact,' Torquatus went on, 'I think you're my doctor.'

'That's right too. Now I'm going to turn you over, which will hurt.'

The next time Torquatus woke up it was in his own bedroom. Definitely his room: the walls had been painted with fantasy temples and colonnades, buildings piled on buildings, all glowing reds and golds and blues. And at the bottom of the little scene a door opened onto a sunlit street, white and hot. He had often wanted to walk through that door, into that hot place. But now he didn't feel like that at all. His back still hurt, but not very much. His hands seemed to be wrapped up in something. But in spite of that he was very comfortable in his bed, and he was happy just to look. Phrases of Fiscilius' last speech went through his head: unquiet spirits - hide any crime in Rome - or nearly. Had Fiscilius' final action been an attempt to lay blame on him?

A slight noise made him turn his head, and there to his delight was Cornelia, sitting in an easy chair, a little piece of white cloth in her hand, which she seemed to be sewing. She didn't seem to be pregnant any more. But of course she wasn't: they had a baby, little Lucius. His son. The sight of Cornelia filled him with profound joy.

'I've never seen you sewing before,' he said, and she smiled very lovingly.

'I've never had a baby before,' she pointed out. She put down the sewing, and came over to the bed and kissed him. He would have liked to put his arms round her, but they were ridiculously heavy, as if weighed down by his bandaged hands.

'How did I get here?'

'In a litter.'

'No, really. How did I?'

She laughed and said, 'Those bodyguards of yours - and I admit I've always thought them a pair of useless lumps of lard - came to your rescue quite heroically. Pulex thought he saw Fiscilius in the street. He told Becco and they dithered for a bit. Then when you didn't come out of the shrine they went in to see where you were. They saw the slab was open, and Pulex followed you down. Becco came running home, and I told him the sewer ran into the Cloaca Maxima: I knew because of all the uproar over moving the shrine. He took the doctor and found a boat, and was about to row up the Cloaca, hoping to find you, when he realised your boat had been landed and you were on the quay. It was Pulex who'd shouted for help. Fiscilius was dead, and the doctor thought you were too, at first - ,' She stopped and pressed her lips tightly together. 'But you weren't.'

'And Pulex,' he asked lazily. 'How did he get there?'

Cornelia laughed. 'Oh, Pulex climbed down the ladder after you, and took to the water. When your boat appeared, he was just behind it, apparently, paddling along with his hair full of crappy water, and crying out that his master was dead.'

'And there was I thinking he couldn't swim.'

They sat in silence for a while, until Torquatus, on the point of sinking back into sleep, remembered the one thing he had to do. He forced his eyelids open again. 'Oh, Cornelia! Would you tell Fiscilia that I've found the rest of her inheritance? She'd better arrange some transport: Fiscilius said he used three ox-carts, but he did have a load of - carrots, was it, or turnips? on top. And cabbages. I can't remember now. What? Oh, it's in our family tomb on the via Salaria.'

He slept.

Author's Note

Nothing would happen without friends, and I want to thank Stacy and Tom for reading drafts of *Unquiet Spirits* . They read critically but kindly, pointing out typos as well as ensuring that Torquatus never found himself in two places at once. Deborah, too, produced the map in the face of glitches which would have put off a less determined woman.

Writing a historical novel always involves difficult decisions. As it happens we know a good deal about what Octavian, Marcus Antonius, Balbus, Agrippa and Salvidienus Rufus actually did, because historians have always been fascinated by this disastrous period between Republic and Empire. For this pre-imperial period the most immediate accounts are Appian's The Civil Wars and Cassius Dio's Roman History.

What we don't know is what their motives were. Nor did Appian or Dio, who were writing considerably later, under the empire. The motives they often ascribe to their actors are ones that made sense in their own contemporary world. We may or may not agree.

The Perusine War happened pretty much as I've described it, though I have brought it to an end a little early, because Cornelia's pregnancy demanded it, and babies don't care about novelists' plot difficulties.

Lucius Manlius Torquatus, the father of my hero, actually existed, as did Aulus' elder brother, also Lucius. The facts of their lives, as given in this book and in Saturn's Gold, the first story in the Roma Capta series, are as I have described them. Aulus Manlius Torquatus himself is fictitious, though there were men called that: cousins, maybe, or uncles.

I have tried to stick to the Latin versions of place-names: yet another list at the back of this book seems like overkill. People's names, too, have been kept in their Latin form. Mark Antony is a Shakespearian character now, and that feels inappropriate here. There are only two exceptions: Pompey the Great is not called Pompeius Magnus, because that might cause confusion with his son Sextus Pompeius; and I am using the name Octavian because although he himself chose to be called Caesar, for us that means his great-uncle and adoptive father Julius Caesar.

To me it's very important not to take liberties with history where it can be avoided. We are lucky enough to live in an era in which wonderful historians have opened up our understanding of Roman slavery, families, the lives of the poor, so we can know a great deal about aspects of Roman life which were once overlooked. I am greatly indebted to them.

But I am writing stories, not history. I take my ingredients and bake my cake, which isn't the same thing as any of those ingredients, or even of them all mixed together. Magic! I hope you like it.

Have you read ***Saturn's Gold***, the first in the Roma Capta series? If not, here's a taster …

During the night the weather changed, and Rome was blanketed in fog: thick, yellowish-grey, acrid with the smoke of a thousand wood-fires. Torquatus tasted ash on his tongue and thought of the pyres up on the Esquiline where the dead were burned. Stephanus would be one of them today: he wondered uneasily what in Hercules' name the old boy had been doing up there on the Capitol, and who had sent him to his death. Was there a murderer in his household? Or could it possibly have been an accident? Under his feet the street was slick with greasy dirt, each cobble a slippery trap for the unwary. A senator ought not to be seen falling down in the street. He put consideration of Stephanus' death aside.

As his party descended from the Quirinal, the foggy air became thicker yet. The smell of the river, with its freight of excrement, animal guts from the meat market, yellowing cabbage leaves dumped by the vegetable sellers, dead fish and live ones, rose up in the Forum to meet the smoke coming down. The broad stairs at the bottom of the Argentarius were covered in wet, grey dirt. This was where Stephanus' broken body had been left to lie in the mud. What was going on in his house? His spine seemed to chill at the thought of slaves creeping about in the dark, their minds filled with hatred.

Perhaps it was only the desolate mood of the place infecting him. The Forum might be the heart of Rome, but it had once been a marsh, and in weather like this still felt like one. He shook himself and followed the slaves with their sputtering torches through the wide space where buildings loomed out of the fog, then sank back into the murk. Here a corner of a temple appeared, sharply familiar, there a colonnade ran regular and ghostly into invisibility. He was careful to walk as he had been taught by his father, upright, not deigning to look at the ground, however treacherous. Even when there was no-one to see.

The slaves cried out and jumped suddenly, their torches smoking darkly, and he himself felt the hairs on his arms rise. Out of the fog, looming down at them, a face had appeared. Its dead eyes stared. Beside its ears two hands seemed to waggle as if in a children's game. He knew that face, and swallowed hard. It would not do to be sick. Tears pricked his eyes. Cicero had taken far too many risks in these recent years, goading Antonius in speeches of great brilliance. Had the speeches been duller, they would have done less harm, but it had become a spectacle, each speech commanding a greater audience, the witty barbs flying out of the senate-house and into the Forum, to become the currency of every market trader or common citizen. He must have known what Antonius would do if ever he had the power. Well, now Antonius had the power, and here was Cicero's head to prove it: bruised, the sparse hair draggled and wet, the tongue stuck out, skewered by a hairpin. This must have been put up during the night, just in case anyone had doubted the Three's intentions.

And there beside Cicero, above Torquatus like gods on their ivory stools were the Three, the great men themselves. Octavian, a small, pale man, the sort you'd never remember in a crowd, Antonius, legs spread, his boxer's face grumpy, looking as if he wanted a drink, and Lepidus, sitting upright, coldly handsome. All three were very correctly dressed in togas and boots, and looked chilled to the bone. Torquatus knew they sometimes chose to come down in the morning to dispense justice, as they liked to call it, but he couldn't believe they'd stay there long on such a dark day. A number of heads on spears loomed out of the mist around them like a spectral bodyguard, though of course each man had a detail of soldiers to protect him too, standing at a not too discreet distance. Below them a pile of heads and bodies, of those not important enough to justify hoisting them onto the Rostra straight away, he supposed, lay in a jumbled heap, blood oozing down across the cobbles in a sluggish stream. The sharp iron smell of it was heavy in the foggy air. Torquatus took a deep breath and raised a hand in greeting. Lepidus returned the greeting ceremoniously, one senator to another. Well, Lepidus at least had no reason to wish Torquatus dead, as far as he knew. Antonius glowered, but nodded. Torquatus thought he probably wasn't important enough or rich enough to be on Antonius' hit-list – but who knew? Who knew? Octavian smiled, lifted a hand, greeted Torquatus quite warmly, for him. It seemed he was alive, for now.

If you enjoy my books, keep an eye on my website at clarebainbridge.com, or email me at peartreepressdevon@gmail.com. I will reply!

Printed in Poland
by Amazon Fulfillment
Poland Sp. z o.o., Wrocław